THE
INTERSECT

When life veers off course, strangers
find comfort and lasting connection

BRAD GRABER

ISBN: 978-0-9976042-0-7

Cover and interior page design: Jeff Brandenburg

Published by Dark Victory Press
brad@bradgraber.com
bradgraber.com

First printing: 2016

Printed in the United States of America

DEDICATION

To Jeff who supported me faithfully. His love and kindness offer the secrets to a happy life.

ACKNOWLEDGMENTS

To all the wonderful friends and family who inspired me to write a novel. For years, stories have been bouncing around in my head. Now, I've found a useful outlet for sleepless nights.

To Steven Bauer of Hollow Tree Literary Services who edited my book. I'm grateful for his focus, skill, and patience in dealing with a novice.

To Jeff Brandenburg who exceeded my every expectation in design and layout and continues to be my friend.

1

....

US Airways Flight #610 took a sharp bounce, jostling Dave Greenway in his seat. It was the 6:00 a.m. flight out of San Francisco to Phoenix. The scent of freshly brewed coffee wafted through the first-class cabin as he planted his size tens firmly on the floor beneath him, hoping against hope, to stabilize the Airbus 320.

It didn't work.

The plane took another nasty hop.

As Dave struggled to hold his cup steady, coffee splashed everywhere. "Dammit, I knew that was going to happen," he muttered, his hand soaked as he downed the last of the liquid.

Again, the plane bucked hard.

A woman nearby let out a muffled cry. Everyone else fell dead silent. An elderly gentleman emerged from the first-class restroom, zipper down, a surprised look on his face, the front of his khakis wet. As he stumbled to his seat, the unlatched door swung freely. A stewardess jumped up to secure it, balancing herself precariously with one hand on the cockpit door.

Perfect, Dave thought, turning a ghostly white. He pulled his seat belt tighter. *We leave earthquake country and die in a plane crash.*

Seated beside him, his partner Charlie nudged him with an elbow. "It's just a little turbulence," he said confidently. "There's nothing to worry about. Hey, check this out." He held up an old issue of *People* that he'd lifted from the airplane magazine rack. Ryan Reynolds offered a seductive stare.

"Very nice," Dave said dryly, still unnerved by the plane's erratic motion. He searched Charlie's angular face for any sign of tension. "How can you be so calm?"

"Thermal inversion," Charlie said, as he returned to perusing the magazine. "It happens over the desert. If you're scared, just look down at your sweater."

For the big travel day, Dave had worn his favorite black pullover, purchased on a whim at a Greg Norman sale. It contrasted nicely with the silver coursing through his mostly dark hair which he wore conservatively parted on the side. The cotton/poly blend with a zippered collar at the neck, sported the signature shark logo encircled by Norman's motto—*Attack Life*—an attitude Dave admired. Dave loved the primary colors of the shark logo and wondered if it was the designer's nod to the rainbow flag.

The plane jumped side-to-side. Dave gripped the armrests.

"There's no point freaking out," Charlie said, still reading, oblivious to the motion, the dark-grey wispy curls atop his head indifferent to Dave's need for order. "Think of it like riding a roller-coaster. Go with the flow. Tensing up only creates sore muscles."

Dave tried to relax. If Charlie was so blasé, there couldn't be any real danger. After all, Charlie had logged hundreds of thousands of air miles. "I take paradise and put up a parking lot," he'd told Dave when they'd met some twenty years earlier at a Human Rights Campaign Fund Dinner. Dave had returned a blank stare as Charlie, tall, tanned, and dapper in a black tux, explained that he worked with developers on site locations for new stores. Since then, Dave had watched Charlie ricochet around the country, providing market research to support trade area development for retailers, investment banks, and anyone who needed predictive sales modeling.

Charlie closed the *People* magazine. He looked over at Dave. "March is really a great time to move to Phoenix. The weather's ideal. And I can finally say goodbye to all those flight delays at SFO. *No more morning fog.*" He practically sang the last few words.

The motion of the plane calmed as Dave assumed Charlie's joyous mood. "No more jumbo mortgage on that tiny Mill Valley house we once called home."

Charlie's hazel green eyes lit up. "Good riddance to those break-the-bank California taxes."

"Adieu to the rain that arrives in November and stays until April. And a fond farewell to those outrageous gasoline prices."

Charlie smiled. "We're going to save a shitload of money."

"We will," Dave agreed as the plane unexpectedly lost altitude. Dave's gut pressed hard against the seat belt. A second later, his bottom reunited with the cushion, and the mood turned serious. "Beware the Ides of March," he mumbled.

"What the hell does that mean?" Charlie asked, perplexed by the ominous reference.

Dave had no trouble explaining. He'd already given it considerable thought. "Gay people flock to San Francisco. Everyone wants to live in the Bay Area. And here we're leaving. And tomorrow, March 15th of all days, I start my new job."

Charlie sought a positive spin. "With scientists predicting *the next big one*, we'd have been crazy to stay. If our home had been destroyed in an earthquake, we'd have still been on the hook to pay off that huge mortgage."

"True," Dave said, impressed by Charlie's ability to turn the argument. "An earthquake is a terrific strategy to minimize overcrowding in the Bay Area," Dave laughed. "But moving to Arizona . . . *a red state?*"

"How do you think red states turn blue?" Charlie's eyes twinkled. "Pioneers like us. One day we'll look back and say, remember when Arizona was red?"

Dave relented. "I guess that's one way to look at it."

"Sure. And there's a large gay community in Phoenix." Charlie reached down and retrieved his black leather briefcase. Unzipping the front pocket, he pulled out a full-color *Phoenix Homes* magazine. "You have to check out these properties," he said thumbing through the pages. "I've already hooked up with a realtor to show us around."

"Show *you* around," Dave corrected. "I'll be in the office tomorrow. Physician practices need to be managed. From now on, my life will be one long operations meeting, physicians in the morning, physicians at night."

"Well, you took the lead in getting us settled in the Bay Area when we left Michigan. Now it's my turn. God knows I'll have plenty of time. With credit frozen, consumer spending down . . . retail's in such a deep slump. Last Christmas was a real bust. I don't think 2010 will be much better. I should have plenty of time to get us set up. There's not much business on my plate at the moment."

Dave felt bad for Charlie. He'd worked so hard to build a successful business. "Well, Obama really pulled us back from the brink," Dave said, still uncertain that the worst of it was over.

"With so many Americans out of work, it's more like a depression than a recession," Charlie observed glumly. "But we should look on the bright side. With such high employment . . . you have a new job. That's freaking amazing."

"It feels really out of step," Dave agreed, still ambivalent about his good fortune. "Kind of unsettling."

"You're nuts. You should be ecstatic."

"I'm too on edge. I have all these crazy thoughts running through my head," Dave admitted, a nervous tingling shooting through his body.

Charlie gave Dave his full attention. "Tell me. I want to hear."

"It's ridiculous," Dave admitted, blushing. "It's too silly."

"Tell me," Charlie insisted. "I want to know."

Dave relented. He hoped Charlie would be understanding. "Okay. Take my car. It's black with a black interior."

"And?" Charlie asked, stifling a laugh.

Dave continued. "It gets brutally hot in Phoenix during the summer. Black retains the heat."

Charlie offered a huge smile. "You're kidding, right? You know you can't get incinerated driving to work." His voice dripped with sarcasm. "There's such a thing as air conditioning. And if it's a real problem, you'll trade that car in for a white one. Problem solved. What else?"

Dave hesitated.

"What else, what else?" Charlie probed, eager to hear the next concern.

Dave took a deep breath. "You know I'm susceptible to nosebleeds. It's dry in Arizona. I read on the Internet that it's the nosebleed capital of the world."

Charlie gave Dave a sidelong glance. "Now you're making that one up."

"I read it," Dave insisted.

"Your body will adjust," Charlie promised. "You'll be fine. So that's what's worrying you? Here I thought you had concerns about the job."

"I should have kept it to myself. Real men never share," Dave sharply remarked.

Charlie placed a hand on Dave's thigh and gave it a gentle squeeze. "Real men who love each other do. Why not look on the bright side? We'll have domestic partner benefits. For the first time, I can get health insurance through you. No more HMO. Hello, Blue Cross Blue Shield."

"Yeah, that is pretty progressive," Dave agreed, "And of all places . . . Arizona."

"That's what happens when you stop working for Catholic organizations."

"True."

"And the roof won't leak. It barely ever rains in Phoenix. And . . . get ready . . . here it comes . . . we can buy a *new house*. We could never afford that in the Bay Area."

Dave perked up. Images of Sub-Zeros, marble countertops, pebble-tech pools, and flagstone patios danced in his head. "A new house . . . wouldn't that be something?"

"We can do whatever we want," Charlie answered, once again opening the *People* magazine and flipping through the pages.

Dave looked over Charlie's shoulder. "My God," he said, pointing at a photo of Gilles Marini. "He looks a bit like you when you were young. You had the same five o'clock shadow and all that jet-black hair."

"I was hot," Charlie agreed. "But if I worked out like you," Charlie rubbed his tummy, "I'd probably drop these last ten pounds."

"Hey, I'm at the gym to manage stress," Dave emphasized, explaining his obsessive need to work out.

Charlie shot him a doubtful look. "Maybe you should try Xanax."

"No drugs," Dave pushed back. "I don't need them," he said, defending himself against what he felt were Charlie's hurtful accusations.

"Dave, there's no shame in medication."

Dave gave Charlie a piercing look. The conversation was over.

Charlie regrouped. "Well, I'm glad we took the first flight out. The sun will be coming up soon. We'll have all day to settle in, unpack, and go grocery shopping."

Dave shifted, stretching his arms overhead to ease the tightness in his lower back. "I hope we like living in Phoenix."

"We'll love it. And if it's any consolation, I'm proud of you. Not many men in their fifties would have the courage to take a new job. It's says a lot about you."

"That I'm an idiot," Dave said tongue-in-cheek, as he twisted about his finger the black onyx ring Charlie had given him years earlier.

Charlie shook his head. "No, you have faith in the future," he countered as the plane suddenly shook violently, the thrust so sharp, it caught both men off guard. Dave grabbed Charlie's hand as the yellow oxygen masks dropped, dangling just above their heads.

"Oh my God," Charlie said, his voice dead serious.

"It's just a little thermal inversion," Dave snapped as he slipped the plastic mask over his head, all the while trying to remember to breathe normally.

* * *

Daisy Ellen Lee was a fixture in her Biltmore Greens neighborhood. Spry and energetic, she attributed her vigor to the Phoenix climate. While others complained about the intense summer heat, Daisy likened herself to the mighty saguaro, the desert cactus that dotted the Arizona landscape. During the summer months the saguaro stood tall, defying the searing desert sun. Come the monsoon season, the prickly succulent miraculously budded, yielding an array of bright red and yellow flowers. Daisy admired the saguaro's resilience. If the saguaro was a survivor, then so was she.

Each morning, Daisy walked the gated community, part ambassador, part drill sergeant, undertaking the morning inspection of the grounds. She was barely five foot two, even with her blond bouffant teased to a fluffy fullness. Final Net held it perfectly in place. From a distance, in her green lululemon yoga attire, she resembled a yellow poppy on the march.

The exclusive neighborhood of Biltmore Greens abutted the grounds of the Arizona Biltmore Hotel, a five-star resort opened in 1929 and visited by United States presidents, the Hollywood elite, and foreign and national dignitaries. Designed in the architectural style of Frank Lloyd Wright, the Arizona Biltmore, and the developments that encircled the property were a much-desired address in Phoenix.

"Well, good Sunday morning. You're certainly up early," called out Sheila, who worked the midnight shift on the security gate. Her bright red hair was pulled tightly back from her moon-shaped face into a neatly knotted bun that rested at the back of her head just above the neck. The severity of her hairstyle matched her uniform of blue polyester pants and jacket, interrupted by a white cotton button-down shirt.

"I couldn't sleep," Daisy admitted, eyeing the broken concrete block on the base of the little gatehouse.

"Is anything wrong?" Sheila asked.

"When are they fixing that?" Daisy pointed at the offending block. She'd complained about it at the last Homeowner's Association meeting.

"Next Tuesday. I received the notice yesterday."

"Oh, that's good." Daisy gently nudged a loose stone back with her foot into the small rock garden that decorated the side of the gatehouse. "And how's your mother feeling? Is her back any better?"

"She's much better," Sheila answered.

"Oh, I'm so glad," Daisy said, checking the chalkboard on the side of the gatehouse. She didn't expect to see her name on the list of residents who had packages waiting to be picked up, but checking the board was as much a habit as retrieving the mail. She laughed at her own foolishness.

"And how are you feeling this morning?" Sheila asked.

"I awoke with such an unusual burst of energy," Daisy recalled. "So eager to greet all the flowers and shrubs and say hello to my four-legged friends. Silly, isn't it?"

Daisy adored the dogs of the Biltmore. Unlike Sheila, who knew every resident by name and house number, Daisy knew the neighbors through their dogs.

"And who have you seen so far?"

"I saw Jasmine go by with her two Dads. And Millie on her way to Starbucks at Fashion Mall with her folks."

"Lovely," Sheila said as the eastern sky started to brighten. "The sun will be up any minute. It's almost time for the shift change. Bert should be here soon."

Daisy repeated the weather forecast from the morning news. "It's going to be eighty-five with lots of sunshine."

A gentle breeze stirred the smell of orange blossoms. Both women inhaled and sighed.

"Spring is in the air," Daisy wistfully acknowledged. "Ah, another year older come May."

"I just hope when I'm seventy-five," Sheila said, "I look as good as you."

Daisy was pleased to see the admiration in the younger woman's eyes. "Yoga," Daisy declared. "Stretching is the best medicine. I'm going this afternoon to a hot yoga class."

"They have hot yoga for seniors?" Sheila asked in disbelief.

Daisy frowned. "It's not a seniors class," she said. "Why would I be in a seniors class?" It irked her that anyone would make such an assumption.

"Oh," Sheila said, seemingly unaware of her faux pas. "But aren't you uncomfortable . . . can you keep up?"

"Absolutely. And I love young people. All tatted, like walking canvasses. You can learn a lot about them based on their artwork."

Sheila giggled.

Daisy bent down to retie a lace. "When you're young, there's so much to occupy your time. Jobs and school . . . oh these young people come and go . . . in such a rush to get to the *next place*. I'm practically standing still watching as life passes by. It can be a bit lonely."

Sheila looked astonished. "You . . . lonely? I don't believe it. You always seem so active. Going to all those meetings for the Democratic Party. And the Breast Cancer Walks. And gathering signatures on the latest petition drive. My goodness. I don't know where you get the energy."

"Well, I do try to stay engaged and mentally sharp. Oh, but I get lonely. I've lost so many friends over the years. I almost hate to read the obituaries. And those poor souls who wind up in nursing homes . . . that's the worst. I guess life's a crapshoot. You never know how it's going to end."

Unnerved by the conversation's sudden change in tone, Daisy decided to move on.

"Well, dear . . . it was wonderful seeing you . . . you have yourself a glorious day," she said sweetly, waving goodbye.

* * *

Charlie stood with Dave at the luggage carousel at Sky Harbor Airport. He placed his right foot on top of the of conveyor belt, staking out his territory as the other passengers crowded about.

"I can't believe the oxygen mask dropped," Dave said. He shook his head as if reimagining the entire fiasco. "That scared the shit out of me."

"Me too," Charlie admitted. "In all my years of flying, that's never happened."

Dave slipped out of his pullover. The change in climate from the Bay Area to Phoenix was already noticeable. "That last hard bounce must have tripped open the compartment."

"Did you see the look on the stewardess's face?" Charlie laughed, remembering the woman's frantic expression. "I thought she'd have a cow."

"Well, to her credit, she jumped right up and tried to close it."

"But you'd already put on the mask." Charlie roared with laughter, capturing the attention of nearby travelers. "Prepared to go down with the plane," he said, index finger in the air.

"Hey, there's nothing wrong with my reflexes," Dave defended himself, now standing behind Charlie. "In a real emergency, I'd have been breathing. You'd have been starved for oxygen."

"Small consolation. In a real emergency, I'd rather not know what's happening."

"Is that why you didn't put on the mask?"

"I couldn't," Charlie admitted. "My heart stopped."

They both laughed, grateful for the release of nervous energy on what was otherwise a stressful day.

"Well, it's all behind us now." Charlie placed his hands on his hips and gently twisted. "Damn those airplane seats." He spied the electronic board. "It's only 9:15. We did okay on time."

"I hope that flight wasn't a bad omen."

"Oh Dave, knock it off. Nothing good comes from a negative attitude. You know, you always *find what you're looking for*. Stop putting out negative vibes. Phoenix is a terrific place. There's culture, it's young and hip. Lots of bars and restaurants . . . we're going to love it."

Dave hated when Charlie lost his patience. "God, you sound like the freaking Chamber of Commerce."

"You've got to look on the bright side," Charlie lectured.

Dave nodded. "The bright side."

Charlie continued. "You've worked hard. We deserve this. In a month, you'll be comfortable in the new job. In three months, you'll feel like you've lived in Phoenix your whole life. Just give yourself time to adjust."

"I know," Dave answered. "I have to go easy."

"You do that," Charlie said as the luggage carousel came to life, "and I'll grab the bags."

* * *

Daisy pulled up to the Biltmore Greens gate in her red Honda Fit. She rolled down her window and greeted Bert who worked the morning shift.

"Bert, it's so good to see you. How are you feeling?"

Bert stepped out of the little gatehouse. "Much better, Ms. Lee. It's kind of you to ask. The doctor told me it was just a touch of sciatica."

"Oh, I'm so glad you're better," Daisy gushed. "I hear that's very pain-ful. "

"Yes, it most certainly is," Bert answered, rubbing the affected leg.

"Well, it's wonderful to see you back."

"Thank you." Bert blushed. "Where are you heading this morning?"

Daisy's voice perked up. "Sprouts. They're having a big sale on pine-apples. They're usually $3.99. Today, they're 99 cents," she whispered in a conspiring voice.

"That *does* sound like quite a sale."

"Would you like me to bring you back one?" Daisy offered.

"Frankly, Ms. Lee, pineapple makes me gassy. I think I'm better off sticking to protein bars."

Daisy had never had a protein bar. She wondered if she'd like it. "Is there anything you might need while I'm out?"

"You're too kind. Please don't bother about me. I'm just fine," Bert replied.

"Well, I better get going then. I'd hate to get caught in noontime traffic when church lets out."

"You have a few hours for that," Bert chuckled, checking his watch. "It's only ten o'clock now. "There's not a lot of traffic on a Sunday."

"But there's nothing worse than driving when the roads are crowded," Daisy confided. "People tailgate, honk their horn, wave wildly at me. I can see them in the rearview mirror. It's so distracting."

"Maybe you're driving too slowly?"

"Oh no, I'm a terrific driver," Daisy said indignantly. "I'm just cautious. My only problem is finding my car in the parking lot."

Bert frowned. "I had an aunt who got lost in a shopping mall. It was quite an ordeal for the family. She was diagnosed with early onset dementia."

"Oh dear, that's terrible. But it's not my memory that's the problem. It's the other cars. They dwarf my little Fit. Last week, my car was parked between a Ford Super Duty and a Chevy Silverado. My Fit looked like a clown car at the circus."

Bert chuckled. "That can certainly be a problem."

"Well, it was lovely seeing you, Bert. I better get on with the day."

"Enjoy the morning," Bert called.

Daisy stepped on the gas pedal and without yielding at the stop sign, brazenly pulled into the intersection, busy thinking about the best way to select a pineapple, by smell or by the ease in which leaves at the crown release. It was too late for her to stop when she finally became aware of the Allied Van Line truck, thanks to the driver leaning down hard on his horn. The squeal of metallic brakes was unmistakable.

* * *

"What do you think?" Dave asked Charlie as they looked about the furnished rental. The relocation company had arranged for the turnkey apartment with its faded beige carpet, old oak furniture, and white walls sporadically decorated with cheaply framed posters of desert landscapes. Dave thought it horribly ugly.

"It'll have to do," Charlie answered, "though I wish we'd talked before you agreed to this particular apartment."

"Why?" Dave asked. "They assured me every apartment is exactly the same. There's a second bedroom for your office. When they connect the Internet, you'll be all set to work. And it's close to shopping and the freeway. Besides, it's only temporary until you find us a house."

"Yes, but we face west." Charlie tapped on the window that looked out onto the community pool below. "That means intense afternoon sun. And with these cheap, single pane windows, it'll get nice and toasty."

"Oh geez, Charlie, I didn't even think about that." Dave was suddenly aware that the room was already on the warm side. He'd have to find the thermostat and turn on the air.

"Well, it's okay. We're here now." Charlie waved a hand, the sign that he was ready to make the best of it.

"How bad can it get?" Dave wondered, setting the thermostat at sixty-eight, upset that he hadn't asked for Charlie's input before he made the final arrangements.

"May is when the heat really ratchets up to triple digits."

There was a violent rumble above as the air conditioning unit situated on the roof jerked into action. A musty odor filled the room.

"Well that settles it," Dave announced. "We're going to have to be in a new house by May."

"Two months isn't a lot of time to find a place," Charlie warned, flopping down on the tan sofa. The expression on Charlie's face warned Dave that the cushions were hard. Charlie poked at the fake potted fern on the oak coffee table. "Are they kidding with this?" He held up the green plant by one of its floppy plastic leafs. "This thing weighs nothing."

"How hard can it be to find a place?" Dave called out as he opened the cabinets in the tiny galley kitchen, finding the glassware and dishes. "We're sitting on cash from our sale in California. We should be able to find a terrific house." He ran a finger over the white linoleum countertop. They'd need to purchase cleaning supplies. "Remember the homes you showed me in that real estate magazine?"

"Too far from your office," Charlie said, bending the plastic leaf on the fake cactus back and forth.

"But they're all new subdivisions," Dave remembered. Some of the houses appeared palatial.

"That's Chandler and Ahwatuckee," Charlie answered, shaking the coffee table to determine which leg was loose.

"Awaa . . . what?"

"Never mind. The Phoenix metropolitan area is huge. We'll need to find something closer to your office so that you don't spend your drive time in bumper-to-bumper traffic."

"Well, you'll find something." Dave was certain. "I have faith in you." He began loading the cheap ceramic dishes directly from the cabinet into the dishwasher. "When you're done over there," he said to Charlie, who was still playing with the coffee table, "how about stripping the bed? I think we better wash everything before we sleep on it."

Charlie checked his watch. "Okay, it's ten after ten now. I say we spend an hour or so working on this place, unpacking, and then head off to lunch."

Dave nodded. "You got a deal."

* * *

Daisy's forehead rested on a deployed airbag. She felt slightly nauseous from the adrenaline coursing through her body. The truck had slowed, and still, the Honda Fit had taken a hit to the passenger side. Daisy's body had jerked hard against the driver's side door before coming to rest. She'd heard a crack, like stepping on a branch in the forest. The sound had seemed to come from deep within her own body.

"Ma'am, are you okay? Please tell me you're okay." A man with a deep, gruff voice pleaded as he removed his Arizona Diamondbacks ballcap to reveal beads of sweat pouring from his brow. "I'll never forgive myself if you're dead."

"I'm not dead," Daisy finally confessed as she lifted her head, face flushed. "I'll be fine." She looked at the expression on the poor man's face and took pity on him. "I'm just a little stunned."

"Thank God," the man said, wiping his brow with the back of his hand. "You really should pay closer attention," he now scolded her. "When was the last time someone gave you a driving test? Jesus. You gave me the scare of a lifetime."

"Ms. Lee, are you okay?" Bert called, running up to the site of the collision, cell phone in hand, the 911 operator still on the line.

"She's fine," the truck driver answered, eyeing the damage to the car. "She's absolutely fine."

"Now you stay still," Bert advised. "The ambulance should be here any minute."

Daisy could hear the approach of emergency sirens. "Oh Bert," she softly said, "I don't need an ambulance." But when she tried to move, there was a gnawing pain in her left hip. She winced as the ache intensified.

"Now please, Ms. Lee. Don't move," Bert instructed as the first EMT approached. "I'm here with you. Don't you worry."

Daisy felt flush. "Oh Bert" were the last words she managed before everything went black.

* * *

Phoenix's well-trained EMTs surrounded the vehicle as Daisy came to. On a scale of one to ten, the pain was fifteen. Daisy cried out in agony as she was lifted from the car and placed on a stretcher. Any movement was sheer torture. The sharp, stabbing sensation in her left hip ruled every breath.

The ambulance ride was a blur.

At the hospital, a young emergency room physician, with blond wavy hair and an angelic smile, provided morphine. Daisy sighed as the drug, injected directly into her IV, immediately took effect. "Thank you," she said, her heart full of gratitude as the pain finally receded.

"While you rest," the doctor quietly advised, "we're going to schedule that hip for surgery."

"Oh dear," was all Daisy could muster. *Surgery is such serious business,* she thought, focusing her attention on the doctor's mouth, watching and waiting for his lips to once again move.

The doctor scanned Daisy's chart as he engaged her in light conversation "The paramedics said you were lucky. Your age . . . the nature of the accident . . . you could have been seriously hurt."

His comment rubbed her the wrong way. Adrenaline surged through her small frame and perhaps due to the morphine, she spoke sharply before thinking. "This isn't serious enough?"

The doctor pulled up a chair and sat beside her bed. "Ms. Lee, your broken hip was not a result of an auto accident," the doctor explained. "We see this all the time. A woman who presents as perfectly healthy suddenly falls to the ground. She thinks she's tripped. She hasn't. It's osteoporosis. The disease generates weak bones and in women of a certain age, fragile hips. You broke that hip in a seated position. It was primed to break."

Daisy could hardly believe her ears. She'd heard of osteoporosis, but she'd always thought such a condition was evidenced by poor posture. She hadn't realized that someone who stood perfectly straight could experience the effects in places other than the spine.

"It could have happened in the supermarket or in the privacy of your bathroom. You were lucky. There were people around. Have you spoken with your primary care physician about osteoporosis?" His warm blue eyes pressed her for an answer.

She folded her hands in her lap, fingers intertwined, like a schoolgirl, politely waiting for the teacher to reveal the day's lesson. "No," Daisy admitted. "I don't have a primary care doctor."

The young physician was unable to hide his surprise. His response was quick and abrupt. "And why is that?"

Daisy hesitated. She wondered if it might be rude to share her theory about doctors with a doctor. She'd always been a confident woman, and yet here, in this antiseptic environment, with everyone dressed in white coats and green scrubs, clearly knowledgeable about things she only guessed at, she reconsidered her opinions.

The young physician awaited her response.

She cleared her throat and lifted her chin slightly, believing a regal posture lent authority to her words. "I think doctors overmedicate seniors. For every complaint, they write a prescription. I don't believe in drugs. I don't think they're good for you. I think they bring on confusion in people my age." She paused and took a deep breath before continuing. "There's nothing in my medicine cabinet besides lipstick and face powder," she proudly boasted. "I've been healthy all my life. Why would I pay a doctor to search for problems where none exist?"

The doctor glared at her. She cringed. She'd angered him.

"Do you realize the risk you're taking? Osteoporosis is a serious condition that should be managed. And at your age, you need a family physician. I hope you've at least had an annual flu shot."

Daisy blushed. She'd passed on flu shots. What was the point? She never got sick.

The young doctor shook his head. He returned to the discussion at hand. "The orthopedic surgeon will stop by later. A counselor will also come by and make sure your paperwork is in order, including emergency contacts."

"Emergency contacts?" Daisy repeated.

"Ms. Lee, you're having surgery. It's a serious matter. We need to know who to talk with in case there's a problem."

"Oh my," Daisy fretted. "I really don't have anyone. My family is back east and we've lost touch."

"No children?"

"No," Daisy confirmed.

"Friends. You have friends?"

"Well, I did, but . . ." and Daisy stammered unable to complete the sentence. She was suddenly very tired.

The doctor bit his lower lip. Daisy wondered if he'd encountered her situation before. An older person admitted to the ER with no available next of kin. How many other seemingly alert, independent seniors found themselves alone during a health crisis?

He stood up. "Okay then. We'll have a social worker stop by. Don't worry about it," he said, leaning over and squeezing her hand.

It was a kind gesture. Daisy appreciated the change in his manner. If only she could remember his name. He must have told her, but then it seemed rude to ask again. Instead, she accepted his warmth and was grateful. Whatever his name, at least there was a heart behind that tough clinical exterior.

* * *

"Isn't this nice?" Charlie said, taking a deep breath and enjoying the fresh air. "We're sitting outside and eating lunch. The sun is shining, the sky is blue. It's not too warm. You can even see Camelback Mountain from here. It's Shangri-La."

The hour in the apartment had made Dave tense; now Charlie was trying to get him to relax, but it was difficult.

Dave nodded grudgingly. "It *is* wonderful."

"And after we eat and go to the grocery store, maybe we'll take a nap." Charlie lifted an eyebrow provocatively.

"We'll see," Dave answered. He looked down at the brunch menu. "Do you know what you're having? What looks good?"

"I think *I do*," Charlie said, his voice throaty. He leaned forward and winked.

"Okay, okay, I get it, Mr. Subtle," Dave answered. "How about we order before we make plans for the rest of the day?"

"Sex will relax you," Charlie coaxed.

"Don't feel like it," Dave said. "Not when I'm upset."

Charlie placed his menu on the table. "A little backrub and you'll be fine."

But Dave was not to be persuaded. "It's best to leave me alone when I'm in a mood."

Charlie said nothing.

"Did you hear me?" Dave asked.

"Okay . . . okay . . . I hear you," Charlie acknowledged. "Just trying to help."

A tow truck passed by. A red Honda Fit was hoisted high in the air, the passenger side punched in. Charlie nodded in the truck's direction. "Check that out. Someone's really having a bad day." Dave turned to see the damaged vehicle. "See . . . we have everything going for us," Charlie continued. "You've got a new job. We're healthy. The weather is terrific. We're so lucky."

Dave nodded, hesitantly.

"We have a great life," Charlie continued.

Dave had to agree.

"You should be more mindful of that," Charlie counseled. "And appreciative, instead of getting yourself all worked up and stressed out. A wrecked car . . . that's a problem."

Dave's appetite improved. "Okay, I'm going to get the Greek salad with chicken," he said, more positively. "That sounds good. And an order of hummus. We can split it."

"Okay." Charlie brightened. He waited for Dave to put his menu down before signaling for the waitress.

"And maybe I'll have a Diet Coke," Dave added.

"How about just water?" Charlie suggested. "We're in the desert. You should be drinking plenty of water," he said, knowing from experience that carbonation and sex didn't mix.

"Okay," Dave acquiesced.

Charlie assumed a Cheshire smile as the waitress approached. *Putty in my hands*, he thought. *He's just putty in my hands.*

2

....

When Daisy awoke, she had no idea whether it was day or night. A bright white curtain created a makeshift space that separated her from the rest of the world. Beside her, an electronic monitor seemed to repeatedly hum, *hello there hello there hello there.*

She felt small, fragile, and very alone.

She inhaled and exhaled in a series of slow, deep breaths. She'd learned in yoga about the importance of the breath to ease anxiety, but now, she was unable to achieve any sense of calm. She was too scared about what might happen next.

Tears came to her eyes as her mind drifted back to the day when she'd begun her journey to this place in the desert.

It was August 12, 1952.

She was eighteen years old, standing on the platform at Grand Central Station in an inexpensive blue traveling suit and matching navy beret, white gloves, and holding a straw purse, all purchased from Gimbel's bargain basement. She'd wanted to go to California but could barely afford the fare to Phoenix. With both parents long gone, she was on her own. Still, it had been a heart-wrenching decision to leave New York City. She adored her older brother Jacob, but her sister-in-law Rose had made it clear that Daisy had to leave.

How different my life would have been if I hadn't . . .

The thought stopped midstream. Buried pain was best left in the past. And yet she couldn't resist a final memory. The beautiful eyes searching her face; tiny hands peeking out from a blue blanket; the smell of talcum powder on his warm, little body.

She held her breath as she remembered.

When Daisy arrived in Phoenix, America was in the midst of a post-war industrial boom. Jobs were plentiful. Phoenix was a sleepy town of mostly one-story buildings. Outside the city perimeter, it was still cowboy country—sunburned men with hats and chaps, horses, corrals, and trails across the desert. Daisy landed her first job as a barmaid at the San Carlos Hotel. For most women of her generation, marriage came before work, and yet marriage eluded her. Men came and went, none staying too long. Daisy adjusted. She bore her disappointments quietly. Life taught her that nothing was guaranteed. If she wanted to survive, she'd have to learn to take care of herself. She'd have to be strong. It had been a hard lesson.

A nurse appeared from behind the curtain.

"Ms. Lee, we're just about ready. How are you doing?"

Daisy was too upset to answer and tried, instead, to smile. The young woman stroked Daisy's arm as she checked the IV, then slipped a pair of socks on her feet. The pain from her hip was gone. The nurse pushed aside the curtain and maneuvered the gurney down a short hallway and into a room with a bright white light. A drug was administered as she was instructed to count backward from ten. Somewhere between nine and eight Daisy found a peaceful freedom from thought . . . a total immersion into the unconscious.

* * *

Dave stifled a yawn. He'd arrived at 7:30 a.m. for his first day on the new job. After grabbing a glazed donut and a cup of coffee, he found an aisle seat in the crowded auditorium where new hires from across the regional market were going through a communal orientation. At the front of the room, there was a large screen. Projected in large white letters against a dark-blue background . . . *The Mission of Bremer Health*. On the stage, a young woman in her late twenties, a manager in human resources, repeatedly checked her watch as Dave took the first bite of his donut. *Dear God*, he thought, savoring the sugary goodness. *When was the last time I had a donut?* He licked his lips and sipped the coffee; the combination, pure pleasure.

As the other new hires settled into their seats, Dave spotted Phyllis, his boss's secretary, entering the front of the auditorium through a side door marked *Exit*. It had been weeks since they'd last seen each other at his final interview. She scanned the auditorium, eyeglasses perched atop her luxurious blond mane, wearing a blue knit dress that seemed a bit too tight for her curvaceous figure. Phyllis appeared stressed as she looked about. Dave wondered what could possibly be wrong. He stifled a second yawn as Phyllis slipped on her eyeglasses, squinted, and then nodded in his direction. She hurried over. "Mr. Greenway?" she asked, kneeling next to his chair.

"Yes," he answered, suddenly aware she wasn't quite sure. Up close, he could see the dark circles gathered under her lovely eyes. He guessed she was in her late thirties.

"I'm so sorry," she said, "but it's been crazy around here. I just processed four job offers last week for new executives. I'm having trouble keeping the names and faces straight."

Dave smiled. That seemed like a lot of new positions. He hoped Bremer was expanding. More jobs, more opportunity.

"Mr. Allman wants you to join the executive team meeting," she said. "You'd better bring your things along. These meetings can run long."

Dave grabbed his briefcase and followed Phyllis out of the auditorium, struggling to keep up as she rushed down the hallway toward the executive boardroom.

"Every Monday morning the executive team meets," she called back to him, miraculously balancing the shifting weight of her ample backside on a pair of six-inch black heels. "The meeting will always be on your calendar for 8:00 a.m. and Mr. Allman expects everyone to be prompt." She touched the knob to the boardroom and then stepped back, nodding to Dave to open the door and go inside.

All eyes turned as Dave entered. He was motioned to a chair at the end of a large conference table. Daniel Allman, Chief Operating Officer of Bremer Health, sat at the head. Daniel made the brief introduction. "Ladies and Gentleman, this is Dave Greenway, our newest vice president."

Heads bobbed and turned. Dave recognized a few of the faces from the organizational chart which had arrived with his relocation packet. The seats at the conference table were filled by hospital CEOs and their medical and nursing leadership. Lesser executives, directors and managers, sat in chairs scattered about the room. Dave had never seen so much high-priced talent gathered in one place for a weekly meeting. He'd researched the market and knew many of the executives had journeyed for hours to be in attendance.

Daniel returned the group's focus to the agenda. As Daniel spoke about financial targets, Dave remembered the first time they'd met. He'd been impressed by Daniel's sheer size. He stood six foot four with the build of a retired basketball player who had filled out after a few years off the court. His huge mitts clasped Dave's hand with an energy that had caught Dave totally off guard.

"I'll be frank," Daniel had said, "I need your expertise to help run this place. Sometimes, I think I'm surrounded by idiots. Right now the corporate office is all over my tail. But I don't give a rat's ass about them. Only the Chairman of the Board has the power to hire and fire me. The corporate office is just so much background noise."

Dave had been charmed by Daniel. He appreciated his honesty. He appreciated his informal manner. But now, Dave wondered how Daniel ran his empire, as he refocused back on the meeting.

"I'm going to ask again," Daniel said, glancing about the room, "who shared this month's financials with the corporate office?"

The tension in the room was palpable as Dave coyly looked about, trying to put faces together with the photos and bios he'd been given. He'd have to know the players if he expected to hit the floor running.

Craig De Coy was the first to speak.

Dave recognized Craig from his brush cut. He was a first-time CEO who had held lesser positions in small, rural, community hospitals.

Craig leaned forward, breaking the line of straight-backed executives who had turned to face Daniel. "Corporate tells us to send the information directly to them. What else can we do?"

"You call me," Daniel said sharply. "I've told you that I'll handle all communications with corporate."

"But they leave us no option," Craig insisted. "They expect immediate turnaround."

"That's ridiculous," Daniel said, his voice booming. "How many times are we going to have this conversation? How many times do I have to repeat myself?"

Daniel looked about as if he actually expected someone to answer the question. There was total silence.

He continued. "If the people in this room are unable to put off corporate, maybe you shouldn't be in the C-suite."

"That's not fair," Craig responded, his face bright red, sounding like a third-grader objecting to a homework assignment.

Daniel scanned the room. His dark eyes defying anyone to speak. "Who else doesn't think it's fair?"

Barely a breath was taken.

"It appears you're alone in that opinion, Craig. Perhaps if you ran your operation as well as you answer to corporate, you'd have hit your budget targets this month."

Craig clenched his jaw. The muscles in his cheeks visibly flexed. Dave wondered how long Craig planned to stay in his job. His future with the company seemed bleak.

Daniel's tone shifted. "How do you think I feel when corporate asks me to explain financials I haven't yet seen? All they want to do is catch me off-guard. Make me sweat." He was now playing the martyr. "Those people don't know how to run a business. They're bean counters. I'm the one holding this ship together. So remember, the next time the corporate office calls, it's the regional office that pays your salary. You do what I tell you," he insisted. "I hired you, and by God, I'll fire you! Is everybody clear on that?"

Dave couldn't believe his ears. Is this how the company conducted its meetings? Like an over-the-top Telemundo drama?

Daniel next held up a packet of handouts. Colored pie charts graphed each hospital's performance according to Medicare's quality standards. Green indicated success; yellow, the need for improvement. Nearly every page was dominated by red.

Daniel focused on Craig. "Your hospital's performance is especially dismal," he bristled.

Craig glanced at his chief nursing officer. A middle-aged, attractive brunette, nervously recounted the steps that the hospital was taking to turn the subpar performance. Dave watched Daniel's face as he listened to the woman. It was quiet, impassive. After three minutes had passed, Daniel suddenly pounded the conference table with a closed fist. The force was so great, that the modem at the center leapt from its position. "Bullshit," Daniel shouted. "This is all bullshit."

The poor woman sat slack-jawed, unable to continue.

Daniel stood up. He held the offending data above his head and glared about the room, like an angry giant reaching for the heavens. "I've had it with these excuses, people. Get ready to change jobs because I won't tolerate this kind of performance."

Executives shifted nervously in their chairs as Daniel headed to the door. Before leaving, he slammed the offending packet into the waste can with such force, that it crashed loudly onto its side and rolled over. The sound, a veritable bomb going off, reverberated throughout the room.

After Daniel's exit, the people in the room gathered up their belongings. Empty pads slid into cases, and unused pens dropped into satchels. One-by-one they rose. Defeated children.

Dave's heart sank. *Bullying to achieve results. What have I done? This isn't the work environment I signed up for.*

"Buck up," Charlie said later that evening. "It was probably a once-in-a-blue-moon meeting. Executives don't behave like that."

"I don't know," Dave said. "There was so much negative energy."

"Dave, you're exaggerating."

"I wish I was. I just hope he doesn't go off on me."

"He won't," Charlie insisted. "You're the fair-haired child. He paid a lot of money to recruit you."

"Something tells me he takes no prisoners," Dave worried. "This guy doesn't play well with others."

* * *

While Daisy's surgeon described the operation as a success, she wasn't quite so sure. The total hip replacement had left her in severe pain, and for the first time in Daisy's life, she welcomed medication. Lots of medication. So much medication, she lost the ability to stay in the moment. One day blended into the next. People came in and out of her hospital room. If strangers introduced themselves, Daisy was too groggy to remember who they were or why they were there.

The nurses insisted Daisy get up and walk. That was the first rule following surgery. She tried. But despite the objections of the nursing staff, the pain from the incision and the dizziness from all the medication forced her back to bed. She wanted to rest. She had to rest.

But resting in a hospital is impossible.

Daisy lingered the maximum number of days allowed by Medicare before a young woman in a white coat visited. She told Daisy arrangements had been made to transfer her to a rehabilitation facility. Daisy couldn't remember the details of the conversation, how the decision was made, or who actually made it, but there was no turning back. The young woman toting the documents had made that very clear. They needed to free up the bed.

Luis, a nurse's aide, showed up the next morning.

A large Hispanic man with a sweet disposition, Luis helped Daisy to sit up. "Pardon me," he said, slipping his huge hands under Daisy's armpits, before pulling her close. She could smell his Paco Rabanne. He gently lifted her, and in one smooth motion, shifted her into the wheelchair he'd placed bedside.

The soreness in her hip was a potent clarifier of the day's activities. It effectively cut through the confusion of the pain medication. She was once again alert to her surroundings.

Luis glided the wheelchair down the hallway, past the nurse's station, to the elevators flanked by floor-to-ceiling mirrors. Daisy couldn't imagine why anyone would install mirrors in a hospital. She caught sight of her reflection. She flinched. She had no makeup on. Her bouffant hairdo looked like a deflated balloon. She'd planned to have her ash-blond color touched up before the accident, but had missed the appointment. Dark grey roots created a two-tone effect.

I look like a psychiatric patient who just had electroshock therapy, she thought sadly.

The elevator doors opened. It was midday and the car was crowded. Strangers stared at her. She took a deep breath and resigned herself to the situation. She didn't look her best and there was absolutely nothing she could do about it. She was at the mercy of her left hip.

A young man with shaggy brown hair wearing a *Jesus Loves Me* tee shirt smiled politely and stepped to the side of the elevator. Luis turned the wheelchair around and pulled Daisy in backward. There was just enough room.

Daisy faced the front of the car. In the reflection of the metallic doors, she could see a girl of six or seven standing nearby, cradling a stuffed floppy-eared white bunny in her arms, sneaking furtive glances at a bald spot on the side of Daisy's head. The child's eyes searched Daisy's crown like an explorer traveling through uncharted waters. Daisy closed her eyes to block the little girl out.

When the elevator doors opened onto the lobby, a stiff breeze blew up from the shaft. The gust caught Daisy by surprise. She struggled to keep the front of the flimsy green hospital gown closed but her fingers were like hardened rubber. The two tiny strings, barely knotted in a bow, unraveled. As the wheelchair advanced, the gown slipped hopelessly out of Daisy's grasp and caught in the mechanism of the wheel. Kindly strangers turned away. Others stared as she fumbled and tugged on the trapped gown, bare breasts exposed.

Daisy blushed crimson.

Luis pulled the chair backward in an effort to release the gown as he reached over Daisy's head to stop the elevator door from bouncing back and forth against the wheelchair. The first bounce had created a high-pitched beeping which had alerted security. Daisy was soon surrounded by uniformed guards.

Luis successfully freed the gown, but the damage had been done. The child who stood at Daisy's side had witnessed the entire debacle. The mother tugged roughly on the little girl's hand before she finally left the elevator.

What had taken less than three minutes to unfold felt as if it had happened in slow motion.

Daisy boldly returned the gaze of those in the lobby who'd been too shocked to look away. She nodded politely, as if it had all been planned. She pretended she was enjoying a ride in an Audi convertible on a warm Phoenix day. And though nothing could have been further from the truth, for that moment, Daisy shifted reality.

"Daisy Ellen Lee?" asked the driver, an African-American man whose bent posture and graying hair hinted he was well past retirement age. He took the paperwork from Luis and quickly compared it to his own documents. "Yup, that's you," the man answered with a warm smile. "You just sit tight and relax."

The wheelchair was rolled onto the van's electronic hoist. In moments, Daisy was lifted like so much cargo. "There you go," the driver said, unlocking the safety and pushing the wheelchair into place, his brown eyes projecting pure kindness and consideration. With a quick snap, he locked the chair. "Now that wasn't so bad."

The hospital disappeared in the distance. Daisy thought, *Thank God, I'll never see those people again* as she tightened her grip on the hospital gown, reliving the experience.

"I'll have you at The Village in no time," the driver called back.

Along the interior walls of the van were large glossy photographs of active seniors. A fashionably dressed woman, silver hair cut in a short perky bob, gaily held a glass of red wine, smiling as if ready to make a toast; a handsome gentleman in a bright green Tommy Hilfiger golf shirt and white shorts was on the greens, club in hand, preparing to putt; an older woman emerged from a hot tub, cap adorned in brightly colored flowers, her smile beaming. The Village promised to offer more than rehabilitation. It professed to be a lifestyle community.

Daisy thought, *The Village . . . now that's a lovely name.*

* * *

Jack Lee broke into a big grin as his 2007 white Ford Escape passed Anthem on Interstate 17 heading south. He'd spotted the olive green marker. *Phoenix – 33 miles.* They'd traveled three days, stopping overnight in St. Louis and Amarillo, some two thousand miles across country from Detroit. Enid, his wife, fast asleep in the passenger seat, was gently snoring. She'd drifted off somewhere south of Flagstaff, leaving Jack alone to thrill at the majesty of the red rocks of Sedona.

Growing up in New York, Jack had often heard about Arizona from his father Jacob who had boasted of having a sister, an aunt Jack had never met, who'd settled in the Phoenix area. Cowboys. Desert. Wide open spaces. Jack fondly remembered his father expressing an interest in visiting, though he never did get west of the Mississippi. Together, they watched *Wagon Train, Bonanza*, and *Have Gun—Will Travel.* Jack could never seem to get enough of the Westerns. And then, in 1985, Jack made his first trip to Phoenix to attend a conference at the Arizona Biltmore. The memory of the beautiful property and the surrounding homes had stayed with him. *I'm going to live here someday*, he thought.

It was a promise he'd been determined to keep.

"Hey, sleepyhead," he said, gently nudging his wife's shoulder, "you've got to see this. The scenery is amazing."

Enid, a petite woman of delicate features, who wore her dark auburn hair in a severe mannish cut, opened her eyes. "My God, it's so bright," she said, shielding her face with her hand. "Someone dim the lights."

"You're just tired. It's been a long trip. But I promise, you're going to love it."

"You didn't tell me you could go blind from the sun." She pulled down the car visor.

"We'll get you a pair of dark shades. Heck, we'll be like movie stars and tint the car windows. '*Who's that?*' everyone will ask. '*Enid and Jack Lee. They're new here.*'"

Enid shifted in her seat. "Are you being funny, Jack?" she said with a withering glance.

"Come on. This is the beginning of a new life. Arizona. Yee ha!"

"Jack," she admonished him, checking her hair in the visor mirror, "you're acting like John Wayne is going to show up atop a stagecoach with guns blazing. Phoenix is a sophisticated city. Last night when you drifted off, I read *Fodor's*. The days of the Wild West are over," she announced with certainty.

"Ah, but nature is everywhere. Just look around. You can see it in the cacti and the desert landscapes. So beautiful. This is a dream come true for me." His voice was barely able to contain his excitement.

Enid sighed. "I don't know why I let you talk me into this. Why not Florida? What was wrong with Boca Raton? I have family there."

"Enid, this is an adventure." Jack sidestepped the perilous trap of commenting on Enid's family. "We can still vacation in Boca."

Enid nodded, seemingly appeased.

Jack caught sight of an eagle soaring overhead. His heart skipped a beat. *Besides*, he thought about Florida, *if I wanted to live in a damp swamp, I'd have moved to the bayous of Louisiana.*

* * *

Jack Lee couldn't wait to get out of Michigan. After thirty years teaching high school history in Detroit, he was terrified that his pension might be affected by the trials and tribulations of Michigan's financial woes. The auto industry was on its knees, with the city of Detroit struggling to find bottom. Sick of listening to the daily drumbeat of financial mismanagement, he and Enid had agreed to sell their historic Indian Village home after the fourth break-in in two years. Each time, they'd been lucky. Neither of them had been home. The following week Jack was on a plane to Phoenix where he made an offer on a two-bedroom townhouse in The Biltmore Terraces; a great property with views of the golf course.

"It's so small, Jack," Enid complained when she reviewed the property online.

Jack was not about to be second-guessed. "We're awfully lucky to have picked up a Biltmore property at such a great price. And this is the time in life when we can do with a little less. Besides, that house perfectly fits our budget."

Another reason Jack had pressed for Arizona was its reasonable cost of living. Too young for social security, he'd seen the value of Enid's trust setup by her father, tumble. Over the years, it had generated enough income to keep Enid in the style she craved. But with the uncertainty of the times, and the bottoming of the stock market, the value of the portfolio was at an all-time low. They'd have to watch their spending.

"It won't be long now," Jack said as the car headed down Missouri Avenue toward 24th Street. "Look at those hedges."

A high wall of greenery enshrined the one-square-mile Biltmore property that included the hotel and surrounding property.

"Oh my God," Enid gasped, her mood suddenly brightening. "You didn't tell me it was so private and lush. It's as lovely as the Boca Raton Hotel and Country Club."

They crossed 24th Street and entered the Biltmore. Enid sat up straight and adjusted her blouse. Jack smiled as she checked her face in the mirror.

"Where's my lipstick?" She searched her bag. "Jack, you didn't tell me it was so exclusive. I should have worn something nicer."

Enid's eyes popped as the car crossed the 18-hole golf course before passing the many mansions that lined Thunderbird Drive. Jack was thrilled that she was so excited. *I knew she'd love it. She just needed to experience it.* A quick right, and the car stopped at the gate of the Biltmore Terraces.

"Hello," Jack said to the redhead who popped her head out of the window to greet him. "We're the Lees. We're new. You should be expecting us."

The woman checked the roster. "Lee, Lee. Oh yes. Here you are. Well, welcome. I'm Sheila. I'm filling in today, but anything you need, be sure to ask."

"So you're new too," Jack said exuberantly.

Enid nudged him with her elbow. It was her cue for him to stop talking to strangers.

"Not exactly," Sheila explained. "I work full-time at Biltmore Greens. I'm just helping out today." She handed Jack a manila envelope. "Inside is a parking pass and a decal for your window. Make sure you place the sticker on the inside driver's side. It allows you access to all the Biltmore neighborhoods."

"Thank you," Jack beamed. "Tell me, is it always this beautiful here?"

"Absolutely," Sheila smiled.

"This is just a dream come true. A dream come true," he said.

Enid's elbow poked him again.

"I know this is an odd question," Sheila suddenly asked, "but are you folks related to Daisy Ellen Lee?

Jack was astonished. "My father had a sister Daisy who moved to Phoenix. I was just thinking about her."

"There must be a million women named *Daisy* in the world," Enid offered. Her tone left no doubt that she was eager to get past the gate.

"But you did say Daisy Ellen?" Jack clarified with Sheila. "How many *Daisy Ellens* can there be?"

"A quarter of a million," Enid snapped. "At least as many as there are Jack Allen Lees."

"She's a lovely woman," Sheila went on. "Now my brother's daughter, my niece Alison, is the spitting image of me as a girl. Every time I look at her, it's like looking in a mirror. You know, Mr. Lee? The more I look at you, the more I think you and Ms. Lee are just like two peas in a pod. You have the same eyes. It's quite unnerving."

"I wonder if she's my aunt," Jack said to Enid, before turning back to Sheila. "Now that would be quite a coincidence. Tell me, which is Daisy's house? I'd love to meet her."

Sheila's expression shifted. "Oh, I'm sorry," she said, a worried look crossing her face. "Perhaps I shouldn't have said anything. I'm not allowed to provide personal information about the residents. But I'll tell you what. Why don't you give me a note with your name and phone number, and I'll make sure Ms. Lee gets it."

"Fine," Jack agreed. "Whatever works." He waited for Sheila to open the gate. "Imagine that," he said, turning to Enid, "I may have an aunt who lives in the Biltmore. A long-lost aunt. Who'd have guessed?"

* * *

Dear Ms. Lee,

My name is Jack. My wife and I have recently moved to Phoenix. I wonder if we are related. My parents were Jacob and Rose. They're gone now, but I remember my Dad telling me about a sister who lived in Phoenix. Is it possible you're my aunt? If so, we'd love to meet you. Please ask Sheila to share with us your phone number. Or, if you'd like to call us directly, I've enclosed my phone number on the back of this note with our address.

Fondly, Jack Lee

* * *

Later that day, Sheila visited Daisy at The Village. She offered a friendly hello to a gentleman sitting in the lobby before realizing he was babbling to himself. She averted her eyes as she passed the white-haired seniors, dressed in their bedclothes, who lined the hallways slumped over in their wheelchairs, fast asleep. The closer she got to the wing where Daisy was housed, the stronger the smell of urine.

She gagged.

Arriving at Daisy's closed door, she knocked. "Ms. Lee," she called out. "Ms. Lee, are you there?"

There was no response.

She knocked again, this time louder, cracking open the door and peeking inside. The room was dark. It was midafternoon and the Venetian blinds were tightly drawn.

Perhaps this is the wrong room, she thought, rechecking the name on the door. No, she was in the right place.

She entered, slowly approaching Daisy's bedside.

Daisy stirred. A weak voice pleaded, "Nurse, I need to go to the bathroom. Please help me."

"Ms. Lee, it's me, Sheila."

Daisy struggled to focus. "Sheila, where did you come from?"

"I've been concerned about you," Sheila said in a sudden pang of guilt. Why hadn't she made it her business to visit sooner? "How are you?" she asked, helping Daisy to sit up.

"Not well, I'm afraid. I've developed an infection and I have a fever."

Sheila's heart sank.

"They're giving me antibiotics."

"That sounds like the right course."

"I don't know." Daisy shook her head. "I'm so tired . . . and I have terrible cramps. What time is it?"

Sheila looked at the wall clock. "It's three."

"How long have I been here?" Daisy asked.

Sheila had no clue.

"How about we open these blinds?" she suggested, tugging on the little white cord. Light flooded the room. "There, that's better," she said, turning back to Daisy. "It's such a lovely day . . ." she began, as her breath caught in her throat. Seeing Daisy in the bright light, she struggled to suppress her shock. Daisy's face looked haggard. The gentle lines which had once graced her friendly eyes and mouth had deepened severely from sudden weight loss. Her skin was white and pasty, a far cry from Daisy's normal rosy complexion. Daisy was no longer the vital, energetic person Sheila knew. She'd become a withered old woman,

"I wish I felt better," Daisy said, adjusting herself in the bed. "But it is so good of you to visit. How kind."

Sheila leaned against the windowsill, unwilling to commit to a seat. The smell of disinfectant permeated the air. She maintained a pleasant, outward demeanor, all the while knowing that something horrible had happened.

"Bert sends his regards," she said in a chipper voice. "We both came to the hospital to visit but you were really out of it. I'm not sure you even knew we were there."

"I don't remember," Daisy confirmed. "Morphine is an amazing drug."

And then Daisy pulled back the top cover of her bedding. Her feet were blueish-red and swollen. Sheila diverted her eyes, fighting the urge to flee. Instead, she retrieved Jack's note from her purse.

"Well, you'll never guess who I met," she bravely said, holding up the note from Jack which after all had been the reason for her visit. "It was the strangest thing . . ." and as she started to tell the story, a young African-American woman sporting a close-cropped Afro appeared in the doorway.

"Honey," the aide called to Daisy, "have you been ringing for me?"

"Oh yes," Daisy answered, relief in her voice. "I have to go to the bathroom."

Sheila, grateful for the interruption, placed the unopened note on the bedside table. "Well, I better be going," she said, concerned her presence might cause Daisy embarrassment. "I need to get home," she lied, eager to escape. "I just wanted to be sure and bring this note."

Mission accomplished, Sheila was out of the room before the aide lowered the bars on Daisy's bed. She moved quickly down the hallway, past those who seemed frozen in time. *Is this what becomes of us?* Sheila thought, rushing to her car. *I'd rather die than wind up in a place like that.*

⋈ ⋈ ⋈

"I'm home," Dave called from the open door, his key still buried in the lock.

He was exasperated. He'd hoped to leave the office early, but cornered at five o'clock, he'd fidgeted his way through an impromptu meeting with Daniel that lasted nearly two hours.

Doesn't he have a wife and a home to go to?

He chalked it up to Daniel's endless need to micromanage.

Charlie stood in the galley kitchen, separated from the living room by an eat-in counter. A small dinette table was within steps. "The roast's in the oven, warming." Charlie came around the counter. "Let me give you a hand with that key. You have to jiggle it."

Dave and Charlie switched positions.

Dave dropped his workbag by the door and headed to the kitchen. "It smells good," he said, spotting the mail on the counter. He looked through the stack.

Charlie twisted and turned, eventually loosening Dave's key before dropping it on the counter. "Hey you," he said approaching Dave from behind. With his arms about Dave's waist, he pulled him in for a hug.

Dave turned, and they kissed. He relaxed into it. It felt damn good. "Sorry about being so late," he apologized. "It's impossible to get out of that building at a reasonable hour. I think this might be the way of life at Bremer."

"I'm just glad you're here. Time to relax."

Dave loosened his tie as Charlie pulled out the roast and placed it on top of the stove.

"So how'd it go today? Any better?" Charlie asked, lifting the roast out of the pan with a large fork to settle it on the carving board.

"Any better than what? The same people, the same meetings, the same Daniel. He has all these questions about the financial performance of the business, which is surprising considering he signed all these terrible contracts. Every lousy deal has his fingerprints on it. And he's so damn angry. He's just a very hostile guy."

Dave spotted an oversized card in the middle of the stack of mail. He opened it. A photograph of two Golden Labs, eyes bright, tongues dangling, smiling the way only Golden Labs seemed to do, stared back at him.

"Well, I have a surprise for you." Charlie pointed at the dining room table, carving knife in hand.

There, sitting on Dave's plate, was a box wrapped with a red bow.

"Oh no," Dave moaned, realizing the card he held had been sent by friends in California. "It's our anniversary . . ."

Charlie smiled. "You make it sound like a terrible thing."

"But I didn't get you anything," Dave said mournfully. "All those early morning meetings and late nights, I kept thinking, *I have to get Charlie a gift*. But I kept running out of time. And then I forgot."

Charlie leaned forward on the counter. "Don't worry about it. You'll take me to dinner this weekend. No big deal."

"Oh Charlie, that isn't right. I wanted you to have something special."

"I *do* have something special." Charlie wiped his hands with a dish towel before pulling Dave into his arms. "I have you. And now, I have Phoenix. Dave, I love it here. This is the best decision we've ever made."

Dave was sorry to hear Charlie say that.

Charlie returned to the galley kitchen. "I couldn't imagine us living anywhere else. I mean, can you believe this weather? In April? It's amazing."

Dave fingered the ribbon on the gift. "I've been thinking this move was a mistake," he said, his voice low, nearly imperceptible. Uncertain Charlie had heard him, he blurted out, "I really can't stand working at Bremer."

Charlie, his back turned to Dave, opened the refrigerator, though he seemed to hear every word. "You just need time to adjust. You'll see. We'll buy a great house, make new friends, and get a dog. We'll have a wonderful life."

"Charlie, I don't know." Dave was heartsick. It had been a long time since he and Charlie had been so far apart on an issue.

Charlie dressed the salad. "You've always been slow to adjust to change. Every new job has been a crisis. Given time, things will smooth over. You'll see. It'll all work out. It's just bumpy in the beginning."

Dave sighed. "I wish I was as optimistic as you."

"Well, you never *have* been," Charlie said. "That word isn't in your vocabulary. You're a worrier."

"But this time it's different," Dave confessed, a hand resting on what remained of the unopened mail, eyes pleading for Charlie to understand. "This is really bad."

"You're upset," Charlie acknowledged. "You've had a hard day. Why don't you go ahead and open your gift."

Dave tore at the paper. *How*, he thought, *can I possibly make Charlie understand?*

The gift was a box of See's Chocolates. Mixed Nuts and Chews. Dave's favorite.

"Well, open the card," Charlie demanded.

Dave opened the envelope. Two tickets to Tennessee Williams's *The Glass Menagerie* at Arizona Theatre Company slid out. "That's nice," Dave said quietly, his words more polite than heartfelt. Upset, he needed to be alone. "I think I'll change before dinner."

Charlie, oblivious to Dave's mood, trailed after him to the bedroom, talking about the small events of the day. The neighbor he'd met in the supermarket. The noise the kids made after school as they played in the pool, screeching with delight. The dog he'd seen from the small terrace off the kitchen as it walked by with its owner in tow. And then, about the afternoon activities househunting.

"Ronaldo and I checked out a few more houses," Charlie said, as Dave dropped his tie on the bed.

"What'd you think?"

"Honestly, not much."

"Why?" Dave asked, removing his white dress shirt and handing it to Charlie, who in turn, stuffed it into a blue, dry-cleaners bag.

"I didn't really like the neighborhood."

"Then why look there?" Dave wondered. "Just tell Ronaldo the neighborhoods you're interested in." Dave stepped over to the en-suite sink in his briefs and washed his face.

Charlie picked up Dave's slacks, folded them, and slipped them onto a wooden hanger. He hung up the tie on the metal rack inside the closet. He placed the black Cole Haan loafers on the appropriate shelf. "Well, that's the problem," he said, emerging from the closet. "I really don't know the neighborhoods. So, we've been checking out North Central and a lot of houses closer to your office. I know you're concerned about the drive."

"The traffic can be tough," Dave admitted, drying his face with a towel, "but I don't want to live too close to the office. I already spend too much time there."

"Physically and mentally," Charlie added.

"So nothing yet?" Dave stepped into a pair of grey Nike shorts.

"Oh, I've seen nice houses, but they aren't for us."

"Too bad," Dave said, slipping on a dark blue tee shirt sporting the logo of the San Francisco Police Department.

"I thought you were afraid to wear that thing." Charlie had bought the tee shirt at a fundraiser during a Bay Area street fair.

"As long as we're staying in, it's okay. Remember when that woman ran up to me in the city and said she needed my help?" Dave smiled at the memory, suddenly longing to be back in the Bay Area.

"How could I forget?" Charlie let out a chuckle before returning to the subject at hand. "Maybe I'll have better luck tomorrow. We have appointments to see five houses in Scottsdale. We'll see how that goes."

* * *

Delirious from a blood-borne infection, Daisy was admitted to an intensive care unit in the middle of the night. The nurse's aide who coordinated the transfer spotted the note lying on Daisy's bedside table. Glancing at the contents, she handed it to the lead EMT. "Mac, this might come in handy." Mac, a stocky guy sporting a crewcut who had played defensive end in high school, shoved the note in his pocket.

That morning at Denny's, after finishing breakfast, Mac pulled the note out when he reached for his wallet to settle the check. "Crap," he said, reading the note. "I've got to get this back to that old lady." But with his shift over, he had no desire to return to the hospital. Instead, he opted to do the next best thing. He pulled out his cell phone.

"Hello, is this Jack Lee?" Mac asked.

"Speaking."

"I'm afraid I have some bad news for you."

* * *

"Oh my God," Jack said, hanging up the phone. He'd been outside planting miniature cacti when his cell phone rang. "She's in the hospital," he told Enid who was stretched out on a lounge chair sipping lemonade.

"Who?" Enid asked, sitting up with alarm. She wore a white outfit; white top and white shorts; a large straw gardening hat rested in her lap.

"Daisy," Jack answered. He examined her face for any sense of recognition. "The woman we thought might be my aunt."

"Oh," Enid said, seemingly relieved, "is that all." She relaxed back into the lounger. Though she'd told Jack she'd help with the planting, after opening the first bag of fertilizer, the smell had put her off.

"She's ill," Jack said, his voice tinged with annoyance. "Here we have a chance to get to know her, and now it gets complicated."

But Enid still didn't seem to care. "That's too bad Jack," she said, checking her manicure. "Jack, we really should have hired someone to do the gardening. It's such a messy job."

Jack wiped the sweat from his forehead. He hated when Enid changed the subject in mid-discussion. Irritated, he ignored her behavior. "Do you think we should go visit her?"

Enid offered a perplexed look. "I don't see why. We don't know her. This seems to be a private matter. What does she have to do with us?"

Jack arched a brow. "I don't know exactly, but if she's my father's sister, I should do something."

"Oh no." Enid waved her hands in the air. "We're not taking on the care of an old woman, someone we've never even met. Forget it."

"Then again, she might not be my aunt," Jack said, his face registering a modicum of relief. "That certainly is possible."

"That's right," Enid agreed. "She probably isn't."

"It would be too much of a coincidence, don't you think?" Jack caught sight of an eagle soaring in the distance. The graceful majesty of the bird reminded him of his Dad's love for everything Southwest. "No . . . I'm going over to the hospital," he reconsidered. "I better just go."

Enid sneered. "And what do you think that'll prove?"

"I don't know," Jack said. "It just feels like the right thing to do."

Enid pressed her lips together. "Okay, but if you're going . . . I'm going with you. Give me a few minutes to change my clothes. You're too soft-hearted for your own good, Jack Lee. Much too soft-hearted."

*　*　*

Daisy's eyes felt like hot coals. She'd tossed and turned, confused, uncertain where she was. She'd tried to remove the IV from her wrist when the ICU nurse entered the cubicle to check Daisy's vitals. Daisy struggled, certain the woman wearing a facemask had come to kill her.

But by nine o'clock in the morning, her fever had broken. Exhausted, she napped on and off.

She was awakened by a gentle touch to her arm. A nurse hovered nearby. "Good afternoon, sweetie. Are you awake?" Her voice was like honey. "Do you remember me?"

Daisy smiled, hoping that was enough recognition.

"I need you to tell me your name and birth date, if you can."

"I'm Daisy Lee," she managed to get out. She then provided her birthdate.

"Good, very good." The nurse smiled and patted her shoulder. "I have a few more questions for you. There's a gentleman here who says he might be your nephew. Do you have a nephew?"

"I don't have any children," Daisy answered, shaking her head from side-to-side, eyes closed.

"No, dear," the nurse tried again. "A nephew. A man named Jack Allen Lee?"

Daisy drifted off.

The nurse touched her arm. Daisy opened her eyes. "Can you tell me the name of your brother?" she asked.

"Jacob," Daisy replied weakly. "Jacob. Is he here?" she asked somewhat confused, her eyes searching about.

"His son is," the nurse answered.

"Oh." Daisy nodded off again.

"Ms. Lee," the nurse gently called as she stroked Daisy's hair. "Do you know a Jack Allen Lee?"

Daisy's head cleared for a moment. "Yes," she nodded, eyes wide open.

"Is he your nephew?"

"Jack," she murmured. She smiled broadly.

The nurse adjusted Daisy's head on the pillow. "There you go, dear. Now you rest."

* * *

Jack took a seat in the cramped medical director's office. The desk was a mess. Freebies from pharmaceutical companies, blank pads and pens embossed with names like Merck and Pfizer were mixed in with scattered pink and yellow papers, and a variety of tiny mechanical windup cars and robots. A white coffee mug with red *We Love You Grandpa* lettering, still a quarter full with black coffee, rested on an open copy of the latest edition of the *New England Journal of Medicine*. Jack wondered how anyone could work in such surroundings. Enid had gone to the restroom. He glanced repeatedly out the open door to the hallway, hoping to catch a glimpse of her as she walked by.

Dr. Mueller, a balding man in his late sixties with fine white hair and a large bulbous nose, shifted a stack of medical records from his chair to the floor near his feet so that he might sit down. "Excuse the mess," he apologized. "I'm the chairman of the hospital's quality committee. I have to review these cases before our next meeting on Friday morning."

Jack nodded in sympathy as if he understood. "My wife should be here any moment," he said, shifting the conversation as he continued to look toward the door. "I'd prefer if we waited for her before we begin. I'm not very good with all of this."

Mueller looked at his watch. "Well, I don't have much time. If it's okay with you . . ."

"Over here," Jack called, spotting Enid.

She stopped midstep. While Jack wore an old pair of jeans with a cotton shirt of bold, red and blue stripes, Enid had dressed for the occasion in a sophisticated olive green dress and white sandals, full makeup and gold jewelry.

Enid took a seat.

"We've spoken to your aunt," Mueller started.

Jack's tone revealed his excitement. "So we *are related*?"

"Ms. Lee confirmed her brother's name was indeed Jacob. And she did recognize your name."

"Really," Jack said enthusiastically. "Are there any other family members? Children?"

Mueller shook his head. "We have no next of kin."

"She never married?"

"We don't know her full history. We just know she's currently single." Mueller's face was stoic.

"When might we be able to talk with her?" Jack asked.

"Her condition is very serious. These superbugs are hard to knock out. She's barely holding her own, though I'm happy to say her fever has come down and she's no longer delirious. We should know more in a few days."

"Oh," was all that Jack could manage.

Mueller lifted the coffee mug, tilted it, looked inside, and then returned it to the desk. "You understand that you have no legal rights to make any healthcare decisions on her behalf."

"Of course not," Jack answered, surprised at the turn of the discussion. "We just wanted to know if she was indeed my aunt."

Afterward, as he and Enid waited for the elevator, Jack was deep in thought. Stepping into the elevator, he couldn't help but acknowledge the obvious, "It's really crazy. I never met my father's sister, and now I have the opportunity, but she may not survive. It's the damnedest thing."

Enid, who'd been quiet and pensive, brightened. "You're probably her only living relative, Jack. If she dies, there could be an inheritance."

Jack was aghast. Leave it to Enid to be focused on money.

"Jack, you might inherit her estate. We could trade up to a bigger Biltmore property. A home in Taliverde. Those homes are one-of-a-kind." There was a gleam in Enid's eye. "This could be quite a windfall."

"Taliverde is well beyond our means," Jack countered, annoyed by Enid's suggestion. "The monthly association dues alone are more than we can afford."

"Daisy's house must be worth some money. I wonder how she had the means to settle in the Biltmore. She must have a sizeable nest egg."

"Enid, I don't think we should be counting her money. After all, we're strangers. For all I know she's living on Social Security."

"Jack, that's ridiculous. No one in the Biltmore is living on Social Security."

"You don't think so?"

"Tomorrow, I'm going to find a lawyer who can advise us."

"I'm not comfortable with this," Jack admitted as they walked through the hospital lobby. "I feel like a vulture."

"Someone has to help her," Enid argued. "She's all alone. She may need us to make medical decisions. We might need a power of attorney. We have a lot to do."

"It's all happening too fast," Jack said, as they crossed the parking lot toward their car.

"And tomorrow, we're going to ask Sheila for the key to Daisy's house. I want to see her place."

"She's not going to give us the key," Jack insisted.

"Oh yes she will," Enid assured him. "You just leave that discussion to me. I'll get those keys and we'll see that house. Mark my words."

Jack had no doubt. Enid could be a dog with a bone, especially when money was involved. As Jack backed out of the spot, his cell phone rang. He fumbled for it in his pocket. "Yes," he said, listening carefully to the other party on the line. "Okay, we're coming back."

"Who was that?" Enid asked.

"The hospital. She's gone into convulsions."

3

....

Anna Garrett was proud of the new addition to her front lawn. She'd recently had the four-foot-wide sign installed between two six-foot-high posts to attract new clients. Commuters on 19th Avenue had to avert their eyes to avoid seeing *Psychic* flashing in bold red neon.

The small bungalow in which she lived and worked had once been part of a residential neighborhood, but with commercial rezoning in the 1980s, and the widening of 19th Avenue, nearby homes had been replaced by office buildings and strip malls crowded with tattoo parlors, wig shops, nail salons, and fast food—Papa John's, Subway, Burger King, and Dunkin' Donuts were all within steps of Anna's front door. Now, with the ongoing recession, empty storefronts had proliferated, providing a haven for the homeless. Anna had spotted strangers milling around the dumpsters and trash cans.

Perhaps, she thought, *it's time for a security door.*

A local handyman had placed a business card under Anna's car wipers when she was at the supermarket. As soon as she touched the card, she had a good feeling about Ernie Gonzalez. She called him, and the following day, Ernie stopped by to look at the job.

Together they stood in Anna's front room, the dedicated space she used to meet with clients. The room held a simple oak table and chairs. The walls were unadorned. A deck of Tarot cards rested in plain sight.

"So, you're a psychic," Ernie said.

Anna felt his eyes take in her five-foot-three rotund frame. She blushed. "I guess that's one way to make a living," he quipped.

Anna was familiar with those who doubted her gifts. "I take it you don't believe in psychics," she said.

"How could I?" he asked. "There seems to be one on every corner in Phoenix."

Anna frowned at Ernie's observation; he was right, of course.

"But I'm glad for the work," Ernie continued. "A paying customer is a good thing."

"But you don't believe," Anna confirmed.

"Well, it's hard to believe. Though I have to say, you certainly look the part."

Anna wore a white peasant blouse that she'd paired with a black skirt. A flowing orange scarf was wrapped about her head in turban fashion. To say she looked odd would be an understatement.

"I wear what feels comfortable," she indignantly answered.

"Oh," Ernie responded. "Me and my big mouth. I should know better than to comment on a woman's appearance."

Anna glared at the handsome dark-haired man. The gentle greying at his temples suggested he was in his mid-forties. His skin glowed with the vigor of someone who worked outdoors.

She closed her eyes and took three deep breaths.

"You don't remember your father," she began. "Your mother told you he died when you were a baby . . . *a car accident* . . . she said. A neighbor helped your mother to raise you. You called him Uncle, but his name was . . . Arturo."

She opened her eyes.

"How could you know that?" Ernie's eyes registered disbelief.

Anna continued. "When your Uncle Arturo was dying, you didn't go to the hospital."

"I was afraid of losing my job," Ernie hastened to explain. "I was working part-time as a bouncer at a local club. I asked to leave, but the bar was short-staffed. I had to stay."

"He wants you to know he loves you and it doesn't matter. He always knew you loved him."

"No . . ." Ernie blurted out, squinting his eyes. "How could you possibly know that?"

"I've always known things I shouldn't," Anna admitted, "ever since I was a little girl."

Ernie stared at her. "So you read minds?"

"I'm not sure how it works. I get . . . impressions."

Ernie slowly backed away from Anna. "I was raised Catholic," he said, a hand in the air. "I still go to church on Sundays. Maybe you're conjuring the devil?"

Anna tried not to laugh. "I always forget. The only people who want a reading are those who schedule an appointment. Everyone else thinks I'm nuts or possessed."

There was an awkward silence. Then Anna came back to the issue at hand. "So what about installing that security door?" she asked.

"Sure, I can do that," Ernie responded.

"And, I was wondering if you do electrical work too? I want those lights that turn on when someone gets too close to the house. Is that possible?"

"You mean motion detectors?"

She nodded.

"Glad to do it," Ernie said.

"And since you're here, I was thinking of painting the kitchen. Any chance you can handle that?"

"You tell me the color, I'll buy the paint, and it will be done."

Anna smiled. It was nice to have a man around the house. Especially one who was good-looking and followed orders.

* * *

"Aunt Daisy," Enid whispered. "Can you hear me?"

Daisy opened her eyes. "Do I know you?" she asked.

It was midday and the lunch tray sat by Daisy's bedside untouched. After six days in Intensive Care, Daisy had finally been transferred to a double room. She was weak, and still slightly feverish; the combination of antibiotics and pain medication had left her exhausted.

An elderly woman sporting a pageboy haircut, occupied the next bed. "We're all loopy in here, dearie," she told Enid. "She'll be fine once she comes around. By the way . . . I'm Mrs. Olive Mulligan." Mrs. Mulligan wore a bed jacket of blue satin. The blue looked particularly flattering in contrast to her white hair. "When I awoke from surgery a few days ago, I wouldn't have recognized my own mother if she'd walked in that door and pulled up a chair."

Enid smiled and ignored the stranger. "No, actually, we've never met," she told Daisy. "I'm your nephew Jack's wife."

"Jack . . ." Daisy's eyes widened.

"Yes. Jacob and Rose's son."

"But where did you come from?" Daisy wanted to know.

"We just moved to the Biltmore from Detroit. The woman at the gate-house—Sheila, I think—told us about your situation. I hope you don't mind me coming to visit."

"Of course she doesn't mind," Mrs. Mulligan answered. "I only wish someone would visit me. My daughter works all day and has her children at night. You'd think her husband could watch those kids so she could come visit her mother." Mrs. Mulligan's voice rose. "It's a terrible thing," she lamented. "A mother's love is never reciprocated. One mother can raise four children, but four children can't take care of one mother."

Enid pretended Mrs. Mulligan wasn't in the room. "Is there anything you need? Anything you want?" she asked Daisy.

Daisy blinked. "Jack . . ." was all she could manage to say.

"Yes, Jack and I are here to help. I've gone to a lawyer, Aunt Daisy. I know you've been terribly ill. He recommended a power of attorney so that we can get you back on your feet."

"Where's Jack?" Daisy asked.

Enid shifted uncomfortably. "He's out-of-town," she lied. Enid had wanted to come alone. She'd met with the attorney on her own and had no interest in including Jack in any of the details. She thought him too emotional about the matter, and too easily swayed by conscience to make the hard decisions that Enid was prepared to undertake as Daisy's representative. "He's in Michigan handling some financial matters, but he'll be back soon. Then he'll come see you."

Daisy's eyes lit up.

"But for now, I need you to sign this document." Enid pulled out the power of attorney from her bag. "This will allow Jack to help you through this crisis. To make certain your bills are paid; that you get the money you need during this horrible ordeal."

"Don't sign anything," Mrs. Mulligan warned. "You don't know this woman."

Daisy closed her eyes. Enid was worried she might fall back to sleep.

"Excuse me," Enid turned to the woman in the next bed, "this is none of your business. No one asked your advice."

"I know what I know," Mrs. Mulligan insisted.

Enid got to her feet and with a hard tug, pulled forward the white privacy curtain that divided the two spaces, blocking Mrs. Mulligan from view. "I need your signature," Enid insisted, placing the document on the bed tray in front of Daisy. "You sign and I'll bring Jack to visit."

"Don't do it," Mrs. Mulligan called out.

"You want to see Jack," Enid asked Daisy. "Don't you?"

* * *

Charlie was unloading the dishwasher when Dave walked in the door. "Gee, you're home early," Charlie said, as he quietly observed the tension in Dave's face. The clenched mouth; the lower lip tightly drawn in. The undeniable anger in his eyes.

"We had a meeting offsite with that dragon lady who runs the health plan," Dave grumbled. "After an hour with her, I couldn't go back to the office."

Charlie changed the subject. He pretended all was fine, as if by wishing it so, Dave would suddenly be happy. "I looked online at a few more houses."

Dave opened the refrigerator. "Anything to eat?"

Charlie blushed. "I was going to go to the supermarket, but got sidetracked. Hey, I'm done with my calls for the day. Let's get out of here. Let's go over to the Arizona Biltmore. We haven't been there yet. We can walk around, grab a drink. They have a terrific bar. And maybe eat dinner. I bet that would cheer you up."

Dave sighed. "Okay, but let me get out of these work clothes."

"Sure, throw on a pair of shorts and a nice shirt . . . Arizona casual."

"Are you sure you'll be okay wrapping up early?" Dave asked.

"Dave," Charlie answered, "business is so slow . . . trust me . . . I'm fine. And besides, this apartment is getting on my nerves."

* * *

Ernie stopped to admire his work. He'd been using a roller brush on the end of a metal pole to apply Marblehead Gold, the deep mustard color Anna had selected for the kitchen walls. He loved the smell of fresh paint, clean and glistening, the way it had of magically transforming a space. *If I could go house to house, block to block, and make everything clean, welcoming, and bright, people would feel so much better about their lives*, he thought.

He closed his eyes and he was ten years old again.

His mother's voice frantically called to him. He ran back into the dark shabby apartment with its worn linoleum and dingy walls. Boxes lined the floor. An old grey sofa, fabric tattered and torn, dominated the center of the room. At night, covered in a white sheet, it would be his bed.

"Hijo," she yelled, the Spanish word for son, "you need to answer me when I call you," she admonished, hands on her hips, a flash of fire in her eyes. She wore her luxurious auburn hair shoulder length, parted in the middle, framing the expressive brown eyes Ernie had come to rely on to read his mother's every mood.

He'd been just outside the door, eager to explore the courtyard and the surrounding area of the two-story, redwood paneled apartment complex. Their unit was at the top of a steep set of stairs, the fifth door to the right along the wooden walkway that encircled the second level. It was their third move in two years. They were always moving. His mother said it was her safety plan.

They can't find you if you keep moving. Always keep moving.

Exactly who *they* were, he wasn't quite sure.

"Where have you been?" She roughly grabbed his arm and pulled him close. She scared him when she was upset. Though she was small in stature, only five feet, she was not to be crossed. "Now you help me put some of these things away," she scolded, glancing about the room, trying to decide where to start.

"I was just walking around, Mama. Just outside the door. But I'm here now. I'll help," he said, offering words that might soothe her. He'd learned through trial and error how to calm her when she was edgy.

"I've told you before, I want you to stay near. Didn't I tell you?" She gave him a sharp look.

He immediately complied. "Yes. Mama," he said, hoping to see her mood soften.

He didn't understand why she was angry. Why her love was so angry. His last words seemed to have worked. She embraced him, squeezing so tightly, she threatened to stifle his breath.

"You're a good boy," she said, finally releasing him from her arms.

She caressed his cheek. He flinched. He didn't trust her kindness.

"What would I do without you?" Her eyes searched his face as if memorizing it. "How would I ever manage?"

He didn't understand her intensity. He only wanted to go outside and play. To be free to run with the other kids who lived in the complex. But he knew she'd not allow that. He'd have to remain separate and alone. He could ride the school bus with the other children, spend his day making friends in class, but once three o'clock came, she wanted him home.

"Remember, Hijo, the neighbors will tell me if you are not home within thirty minutes once school is out," she warned him.

Which neighbors might tell, he had no idea? And though they didn't yet know the neighbors, he dutifully obeyed his mother. Better to obey than risk her wrath. And when she arrived home at five o'clock after tending to the homes of rich white people, she expected him to have completed his homework and be ready to talk with her as she made dinner.

The boxes labeled *cucina* were empty. Ernie had unwrapped and handed plates, glassware, pots and pans to his mother. Most items had found their way to a cabinet. Some, like the large pot Maria used to make soup, sat out on the stove, empty, waiting to be filled with the scraps Maria collected through the week from her employer's kitchen. Leftover meats, vegetables, food that she saw no reason to toss in the garbage.

"Now go wash your hands and change your pants. It's time for church," she scolded.

"Do we have to?" Ernie whined, hoping Maria might be convinced instead to go to the park.

She flashed her eyes. "The Lord made Sunday for church. Now hurry up or we'll miss the bus."

He knew better than to upset her. He washed his hands in the kitchen sink, using a dish towel to get them dry. Maria laid out his church clothes on the sofa, and waited as he kicked off his Keds, stepped out of his shorts, removed his tee shirt, and slipped into the clean white shirt and black pants. Then with a rotation of her finger, she directed him to turn around and face the wall so that she could change her clothes. When Ernie was finally allowed to turn back she had on a blue dress, high heels, and white gloves. She was elegantly transformed. He thought her the prettiest mother in the world.

"Mama, why don't we own a car?" he asked as he tied the laces of his church shoes. "Everyone else does."

"We're not like everyone else," Maria answered, running a brush roughly through his hair.

"We're of Mexican descent," Ernie said proudly. "I know that. Most of the kids I go to school with, their parents are also from Mexico."

Maria's expression shifted. There was a sadness about her eyes.

"Mama, what's wrong?" he asked, his innocent question hanging in the air between them,

"Ernie, there's something I should tell you. You're old enough now to know. You're practically a big boy."

"I *am* a big boy," Ernie insisted.

"Yes, you are," she said, taking his two hands in hers. "Promise me that what I am about to say will be kept a secret."

"We're poor," Ernie acknowledged. "I already know that."

"Yes," Maria answered. "But it's more than that." She hesitated. She looked deep into her son's eyes. "We're not American citizens."

"Because we're Mexican," Ernie said, certain he understood the reason.

"No, Ernie. Because we entered the country without proper legal documents."

Ernie was startled. He had no clue what to make of this new information.

"We're *undocumented aliens*," she emphasized.

Ernie failed to grasp the meaning of her words. He was confused. "Aliens are from outer space."

Maria laughed. Ernie loved science fiction. His favorite television program was *My Favorite Martian*. She'd even allowed him to watch *The Outer Limits*. The show frightened him, but each week he begged to watch it. "Honey, it means we're in this country illegally. Against the law."

"Illegally." The word stuck in his throat.

"You must keep this to yourself. Do you understand? It is no one's business. It's our secret. If anyone finds out, we could be deported."

Ernie had no idea what his mother meant by deported but he'd already heard enough. He decided not to ask any more questions.

"Not a word," she said.

"No," Ernie echoed. "I'll never tell anyone. I promise."

* * *

As much as she hated to, Daisy pressed the buzzer to summon an aide. She was relieved to see it was Armella who came.

"You've had a rough time, sweetie," Armella said, helping Daisy onto the bedpan. "I'm glad you're back from the hospital. Now we can work on getting you better."

A heavy, dark-skinned Haitian-American, with a tight, curly weave that cascaded like a black waterfall from the top of her head down to her shoulders, Armella had perfected the art of being upbeat no matter how unpleasant the task. She was among a group of nurse's aides on whom Daisy was increasingly reliant for *the acts of daily living* at The Village.

"Those super bugs are scary," Armella whispered. "People die from that shit. Now shift," she ordered.

Daisy moaned. The hip hurt like hell. Unlike other hip replacement patients who'd begun physical therapy right away, Daisy had been delayed. The ten days in intensive care had interfered with the recovery process.

Armella was undeterred by Daisy's discomfort. "Last week, Mr. Shapiro developed a nasty infection on the bottom of his foot . . ."

Daisy winced. Balancing herself on the plastic form was extremely uncomfortable. The day before, she'd wet the sheets when she accidently slipped off, requiring the bed to be remade. She hated to put anyone to all that bother. This time, she concentrated to make sure the pan was centered.

"Oh, the smell from that foot was terrible," Armella continued. "And then you'll never guess what happened?" She giggled. "I was on vacation for a week, and when I got back, I checked on Mr. Shapiro's foot and Lord . . . it was gone. No one had told me. Oh, you should have seen the look on my face. I nearly fainted. But that's diabetes, honey. You're sure lucky you don't have diabetes."

Daisy listened politely, not sure how her hip and Armella's story meshed.

"You listen to the doctor and get out of here as fast as you can, baby. The longer you stay, the greater the likelihood you'll never leave. And you don't want to live here, do you, honey? You don't want old Armella to always be helping you with your bathroom chores."

Daisy agreed.

Armella assumed a stern expression. "Honey, don't join this legion of lost souls. The only way out is to relearn what once came natural. You'll have to get up and walk." Daisy shifted her body, signaling to Armella that she was done. Armella reached under Daisy and removed the bedpan, examining the contents. "Good girl. We're having no problem passing fluids. I'll just clean this out. While I'm gone, you think about what I said."

Daisy didn't need to think long. She had only one wish . . . to escape. But that would require she get out of bed on her own and she wasn't quite certain that would ever be possible. At least not in the immediate future.

* * *

Ernie made a right off Thomas into The Home Depot parking lot. He was surprised to see so many day laborers lined up on either side of the driveway so late in the afternoon. Before the recession, when the trades were busy, labor had been scarce by 8:00 a.m. Trucks pulled up in the wee morning hours and loaded up those eager to work. From construction to landscaping to roofing, there had always been plenty of jobs for laborers in Phoenix. But with construction at a standstill, the Home Depot lot had become the latest haven for the unemployed. Dark-skinned men loitered about, in need of a shower and a change of clothes. Discarded plastic cups and paper bags from McDonald's, Sonic, and Jack in the Box blew in the wind.

The men waved and called out as Ernie drove by.

I'm not like them, he thought. *I run my own business. I have clients.* And yet, even as he professed to be different, he knew the truth. At the very core, they were all his brothers . . . undocumented immigrants.

After years of working all day and going to school at night, he'd graduated from Arizona State University with a degree in Hotel Management. It had been a noble idea, but perhaps futile, since, without a Social Security number, Ernie couldn't get a job in his chosen field. He started a business as a handyman, doing odd jobs at competitive prices, everything from drywall to plumbing, trades he'd learned working his way through ASU. For years he'd made a respectable living. He was well-liked and reliable. Then in 2008, when the economy tanked, Ernie struggled. Without a steady income, he could no longer afford to pay for his mother's apartment and living expenses.

"Mama, move in with me," he reluctantly asked, hating the idea of once again living with Maria, her strong personality, and those dark, questioning eyes, dissecting every word for a hidden meaning. But he had no choice. She was blood. "At least until things get better," he added, confirming it would not be permanent.

"No, Hijo." Her eyes flashed annoyance. "You don't really want me. I can see it in your face." She smiled bitterly, patting herself on the chest. "God gave me two good hands. I can work. We're a proud and independent people. Don't you forget that, Ernie Gonzalez."

True to her word, Maria found a job at Taco World, two blocks from her tiny apartment. For twelve hours a day, five days a week, she seared beef and chicken, made guacamole and salsa, and chopped lettuce and tomatoes in a hot kitchen alongside other women like her.

Ernie was relieved that she was able to support herself, yet the guilt weighed heavily. "As soon as I'm back on my feet, you're quitting that job," he told her.

"Ernie," she said, her tiny frame planted solidly on the ground, her hands anchored to her hips. "Life has its ups and downs. It will get better. You'll see. This isn't your fault."

It is my fault, he thought. *I've failed you. I've failed myself.*

And then, as if things weren't bad enough, the sky fell in.

It was the lead story on the Phoenix *CBS Evening News*. Taco World raided by Sheriff Joe Arpaio. Ernie watched in shock as Maria, caught on camera, along with ten other undocumented immigrants, was led out of the restaurant in handcuffs.

She should be sitting by the pool enjoying her life, he thought. *Not in some God-forsaken rented room in Nogales, Mexico.*

Maria's deportation was a new low. A new indignity. Ernie thought he'd become accustomed to the difficulties of being undocumented. *All I ever wanted was a driver's license*, he thought. Now his wish for a driver's license seemed trivial.

Ernie blamed himself for his mother's deportation. Had he been a better son, more successful, it would never have happened. But the deck had been stacked against him.

I look just like everyone else. I speak English with no discernible accent. I dress well. No one could possibly know that I'm anything but a United States citizen.

And that was exactly what he wanted people to think. He didn't need a birth certificate or a Social Security card to prove he was a full-blooded American. His status should be obvious based on his intelligence, ingenuity, and drive. Ernie felt blessed to live in the greatest country in the world. He was grateful his mother had brought him from Mexico. Legal documents could never change what was in his heart.

Ernie was an American.

His belief had trumped all . . . up until the moment of Maria's arrest.

Ernie pulled into a parking spot at The Home Depot and turned off the car.

Sure, Arpaio doesn't bother you if you're hanging around, begging for work . . . a starving vagrant. As long as you're miserable and know your place, he leaves you alone.

* * *

Daisy took a deep breath. June, her physical therapist, was much too young to understand the pain and discomfort she was experiencing.

"You can do this," June insisted.

Daisy felt lost.

"Just break the movement down into small steps."

Jesus, Daisy thought. The pressure to do as she was told, to be a pliant and responsive patient was overwhelming. And though she struggled inwardly, Daisy remained restrained and polite. It took all her energy not to complain. Not to reach over and slap June across the face. Not to direct her fury onto the one person who was actually trying to help her—June with her trim figure; June who looked as if she could complete an Iron Man Triathlon; June and her perky attitude.

The regimen of bending and stretching exhausted Daisy. She found it awkward and humiliating, struggling to get movement into her hip joint, sweating profusely and periodically breaking wind. "Oh dear, there I go again," she winced with the release of three sharp toots.

"This is difficult work. It's all natural. Don't give it another thought," June offered.

But Daisy couldn't help but give it all her thought. Like any unpleasant experience, the physical therapy sessions seemed endless. And though Daisy did her best to comply, by the end of the second week, she'd barely progressed. Ten sessions down and the mental anguish of being some-place other than home was taking its toll.

Daisy struggled on.

When she extended her left leg, tightness ran up her thigh, directly to her lower back. She tried to pull herself up to a standing position. The ache in her hip prevented her from getting to her feet. She had an ominous suspicion she was failing to recover, that the rehabilitation wasn't taking. She was able to stand only if June provided a generous heave-ho. Once on her feet, Daisy supported her full weight on the metal walker, where she gingerly dangled for seconds, before she sat back down with a hard thump. For someone who'd been fiercely independent, this was no way to live.

"Just put your weight on your right foot," June prodded. "Pull your left leg up. Concentrate. Think it through."

Daisy felt trapped. Her body refused to follow the simplest commands. With each passing session and every failure, she felt herself growing smaller, withdrawing deeper inside; she was closing down. Polite conversation no longer interested her.

Can there be a time limit on rehabilitation? Daisy wondered. *Can someone actually fail to rehab?*

She knew that with some old buildings, it was just too late to fix their foundation, pour a new concrete floor, add drywall, or tend to the roof. Was the human body like that?

She doubted she'd ever be the same again. And though she'd spent a lifetime as a fairly positive person, dark clouds gathered. Only sleep provided a reasonable escape, the kind of sleep in which, upon waking, dreams are forgotten and grogginess remains.

Daisy was trapped in a nightmare.

She was becoming a resident of The Village.

* * *

"It's all done," Enid announced, stepping out onto the balcony of their townhouse which overlooked the golf course. The grading of the property had placed the balcony thirty feet from the course and four feet above the green, offering the Lees a perfect view of the sixth tee, just off to the right, some ten feet up the fairway.

Jack was lying on a recliner in grey sweats and a tee shirt, the newspaper spread out before him. He faced the tee, periodically watching as golfers stepped up to take their swing. It was eleven o'clock. Enid had just returned from a meeting with a realtor at Daisy's place. Jack's grey hair was disheveled, a bedhead mess. He hadn't yet showered. She sipped a tall glass of ice tea that she'd poured for herself in the kitchen, irked at Jack's apparent laziness.

"I signed the paperwork to list the house," she clarified, proud of her accomplishment.

"That was fast," Jack said, scanning the paper. "Are you sure about this whole thing? Maybe you're rushing it."

"Fast? There was nothing fast about it. It's been an awful lot of work."

"Well, you were the one who insisted on *taking charge*," Jack answered, finally looking up. "You could have waited until she was better. That's what I suggested before you decided that you knew best."

Enid's eyes narrowed. "*If* she gets better, Jack. You watch. Those hospital bills will be coming in soon. Someone has to handle the paperwork." *The least you could do is be appreciative*, she thought.

In the distance, a white golf cart glided down the fairway. Jack watched as three men wearing brightly colored shirts emerged, laughing.

Enid ran her tongue over her two front teeth. The tea seemed sweeter than usual. She'd been too heavy-handed with the Splenda. "You know, she never purchased Medicare Part B insurance."

"What?" Jack asked, removing his reading glasses and rubbing his eyes.

"Part B, Jack," Enid repeated, bothered that Jack had not been paying attention. She rolled her eyes as she looked over at the first guy stepping up to the tee. She sipped her drink and wondered how many of the men playing through were single.

Jack gave her his full attention. "What are you talking about *now*?"

Enid bit her lower lip. "Why am I doing all of this work Jack? She's your aunt. Why aren't you helping?"

"Enid, you're better with details. Besides this whole thing *was your idea.*"

"Jack, someone has to help her. God knows I didn't want to do it. But she's your family and besides how long does she really have left? I'm just taking care of what we'd need to do if she died tomorrow." *Why do I put up with you, Jack? You're such an ass.*

The first golfer teed off. A powerful swing and with a whoosh, the ball went sailing toward the green.

Jack changed the subject. "The end tables look great in the living room."

"I couldn't sell those tables. The wood is so beautiful. I'm sure she'd prefer we take the antiques. The other items, I'll unload once the house sells. This way it will show as if someone still lives there."

The second golfer teed up. He took a swing. The ball drifted to the right of the fairway, heading toward a sand trap. Jack winced in sympathy. "And what about the china and silver?" he asked. The open boxes, stuffed with tissue paper, sat on the floor of the Lee dining room. Beautiful white Rosenthal plates decorated with elaborate bouquets of pink and blue flowers had not escaped Jack's notice.

"You'd get nothing from the dealers. I thought the Rosenthal would look especially pretty for the holidays." She watched the third man bend over to place his tee in the grass.

"And the oil paintings . . ."

Daisy had a series of landscapes by a variety of artists. Lesser known works. Not to Enid's taste. "There was no real value there. A dealer offered to take them."

"And what did you do with the cash?" Jack asked, standing up. He turned to look out on the green. The third golfer adjusted his stance in preparation for his swing.

"It's safe in a checking account. That's how I'm paying the bills," she said, as the golfer raised the club high in the air.

"It sounds like you have everything under control," Jack said as the golfer brought the club down and sharply sliced the ball, sending it veering off to the left, directly toward the Lee balcony.

Enid screamed as the golf ball hurtled toward them. Jack covered his head with his hands. She fell to her knees, ice tea spilling on her blouse as she struggled to keep a hold on the glass. The ball hit hard directly above their heads, just missing the sliding glass doors, bouncing over the deck and coming to rest in a bush below.

"Jesus, could that have been any closer?" Enid cried, adrenaline coursing through her body. The near miss had terrified her. Her guard down, she confronted Jack. "Goddammit, Jack, why is it I have to do everything around here? You should go see her. She's bedridden, incapable of going to the bathroom on her own. It's a terrible way to live out one's last days."

"I did," Jack said. "But she was asleep and I didn't want to wake her. God, that place smells awful. And all those sad faces. It's just too scary to imagine anyone having to be there. Maybe she'll still be okay."

"Jack, don't be such a child. Face reality. You break a hip, there's a hospitalization, then an infection. You survive but fail to rehab," Enid rattled off matter-of-factly. "You catch a cold, or another bug, which are rampant in those places; pneumonia sets in, and because you're in a weakened condition, you die."

"Excuse me," called a man from below. He stood on the other side of the iron fence that separated the course from the Lee's property. "Have you by any chance seen my ball?"

"You nearly killed us," Enid snapped. "Now get the hell out of here and take some goddam golf lessons, you maniac."

The golfer quickly retreated.

Jack glared at her. "What's wrong with you? Where do you come off speaking to anyone like that?"

"Like what?" Enid asked, knowing full well that she could be belittling.

"I don't like it when you're harsh, pretending to be an expert in everything. Like the way you've planned Daisy's demise."

Enid flinched. "Are you implying that I had anything to do with that old woman's illness?" She contemplated throwing what remained of the ice tea in his face.

"Of course not," Jack said, sarcastically. "I just hope you're not going to visit her when you have a head cold."

He smiled at Enid. It was an evil smile.

"Funny, Jack," Enid sneered, irritated by his dark humor. "At least then, we'd have a nest egg instead of your measly monthly pension." She took the last sip of her ice tea, taking a small cube into her mouth. She grinded on the ice, all the while glaring at Jack.

"Enid," Jack said coldly, calmly, "if you don't like living off my pension, you should have planned to go to work years ago instead of choosing to stay home and do nothing."

Enid didn't miss a beat. They'd had this exchange before. "I can't help it if the money in my trust was depleted. I had no idea the market was going to crash. Call Washington; blame Obama."

Jack pushed back. "You spent the money in that account on your shopping, luncheons, and charity events. You spent it like you thought it would last forever. Everything had to be first-class. You never compromised. We could have lived within our means, but you had to drive a Jag, live in a wealthy enclave of Detroit, and belong to the best clubs in Grosse Pointe. And all those fundraisers for the Republican Party. What business do you have being a Republican?"

"Those are my friends," Enid insisted, leaning against the railing of the balcony as if cornered.

"Well, your friends *squandered your trust.*"

Enid's temper flared. "When I agreed to marry you, I didn't agree to live within your means. I expected a beautiful home, not a townhouse. I hoped for the better things in life. Not this glorified apartment."

"Well, take a good look," Jack shouted waving his hand about. "This is as good as it gets. And, I might add, plenty of women would be happy to have it."

"Perhaps," Enid shouted back, "but I'm not one of those women. Maybe your first wife would have been enamored . . . not me."

"I'll be damned if I'm going to listen to you say anything about Betsy. If Betsy had lived, I'd never be in this situation. I'd never be married to you. If Betsy had lived, my life would have been different," Jack said opening the sliding glass door and storming off, leaving Enid alone on the balcony to close the door behind him.

* * *

Sheriff Joe Arpaio stood before a group of reporters and promised to clean up Phoenix—to get rid of undocumented immigrants. Ernie watched it all on the *Evening News*. The sheriff's face registered no emotion; his jaw was set, his tone unaffected. *The man has no soul*, Ernie thought as the sheriff promised to ferret out any businesses that knowingly hired illegal workers.

The threat was direct and certain.

Ernie grimaced as the station played a tape of men and woman of Mexican descent being rounded up and arrested at a local car wash. *I've been to that car wash*, Ernie thought. *Those people work so damn hard. Who's going to do that job in the Phoenix heat?*

Ernie's blood boiled.

Though it had been weeks since Maria had been captured in Sheriff Joe's raid, the injustice still burned in Ernie's gut. Maria's landlord had quickly changed the locks on her door. Within a day, he'd emptied the contents of the apartment. What couldn't be sold was given away to the landlord's relatives. Maria's two-year-old apricot poodle, Tomás, was gone. Ernie begged the landlord to tell him where the dog was. He knew his mother would be devastated by the loss. But there was nothing Ernie could do. He couldn't reason with the landlord and he couldn't call the police. He was at the man's mercy. "Undocumented immigrants have no rights," the landlord told him. "Now don't bother me or I'll report you to the authorities."

Ernie was distraught. He couldn't leave Maria in Mexico.

I need to hire a mule to get her back into the country, he thought, *someone who can safely lead her over the border and into the United States.*

He needed five thousand dollars and he needed it quickly.

Ernie went through the plan again in his mind. He'd arrive at the Bank of Arizona at two in the afternoon. It should be quiet then. He'd wear the black fright wig he'd bought at Walmart. He'd pass the note to the teller, demanding the money. Hopefully it would go smoothly and he'd be able to get out of there without anyone getting hurt. Ernie cringed at the thought of anyone getting hurt. Just to be sure, he'd refuse to bring a weapon. He didn't want to tempt fate.

There's no other choice. What can I do? I can't leave my mother in Nogales. I have to get her back here. I have to.

4

....

"Charlie, I'm dead tired," Dave complained, the phone pressed to his ear. He sat at his desk surrounded by contracts and financial projections. "I've been in meetings all day. I can barely focus." He swiveled his chair about, turning his back to the pile. He looked out the window of his third floor office. There, he had a dead-on view of the employee parking lot. Daniel was crossing the lot, heading to his Lincoln Town Car. Dave glanced at his watch. It was three o'clock.

He refocused.

"I'm in no mood to look at houses. I'm swamped here. I just want to go home."

"But you have to see this one," Charlie begged. "It just went on the market in the Biltmore. Ronaldo says it's perfect for us."

Dave looked at the stack of physician contracts he still needed to review. *How many of these can I get through before the end of the day?* "I don't know Charlie. Why do we have to do this on a Friday night?"

"Dave, the appointment is for *five in the afternoon*," Charlie confirmed. "We can meet at the house and afterward go to dinner. Ronaldo will pick me up at the apartment and drive me over. We'll meet you there. You can relax afterward."

Dave gently rocked in his chair. "I don't know if I can be there by five o'clock."

"Please," Charlie pressed. "This is important."

"Okay," Dave finally acquiesced. "But I'm telling you, if I don't like the outside of the house, I'm not going in."

There was a moment of silence between them. Dave's eyes followed Daniel's car as it exited the lot, turning the corner and disappearing from view.

"Why are you being so difficult?" Charlie asked.

Dave was in no mood to be analyzed, unwilling to deal with another conflict in a day already filled with challenge. "Okay, okay. I'll see you at five."

* * *

Dave arrived twenty minutes late for the five o'clock showing. He spotted the white Cadillac Escalade with the personalized license plate *Home4U*, waiting just outside the Biltmore Greens gatehouse. Dave tapped his horn and with a wave from the driver of the Escalade, followed the realtor's car into the development past the security gate.

Dave nodded to Ronaldo as Charlie introduced the two. With a dark five o'clock shadow and black wavy hair, Ronaldo bore a striking resemblance to Mark Consuelos, the hunky husband of Kelly Ripa. As Ronaldo struggled to open the front door, Dave checked out the hot Brazilian's tight white jeans and fitted periwinkle blue Polo shirt.

No wonder Charlie's having such a ball looking at houses, Dave thought as Charlie chattered away about the property. "Just look at those orange trees." Charlie pointed out along the side of the house. "And the baby palms lining the driveway."

Dave's stomach growled. He'd missed lunch due to back-to-back meetings. *I wonder if they have any Hershey's Kisses or chocolate chip cookies.* Such snacks, left out for potential buyers, had fueled his interest in most of the open houses Charlie had dragged him to on the weekends. *I'm so hungry . . . I'd buy the next house with a plate of Oreos on the counter.*

Once inside, Ronaldo, waved his hands in Vanna White fashion. "Just look at that fireplace." His voice was deep and sultry.

Dave scanned the sunken living room, but his eyes mostly admired Ronaldo's broad shoulders and formidable build.

"It's beautiful . . . just as I told you," Ronaldo said in his sexy Portuguese accent. "Everything you could ever imagine."

Dave nodded. "Beautiful," he said as he walked away to check out the rest of the house.

Charlie followed closely behind.

"Why didn't you tell me about Ronaldo?" Dave whispered as they walked out of Ronaldo's earshot, past the dining room, and into the kitchen that opened onto an intimate family room. It was a good-sized kitchen with lots of cabinet space. "These need to be redone," Dave said, touching the faded oak cabinets. "Very dated."

"Some paint, a granite countertop, and we're good to go." Charlie responded.

A picture window above the kitchen sink offered a view of the back-yard pool and the golf course beyond. "Pretty," Dave said looking out. "So what's the story on Ronaldo?" he asked looking at Charlie, eyes raised suggestively.

"What's there to tell?" Charlie answered casually as he opened the dishwasher and looked inside. "He's young . . . I wonder how old these appliances are? I suppose we could always replace them."

Dave had already moved on to the family room.

Dave peeked through the heavy red velvet curtains that concealed the sliding glass door to the backyard. "Where are we? Tara?" he said, pulling the curtain back to allow natural light to flood into the room, fingering the soft curtain material, wondering how it might feel on his naked body. He unlatched the slider and pulled the door open. "Charlie, I'm going to check out the backyard."

The backyard was beautifully landscaped with small palms and cacti. Lush red and purple bougainvilleas covered the tall walls that separated the home from the adjacent property on either side, blocking any view of the neighbors. A black fence, finished off the backyard, and mixed in with the desert vegetation, separating the property from the green golf course.

It's like the Garden of Eden back here, Dave thought. *So private.*

Charlie caught up to him. Together they stood looking into the pool. The water was dark green.

"The pool needs to be drained and cleaned," Dave said.

"Yup," Charlie agreed. "But I love the blue and white tile around the border. Very Southwest. And probably expensive. What do you think?"

"He's got quite an ass on him," Dave said, once again referring to Ronaldo. "Can he wear his clothes any tighter? Where does he shop? The children's section? And what was he before he was a realtor . . . a porn star?"

Charlie tilted his head, offering Dave a disapproving look. "Can we be serious and please focus on the house?"

"I'm just saying . . ." Dave answered, rolling his eyes suggestively before heading back inside and down a short hallway past a full bath that abutted two bedrooms.

Charlie followed closely behind.

"This one's perfect for your office," Dave said, walking into the larger bedroom. A bold floral print on the queen-size bed screamed *grandma*. White doilies covered the pillows. "Nice touch," Dave chuckled, lifting one of the doilies and placing it on his head. "How do I look?"

Charlie scowled his disapproval. "Stop it. Do you want Ronaldo to see you? Put it back."

Dave held the doily up between them and looked through the tiny holes. "I wonder how he'd look wearing this thing. Maybe we can make it into a teeny weeny bathing suit and he can come over and go swimming."

Charlie grabbed the doily out of Dave's hand and placed it back on the pillow. "Come on. Let's see the rest of the house."

Reversing their tour, they walked past the family room, kitchen, and dining area towards the front door, where they spotted Ronaldo in the living room sitting on an avocado green sofa, chatting away on his cell phone. Charlie hadn't seen that color green in a long time. Ronaldo waved as they passed, a serious expression on his face, and though they could not hear his words, his manner seemed intense and abrupt.

"What do you think that's about?" Charlie asked Dave after they passed by. "He must have an emergency with a client."

Dave quickly responded. "He's suing his dry cleaner for shrinking his clothes."

Charlie laughed. "His clothes are awfully tight. I hadn't noticed that before."

"Then you must be clinically dead," Dave joked as he stepped into the master bedroom. The ceiling was painted a pink blush. Roses combined with red, white and blue striped wallpaper adorned the walls. A canopy bed stood at one end of the room. Dave gasped as his eyes scanned the dated decor. "Oh my God," was all he could manage.

"It's a good-sized master bedroom," Charlie pointed out, coming up behind him.

"Check out the wallpaper. All this flowery stuff. Geez. It's everywhere."

"Paper can be removed. We should be looking at the footprint of the house. Does the flow work? Do we like the property? Is the location ideal?"

Dave had to acknowledge that the bones of the house were pretty spectacular. After weeks of Charlie searching, Dave sensed they'd finally found the right house. Ronaldo ended his call as they wandered back into the living room.

"Look up," Ronaldo said as he pointed to the wooden beams that lined the vaulted ceiling. "This house is fabulous. Everything you could ever want."

Charlie looked up. "Dave, this wood is pretty amazing."

Dave stared at Ronaldo's crotch. "Yes, nice wood," he said, enjoying the double entendre.

"And there's even grass out back for Timmy," Ronaldo added.

Charlie had recently bought an apricot poodle on Craigslist. The previous owner had been an elderly woman who had died suddenly. "I wish I could keep him," said the woman's landlord who had handled the transaction. "But I have no room. He's purebred. I don't have the AKC papers, but just look at him. He's perfect. And housebroken." The dog was so sweet that, for two hundred dollars, Charlie couldn't write the check fast enough.

"So Dave, what do you think?" Charlie asked, eyes bright with excitement.

"If you don't purchase this house today, I will buy it myself," Ronaldo gushed as he linked his arm with Charlie's. "I promise I will," he said, gently shaking back and forth as if attached to a vibrator.

"It does seem perfect," Charlie agreed, now moving in unison with Ronaldo.

"I suppose," Dave replied, looking carefully about, wondering if this was the right time to buy. If perhaps, he needed to rethink Phoenix.

"What's wrong, Dave?" Charlie asked. "I know you. You don't sound excited."

Ronaldo appeared alarmed; his smile gone; those gorgeous white teeth banished to the recesses of his mouth.

"Oh, it's not the house," Dave acknowledged.

"Then what is it?" Charlie wondered.

"Ronaldo, can you please give us some privacy?" Dave asked.

Ronaldo headed to the kitchen. Alone with Charlie, Dave admitted his concerns. "I don't know, I just . . . to take all this on, and then—if I don't want to stay in my job, we're going to have to sell and relocate all over again. I just don't feel comfortable buying a house right now."

Charlie glared at Dave. "So what do you want to do, Dave? Start job hunting? It's been less than two months. Do you want to move somewhere else? Seattle, where it rains constantly? Boston, with those winters? Miami, with all that humidity? Phoenix is perfect for us. We both like it here."

Dave bit his lower lip. "I'm not sure what to do. I don't want to move again, but if this job doesn't work out, there aren't a lot of executive jobs here for me. All my contacts are in California or the Midwest. I'll have to do a national search. What other choice will I have?"

Charlie was adamant. "We need a house to be comfortable. Once we have a home, it'll ease your adjustment. You'll see. You'll feel better about the job once you have someplace to call your own."

Dave weighed the options. Either they could continue to live in a cramped two-bedroom apartment or they could live in the Biltmore. It didn't seem like much of a choice. If he was working in Phoenix . . . it only made sense to have a home in Phoenix.

"Okay," Dave relented. "You win."

"Yeah," Charlie shouted. "We did it. We found our new home."

Ronaldo was back in the room, gushing with joy. "Now that you two have made up your minds, let's have a big hug," he commanded, arms extended wide.

Dave may have had second thoughts about the house but he had no doubts about hugging Ronaldo as the realtor's powerful physique pressed up against his own.

* * *

As Director of Physical Medicine and Rehabilitation at The Village, Bonnie Devlon held staff meetings once a week to review the team's progress. An attractive blond in her late thirties, Bonnie had suffered a painful tear of her Achilles tendon as a young athlete in her sophomore year attending Duke University on a track and field scholarship. She'd landed *hard* on her right foot following the ninth hurdle in a 60-meter indoor trial. On the tenth hurdle she felt the snap and dropped to the track in agony. Surgery, and a slow and painful rehabilitation, led her to a career path in physical therapy. With her days of athletic achievement well behind her, her once hard, muscled physique had transformed into that of a shapely, sultry woman. The glint in her blue eyes hinted at an emotional intelligence, which after business hours, morphed into playful sensuality.

"Okay, let's get started," Bonnie said, glancing at her watch to note the time. "We have a lot to get through this afternoon. It's three o'clock. Let's see if we can wrap this up in two hours."

Conversation among the five therapists at the conference table stopped. All heads turned as Bonnie eyed the agenda.

The first case up for discussion was that of Ms. Daisy Ellen Lee. Bonnie glanced about and immediately caught sight of June's long brown hair, luminescent in the fluorescent light. The only natural brunette in the bunch, June still wore her hair like a college student, hanging freely about her shoulders. Bonnie felt a twinge of jealousy. *Ah, to be that age again. No salons, no make-up, and with a metabolism that cared little about what you ate. I bet she looks absolutely lovely when she wakes up.*

Bonnie cleared her throat. "June, you're up first. Tell us about Ms. Lee."

Only twenty-three years old, June was the new hire to the team. The Village was her first job since completing an internship following graduation from Washington University in St. Louis. As June glanced at her notes, she tucked her long silky hair behind her ears, revealing a flawless complexion.

"Just take your time and you'll be fine," Bonnie coaxed, rolling a Marriott Courtyard pen between her thumb and index finger. The challenge of presenting a case before a team of professionals was a rite-of-passage.

June took a breath. She clasped her hands together, fingers interlocked; she straightened her back and shifted ever so slightly in her seat. "Well," she began, "we've been following the appropriate exercises for hip replacement, and still, Ms. Lee remains extremely weak and unable on some days to do much at all."

June's voice was light. Bonnie leaned in to be sure to catch every word.

"She's unable to stand without assistance and complains about the hip quite a bit. She appears resigned to the current state of her condition. Frankly, I'm worried about her progress going forward. I've done the best I can, but it's been difficult to get through to her. She's a lovely lady," June quickly added, "but she remains unresponsive. Disconnected."

For Bonnie, it was important that June be clear about her observations. That was the whole point of the Wednesday meeting—to make certain the cases were discussed accurately, progress noted, and when needed, guidance administered by the team.

"Does Ms. Lee have early stage dementia?" Bonnie asked, knowing full-well that the consulting physician had not indicated dementia in Daisy's chart.

"No, she's aware," June countered, tilting her head slightly.

"Then what do you mean by *disconnected*?"

June blinked twice. "Well, she follows simple conversations but she doesn't speak much. She's detached. She doesn't have that fire in her belly to get well." June paused and took a deep breath, "She's not motivated. She'd rather go back to bed. I'm just not getting her full commitment."

"Have you confronted her about the behavior and its implication for her future?" Bonnie asked.

"No." June admitted, looking down, her face breaking into a soft blush. "I haven't." And then in a barely audible voice, she whispered, "She reminds me so much of my grandmother. I want to be respectful. I was hoping she'd come around."

Bonnie understood. Even so, she had to set June straight.

"Her age," Bonnie reminded the group, "has nothing to do with her getting well. Working as a therapist in The Village requires us to be mother, father, sister, brother to our patients. And sometimes we need to kick a little ass. I know it's awkward. But that's what they pay us for."

"Honestly, I've tried to talk with her . . ." June's voice trailed off. "But she's just not speaking much." June's eyes welled with tears.

Bonnie slid the box of Kleenex down the table. Tears were part of the workplace when dealing with difficult clients and young, overly-sensitive, therapists.

Bonnie redirected the discussion back to the case. "Is she someone who, in your professional judgment, will benefit from further physical therapy? What's your recommendation?"

"I'm not certain," June admitted.

"Well, if we stop physical therapy, there's no alternative but to move her to long-term care. Is it time to make that decision?"

"I don't think so," June said, using the back of her palm to wipe away her tears.

Oh to be young, Bonnie thought, *when the world can so easily break your heart.* "How about if we team up on this?" Bonnie offered, exploring June's face for any signs of resistance. "Sometimes we need to do that with tough cases. I can take the lead and you can pick up one of my more difficult patients. I'd certainly welcome your help and insight."

June's face brightened.

"Okay then, that's what we'll do," Bonnie said, glad to have diplomatically resolved the issue. "If we don't push Ms. Lee, she's going to wind up permanently disabled and living in that wheelchair. Our goal is to get her back on her feet. The clock is ticking. The longer she lingers in that chair, the longer she believes she's unable to walk. We have her life in our hands."

Bonnie made a notation on the agenda about the decision.

"Okay. That takes care of Ms. Lee. Fourteen more cases to go," she said winking at June.

* * *

When Dave and Charlie arrived at Empire Title, they were shown to a private conference room. Dave paced nervously as Charlie relaxed in a plush Herman Miller chair.

"Hey," Charlie said, grabbing Dave by the arm. "Chill out. It's just a closing. We've done this before."

"I know," Dave acknowledged, releasing a sigh. The room seemed short on air, the walls pressing in. He wished he hadn't agreed to go along with the purchase. It felt all wrong, but Charlie seemed so happy.

"We'll just sign a few papers and then go over to the house and celebrate."

Dave didn't answer. He was lost in thought. *Was this really the smart thing to do?*

"I really wish you'd sit down. You're making me nervous."

But Dave couldn't sit. His future was sealed. Stuck with the job in Phoenix and the shouting, pompous, unreasonable Daniel. Assigned a front office in the looney bin.

"Come on," Charlie insisted. "Sit, before you wear a hole in the carpet."

A secretary popped her head in. "Is this the Biltmore Greens closing?" she asked.

"Yes," Charlie and Dave answered in unison.

"It's over here," the woman called behind her.

A couple appeared at the threshold of the conference room. Dave thought them only a few years older than he and Charlie. The man seemed relaxed in blue jeans and a Tommy Bahama Hawaiian shirt. He wore his white-grey hair clipped short as if he'd just come from the barber. He offered a friendly smile. Dave immediately thought him handsome. The woman by his side projected a strong, bold presence; with her red hair pulled severely back from her face, she was impeccably outfitted in a white summer dress, though Dave thought her make-up a bit heavy for daytime.

Charlie and Dave stood up.

The woman stepped forward with her hand extended. "Hello, I'm Enid Lee, and this is my husband, Jack."

Charlie took her hand. "Charlie Huff. And this is my partner, Dave Greenway."

Dave waved, forgoing the handshake, aware of the many germs passed among strangers.

"Business partners?" Mrs. Lee asked as she took a seat at the conference table.

"Domestic partners," Dave clarified as he sat down across from the woman, instantly irritated at her surprised expression. *We're always coming out*, Dave bitterly thought.

"Everyone's a bit early," the secretary announced. "We should be getting started in a few minutes. In the meantime, please make yourselves comfortable." She slipped out of the room.

Dave had no interest in engaging in any discussion with the couple. Instead, he turned to Charlie and smiled, suffering through an awkward silence, hoping someone from the title company would appear to move the proceedings along.

"So where are you boys from?" the woman asked Dave as she began to search through her handbag. "I have this awful tickle in my throat," she admitted, retrieving a yellow sourball which she slowly unwrapped.

To Dave, the crinkling of the cellophane was like nails on a chalkboard. He just stared at her. She, in turn, offered him an inquisitive expression as she waited for the answer to her question.

"The Midwest mostly," Charlie answered, filling in for Dave. "Recently the Bay Area."

"Oh, the Bay Area," the woman swooned, examining the sourball as if it was a cherished piece of jewelry. "I love the Bay Area. We spent our honeymoon there. Why would you boys ever want to move?"

"Dave got a new job," Charlie quickly responded "And the Bay Area is so expensive . . ."

"Fisherman's Wharf, those lovely little trolley cars, and Boulevard. Have you eaten at Boulevard? It's just heaven." The yellow orb remained between her two fingers, perfectly capped on either end by pink nail polish.

"Now there's a *pricey* restaurant," her husband digressed. "A special occasion, okay. An institution, certainly. But at those prices, I'm sorry . . ."

His wife cut him off. "It's such a romantic city. We just love it."

Dave wondered what Charlie was thinking about these two. The man seemed nice, down to earth. She, a snobbish bore.

"Jack and I moved here from Detroit," she said. "We'd never go back. It's too awful. All that poverty."

"Depressing," Jack added.

"Dave's actually from Bloomfield Hills," Charlie explained. "We met in Detroit."

"I love Detroit," Dave interjected. "We still have friends there."

"You love it," the woman admonished Dave, "because *you didn't live in Detroit.* You lived in Bloomfield Hills. How can anyone love Detroit?" She rolled her eyes, the sourball still in her hand. "Jack, aren't these boys too cute. They love Detroit. All that crime, and all those . . ." and she caught herself in mid-sentence.

"You don't like African-Americans?" Dave asked.

Waving the sourball before them, the woman clarified. "Not the sort in the inner city."

Charlie shifted in his chair.

"How long have you boys been in Phoenix?" Enid asked, changing the subject.

"Excuse me," Dave said, "but you keep calling us boys. How old do you think we are? Ten? Thirteen? Sixteen?"

"What?" The woman turned to her husband, giving him a confused look. "I'd guess mid-fifties."

Dave took a deep breath. "Then why are you referring to us as boys? I find that insulting. Don't you think that's insulting, Charlie?"

The blood drained from Charlie's face. Dave didn't care if Charlie was uncomfortable. He was annoyed. The woman's false familiarity had gotten under his skin.

"Charlie and I aren't boys. We're grown men."

"I hadn't realized . . ." Mrs. Lee stammered.

"You have to forgive Dave," Charlie said, coming to the woman's rescue. "He's been working so hard and we got up really early." Charlie glared in Dave's direction. "Dave meant no offense."

"Well, no one ever complained before," the woman said. "I think *boys* is kind of endearing. Don't you, Jack?" She popped the sourball into her mouth.

Charlie closed his eyes and dropped his head to his chest in defeat. Dave smiled. There was no way of saving Enid Lee.

* * *

When Bonnie first met Daisy, as she did all new patients to physical therapy, the older woman had exhibited a cheerful, upbeat energy. Her smile had almost been infectious, so eager was Daisy to please. But by the time Bonnie assumed her care, Daisy's demeanor had significantly altered. She was withdrawn and sullen. She engaged in polite conversation when prodded, but mostly spent her time in a wheelchair in the solarium, talking to no one, staring off into space. Bonnie wondered how to light a fire under her new charge. What would it take to get Ms. Lee bending, stretching, and reaching for a walker, a cane, and then her personal freedom? There had to be a carrot to get Daisy motivated.

Bonnie believed a good physical therapist in senior care had to act as a psychologist in addition to being knowledgeable about treatment protocols. Understanding the patient's mindset and lifestyle was as important as the right exercises. Without such an understanding, there could be no progress.

"There's no labor and delivery wing at The Village," Bonnie reminded her team. "No one was born here. Our clients once had active and productive lives. It's our job to make sure that, despite a physical set-back, they return to those lives."

The men were easier to inspire.

For veterans, Bonnie referred to the war years. Being reminded of a past challenge on the field of battle was often enough to awaken the powers of resiliency. Former athletes responded to the *just walk it off* machismo. And when all else failed, Bonnie resorted to male pride. A sweet remark, a well-placed compliment, and most men struggled to their feet, despite the pain. They didn't enjoy appearing weak, uncertain, or afraid. Playing off those innate traits made working with men predictable.

Women, on the other hand, were more emotional. Tears flowed easily and often. And though Bonnie understood the struggle, tears would not get anyone up on their feet and walking. Women needed to trust the therapist. There had to be a bond that allowed for the sharing of confidences, concerns, and fears. Some were motivated by rhetoric pertaining to childbirth. *If you could live through that pain, this is nothing.* Others were inspired by being reminded that they were the matriarchs of their families. Y*our husband needs you. Your family needs you. Your grandchildren need you.* Professional woman discussed their careers and the challenges they'd faced. Bonnie had found that reminding her patients of successful experiences in their past was mostly what was needed to begin the painful work ahead.

Bonnie reviewed Ms. Lee's chart and was dismayed to find that June had failed to complete the department's intake survey which outlined the details of Ms. Lee's life. The clinical notes informed on Daisy's age and condition, but such facts shed little light on the patient's humanity.

As Bonnie walked the facility, she eyed those residents who were confined to wheelchairs. Many had passed through her department at one point in time. While hospitals worried about patients catching super-bugs, The Village worried about depression. Those accustomed to being fed, washed, and changed ran the risk of being infantilized, ultimately surrendering to long-term care. Bonnie struggled with her failures. *Where had these men and women been five years ago? Ten years ago? What were their hopes and dreams? Were they shocked by their present circumstances?*

It broke Bonnie's heart to see the bewildered faces of those lost to their infirmities. She recognized that anyone could be transformed into an invalid in a matter of seconds by a stroke or an aneurysm. Dementia, a slow, more frightening route, seemed to take hold, erasing any sense of the patient's individuality. When life was considered in five-year incre-ments, physical changes in seniors could indeed be overwhelming.

Bonnie knew what she had to do. She'd have to be brutally direct with Ms. Lee. Face the hard facts. No more pussyfooting. Either the woman was going to work harder than ever before or she needed to permanently change her address to The Village. Time was running out. Bonnie would have to tell her the truth and risk scaring her right out of that wheelchair.

She hoped Ms. Lee would thank her later.

* * *

Anna didn't hear the doorbell over the whistling of the kettle. Tea in hand, she was startled by footsteps on her porch. It was seven at night. Peeking through the blinds, she saw a young man, tall and handsome, his face composed of the sharp, angular features that defined only the best-looking men. He was examining the porch swing, fingers pressing on the green cushion, seemingly testing it for comfort, as if he planned to sit down. But he didn't. Instead he brushed off the sleeve of his denim jacket, pulled the cuff firmly down so that it reached the top of his wrist, only to reveal a large tear in the right shoulder of the jacket. Anna guessed it was the style, like the torn jeans she'd seen worn by other young people. The young man caught his reflection in the glass. He ran a hand over the top of his head and smoothed out his long black hair, which was pulled into a ponytail.

Ah, she thought, *my neon sign is working its magic.*

"Please come in," she said, opening the door. "I hope you haven't been waiting too long."

Like every psychic, Anna had her own glossary of signs to decipher spiritual messages. Flowers were generally a welcome gift offered to a loved one. Doves suggested that all problems would be resolved to the client's satisfaction. Shifting sands meant that the journey ahead was fraught with challenges, but critical to growth and development.

But channeling spirit was not a linear art. Messages arrived suddenly, rapidly, often randomly and out of sequence. Rarely did a spirit visually present. Instead, Anna mentally connected with the entity, intuitively sensing an energy just before messages from spirit formed in her conscious mind.

It was a complex game of mental telepathy.

Anna's grandmother had been the first to explain her special gifts.

"Now don't be frightened," Grandma Ruthie had told her when she was a child. "All they want is your help. If you don't want to be bothered, close your eyes and think to yourself, *not now*. The spirits will wait until you're ready."

"But how will I know what they want?" the little girl asked.

"There's no way of absolutely knowing," her grandmother had said. "You'll sense it. They'll tell you in ways *you can understand*. Then, when you share those messages, you'll feel an inner glow. Your soul will vibrate. That's God's way of congratulating you on a job well done. And that's the most important part of the gift . . . to help others."

The little girl hugged her grandmother.

"Now remember, if you ever need anything, just think of me. I'll be right beside you."

That afternoon, when Anna had gone with her parents to the funeral home, she couldn't be sad. The others had cried for Grandma Ruthie but for Anna, there would be no final goodbyes. Her grandmother visited often. And as Grandma Ruthie had promised, as often as Anna wished.

As Anna had grown into a young woman, she'd kept her grandmother's words close to her heart. *This is a great burden and a wonderful gift. Treasure the responsibility and it will take care of you through your darkest days.*

"Please take a seat at the table," Anna instructed the visitor to her front room as she lit an incense candle. Lavender flooded the space. The young man shifted nervously as Anna sat across from him and started to explain the origins of her gift. It was her introduction before discussing her fees. As she reviewed the concept of her unique glossary of signs . . . she saw an open window . . . emotional issues unresolved . . . an empty corridor . . . loneliness in its purest form . . . butterfly wings rapidly beating . . . an unbalanced energy. Anna immediately sensed something was terribly wrong; the young man was in some kind of trouble. She leaned forward and innocently asked, "Young man, are you alright?"

Mouth tightly shut, features set, his eyes transformed as he stared at her. A darkness had settled over her guest. She spotted a tic in his left eyelid. A minor flutter, most curious as it was sudden. He reached into his inside coat pocket and pulled out a small black object. At first, she thought it his wallet. Then, perhaps an eyeglass case. With the press of a tiny silver button, a switchblade was revealed. His voice cracked as he pointed the knife in her direction. When he spoke, his face broke into a startled, surprised expression which seemed to mirror her own. "I'm here for your cash," he said in such an innocent voice that Anna didn't quite grasp the urgency of the demand. Denial held her firmly in her seat as her mind processed the sudden turn of events. Inaction only escalated the exchange. His eyes widened, the whites now visible, as he leaned across the table and commanded her. "Get me all your cash. And be quick about it."

Anna leapt to her feet, the chair beneath her falling sideways, coming to rest against the wall. The young man sharply flinched at her sudden motion, pushing his chair backward, almost losing his balance.

Move slowly, she thought. *Don't frighten him. He's already scared.*

But there was no easing her panic. She could feel her blood pressure rising even as she struggled to find her voice.

"There's cash in my purse. It's in the bedroom," she offered.

He was on his feet beside her. "Get it," he demanded, his voice quivering, the sharp edge of the blade glistening.

She desperately wanted him to leave, but at the moment, wasn't sure who was more frightened, she or the intruder.

They moved in unison to the rear of the house. The stranger's energy flooded the hallway. She was overwhelmed by the irony; someone threatening to hurt her was in so much pain of his own. *He's upset by all this, confused, traumatized by his very actions, wishing he had never rang the doorbell. Hurting and in desperate need of kindness.*

She located the purse. He grabbed it from her. In that moment, their energies connected. She experienced a series of spontaneous flashes. The face of the stranger's father . . . angry and disapproving . . . the mother . . . cold and distant. Anna absorbed the fleeting images of a troubled family life while he stood but a step away.

Her wallet contained fifty-six dollars. On seeing the paltry contents, the young man became agitated. Anna caught the look in his eyes. He was desperate. And then, from the front of the house, came a familiar voice. Ernie was calling her name.

"Anna, I'm here to finish up."

"Ernie," she gasped. "Ernie, don't come back here."

But it was too late. Ernie was in the doorway. He rushed the intruder, knocking him down and sending the knife into the air.

"Call the police," Ernie shouted, landing on top of the intruder's chest and planting a knee into the struggling thief's shoulder. "I've got you now, you son-of-a-bitch."

Anna grabbed her cell phone and dialed 911. Behind her, on the floor, were the cries of a wild animal writhing in pain.

*　*　*

"Get off me," the young man shrieked as Ernie used all his weight to press his knee ever deeper. "I give up. You're killing me."

Anna stood by with her hand clasped over her mouth.

Ernie held fast. "What were you doing with that knife?"

"I wasn't going to hurt her." Tears rolled down the young man's face as his head rocked from side-to-side as if searching for an escape from his pinned position. "I needed money. I wasn't going to hurt her." He struggled mightily beneath Ernie's brute force.

"Like hell." Ernie pressed down again. "If I hadn't walked in, you were going to stab her. Admit it."

"Please . . ." the intruder begged, perspiration soaking his brow. "I was only trying to scare her. I'd never hurt anyone. I swear."

Ernie could see the terror in the young man's eyes. He could sense the remorse in his voice. The closer he looked at the face, the more he realized he was dealing with a teenager. Ernie pulled back, easing the pressure on the kid's shoulder. "How old are you?" he asked, his tone giving rise to the suspicion that the adult beneath him was actually much younger.

"I'm fifteen," the boy cried, rubbing his shoulder in pain as Ernie shifted his weight on to his knees, straddling the kid.

Anna gasped. "Fifteen. What are you doing with a knife? Are you crazy? You could hurt someone."

The response came out in a rush of sobs. "I was desperate. My parents kicked me out weeks ago. I've been living on the streets . . . and then I saw your sign . . ."

"Oh God," Ernie said. "He's just a kid. A poor, screwed up, kid."

"What should we do?" Anna asked Ernie as the sirens of the approaching police cars blared in the background.

"He *was* wielding a knife," Ernie reminded her, the kid still firmly beneath him.

"I know . . . but fifteen. He's a baby. We can't turn him over to the police. We should be helping him."

Ernie rolled his eyes. "Helping someone who just tried to knife you?"

But Anna wasn't to be dissuaded. "I just don't feel right about this. Look at him?"

Ernie looked down into the young man's frightened face. He was no longer the menacing threat he'd been just moments before. Ernie softened just as he heard footsteps charging down the hallway. Two officers, fully armed, guns cocked, burst into the room. They pointed their weapons directly at Ernie.

Ernie flinched.

The teenager pushed Ernie backward, sending him tumbling to the ground.

Anna screamed.

Suddenly there were two more cops in the room. Then four. Ernie saw one pull Anna out the door. When Ernie looked up, the cops were hovering over him. "Stay where you are," one cop yelled. "Don't move."

Ernie raised his hands in the air. "Don't shoot," he said, struggling to remain calm.

Amidst the confusion, the kid backed out of the room. Ernie spotted him turning toward the rear hallway.

"He's the one you want," Ernie shouted. "He's the guy."

But it was too late. Ernie looked about. Cops everywhere. He started to panic. The kid was gone. Anna was gone.

My God, he thought. *They think I'm the criminal!*

* * *

Out on the sidewalk in front of her house, Anna rubbed her arm. The cop who'd pulled her out of the bedroom had yanked her with such force, she feared she'd have significant bruising.

"Ma'am, can you tell me your name? Is this your house," the young policeman asked, notepad ready.

Anna nodded, distracted as more cop cars arrived, red lights whirling, sirens screaming, one car boldly jumping the curb and coming to rest on her front lawn.

"Oh my grass," she complained. "Look what they're doing to my yard."

Anna raced over to the car on her lawn, arms waving in the air, trying to get the driver to back up.

The officer who'd been talking with her was now on his cell phone. "Yes, I have the homeowner with me. She appears to be in shock. We better get an ambulance," the officer suggested.

And then Anna spotted the young assailant sneaking along the side of her property.

"He's escaped through the back door," she shouted to the cop with the notepad, but her voice was drowned out by the advancing ABC News Fifteen helicopter, propellers whirling, hovering overhead. Anna looked up, instantly blinded, shielding her eyes from the helicopter's bright lights as they swept back and forth across the action below.

* * *

"On your knees," the officer commanded Ernie.

Ernie did as he was told. *As long as I do what they ask, I'll be fine*, he thought, hands still in the air.

"Do you have any weapons?"

"No," Ernie answered. "*Listen*. It wasn't me; it was that *kid*. Ask Anna! She's the homeowner."

"Shut up and get down on your stomach," a burly officer ordered, positioning a foot onto Ernie's back and shoving him hard to the floor. Ernie let his body go limp. He didn't want to be seen as putting up any resistance. One cop held a Taser. Ernie swallowed hard. He knew about Tasers. They could bring on a heart attack in a man his age.

They cuffed him from the back and then pulled him up to his feet. Ernie heard the arrival of a helicopter. The room was suddenly brightened by the helicopter's sweeping illumination, as if someone was shining a flashlight into the room, a flashlight that had searched in the darkness of the Phoenix sky to uncover an undocumented immigrant hiding on 19th Avenue.

"Okay, we've got this under control," the officer shouted to the others in the room. "He's cuffed."

* * *

"No!" Anna screamed. "Not him!"

She watched helplessly as Ernie was pushed into the back of a patrol car. Lights flashed everywhere. The reporters had arrived with their cameras to join the helicopter still circling overhead. The police had closed off 19th Avenue. Traffic was at a dead halt. Anna grabbed at the policeman closest to her. He was talking to dispatch. "You've got the wrong man," she screamed, barely audible over the helicopter propellers. "He was trying to help me."

"Ma'am, you need to calm down," the cop answered in a sharp tone as he turned away to continue his call. "We have this all under control," he said to whomever was on the other end.

"But it's the wrong man," Anna insisted. "That's my handyman."

The cop shrugged, unable to hear her amid the noise. And then the images began to flash in her head.

Oh my God. That young boy's going to kill himself.

She sensed the intensity of his desperation.

He's going to jump.

She had to find the boy. If she didn't, she feared his death would be forever emblazoned on her conscience.

* * *

Anna saw the ledge . . . the teen sitting, hands pressed flat, gently rocking, balancing precariously. She sensed his determination. His strong intention to end his life.

The pain in her head was blinding.

She had to stop him.

Gut instinct compelled her forward.

She slipped away amid all the commotion and headed to the highest point in the neighborhood. The Church of the Beatitudes. The back door was open. She found the circular metal stairs that led to the top of the steeple. She heard a muffled wailing echoing from above. She looked up into the darkness. *Dear God*, she thought. *How am I going to climb all these stairs?* She closed her eyes and gathered her determination. There was a soul to be saved. That alone justified the monumental effort.

Her small feet fit easily on the tiny winding stairs. Five, eight, ten steps. She had to stop and catch her breath. Fifteen, twenty, thirty steps. Her right hand throbbed from tightly gripping the railing. Fifty, sixty, seventy steps. Her shoulder screamed out in pain as she stopped counting and forced her gaze upward knowing full well she was far from solid ground. Her brow was damp. Her arm ached from pulling her body weight up with each advancing step. Weakness gathered at her knees. Her joints demanded rest. Waves of nervous energy shot through her short, hefty frame, as she struggled ever upward continuing to climb the stairs, determined to get to the top. Two stories, three, four. How high had she gone? She had no idea. She dared not look down. Only upward into the darkness unraveling before her with each step along the twisting stairway.

She approached the final turn. She was once again on solid ground at the top of the bell tower. The space was nothing more than a series of open ledges with alternating solid walls. Her back pressed against one wall as she struggled to catch her breath. A gentle night breeze momentarily soothed her. A massive bell hung just above, poised to chime on the hour. She had twenty minutes.

Still light-headed, she looked about. She spotted the back of her young intruder perched on one of the open ledges.

He glanced over his shoulder. He eyes red, swollen, edgy. He was primed to jump.

"Go . . . a . . . way," he slowly articulated, desperation embracing each syllable.

Anna gathered her wits. "Come down from there," she demanded, fearing she might faint even as she mustered her most authoritative voice. "Nothing is going to happen to you. You're safe from the police."

"Go away," he repeated, leaning forward as if searching for a spot to land below.

Her heart beat wildly in her chest. She hoped she wasn't about to have a heart attack. "I'm not leaving without you," she managed to say, her calves still burning from the steep climb.

He scooted forward on the ledge inching his way toward oblivion. His long black hair hung down about his shoulders. "You don't understand . . . I want to die," he said, a trembling in his voice.

Her mind raced. *What can I say to stop him? I must stop him.*

"Talk to me," she begged. "Help me understand."

"I'm tired," he wailed, rocking back and forth.

Slowly she inched forward towards the center of the open space, moving away from the safety of the wall which moments before had been her only security. "Whatever you're struggling with," she began, her kind eyes firmly upon him, "there are good people who can help. You mustn't give up. You're not alone. That's just an illusion. All you need do is look around and have faith."

Her maternal instinct kicked in. She'd never missed having children, never wanted any, but now, every fiber of her being desperately wanted to protect this boy.

"I've climbed all these stairs and I'm terrified of heights," she admitted. "*Terrified*. But I did it. And I'd do it again. Because you're important. Every human life is important."

The boy wrapped his arms about his heaving chest. "Why should you care about me? You don't even know me?"

"You're young," she said in a soothing voice, "and the young feel everything so deeply. But every pain, every sorrow, is just another guidepost on the journey to becoming who you're meant to be. You have the power to do anything with your life."

"I can't change who I am," the boy answered.

"Of course you can," Anna responded. "You can be whomever you want to be."

"I'm gay and I can't change. I can't be straight," he insisted so desperately that Anna rocked back on her heels.

She steadied herself. "Well, who says you need to be straight?" she said indignantly.

"My parents . . . they threw me out of the house."

Anna was momentarily speechless. "Well," she said, recouping, "then you're better off without them. Parents who turn their backs on their children aren't worth a moment's regret," she said defiantly.

"But how will I live? I can't go back to the streets."

The answer tumbled out of Anna before she had a moment to think. "You'll stay with me. That's all," she said, as if it was the only logical conclusion.

The boy turned to look at her, his face transformed from pure anguish to overwhelming shock. "I don't believe you'd take me into your home after what I put you through tonight."

"Yes," Anna said, chin held high, astonishing even herself. "I most certainly would. If I'm good enough to rob, well, then I should be good enough to stay with," she said fully appreciating the irony of her remark. "You have my word." She extended a shaking hand. "You're welcome in my home."

The teen rotated about on the ledge. He was now facing inward.

"How do I know I can trust you?" He stared at Anna as if he was seeing her for the very first time.

She smiled. "You don't, but then, I wasn't the one wielding a knife."

The teen ignored her sarcasm. "You would really let me stay with you? You would do that?"

"I would do that," she repeated, wondering what in heaven's name she was getting herself into.

Much to her relief, the teen slid off the ledge and back inside.

"Now, we need to get down from here," she said, "before this damn bell goes off," and as if by royal command, the teen followed Anna on the slow descent to safe ground.

"By the way, what's your name?" she finally asked.

"Henry. I'm Henry."

"Hello, Henry. I'm Anna."

5

....

Ernie Gonzalez spent the night in the Phoenix lock-up on Third Avenue. The large room held twenty detainees. Ernie sat on the floor, back up against the hard cement wall, wide awake, watching the other men, alert to any potential aggression. The place reeked of alcohol and dirty socks. So thick was the smell that Ernie could taste it.

The tension in the cell was palpable.

Men bruised and bloody from the night's escapades, bragged about resisting arrest and sported the injuries to prove it. Others, unable to sit still, acted out wild hallucinations, sweating and mumbling incoherently. Ernie guessed they were struggling with withdrawal from illegal substances. One man who screamed about seeing rats was knocked to the floor where he laid in a human heap, passed out.

Ernie's stomach was in knots. He silently prayed for protection. *Sweet Jesus . . . I beg of you . . . I know I've sinned . . . I've strayed from my faith . . . but now . . . I am recommitting myself. Please,* he whispered, *let me go home.*

Ernie was grateful the cops had taken his wallet and watch as he glanced about at his unsavory cellmates. He'd never been inside a police station, let alone a jail. He'd always steered clear of the police, and since the passage of State Bill 1070 by the Arizona Legislature, that respect had turned to a deep-rooted fear. Any Mexican who the police deemed suspicious could be stopped, interrogated, and deported. And though Ernie looked as American as the next guy; camouflaged in expensive

Nordstrom clothes; hair well-coiffed; he remained at heart, a frightened, undocumented immigrant of Hispanic origin.

"Gonzalez," a cop's voice called out as the door to the cell opened.

Ernie, startled, got to his feet.

"Hold out your hands," the officer, a giant of a man directed, cuffing him. "Come with me."

Ernie's heart beat wildly as he was led to a small, white, conference room. A fluorescent light burned brightly overhead. Ernie blinked as his eyes adjusted to the intensity. His coffee-colored skin seemed to be even more pronounced against the stark whiteness of the room.

He blushed with shame.

The officer pointed, and Ernie took a seat at a small, round table. The officer sat across from him. Paperwork was already on the table. The smell of Starbucks hung in the air. Ernie spied a discarded cup in a trash can by his feet. He wondered what he had to do to get a cup of that coffee. The pungent aroma teased his senses. Saliva pooled in his mouth as he anticipated the smoky flavor of the hot, dark liquid.

Warm blue eyes encouraged him to let down his guard. "You might as well tell us the truth about last night," the cop said. "We already know what happened."

The cop had a kind face. He was a redhead, an unusual hair color that Ernie imagined probably attracted a lot of unwanted attention when he was a kid. Perhaps he was someone who understood what it was like to be different. Ernie twisted the cuffs that rested on his lap. He had a rush of nervous energy. He had to convince the man he was innocent.

"Hey you've got the wrong guy," he said shrugging his shoulders, trying to affect a nonchalant manner. "I was just an innocent bystander. If you check with Ms. Garrett, you'll know I've done nothing wrong."

The cop tilted his head slightly as he lifted his chin. "You're in the United States illegally. Am I wrong about that?"

Ernie clenched his back teeth. For a moment he feared that he'd locked his jaw, but then, it released. "I've been here since I was eight years old. That's over thirty-five years. I'm as American as you are," he said, smiling, hoping his air of pressed confidence might win the day.

The cop glared back at him. "You're an illegal alien," he restated as if Ernie hadn't heard him the first time.

Ernie defended himself as if his status was up for discussion. "I've always worked . . . I own a business," he said proudly. "No one ever handed me anything. I've always stood on my own."

A silence hung in the air as the cop rubbed his chin. "Well, that's a matter for the Immigration Court," he finally said, breaking his silence. "Now we can either do this fast and easy, or we can drag it out," the cop said. "You tell me. We have you for *breaking and entering*. We can send you to a federal detention center, where you can sit and cool your heels for months before we ship your ass home to Nogales or you can make it easy on yourself," the policeman said.

Home, Ernie thought. *But this is my home.* "Can I get an attorney?"

"Sure," the cop smiled. "But why spend money on a case you can't possibly win, assuming you even have the money."

Ernie felt the cuffs tighten on his wrists. He pulled against them. They were real. Real metal. Shock set in. His funds were already tapped out. And with no bank account to draw on, his home already in the process of foreclosure, his mother in Mexico, there seemed no point in fighting.

The slide had been swift. What had been his life was now over. A day before, he'd been like any other American. Living quietly, working, going to the grocery store, putting gas in his car. Now, the world had turned inside out. His worst fears had come to pass. And though he didn't quite know what lay ahead, nothing would ever be the same again.

"Is there anything I can do?" Ernie appealed to the officer. "Surely there must be something . . ." He asked, his voice trailing off.

"You can get yourself prepared for a change in the weather," the officer said sarcastically as he stood up. "Mexico is hotter than hell this time of year. And very humid."

* * *

There was a knock at Daisy's door. A statuesque blond in a white clinician's coat, I.D. badge hanging from a front breast pocket, stood in the doorway with an empty wheelchair. The woman smiled brightly as she entered the room. Daisy thought she looked like a slightly older Grace Kelly from Alfred Hitchcock's *Rear Window*. Regal; self-assured; glowing with vitality.

"Ms. Lee, my name is Bonnie Devlon. I'm in charge of physical therapy and rehabilitation at The Village and today, I'm your physical therapist. May I come in?" she asked, proceeding forward without Daisy's consent.

"Where's June?" Daisy asked, alarmed by the sudden change. "June's my therapist," she announced to the stranger whose take-charge demeanor seemed threatening.

"She and I will be working together on your treatment plan," Bonnie said, placing the wheelchair next to Daisy's bed.

Daisy frowned. "She hasn't been fired, has she?"

Bonnie helped Daisy to sit up. "Fired? Now why would you think that?"

"It isn't her fault that I haven't gotten any better," Daisy volunteered. "She's a sweet young girl."

"Yes, we all like June very much," Bonnie said, guiding Daisy's legs over the edge of the bed. "Now how about you scoot down a bit? There we go." With a firm lift, Bonnie swiveled and placed Daisy in the wheelchair. "Good. Now we've got a busy day planned. We'd better get started."

Daisy visibly recoiled. "Well, I'm not so sure that's a good idea."

The therapist crouched down in front of Daisy. With one hand holding onto the wheelchair, she balanced herself. Their eyes met. "And why is that?" Bonnie asked. "Aren't you feeling well?"

"I'm just not up to it," Daisy said, though the truth was that she preferred June, the meek therapist, who had enormous patience and an understanding of Daisy's limitations. June had been so kind, so sympathetic. Daisy was uncertain what to expect now that June was out of the picture.

"Ms. Lee, it's my job to work with you, and unless there's a very good reason why you're unable to do so this morning, *we are going* to physical therapy." Bonnie's tone was firm. "Our goal for you is to have you on your feet in three days. In five days, you'll walk across the room on your own. In ten days, you'll be dancing like a young girl again. We're going to get you out of The Village as soon as we possibly can. You'll see how easy it is once we work together. Now, our time on the mat begins at 9:00 a.m. and it's already 8:50."

And just like that Daisy's experience at The Village shifted.

* * *

By noon, Daisy was completely exhausted.

"I know this is hard work," Bonnie sympathized. "Grit your teeth, and if you have to, scream." Bonnie looked about the gym. There were only two other clients at the moment. "This is the place to do it. Push back on the pain. Work through it. Think about going home. Don't worry how long it takes. Soon, we'll have you walking with a cane, head held high."

"I wish I could believe that," Daisy admitted, a tear escaping the corner of her eye. She missed her home. She missed her life. Mostly, she missed her independence.

"I've been doing this job for fifteen years. You listen to me. It's possible. We're going to do it together. If I have to tie a rope around your waist and pull you across the room, we're going to do it."

Daisy laughed at the image. "You really think so? You really think I'm going to be able to get up and walk out of here?"

"Sure. Why else would I be working with you? Now stop thinking about what you can't do and start thinking about what you're going to do. Imagine yourself walking. Make your muscles perform. Imagine it. The mind is a powerful ally."

Lying on her back, Daisy gritted her teeth and raised her left leg in the air. She pushed back as Bonnie's hand provided light resistance. "I refuse," she grunted, "to give into this. I refuse to be an invalid."

Pleased, Bonnie smiled. "That's my girl. Now switch legs."

Daisy gave it all she had. *I'm walking out of here and going home. I'm not going to spend the rest of my days strapped to a bed.* Daisy's leg shot up with force.

"Now we're getting somewhere," Bonnie responded. "Good for you. I want to see more of that pushback. We're on to you now. You can do it. You're going to walk. The day is coming."

Daisy was grateful to whatever higher power had brought the tenacious therapist into her life. For the first time in weeks, she felt hopeful. The old zest for living surged through her veins.

This was Daisy's second chance at life and she intended to grab it with both hands.

If wishes came true, she wished to dance.

* * *

Anna was exhausted. She'd spent the afternoon calling lawyer after lawyer to see if she could retain counsel for Ernie. She'd searched through the phone book to find a law firm that specialized in immigrant rights and false arrests. She'd tried the firms that advertise on television. The jingles still played in her head. *Call Lerner & Rowe it's the place to go . . . call 9. . .7. . .7. . .1. . .9. . .oh. . .oh.* But such firms specialized in accident cases. None were prepared to take on the City of Phoenix in a false arrest charge.

"The matter has been turned over to Immigration and Customization Enforcement," the desk sergeant had told her at the police station. "He's an undocumented alien. He has no place in this country."

Anna was dumbstruck. "But he saved my life."

"Ma'am, for that I'm glad, but it doesn't change the facts of the matter."

"Surely you can make an exception. He's an innocent man."

"Innocent? Anyone in this country illegally has broken the law," the officer explained. "When undocumented immigrants get involved in public scuffles, it's our duty to turn them over to the authorities and make sure that they're deported."

This is all my fault, Anna thought. There had to be something else she could do. She closed her eyes and prayed for a miracle. *Surely a higher power will see the injustice in all this. I'm not alone*, she thought. *There must be a way to make this right.*

* * *

Dave struggled to make the new job work.

Daniel had made it clear that financial improvements needed to be made. Dave had spent considerable hours combing through the physician practices. In the course of the review, he'd uncovered a number of physicians being paid full-time for part-time work. He'd found practices that had been purchased despite weak volume, office locations that were hidden at the rear of medical complexes, and physicians who had placed a hold on their schedules while they collected income guarantees. The more Dave learned, the more challenging the turnaround seemed.

"I really don't like this," Dave said in a one-on-one meeting with Daniel. "I get to clean up the mess, and in the end, the physicians won't want to work with me. They'll just think of me as the bad guy."

Daniel wasn't listening. He was busy reviewing the practice's latest volume report. Dave had pulled together the document to provide a daily snapshot on each physician's performance. "I can't believe this," Daniel said. "Some of these practices have only two or three patients per day. How can that be?"

"Whoever was responsible for building the network wasn't paying attention to the details," Dave offered, assuming Daniel had been responsible.

"That goddamn bitch," Daniel seethed.

Dave had no idea to whom Daniel was referring.

"Mossy Bitnow in corporate lied to me. She made every recommendation."

"Well, that explains the angry phone calls from Mossy," Dave said. "Every time I tell her about a change we need to make in the network, she gets defensive. I had no idea why she was pushing back so hard."

"Don't tell her a thing," Daniel snapped. "Don't take her calls. I don't want any changes to go through her."

Dave remembered Daniel's tirade at the first executive meeting about the corporate office. "But corporate needs to approve all changes in accordance with the compliance software that manages our physician contracts."

"From now on, I'll handle all communications with her," Daniel insisted. "You tell me what you need and I'll get it done."

But the calls from Mossy didn't stop. Soon Dave came to understand that every decision regarding the physician practices would be scrutinized, disputed, and blocked by Mossy through her position. The corporate office consistently trumped Daniel's regional office. The nights passed with Dave tossing and turning, frustrated by his inability to make reasonable changes to the business line. He'd leave the bed at two in the morning, determined to get his job done without being destroyed in the war between Daniel and corporate. *It's madness,* he'd think camped out on the sofa. *Pure madness.*

* * *

Daisy became accustomed to Bonnie's dictatorial style.

"Now come on, Ms. Lee, bend that knee. I know you can do it," Bonnie coaxed. "You had a hip replacement. You didn't break a kneecap."

Tears rolled down Daisy's face. The weakness in her limbs was alarming. In her youth, she'd been strong, able to dance for hours. "I'm doing the best I can," she whimpered.

Holding on to the parallel bars, Daisy worked her way forward. She willed her left leg to move along with her left hip. She focused her mind on her muscles. With concentration, and memory recall, the movements came back. The pain was still present, primarily a side effect of joint stiffness, but there was progress. She most certainly *would* walk again; she could feel it. It might not be today, but it would happen. And that was all the encouragement Daisy needed. *One day at a time. I'll do this one day at a time*, she thought, her determination solidifying.

"Okay, Ms. Lee." Bonnie held on to Daisy as she slipped back into her wheelchair. "You rest a bit. Close your eyes and just relax and I'll be back in no time." Bonnie caressed Daisy's shoulder. "You just have a quiet moment Ms. Lee before we move on to the next set of leg lifts."

"Bonnie." Daisy gently touched the younger woman's hand. "Would you please call me Daisy?"

Bonnie smiled. "Are you sure?"

"Yes, I'd like that."

"Certainly . . . I'd be glad to, Daisy."

Bonnie crossed the room and knelt by the wheelchair of an older gentleman. Daisy had seen the man in the rock garden, his wheelchair parked in the afternoon sun, head tilted back to catch the sun's rays. In the bright sunlight, the man's face had taken on an expression of pure joy. He seemed almost young again. Daisy had envied that private moment of escape.

"I can't," the older man said loudly. "I can't do that."

Daisy had a perfect view of the scene.

"No, not today," he repeated.

Daisy appreciated how easy it was to lose one's temper with Bonnie. The therapist was just so insistent that sometimes it made you angry. She'd push and push until she goaded you into doing exactly as she commanded.

Daisy smiled when the older man finally struggled to his feet. Daisy had no doubt that Bonnie would prevail.

The man leaned his full weight on the walker. Bonnie had one arm around his waist, guiding him along. The man slowly lifted one leg, then the other, progressing in Daisy's direction. With each step, Daisy could hear the man's labored breathing.

Daisy tried not to stare, but she couldn't help herself. The man was looking down, so he didn't see her. But from Daisy's seated position, she had a view of the strain on his face. She recognized the pain. He looked so different from when she'd spied in the garden. As he drew closer, her heart went out to him.

"One more step, Mr. Fenton and then we'll turn around. One more step," Bonnie repeated, her tone encouraging, yet firm.

Mr. Fenton stopped within two arm's lengths of Daisy before he looked up and spotted her watching his progress. Slowly, Mr. Fenton straightened his posture. He tightened his grip on the walker. The old man who had worked so hard to cross the room faded away. A vibrant figure appeared in his place, smiling as he greeted the lady before him in her wheelchair.

"Hello, I don't believe we've met." His voice was steady and self-assured.

"Hello," Daisy said, smiling.

The man's face took on the same joyful expression she'd seen in the garden.

"I'm Lyle. You must forgive me for not asking you to dance. You see, at present, I'm learning how to walk. But when I do, you must promise me the first dance."

Daisy tilted her head, touched by his gallantry. "Well, that depends on whether I'm up on my feet by then."

"Mr. Lyle Fenton," Bonnie interjected, "may I introduce Ms. Daisy Lee." Bonnie smiled from ear to ear.

"Ms. Lee, how delightful." Lyle cocked his head to the right and nodded. "How long have you been here?"

"Too long, I'm afraid," Daisy responded.

"Well then, we both have something wonderful to look forward to . . . *leaving*."

Daisy laughed. *What a charming man*, she thought.

"And now, if you excuse me, dear lady, I really need to hobble back to the other side of the room. But please know that as I do, I will be thinking of your lovely smile."

With that, Lyle lifted the walker and swiveled on his heels. Bonnie turned to look at Daisy and winked, mouthing a silent *thank you*. Daisy wasn't exactly sure what she had done. Later that day, Daisy learned that under Bonnie's directions, Lyle had been placed at her table for meals. While Bonnie provided the exercises, vanity provided the motivation.

⁕ ⁕ ⁕

Standing off in the corner of The Village's dining room, Bonnie leaned against the wall and watched Daisy and Lyle as they lunched. Bonnie's eyes shimmered when Lyle held the breadbasket for Daisy, smiling with the exuberance of a schoolboy, waiting for her to make her selection. *He's such a gentleman*, she thought, as Lyle reached down to pick up Daisy's napkin which had accidently slid to the floor.

Bonnie's heart melted.

It's never too late, she wistfully thought. *Love can come at any age.*

The change in Lyle had proven miraculous.

He'd had his pants pressed and taken to wearing freshly laundered shirts with starched collars, an ascot knotted and stuffed in the opening of the neckline. The Village barber had shaved off the stray wisps from his bald head, leaving a shiny dome, smooth and clean. The bouquet of black hairs that had once sprouted from his ears were no longer visible. He'd assumed the scent of Old Spice.

They're adorable together, Bonnie thought as she considered her past relationships. Greg, the man she'd met in college who wanted to marry her but whom she didn't love. Steve, the medical intern she did love, but who was a serial cheater. Herb, the rebound guy who gave her crabs. Roger, the man she'd spent five years with before discovering he was bisexual. A sea of faces passed before her eyes . . . blind dates, pick-ups, one-night stands.

They'd all left their dirty little imprints on her soul.

She no longer trusted she'd ever marry. Such things happened to other people. She'd long ago decided her career would be her sustenance. Helping others would be the substitute for a loving relationship. And yet, as she watched Lyle and Daisy, she realized she wanted more.

He absolutely adores her, Bonnie thought. *The way he looks at her . . . if a man ever looked at me that way . . .* She was unable to finish the thought, her desire to be in love magically rekindled.

* * *

Enid prided herself on all she'd done for Daisy. When speaking with friends in Michigan, she was the long-suffering hero in *The Daisy Tale,* the do-gooder whose efforts went unappreciated and unnoticed. "What else could I do?" she'd say, full of false modesty. "It was an awful lot of work, but the poor dear is alone in the world. Someone had to step in and help."

And so she did.

For safekeeping, Enid had parked the proceeds from the liquidation of Daisy's property into a private bank account that included neither Daisy's nor Jack's name. She reasoned that Daisy, in her diminished state, would have no reason to access the funds. As for Jack, Enid thought he was notoriously bad with money. She couldn't take the chance he'd squander the assets. Retirement had turned out to be an expensive proposition, and with the stock market decline and the unending recession, the prospect of augmenting her lifestyle at Daisy's expense, proved irresistible. At the very least, as sole power of attorney, she was entitled to an executor's fee, though the exact percentage of the estate seemed to vary based on Enid's whim and desires.

And then Enid received a call from The Village. She'd assumed it was bad news, since the social worker requested to meet that very afternoon to discuss Daisy's condition.

I knew this day was coming, she thought. *Poor dear has taken a turn for the worse.*

Enid arrived after lunch and was shown to a tiny office.

"Your aunt is doing remarkably well," the social worker said as Enid took a seat. "But before she can return home, we need to make some decisions together."

Enid couldn't believe what she was hearing.

"Due to her age, we should schedule a series of follow-up home visits. If she were my aunt, I'd feel more comfortable with someone coming to look in on her regularly. I can refer you to a wonderful home health agency with whom you can make those plans."

Enid said nothing, too surprised to respond.

"As for her mobility, we've really been impressed with how she's bounced back. She seems very strong. We're all so happy for her. It could have gone the other way. For a while it looked like your aunt was going to be a long-term resident."

Enid could no longer control her emotions. She burst into tears.

The social worker came around from behind the desk and sat in the chair next to her. "I know," she said in total sympathy. "It's such a relief when they do well. Your aunt is going to be absolutely fine. She's really very lucky." She offered Enid a tissue from the box of Kleenex on her desk. "It's a good day when we prepare for them to go home."

* * *

Bonnie sat with Daisy in the lobby of The Village. They waited for the cab to arrive.

"I'm really going to miss you," Bonnie said, clasping Daisy's hand. "Now, don't forget. We're having dinner together. I'll pick you up on Thursday."

Daisy nodded.

"My goodness, I'm tearing up," Bonnie laughed, waving her hands in front of her eyes. "My mascara . . ."

Daisy beamed with pride. She was walking again and she owed it all to Bonnie. Bonnie had done exactly as she'd promised. She'd pushed and pushed until Daisy was back on her feet.

"I said you'd be fine in no time," Bonnie reminded her.

"I couldn't have done it without you," Daisy admitted.

"But you *did* do it. You worked so hard."

"Yes," Daisy acknowledged. "I reached down and found the light you talked about. It was there. A bit dim, but still flickering."

A yellow cab pulled up to the entrance. The two women stood to face each other.

Bonnie hugged Daisy. "Now you take care of yourself. Let's not see you back here."

Daisy had no intention of ever returning to The Village with its bed-pans and institutional odors. "Bonnie, please do me one favor," Daisy asked. "Keep an eye on Lyle. He's a wonderful man. I want to be sure he'll be okay."

"If it eases your mind any, I'm certain he'll be discharged in another week or so."

"That's a relief," Daisy admitted. "I hated the thought of leaving him here."

"You can always visit."

Daisy didn't want to offend Bonnie, but she didn't want to visit. She wanted to move on with her life, to try to forget her days at The Village and how close she came to being a full-time resident.

"I just can't," she admitted. "I can't."

Bonnie pursed her lips. "I guess this is a pretty glum place . . . that's alright," she said, giving Daisy another hug. "I understand. He won't be alone," Bonnie assured her. "I'll make certain of that."

"Bless you," Daisy replied.

The yellow cab beeped its horn.

"Well, this is it," Daisy said, reaching for her bag.

"Sweetie," Bonnie said, looking at her watch, "are *you sure* you're okay going home on your own? You'll need to go food shopping, maybe do some light housework. How about waiting till five o'clock. I can drive you. And then, we can do it together."

Daisy shook her head no. She was eager to be on her own again. Away from other people. It had been months since she'd had any privacy. Though she appreciated Bonnie's concern, she wasn't a child. Even the best of friendships needed boundaries. "I'll be fine," she asserted. "It's time to get back to my life."

"Okay. You're a big girl," Bonnie conceded. "Now you have my cell number," she reminded Daisy. "Don't hesitate to call me should you need anything. Promise me."

Daisy promised.

The cab beeped its horn once again.

Daisy came in close for one more hug. "Thank you so much for everything. You saved my life." And then, without another word, they parted, Daisy walking through the automatic sliding glass doors.

"No," Bonnie called out after her. "You saved yourself."

6

....

Charlie cursed the noise. He'd just gotten off a conference call with the CFO at Ann Taylor Loft who'd requested a retail study to project the sales volume for eight new stores to be opened in the coming months. Fortunately, Timmy had fallen asleep under Charlie's desk at the start of the call. Now someone was coming up the walk and Timmy was wide awake, yelping, jumping, on full alert.

There was no need for a doorbell when Timmy was in the house.

"Coming," Charlie yelled as he rushed the front door, certain no one could possibly hear a word over Timmy's enthusiastic high-pitched shriek. "Almost there," Charlie shouted as Timmy, by his side, released a final ear-shattering screech which could only mean . . . *the boogey man is here . . . don't open the door.*

Charlie opened the door.

Before him stood a petite older woman in a fashion-forward denim skirt and a lime green top. Her silvery grey hair settled about her head in a feathery halo, exposing a pair of silver hooped earrings, surprisingly sexy on a woman in her seventies. She eyed him peculiarly and smiled. He'd no idea who she was.

"Hello," he said.

"Hello?" she answered, more a question than a greeting. "Are you staying here?" the woman asked, clearly perplexed. Around her right wrist was a beaded orange bracelet which held two keys. At first glance, Charlie wondered if she'd tried to use her keys to open the door . . . but then thought . . . keys worn as bracelets . . . *Life Alerts* passing as lockets . . . that's just how the older generation rolled . . . and dismissed any further concern. After all, when he worked at home, he preferred his landline, but still walked around wearing his Bluetooth while he carried his iPhone on vibrate in his pocket.

"Yes, I live here," Charlie answered, somewhat annoyed. He wanted to be respectful, but with Timmy whimpering behind him, and another conference call scheduled in the next ten minutes, he was impatient. He had no time to deal with an elderly neighbor. "May I help you?" he asked, this time his voice denoted an edge.

"I'm not sure," the woman answered, looking at the front of the house as if trying to determine if she was in the right place.

Charlie noticed the suitcase. Immediately he understood. She was expecting to see Dave. This had to be Dave's Aunt Gertrude from Queens. Charlie had never met that side of Dave's family, but he'd often heard about Dave's beloved Aunt Gertrude and how she wanted to come for a visit.

"Oh, please come in." Charlie's tone softened as he grabbed the woman's suitcase. "Dave will be so surprised. He's told me all about you," Charlie chirped away. "Don't let Timmy scare you. He wouldn't hurt a fly. Just look at him."

Timmy peeked out from under the dining room table where he'd retreated for safe cover.

"He's shy." Charlie stated the obvious. "Don't look at him and he'll eventually come up to you."

Before the woman could respond, Charlie showed her to a cushy chair in the living room.

"We had no idea you were coming. You must be exhausted."

He watched as she studied the room. Charlie and Dave had acknowledged early in their relationship that they lacked the decorating gene. But the house still looked great. Their success was called a *professional decorator.*

"We had lots of help," Charlie laughed. "It looks nice now but when we moved in, the place was awful. Flowered wallpaper everywhere. Not quite our style."

"Oh, I see. Well this room is lovely," the woman said, her shoulders dropping a bit.

Charlie picked up on his guest's low energy. He remembered that long trips exhausted his mother. "I bet you could use a nap. We have a beautiful guest room with a private bath. It's very homey. How about you go lie down and rest and I'll call Dave and make sure he comes home early so we can all visit?" And without any hesitation, Charlie picked up the woman's suitcase and directed her to the guestroom.

Charlie called Dave. "You'll never guess who's here. It's your Aunt Gertrude."

"Aunt Gertrude?" Dave said in amazement. "My Aunt Gertrude wanted to visit when we moved to San Francisco, years ago."

"Well, she's in Phoenix now," Charlie said, proud of himself for managing the whole affair on his own.

"Not my Aunt Gertrude," Dave confirmed.

"It's a surprise, Dave."

"That would be some surprise. My Aunt Gertrude is long gone. She's resting in a cemetery out on Long Island. I doubt she had the wherewithal to dig herself out and come for a visit."

"Oh my God," Charlie said, horrified at his own folly. "Then who's that in our guest room?"

"Dammed if I know," Dave answered.

* * *

When Dave arrived home, Charlie was in a panic. With his reading glasses perched atop his head, Charlie's wild grey curls seemed more out of control than ever. "You're really losing it," Dave joked as Charlie touched a finger to his lips, suggesting he lower his voice. Dave took the hint. "How could you think my Aunt Gertrude was still alive?"

Charlie shrugged. "You talk about her . . . I just assumed."

"I talk about my folks. You do remember they're dead?" Dave asked sarcastically.

"Well, I knew your folks. I was at the funeral," Charlie shot back.

Dave conceded the point. "Well, what to do now?"

Charlie paced the kitchen. "I'm not sure."

"Well, we have to do something," Dave said loudly.

"Keep your voice down. You might wake her. She's resting."

Dave was speechless. It was just like Charlie. He had a heart of gold. He didn't want to wake the crazy lady sleeping in their guest room.

"Okay, the damage is done," Dave conceded. "I'm sure there's a reasonable explanation. We'll wait till she comes out of the bedroom, and then we'll get to the bottom of it."

"She's been in there for nearly two hours and I haven't heard a peep," Charlie warned. "She might be in for the night."

"What if she's dead?" Dave asked.

Charlie rolled his eyes. "Let's not borrow trouble."

"You said she was really old? It's possible." Dave rubbed his hands together. Any sense of amusement over the situation evaporated.

"Can we please be serious?" Charlie asked.

"I guess we could call the police," Dave offered.

"That seems extreme. I'd hate to see her get into trouble. After all it was my fault," Charlie admitted.

"We could knock on the door," Dave suggested.

Charlie nodded in agreement. "I like that. It's respectful."

"Okay, go ahead," Dave said.

"I'm not doing it," Charlie replied.

Dave pointed an index finger at Charlie. "You got us into this."

"I can't. What if we scare her?"

"It's a knock on the door, I didn't say break it down."

As the two men bickered, a mature woman in a pink satin robe and matching house slippers casually walked into the kitchen. Charlie and Dave stopped in mid-sentence.

"Please, don't bother about me," she said. "I'm just fine. That's a wonderful guest bed. And those sheets are simply heaven."

Charlie beamed. "Five hundred count. It makes all the difference. Dave is so practical. He wanted to get 250 but I told him *250 is too scratchy*. Five hundred is luxurious."

"Yes," the woman agreed, "very luxurious. Rip Van Winkle would have slept another hundred years in that bed."

"Or Rita Van Wrinkle," Charlie said nervously.

Dave cleared his throat. "You'll have to excuse Charlie. When they handed out humor in heaven, he was on a different line."

"Oh, but he's so sweet," she said admiringly.

Dave resisted laughing out loud. Charlie's eyes sparkled with delight. She thought Charlie was sweet and Charlie loved to be admired. If someone liked Charlie, well, that was all he ever needed to welcome them as a friend. And yet, Dave, too, felt oddly at ease in her company. The desire was overwhelming to put his arms around her slender frame and hug her.

"This is really awkward," Dave finally said. "I hate to ask, but we have no idea who you are. How do we know you?"

Charlie tried to soften the question. "*Do* we know you?" he asked, offering his warmest smile.

With barely a moment of hesitation, the older woman delighted in the question. "Why, my name is Daisy Ellen Lee. And this is my house."

"You mean this used to be your house," Dave clarified.

"It *is* my house," Daisy answered, her expression steady and assured. "You two must be renting."

"That can't be possible," Dave said firmly. "We own the house. We have a mortgage and pay property taxes."

Daisy was visibly shaken. "But how can you own my house?" she asked, as if there could be a reasonable explanation. She looked about the kitchen, seemingly noticing for the first time all the changes. The new Bosch appliances and the granite countertop. "Well then that explains why the wallpaper is gone in the guestroom . . . and all the changes in the kitchen. But I don't understand? This is *my home*," she said with such certainty that Dave almost believed her.

"Maybe we all better sit down," Charlie suggested, leading Daisy over to the kitchen table and offering her a seat.

Daisy sat down, her expression one of shocked bewilderment. "I never agreed to sell my house."

Dave and Charlie sat on either side of her. The guilt was overwhelming, even though Dave knew they'd done nothing wrong. Still he felt awful. A complete stranger, a seemingly kind and helpless woman, was claiming their home was still hers. He felt as if he'd stolen the house right out from under her. "But you must have signed papers," Dave reasoned. "No one can sell your home without your consent."

"Well, I don't recall signing papers. I definitely wouldn't have agreed to it," Daisy answered. "Oh, you two must think I'm just a ridiculous old woman who hasn't a clue about what she's doing. I've been ill these past few months. First I broke my hip . . . then I had an infection and needed to be hospitalized. I thought I'd never walk again," she admitted to the two concerned faces as her eyes grew damp. "Oh, I must sound like a babbling fool."

Charlie handed her a napkin to wipe her eyes.

"Did you sign a power of attorney?" Dave wondered.

"When I was first in the hospital, I signed some documents. Enid, my nephew's wife, brought them over. I thought they were for a Living Will. But I was on a lot of pain medication."

Charlie and Dave exchanged glances. Having met Enid at the closing, Dave had his suspicions. But it was hard to imagine anyone could be so greedy and heartless. Yet, there could be no other explanation.

* * *

Jack wished he'd put his foot down earlier, but now it was too late. He thought, *what business do I have at a Republican fundraiser?* Valet ticket in hand, he watched as his 2007 red Jaguar pulled away from the curb. Before him, a long set of stairs led to the Fairmont Scottsdale Princess and its largest ballroom. Enid had insisted that he get the car washed before the event. *Six dollars to valet*, he had spotted the sign on the valet stand, *two more for a tip. Eighteen for a wash.* He quickly added the figures. "I must be made of money," he griped at Enid, who out of earshot was already rushing up the marble steps.

Governor Jan Brewer was in the midst of her speech when Jack and Enid were ushered to their appointed table at the back of the room just across from the kitchen. The place was crawling with politicians. Jack had caught a glimpse of Senator John McCain sitting alongside Representative Ben Quayle as they passed by one of the better tables upfront. Jack couldn't help but be annoyed by all the frivolity. *They're all smiling and betting against Obama . . . that the 2008 economic slide will continue. That the man will never see a second term. And instead of helping him turn around the country, they're gleefully hoping he fails. Willing to sacrifice everyone else for their petty political gains.*

They took the last two seats at the table, nodding politely to the others who observed their arrival. With their backs to the podium, Enid snapped at Jack. "It's your fault we're late. At $250 a plate, you should have known the function started at five o'clock and not seven. Why do I listen to you? I should have checked those tickets when they were on the counter."

"Two-fifty? You mean this is costing five hundred dollars?" he said, loud enough to attract the attention of the couple to Enid's right. "We can't afford this. Where in hell is the money coming from?"

"I'm not about to explain it all to you here and now." Enid looked about to see if the others at the table were listening. No, they seemed to be engaged in the governor's speech. "Just sit quietly and behave yourself," she instructed, the glare from the bright, white light of the kitchen blinding as the waiters rushed in and out of the swinging doors into the dimly lit ballroom. When their plated entreé finally arrived, the other patrons at the table were finishing their crème brûlée. The chicken Milanese was cold and rubbery.

"This is awful," Enid whispered to Jack.

"Serves you right for spending money we don't have," he said under his breath, for her ears only.

"How do you expect to meet the right people if we aren't seen in the right places?" Enid whispered.

Jack ignored her.

Jan Brewer recounted her successes managing illegal immigration and balancing the state's budget.

The crowd cheered.

Jack leaned over to Enid. He'd read about the budget cuts to the Arizona Medicaid program in the newspaper. "She did that on the backs of the people who needed kidney and heart transplants. And she has the nerve to talk about Obama's *death panels*."

Enid shot Jack a dirty look. "Why should the state pay for that? Those people should have taken better care of themselves. It's not a bottomless well, Jack. We can't provide health coverage to everyone. We'd all go broke."

Jack thought it an odd comment from a woman who'd just spent five hundred dollars to attend a fundraiser.

Soon the evening's formal agenda was over. Enid dashed off to the powder room. "Stay by the table so I can find you when I get back," she called.

Jack ignored Enid's instructions. He wandered around the large ball-room. The band played "Satin Doll," and Jack, an avid jazz enthusiast, approached the bandstand to watch the musicians mesh the melodic sounds of the lilting horns with perfect piano syncopation. There, enjoy-ing the music, he noticed a beautiful blonde across the way.

She smiled.

Jack was immediately attracted. There was something warm and friendly about her. He nodded.

The woman held her hands out. An invitation to dance.

Jack walked over, placed one hand in hers, the other about her waist. Wordlessly, they swayed to the music, bodies in sync, silently, rhythmi-cally, winding their way across the floor.

It was the most romantic, spontaneous moment, in all of Jack's life.

When the music ended, the audience clapped, but the two lingered in each other's arms, Jack's fingers intertwined with the blonde's, enjoying his reverie.

"I think the song's over." She laughed. "You can let go now."

"Oh, yes," Jack said, as if awakening from a dream. "I don't know what came over me."

"It's the music," she said. "It's so wonderful. And you dance so beauti-fully. It's a pleasure to meet a man who knows how to move on the floor. You must go dancing quite a lot."

Together they strolled toward one of the bars set up in the corner of the room. There, they joined the long line of those waiting.

"Actually," Jack confessed, "I don't. When I was younger I did. I guess you don't forget."

"No, I guess you don't," she agreed.

"My wife isn't much of a dancer." Jack winced. He wasn't sure if it was because he felt disloyal speaking negatively of Enid to a total stranger or that he'd even brought up the existence of his wife, but either way, he felt guilty.

"Well, too bad. She's missing out on something special."

He sheepishly introduced himself. "My name is Jack. Jack Lee."

"Jack, it's lovely to meet you."

"And your name is?"

"Bonnie Devlon."

"Bonnie," he repeated.

"Yes." Her blue eyes sparkled.

"And what brings you here tonight?"

"A girlfriend had an extra ticket."

"So you're not a Republican?"

"Heavens no," Bonnie said. "But I do love the chance to get dressed up. What about you?"

"Oh, I'm here exclusively for the music," he answered, completely mesmerized. "Well then, I'm glad I came tonight. It was worth it just to meet you."

"Jack," she teased, checking out his wedding ring, "you're a married man. Your wife wouldn't approve of you talking to a strange woman."

"But you're not exactly a stranger," Jack pointed out. "I know your name and we've danced together."

Jack caught sight of Enid. She was back from the powder room and searching for him. He hoped he'd have a few more minutes alone with his new friend. To do what, he wasn't sure. Perhaps just to talk. It'd been a long time since he'd been so charmed by a lady. But the moment wasn't to last.

"Jack, here you are. You're always wandering off," Enid scolded, ignoring the young woman to whom Jack had been speaking. She tugged hard on his sleeve. "We've got to go. I don't feel well. I'm having some kind of allergic reaction."

Jack's eyes darted from Bonnie to Enid and back. He felt completely helpless.

"We have to go now," she whispered. "I need my decongestant. I can barely breathe."

Jack acquiesced.

Bonnie nodded at him. Her ebullient smile transformed to one of sympathy. Jack read the change in her attitude. He too felt sorry for himself.

Jack sighed as they hurried to the valet stand. Meeting Bonnie had been a miraculous experience. How could a stranger make him feel so amazing? And why did his own wife make him feel obligated, put upon, and annoyed?

As the car pulled away from the curb, Enid asked "Who was that blonde you were standing with?"

"A stranger. No one really," Jack replied.

"She looked at you as if you *were* someone," Enid casually remarked as the car crossed under Highway 51 at Scottsdale and Bell Road. "Oh these lovely lizard designs," she said, admiring the carvings used by the Arizona Department of Transportation to beautify the roadway's underpass. "Aren't they magnificent?"

And just like that, any discussion about the stranger talking to Jack was forgotten.

* * *

"Now listen," Charlie said, glancing quickly over at Dave as he directed his comments to Daisy, "don't you worry. We'll figure this out. But for now, you must be hungry. Have dinner with us. We have some beef stew I made yesterday. I'll just heat that up. And Dave will make a salad. And, if it helps, we'll open a bottle of red wine."

Daisy's eyes glistened. "You'd let me stay for dinner after I barged in on you like this?"

"Barged in?" Dave instantly corrected her. "We invited you. And when we invite someone, well, they're invited."

Such nice men, Daisy thought, moved by the gesture. And since she really didn't have anywhere else to go, she settled in as the two scrambled about preparing the meal. Dave, as promised, opened a bottle of merlot. Daisy sampled it and thought it simply wonderful.

"You both are really too kind," she intoned thinking *what excellent husbands they'd make and so good looking.* Daisy was especially taken with Charlie's big brown eyes.

After dinner, Dave poured Daisy a cup of coffee. "Now don't you feel better?" he asked as Charlie cut into a warm apple pie.

Sure enough, Daisy did. Maybe it was because Charlie and Dave were such sweet men. Or because they'd taken an instant liking to her. Perhaps it was the wine working its way through her system. Or maybe it was something else. There was a warmth in the house. A lovely feeling of family.

Daisy watched the two men clean up. Dave wiped the counters while Charlie rinsed the dishes and loaded the dishwasher. They worked well together. Each had his respective kitchen duty. One completed a small task left undone by the other, like shutting a kitchen drawer or turning off the tap water. It was a perfectly timed ballet. There was a harmony in the movements. Grace in the flow.

Daisy noticed the special relationship between the two men.

They seemed to be more than just roommates. Almost brothers. And though Daisy wasn't at first aware of the nature of their relationship, slowly she came to realize, as the two men interacted, that it was love that bonded them. Charlie and Dave loved one another. Daisy sensed their love in the way the two men looked at each other. She could hear it in their voices. And though she'd never been in the home of a gay couple, she was struck by how wonderful it all was. To Daisy, these two beautiful men were simply the ideal dinner hosts. She was truly delighted to be in their company.

* * *

Henry tossed and turned, unable to sleep. The room was too hot; there were too many blankets. He threw them off. His chest was wet with sweat. Fully awake he could see it all in his mind's eye: his father, had him pressed up against the wall of the dining room, Henry struggling to catch his breath as his mother screamed in the background *let him go . . . let him go.*

He'd been surprised by his father's reaction. They'd just sat down for dinner. His dad had been working on his second scotch when Henry broke the news. Henry wasn't trying to freak them out. He just thought the time was right to be honest about who he was.

"There's no way you're gay. I don't believe it. You're too young to even know." His father's breath reeked of alcohol as he clutched Henry's shirt collar in a tight fist, hiking it up, exposing Henry's stomach, a gold wedding band planted in Henry's chin, forcing his head up.

But Henry knew. He'd always known.

His father was relentless. "So you're telling me that you hate women?" He twisted Henry's shirt ever tighter, emphasizing the importance of the question.

Henry pressed forward against his father's arm, trying to catch his breath. He needed to get free, but his father's grasp was firm. "Dad," he croaked, struggling to release himself from his father's grip, "I don't hate women."

His father's eyes burned with fire. "And you're telling me that you don't want to be with a woman?"

Henry didn't know what to say. Wasn't it clear that when he said he was gay that he had no interest in sex with women? Did his father think that by rephrasing it, Henry would suddenly discover he was really straight?

"I'm gay," Henry repeated, still shocked at his own admission, one that he'd uttered to his parents for the first time just a few moments before. Saying it for a second time didn't feel much better.

Henry's mother, to the left of his father, pulled on her husband's arm with such force that two buttons popped off Henry's shirt. His father stepped back and she moved forward.

"Why are you telling us this now?" she demanded to know. "Are you trying to destroy this family? Is that why you wear your hair so long?"

Henry adjusted his shirt, running his fingers through his hair, which had become disarrayed in the physical exchange. He was speechless. What did the length of his hair have to do with being gay?

"It's just who I am, Mom," Henry answered, unnerved by the vitriol of their reaction.

"No son of mine is gay." Henry's father shouted as he stepped back into the mix. "I won't allow it."

Henry stared at the both of them in disbelief. Their reaction to the news had nothing to do with him and everything to do with them —his news, they thought, said something about *them*. "There's nothing to be ashamed of," he tried to explain, sidestepping the two and moving toward the hallway so that he was free from the confines of the room. "It's not your fault. It's just who I am."

But his father would have none of it. "I'll be damned if I'm going to have a little cocksucker in my house."

"That's disgusting," Henry's mother said as she grabbed Henry by the arm and pulled him closer.

"Not as disgusting as your son," Henry's father shouted from behind her.

"Henry, stop this now," his mother insisted, shaking him by the arm. "Tell us you're joking. This isn't true."

"I can't." Henry was exhausted. "It *is* true."

She landed a hard slap across his face. Henry was startled by the intense physicality of her reaction. She attempted to slap his face again but this time Henry grabbed her wrist in midswing, stopping her. The two struggled.

"You lousy kid." His father pulled the two apart. "How dare you put your hands on your mother?"

"I wasn't," Henry screamed, frustrated, upset and losing it.

Henry's father grabbed him by the back of his shirt collar and pulled him roughly toward the front door. There was the sound of ripping fabric as Henry felt his collar come loose from the shirt's yoke. "What are you doing?" Henry yelled, trying to maintain his balance as he was dragged along the hallway.

"Not in our home," his father shouted, opening the front door. "Go find somewhere else to live," he said, shoving Henry out into the cold night air before slamming the door so loudly that Henry sat straight up in bed, his heart pounding.

The sheets were soaked.

I should have kept my mouth shut, he thought. *I never should have told them.*

* * *

"It's about time," Anna said, her hair up in curlers, in a long yellow terrycloth robe, as Henry emerged from the second bedroom and made an appearance in the kitchen. "I thought you were going to sleep all day."

Henry blushed. He wore a pair of jeans and the same tee shirt from the night before. His long hair was wet. Anna had heard the shower running.

Well at least he has good hygiene, she thought, wondering if she'd be able to pick him up some basics, like underwear, socks, shirts, at the Goodwill Store. "I've got cereal and juice on the table. I hope you like Frosted Flakes."

Henry nodded. "I want to thank you," he began, "for being so kind. I don't deserve it." He gently touched a yellow Gerbera daisy that Anna placed on the table to make it all seem cheerier.

"You did scare me," Anna admitted hovering near the oven.

"I know," he said, looking down into the bowl of cereal. "Wow. You added blueberries. I love blueberries."

"I have some corn muffins too," she said, pleased he appreciated her effort. "They should be ready any minute."

"I really do feel bad about the whole thing," Henry said, mouth full of flakes. "I've been living on the streets for three months . . . I'd almost lost my mind. I've done some things I'm ashamed to admit . . . just to survive. It was terrible."

"I'm sure," Anna said, not wanting to appear too curious.

"I went through garbage cans for food. I begged for money. And then there was this older man." Henry closed his eyes as if trying to erase an unpleasant memory. "I shouldn't be talking about this."

Henry had Anna's full attention. "Well, you're safe now. That's all that matters."

"Am I?" Henry asked, digging into the bowl of cereal, the spoon clanging against the dish.

"I told you," Anna reminded him, "you can stay here as long as you need to. But you're going to have to go back to school. That's a requirement."

Henry nodded. "I remember. But why would you take in a total stranger? Why are you doing this for me?" He sipped his juice as he waited for the answer.

Anna's thoughts turned to Herbie, her boyfriend in high school. He'd been just about Henry's age when he started to experience intense bouts of depression, locking himself away for hours in his room. The family had no idea what was wrong. They thought it was just a phase.

Henry was watching her. "Are you okay?" he asked, as she stood perfectly still, her eyes closed.

Parents can be such a bother, Anna had thought back then. *He just needs time alone. There's nothing wrong with him.*

The day Herbie hung himself from an apple tree in the backyard after failing to make the high school football team was the worse day of Anna's life. It had been a complete shock. She'd felt somehow responsible. That was the day when she started to put on weight, eating to soothe her guilt.

"It's hard to explain," she began, drying her hands with a dish towel, avoiding the real reason for her kindness to Henry, "but I have these gifts. I can connect with the spirit world. And that allows me to see past all the nonsense of the physical plane. Those souls who end their lives prematurely tend to regret the decision. It prevents them from finishing important business. Things they wanted to complete while still here on planet earth. You've just temporarily lost your bearings. That's all. And if I can help you through, well, I'm glad to do just that."

"Oh . . ." Henry said with an undertone of mockery. "I see."

Anna ignored his reaction.

"Well, I'm not much for the occult," he said.

Anna gave it one more shot.

"Most people think they're alone. They struggle . . . they get depressed . . . they make decisions about their lives based on a specific moment in time without any consideration for the flow of life. There's always change. Good and bad. And through it all, you're never really alone."

Anna pulled a tray of muffins out of the oven. A wonderful smell engulfed the room.

"Did you know that when you ask for help there's always someone nearby? You may not see or hear them, but they're always there," she explained.

Henry nodded matter-of-factly. "I'll have to take your word for it."

"All you have to do is ask and help is provided."

Henry offered Anna a serious look as he bit into a corn muffin. She was certain she'd convinced him. Then his face transformed. He had an important question, perhaps about the universe. She was ready to answer.

"Is there any more butter for the muffins?" he croaked, coughing a bit before downing what was left of his juice. "They're kind of dry."

* * *

Anna was determined to see Henry thrive. She enrolled him as a freshman in high school and arranged for tutoring services.

"Your education is the most important thing," she emphasized. "We've got to get you back on track. And I want you to meet twice a week with a therapist."

"Twice a week?" Henry furrowed his brow. "That's sounds pretty expensive."

"Now don't you worry about the cost. I have a regular client who's a therapist. We'll barter services."

Henry's eyes popped. "A therapist who believes in the occult? Isn't that a bit odd?"

Anna held her head high. "I don't see why. I have clients from all walks of life. I even have an oncologist who comes in every other month. There's always a long line of souls waiting to communicate with him."

"But a therapist?" He asked. "I thought they believed in talking through your problems."

"A therapist is a human being too," She blithely responded. "They've had mothers and fathers, and plenty of them struggle with those relationships. In a way, a therapist and a psychic are in the same business. The therapist works through family issues while everyone is here on earth. I get them, when members of the family have crossed over."

"I don't know," Henry answered. "I'm not much on talking with strangers."

"It's part of the bargain," Anna said. "Non-negotiable."

Henry shrugged his shoulders. "Okay," he acquiesced.

"Now I want you to give me your parents' phone number," she pulled out a piece of paper and a pen from the kitchen drawer.

"Why do you need that?" Henry asked.

"Never mind why. What is that number?"

"Not until you tell me why."

She cocked her head. "I want to be sure that your family knows you're safe."

"They don't care about me," He quickly said.

"I don't believe that," Anna insisted. "If you're going to stay here, your parents must know where you are. Now give me the number."

Though Anna hadn't said so, she was determined to reunite Henry with his family. That only seemed to be the right thing to do.

Parents don't love their children conditionally. They must be sick with worry. Whatever caused the rift can be mended. As long as there's love . . . she was certain . . . there was a way.

* * *

Bonnie was at her desk when she received Daisy's call. "Are you kidding me?" she said, astonished as Daisy described the sale of her house. The pencil in Bonnie's hand snapped in two. "That's outrageous. Have you spoken with your nephew?"

"I can't get ahold of him. The security guards told me they're out of town on vacation. I've left messages asking him to call me."

Bonnie was in a rage. "We have to do something about this. Have you consulted a lawyer?"

"I haven't yet," Daisy admitted. "It's all been such a shock."

Bonnie clenched the phone so tightly her knuckles turned white. "Don't wait too long. In the interim, you should move in with me."

"I thought of that. Do you have a spare bedroom?" Daisy asked, never having been to Bonnie's.

"It's a one-bedroom condo. But we can make it work. I'll take the sofa. We'll manage."

There was silence on Daisy's end of the phone. Bonnie thought, *it will be awfully tight with two people.*

"No dear, that's a lovely invitation, but I can't let you do that. You work hard and you need your rest. I think I'll stay with Dave and Charlie until I decide."

"But how can you?" Bonnie asked, leaning forward, both elbows on the desk. "Those men stole your home."

"Oh no," Daisy insisted. "They had no idea."

"Oh Daisy, I don't believe that."

"You'll meet them Thursday night when you pick me up. You'll see. They're just the sweetest guys."

"I don't think so." Bonnie had no intention of fraternizing with people she considered Daisy's enemies. "I'll just wait outside in the car for you to come out."

"You must come in," Daisy went on. "I insist. You'll see. They're wonderful."

Bonnie held her ground. "No. I don't think so."

"Please," Daisy pressed. "Do it for me."

Bonnie finally relented. "Okay, but promise me you'll think about what I said. You need to find an attorney. Don't let too much time pass before you act."

"I won't," Daisy promised.

* * *

"I thought we were going out to dinner," Bonnie whispered, stepping into the hallway of the home with its marble floors and arched ceilings.

Daisy's face lit up. "Dinner here will be so much nicer. When you get to know Charlie and Dave, you're going to love them."

"I don't know." Bonnie shook her head, uncertain. "This isn't what we agreed to," she said, annoyed at the change in plans.

"Trust me," Daisy coaxed, giving Bonnie's arm a tug. "You're in for a treat."

Despite Bonnie's objections, Daisy led her past the step-down living room with its warm earth tones and handsome concrete fireplace, past the dining area where the table was set with a blue linen tablecloth, red votive candles, and fine bone china, which Bonnie barely had a chance to admire before arriving in the kitchen. The aroma of garlic bread assuaged Bonnie's resistance as two men, busily engaged in getting dinner together, turned to greet her.

"This must be Bonnie," said the tall good-looking one wearing a baby blue V-neck Daniel Cremieux cotton shirt and khaki shorts. The grey, wispy curls atop his head added a boyish youthfulness to his handsome face. When he smiled, his grin was bright and electric, generating a warmth which was immediately disarming and endearing. Positioned by the stove, he said, "Welcome. I'm Charlie. I hope you like lasagna. We have one in the oven and we just opened a terrific bottle of wine." He held up his wine glass, as if making a toast. "I hope you like merlot."

"Hello," Bonnie said glancing downward, suddenly shy and awkward. "How nice of you to make dinner," she stammered, regaining her composure. "I feel terrible," she said, glancing over at Daisy who'd taken a seat at the granite counter that divided the kitchen from the family room and doubled as a bar, where a platter of brie, assorted crackers, and red grapes became her focus. "*Had I known you were cooking*," Bonnie said with a slight undertone of irritation as Daisy popped a grape into her mouth, "I certainly would have brought something."

"Nonsense," said the other man, standing nearby decanting the wine. He came around the island with two wine glasses in hand, filled halfway. He placed one before Daisy. "Madam," he said cheerfully, bowing his head. He too was attractive, but unlike Charlie, was more formally attired in a yellow dress shirt, grey slacks, and a pair of beautiful brown Mezlan dress shoes polished to a high sheen. His dark metallic grey hair was neatly parted on the side and seemed to glisten under the brightness of the recessed kitchen lights. Bonnie guessed he'd just arrived home from the office, had ditched his tie and jacket, and was settling in for the evening before offering to help out in the kitchen. "I'm Dave," he said, handing Bonnie the other glass of wine. She could tell by the broadness of his shoulders, and the way his shirt pressed against his chest, that he was well acquainted with the gym. "Welcome, and do drink up." he said, in a conspiratory manner, playfully arching a brow. "We really never know how that lasagna will turn out."

"Now come on," Charlie said, seemingly surprised by the comment. "Be nice. You know my lasagna can be tasty."

Dave looked over at Charlie. Then back at Bonnie. He crinkled his nose. "But the more we drink . . . the better chance we have that it might *actually be* delicious."

Bonnie couldn't help but giggle as Daisy burst into laughter.

After two glasses of wine, Bonnie let her guard down. And whether it was the wine, or the charming company, Charlie's lasagna turned out to be fantastic, the best she'd eaten in a long time.

As Dave and Charlie stepped away from the table to clean up, Bonnie and Daisy retreated to the family room. "They are lovely men," Bonnie admitted, conceding Daisy's point. "I didn't think it was possible."

"I told you." Daisy beamed.

"And they obviously adore you," Bonnie confirmed, watching her tone so as not to be overheard by her two hosts.

"Well really," Daisy said, in mock approbation, hands in the air, palms facing up. "What's not to love?"

7

Ernie Gonzales had no memory of ever living in Mexico, which made the sight of Nogales even more startling.

As a poor Mexican kid raised in North Central Phoenix, he was accustomed to paved streets, manicured lawns and homes constructed of solid materials. Crossing the United States border was like stepping into another world. Before him lay a shantytown of corrugated tin roofs, and windows and doors cut at such odd angles that he imagined it had all been designed by the surrealist Salvador Dali. These flimsy wooden shacks were scattered about the hills like the tumbleweeds that blew through the Sonoran desert in July and August, pockmarking the landscape, assaulting Ernie's aesthetic senses. As a man who'd made a career in the trades, he found it hard to believe anyone lived in such ugly, rudimentary shelters.

He knew his mother's address, and after stopping at a local mercado, had been given directions to cross the train tracks which bisected through the downtown area, and head southeast. He passed an alleyway filled with open trash cans, spotting the railway crossing just up ahead. The stench of rotting garbage filled his nostrils. Rats scampered about making a meal of whatever they could find.

He'd known fear as a child . . . fear of his mother's temper . . . fear of discovery . . . but this fear had a morphed intensity. It permeated his very being like an alien entity, contaminating each cell with a fervid ferocity. His limbs felt numb, his breathing shallow, as he lumbered along in a daze trying to come to terms with the dark pit into which he had fallen.

Stripped of all possessions, the descent had been unimaginable. He'd have to start all over again, and figure a way up and out. He'd have to survive, if only to take care of his mother. But as he made his way along the filthy streets of Nogales, he wondered if he had the resilience, the strength, to overcome the curveball life had thrown at him.

I've got to get ahold of myself, he thought, agitated, frightened, struggling to maintain his composure as he walked through his own worst version of the *Twilight Zone*.

"Hijo," Maria shrieked when she saw him, her eyes lighting up. "Why are you here? Are you all right?" She wrapped her arms about his waist and pulled him close, her head against his chest, his head resting atop hers.

He broke down and cried, releasing the intense emotions he'd held so tightly in check since the night the Phoenix police had taken him into custody. "I've been deported," he wept. "I've lost everything."

They stood together, a family reunited against the world's indifference with only each other's good will to rely upon. He was a child again for a brief moment, protected, secure, cherished . . . safe from the nightmare.

And then the moment was over.

Maria slipped her hands between them, and with a sudden push, shoved him away. He was caught off-guard as he struggled for balance. Once settled squarely on his feet, she stepped forward and delivered a fast, powerful punch to his midsection. He stumbled backward, hunched over, held his gut, and gasped for breath.

"Stand up," she shouted, her voice piercing the reunion. "Stand up, you coward."

He could only stare at her as if she'd grown another head, holding his belly, slowly recovering from her outburst.

"Stand tall," she growled. "Be a man."

"My God," he said, gathering his breath and rising to his full height, "are you freaking insane?"

"Shut up," she said, coming in closer, threatening to hit him again. Fist in the air, she raged. "Do not ever cry again in my presence. You are not a child! I don't want your tears. I want your outrage. I want your strength. I didn't raise you to give in. I raised you to be a man."

He listened and he remembered. He remembered the mother who took no prisoners. The woman who beat him when he came home from school with a black eye. The woman who grabbed his arm too tightly when she wanted him to behave in a certain way. The many bruises she'd left on his body before he learned to keep his emotions to himself. The woman who had no pity for weakness of any kind.

"Tomorrow you'll look for a job," she insisted, finger jabbing hard into his chest.

"And where are *you* working?" Ernie asked, backing away, remembering all too well that Maria's job at Taco World had come to no good.

She was silent.

"Who has taken care of you while you've been here? Answer me," he said angrily, knowing full well that she'd relied solely on his financial support since she'd been deported. "And what happened to your *two good hands*? Why aren't you working?" he asked in a venomous tone.

The steel frame of the woman he'd called Momma softened. Her shoulders dropped and rounded. "I can't work," she surrendered.

"Why?" he asked, confused by the shift. There was fear in her eyes. He'd never seen her afraid.

He took a good look at her.

With no make-up, hair greying, she was small, fragile, face heavily lined. Why hadn't he noticed it when he first saw her? She was tired. Older. He'd been so overcome by his own emotions. So focused on his crisis. But now, looking at his mother, he realized she too bore the scars of her forced relocation.

"I'm frightened," she admitted, stepping back to sit down on the creaking cot against the wall.

He looked about the room. Here, she was as a wax figure in a dark, shabby tableau. The tiny space evoked a claustrophobic feeling. An opaque window, perched high on the wall, offered little natural light. There was a chrome-legged, pink, speckled Formica table from the 1960s, the top stained and discolored, the padding of its two chairs heavily scratched. In the corner, a sink, pipes exposed, two shelves above for glassware. A shoddy dresser and a cot completed the grim set. On top of the dresser, a hotplate, and some canned goods.

"You . . . frightened?" Ernie had not seen this side of Maria.

She looked up. The fear replaced by sadness. "I had thought all of this was behind me," she said. "Now, I'm back to the very beginning. I'm too old, Ernie, to start again. I just can't do it."

Ernie was astonished. His mother had never seemed too old to do anything.

"That's ridiculous," he said, kneeling beside her, finding strength in her weakness.

A dark-brown cockroach, resting at the foot of the cot, scampered up a metal leg and crossed the grey woolen blanket on which Maria sat. "Mios Dios," she cried out, as the tiny creature raced past her, making its way to the wall and up toward the ceiling. "I will not be stuck in this hellhole," she whimpered, tears running from her eyes. "I'm your responsibility, and it seems to me," she said as she looked about the filthy rented room, "you'd better figure a way to get us out of here."

* * *

Ernie found a job as a bouncer at Chica's, a seedy strip club near the Warehouse District, housed in a dilapidated shack that at one time had been a makeshift barn for boarding horses. He kept mostly to himself, uncomfortable with the underage girls and Chica's ties with the drug cartel. His goal . . . earn enough cash to cover rent and food . . . and eventually buy two bus tickets to Puerto Vallarta, where he hoped to obtain employment at one of the many tourist resorts.

It was five o'clock in the morning, still dark outside, when Ernie came in. He was beat. Maria, lying in bed, was awake.

"Did they pay you?" She shifted the pillow beneath her head.

"Are you getting up?" he asked, deflecting the question as he slowly slid down the wall to the floor, too exhausted to stand.

"I'm getting up," she said, drawing back the grey woolen blanket. Wearing an extra-large tee shirt she'd purchased from a local market, she placed her feet on the floor and winced. "Getting old is for the birds," she complained as she reached down and rubbed her ankles. "So . . . did they pay you?" she asked again, seemingly distracted by her morning aches and pains.

Dead tired, Ernie shook his head no.

She sat straight up, hands poised flat on the edge of the bed, fingers outstretched. She seemed more alert. "When? When will they pay you?" she asked, her tone taking on a sense of alarm.

"I have no idea," Ernie freely admitted, disgusted with the job, annoyed at the questions, and too tired for a conversation.

"It's been a week already. They promised to pay you!"

"I know," he said, wearily kicking off his Nikes. His feet ached from standing all night. "They told me yesterday I'd get paid today but the big boss didn't show."

Ernie had never even met the boss. A guy named Julio had hired him in the morning for the night shift. Now he wondered if they were toying with him. Had they sensed his desperation and taken advantage of his situation. *How many bouncers at Chica's ever got paid?* Bartenders and dancers touched money. They could always ferret away something when no one was looking. But there was no entrance fee to the club. It wasn't that kind of a place. Ernie never touched cash.

"They keep stalling," he admitted, mostly to himself.

"We don't work for free," Maria said, the frustration in her voice unmistakable. "We need to eat. And the landlord was here last night. We have forty-eight hours to pay up. After that, we're on the street."

Ernie was too tired for ultimatums. Instead he asked, "Are you done with that bed?"

Maria stepped on to the bare floor, relinquishing the cot.

With a sigh, Ernie rose to his feet. He slipped out of his only shirt. It reeked, though that hardly mattered anymore. He undid his belt; his jeans dropped to the floor. Maria watched, not bothering to turn away. He'd already dropped a few pounds, not surprising for how little they ate; he was hungry most of the time. He sat down on the creaking metal cot. The thin mattress provided scarce protection from the sharp, uneven coils.

This was the bottom. He was sure of it. It could get no worse.

"What are we going to do?" Maria demanded, lingering nearby.

Ernie had no answers. He just wanted to sleep. To be left alone.

"No, you don't," she said. "You don't sleep until we figure this out."

He ignored her, rolling on his side to face the wall.

As he drifted off, he was startled by a barrage of punches to his shoulder and arm. Jolted, he rolled over to see his mother, fists in the air, leaning over him. Each clenched hand was no bigger than a small apple. Quickly he was on his feet. His heart lurched, his pulse raced, the blood pounded in his temples. He hovered over her, his rage threatening to annihilate her. She cowered. He didn't recognize her. He didn't recognize himself. He struggled to gather his wits.

She backed away.

"Don't you ever hit me again," he said in a low, forceful growl, "Or God help me, *I will kill you.*"

* * *

He took a shortcut from Chica's on his way back to the rented room. The big boss had shown up and counted out enough pesos to barely cover Ernie's living expenses for the week. And then, in the darkness of the early morning, he tripped over a body lying in the tall grasses by the railroad tracks. At first, he thought it was a bum fast asleep, but the stench, horrific, cutting, told him the man had been rotting in the Mexican heat for days. He'd heard of bodies found by the tracks. Informants, cops, drug smugglers who failed to play by the cartel's rules. Death could be swift. He held his breath, swallowing hard to keep the contents of his stomach in check, and searched the corpse. A wallet. A watch. A ring. He removed the jewelry. He ripped at the blood-soaked shirt and found a chain caked with blood so thick it had formed a crust over the gold cross it supported. In the dark, his hand brushed shards of bone where the butcher had hacked off the head.

He threw up.

Covered in the stench of death, rotting flesh on his hands, vomit on his clothes, he pulled the gold chain off and stuffed it in his pocket along with the rest of the booty, racing back to the room, certain that his luck had just changed.

* * *

They arrived in Puerto Vallarta after a two-day bus ride from Nogales. Ernie and his mother had hardly spoken during the trip. The dynamic of their relationship shifted markedly in Nogales. His focus had been solely on the journey, pushing forward, desperate to emerge from the current misery that was his life. As for his mother, he no longer cared about her frame of mind. He only had enough energy to sustain himself. As long as she was beside him, he had met his obligation. The rest would have to take care of itself.

On the outskirts of the coastal town he found a cheap room with two beds in a gray cinder-block building where Maria stayed while he searched for work. The street was unpaved, and each passing car stirred up its own cloud of dust. During the day, feral dogs wandered the empty roads, ribs exposed, hunting for their next meal. An animal lover, the sight of the skeletal mutts broke Ernie's heart.

"Are you going to be alright?" Ernie asked Maria as he prepared to leave that first morning to find work.

She, still in bed, searched her son's face as if he held the answer to his own question. "What's there to do?" she said in a hushed tone. "But lie here and die."

"I haven't time for this," Ernie said, his frustration clear. "You've got to stop feeling sorry for yourself."

"I can't," she said, slowly sitting up, resting the weight of her small frame on her elbows, "And I won't. I did nothing to deserve this. I am a good person. I worked hard all my life. I raised my child all alone. This isn't my fault."

She spoke as if Ernie was a stranger and she was trying to persuade him of her innate goodness. He nodded in agreement, hoping that might ease her anguish. "I have to go," he said, leaning down and kissing the top of the head. "I'll be back later."

He was relieved to leave. Relieved to close the door behind him.

Finding work wasn't easy.

Ernie did odd jobs, mostly road construction, spending long hours in the blistering sun, shoveling gravel into potholes, topping the piles with hot tar. It was backbreaking, dirty labor, but it kept food on the table. And each day Maria receded deeper and deeper within herself until she seemed to disappear completely, no longer the mother who'd raised him. But he had no time to focus on Maria. His shoulders ached from the weight of the shovel he pushed, lifted, and rotated, ten hours a day. At night, hands swollen and stiff, he struggled to grasp a glass of water, uncertain he could maintain his grip long enough to quench his thirst. He had just enough heart to survive, to work the week and collect a paycheck.

On the downtown streets, shovel in hand, potholes to be filled, he spotted a man wearing a baseball hat with the Arizona Diamondbacks insignia. Then he noticed other hats . . . other teams . . . Los Angeles Dodgers . . . San Francisco Giants . . . New York Yankees. Women in bright, sporty summer dresses, hair pulled back to expose their necks to the warmth of the Mexican sun, hurried past the mess and noise of Ernie's work. Stylish eyeglasses hid their uncaring faces as they clustered together to giggle and laugh at some private joke.

How lucky you are, he thought, his back on fire, his fingers pulsing. *To you, Puerto Vallarta is a delightful vacation. A hotel room, a few good meals, some swimming and sun. Maybe, if I could go back to the States, I'd be smiling and carefree too.*

Ernie resisted the urge to plead his case to every American who passed. To let them know that he'd been unfairly evicted from his home, forced out of his country, and moved into accommodations and a way of life that made the worst American ghetto seem like a paradise. Perhaps if his fellow Americans knew of his plight, they'd press for immigration reform. But would they believe him? Or even care? Would they recognize the United States was his home too?

His heart cried out. *I'm one of you. Help me. I'm trapped here. I'm an American.*

And then Ernie realized he too was invisible, no better than the dirty peasant children, begging for food, selling sticks of chewing gum on every corner. He'd been swallowed whole by Mexico and transformed, his life no longer his own. He was cursed; he was certain God had turned away from him.

At night, he closed his eyes but didn't sleep.

The city of Phoenix loomed before him. He remembered the America he loved—the standard of living, the promise of advancement with hard work.

I have to get out of here. I can't stay in this poverty or I'll go crazy.

He wanted to cross the border and make his way back to Phoenix, but he wasn't on his own. Maria needed him. And though his childhood had been strict, his mother demanding, often overbearing, he felt a loyalty that could only be explained by two people who find themselves alone in a world of darkness. He was unwilling to risk her safety in an attempt to re-enter the United States illegally.

The return to Mexico had already proved far too taxing.

She now rarely spoke unless spoken to.

His strong vibrant mother had given up. He understood. A dark undertow threatened to pull him into a black bottomless vortex. *I have to forget about Phoenix. About the United States. I have to see what's in front of me now. Work with what I have. I have to figure a way to be successful in Mexico.*

And so Ernie redoubled his efforts to find professional work. He prepared resumes and sent out inquiry letters. *Maybe*, he fantasized, *if I'm lucky, I'll land a job with an American-based company. It's possible*, he thought. *It has to be possible.*

* * *

Dave placed a dinner napkin on his lap. "God, I hate my job. That company is wearing me down. All these years, I've always loved my career. Now, I'm counting the days and the hours," he complained to Daisy who sat directly to his right. "I feel like they're sucking the energy right out of me."

Charlie hovered nearby with a pitcher, filling the water glasses.

"In the morning, as soon as I park the car, this unbelievable feeling comes over me. I just want to escape. I want to hop onto Highway 51 and drive," Dave rattled on. "There's this annoying tightness in my chest . . . I'm practically struggling to breathe. I swear . . . that job will be the death of me."

The conversation seemed to be the same every night, and though Charlie had asked Dave to leave his work at the office, Dave was completely immersed in Bremer. The politics, the personalities, the business decisions. Letting go of the frustration and the drama was proving nearly impossible.

"If they'd only let me do my job, I know I could fix the financial problems," he'd mumble, mostly to himself. "But they block me at every turn. And then they want to know why the performance isn't improving. It's enough to make you insane."

"I'm so sorry. That sounds just awful." Daisy reached over and gave Dave's hand a pat.

Dave caught Charlie's look of irritation. Eyes narrowed, downturn mouth, Charlie wasn't subtle. He'd just brought to the table a platter of sliced heirloom tomatoes and mozzarella sprinkled with fresh basil in a light balsamic vinaigrette.

"Caprese salad!" Daisy said. "Oh, how lovely, Charlie. It looks fabulous."

Dave served himself as the conversation turned to the growing number of mass shootings in America. Charlie and Daisy discussed the GOP and its position on gun control and abortion. As Dave listened, his mind wandered back to Bremer.

"Well it seems to me," Daisy said with conviction as she prepared the perfect bite-size forkful of tomato and mozzarella, "if you're against the killing of newborns then it only makes sense that you'd want stricter gun control laws."

"Well that's the rub," Charlie said, passing the bread. "Those people . . ."

"Those people?" Daisy interrupted him. "Charlie, it's not the American people who make these crazy stands about gun rights. It's the politicians. They are so disconnected from reality."

"But Daisy," Charlie added, "Americans support the politicians."

"Oh, I don't believe that," Daisy argued. "Perhaps the vocal minority who have membership in the NRA. But even among that group, I'm certain there's a silent majority that understands this isn't about Second Amendment rights. I blame Reagan. He was the one who defunded mental health services in this country. Made it impossible to find care for the psychotic. And now anyone can buy a gun."

The difference of opinion brought Dave back to the office. The circular arguments; Daniel's endless grandstanding; the war with Mossy. As Charlie and Daisy bantered back and forth about the American electorate, Dave raised his fork in the air, and in the middle of his inner dialogue, spoke aloud: "No matter how I want to fix things, Mossy blocks me. She's committed to every failed practice site and under-performing physician. Of course, she approved all those decisions, and making any changes would be like her admitting failure. But she doesn't have to account for the financial performance on a weekly basis. That's for me to explain, and still, the corporate office doesn't get that she's screwed it all up. I just can't figure that one out."

Charlie and Daisy ceased their discussion. Charlie sipped his water and shifted in his chair. He looked like he was about to say something and then thought better of it. Daisy wiped her mouth with her napkin.

"I started at six this morning," Dave complained, his monologue underway, "meeting with the surgeons, and then I worked through lunch, meeting with the family practice doctors. I thought I'd made some progress until I discovered later in the afternoon that Mossy had been calling the doctors, undermining every constructive conversation. She's a total bitch, wreaking havoc; Daniel is shouting at the staff, intimidating everyone."

Daisy and Charlie exchanged looks. Dave understood they wanted him to stop. To change the subject. That he was becoming a bore. But he couldn't help himself.

"I try to leave it all behind at the office," he said mostly to Charlie. "But then, three o'clock in the morning, I'm wide awake, staring at the clock. Wondering how I ever managed to get myself into this awful spot."

"Well surely," Daisy said, "there must be something that you like about the job. It can't all be bad."

"I like the people who report to me," Dave answered. "I enjoy working with them."

"Well that's something to be happy about," Daisy said, turning her attention back to the salad. "Oh Charlie, this is really delicious. Is that coarse kosher salt I taste?"

Charlie nodded.

"But no matter how much I try," Dave continued, "I can't figure out how to win Mossy over. How to get Daniel to behave like a professional."

Daisy politely smiled at him. Across the table, Charlie pushed his salad plate away. "I know you're frustrated . . ."

"They're paying me all this money," Dave said, finally putting his fork down, "and I don't get to make a single decision. I'm responsible for the financial performance but I can't implement any changes. It's fucking crazy."

Charlie sighed. "Dave, now come on. You're trying my patience. Are we going to talk about this all night? Enough is enough. Eat your salad. It's your favorite. I think the heirlooms are amazing."

Dave sighed. He had no appetite. "I made a mistake coming here," he said emphatically, sick at the very thought of another day at Bremer. It was a statement he'd repeated often since arriving in Phoenix.

"Don't go there, Dave, please," Charlie said shaking his head, sitting back in his chair, arms crossed.

"I can't help it. I hate working at that company. I should have my head examined for agreeing to move to Phoenix."

Daisy reached over to touch Dave's hand but he pulled it away.

"Let's not travel to the *Land of Regret*," Charlie begged. "There's no sense in beating yourself up over events that can't be changed."

Charlie had coined the phrase *Land of Regret* to describe Dave's compulsion to rehash decisions, to second-guess himself. In the *Land of Regret*, options not pursued were always better. Dave knew *The Land of Regret* drove Charlie nuts.

"So what if the job doesn't work out?" Charlie asked. "It doesn't matter. In the long run, we're exactly where we should be. Living in Phoenix."

"That's right, dear," Daisy seconded. "Don't be so hard on yourself. Sometimes, what seems to be an error in judgment turns out in hindsight to be the best decision we've ever made. You don't really know yet. It's all too close and personal."

Dave took a deep breath. "I don't know."

"Well I do," Daisy said. "When you've lived as long as I have, you understand that what seems life shattering, is barely a moment in time when viewed with perspective. You're taking this job far too seriously. It's not your life. These people you're stressing over aren't worth your energy. Trust me. Wherever they are now, they're enjoying their evening. You're the furthest thing from their mind."

Dave refused to listen. "The guy who held the job before me was there only five months. That should have been a red flag. How could I have been so stupid?"

"Water under the bridge," Charlie answered. "It's all water under the bridge," he repeated, his fork claiming the last of the mozzarella on the platter, continuously circling it about, soaking up what remained of the vinaigrette, before popping it into his mouth.

* * *

Jack and Enid returned home from their two-week vacation in Boca Raton. Jack collected the mail from the guard gate, which the post office had delivered in a large white plastic box. By the time he slipped his key in the front door it was midnight.

A folded note, shoved into the doorframe, dropped to the ground. Enid picked it up. Fliers for replacement windows or roof repair were common, often provided by vendors doing work in the neighborhood. Enid tossed the folded paper on the kitchen counter along with her keys and headed upstairs to the bedroom to unpack.

Jack slid Enid's keys aside and dumped the accumulated mail onto the green ceramic counter. Bills and junk mail fanned out like a magician's deck of cards, burying the note.

Jack's stomach growled.

He'd discovered within the first year of his marriage, Enid's penchant for hiding Oreos, Chips Ahoy, and Honey Maid Graham Crackers. Ever since, he'd played along, searching for the treasured booty, going so far as to replace a box of cookies if he overindulged.

He rifled through the oak cabinets.

Enid typically hid cookies behind the gallon-size bottle of Costco's Kirkland Olive Oil which she used to refill her pricier bottle of McEvoy Extra Virgin Olive Oil. It was a habit she'd acquired living in Michigan. An attempt to impress friends. *Typical Enid*, Jack thought. *Like anyone really cares which olive oil we use.*

He spotted the Kirkland.

There were no cookies behind it.

He turned his attention to the Harvest Gold Kenmore refrigerator. When Enid first saw it, she'd pressed for a total kitchen remodel. Jack thought it ridiculous considering she barely cooked. "Just look at this kitchen," she complained, one hand on the mustard GE wall oven, the other on her hip. "It's an antique gallery. We should donate these appliances to Henry Ford's Greenfield Village as an example of a midcentury modern."

Unwilling to give into her, Jack pushed back. "Which by the way," he pointed out, "is back in style."

Enid's face puckered up. "Oh Jack, we can't live like this."

Jack stifled a laugh, coughing instead. "These appliances will last forever . . . you know they don't make appliances like they used to."

"And there's a good reason." Enid flipped open the oven door. "This isn't self-cleaning. Look at that caked-on crud. I'm not cleaning this. Forget it."

"Then I'll do it," Jack had volunteered, determined to prove Enid wrong. "A little Easy Off and that oven will sparkle. All I need are some Playtex gloves."

Jack laughed at the memory of the conversation. How upset Enid had been. "A little Easy Off," he repeated aloud, enjoying his quick-witted response.

He turned his attention to the refrigerator. *Now let's see what we have here.* He opened the door. The light was out. As he leaned in to check the bulb, assuming it needed to be replaced, he was overcome by the acrid aroma of rotting food. Gasping for air, he pulled his head out of the rancid sarcophagus and slammed the door shut.

The damn thing has died. It must have been out the entire two weeks we were gone.

"Enid . . ." he called out, before realizing she was upstairs, probably in the midst of her nightly ritual of applying face cream to remove her make-up.

It was late. There was little to do at this hour. Little he wanted to do. He decided to let it be. There'd be time enough to deal with it in the morning. After all, he'd already suffered two weeks in Boca visiting Enid's stepsister Rona. That had been torture enough. He was tired.

And so without even a sticky note of warning, Jack switched off the kitchen light and headed to bed. He smirked with delight at the thought of Enid encountering the horrid smell. The thought of her sour expression had him giggling as he made his way up the stairs.

* * *

The next morning at 6:00 a.m., Daisy sat and waited on the Lee's front porch, admiring their black rattan sofa and its comfy, bright red cushions.

On her morning walk, Sheila had alerted her to the fact that the Lees had returned home.

"I stopped at The Terraces before starting my midnight shift at Biltmore Greens. Danny, the new guard," Sheila's eyes beamed with excitement, "is kind of sweet on me."

"Oh," was all Daisy could manage as Sheila went on and on about Danny.

Glancing down, Daisy spotted the concrete block that had been in need of repair the morning of her car accident so many months ago. A new grey block was now in its place, lighter in color than the surrounding ones.

"It was late . . . about a quarter to twelve when the Lees pulled in," Sheila remembered. "And look at you, so healthy and strong now," Sheila gushed. "It's just marvelous."

Daisy managed a smile.

"Now they typically walk in the morning . . . a bit later than you." Sheila checked her watch. "You might just head them off if you go over there now. Oh, I bet they'll be thrilled to see you."

Daisy traced the pattern of the rattan with her index finger. She hoped to remain calm when the couple finally emerged. She needed to understand how it had all happened. How she'd lost her home and possessions. She didn't want to raise her voice. She didn't think it would be helpful. But she wasn't sure she could remain calm.

A grey dove landed nearby. The bird fluttered its wings and bobbed its head as if wishing Daisy a good morning. "Aren't you lovely," Daisy said just as she heard loud voices coming from within the house. Two adults screaming. The dove took off. Daisy couldn't make out what was being said, but the shouting was growing ever louder.

The door opened.

Daisy held her breath as the two appeared in the doorway; the man in tennis whites; the woman in black leggings and a bright pink top. They didn't see her.

"I don't care what you say," the woman snapped as she stepped outside. She held a tissue to her nose. "That awful smell . . . I'll never get that stench out of my nose." She lowered the tissue and took a deep breath.

The man stood at the threshold, leaning against the doorframe. He had a smug grin. The woman turned about to face him, her back to Daisy. "We're gutting that kitchen," she said loud enough for all of Phoenix to hear. "If you expect me to live in that glorified apartment, then you're going to have to bring it up to my standards."

"Okay . . . we can redo the kitchen . . . but no *Wolf* appliances," the man said, index finger pointed in her direction. "We'll go to Sears and price out appliances that fit our budget. And we'll hire a handyman to paint the cabinets. We're not ripping out perfectly good cabinetry."

"Stop telling me what to do with *my money*," she hissed, stepping forward and grabbing the man's index finger. "And get that goddamn finger out of my face before I break it off." She yanked the finger swiftly down as if she was playing a Vegas one-armed bandit. "I'm tired of you always telling me what I can do . . ."

"Hey," he whined, pulling his finger from her grip. "That hurt."

"Good. I'm glad. Maybe you'll learn to keep your freaking fingers to yourself," she exploded as she turned on her heels.

"Good morning," Daisy said as she caught the woman's eye. "I trust you both slept well. Did you see my note?"

"Daisy," the woman said, blushing a deep crimson. "What on earth are you doing here? What note? Did you leave us a note?"

Daisy rose from the sofa to her full height of five feet two inches and walked over to the couple perched atop the basket-weave *Welcome* mat trimmed in black rubber. "You must be Enid," she said, taking in the red-headed woman's features. The pale skin and freckles. The boyish figure. The lines about her face that hinted at too much sun exposure for someone so fair-skinned. The slack in her jaw that, despite her youthful presence, revealed she was older than the man who stood next to her.

If it were ladylike to spit, Daisy would have done so right in Enid's eye.

"Why, yes. Daisy . . . you remember me," Enid stammered. "I visited with you at the hospital and at The Village. I've been taking care of all your paperwork, paying your bills, handling your affairs. We didn't think you'd ever walk again."

Daisy did a quick spin. "As you can see, I am perfectly fine. It's amazing how the body heals given time and the right care."

"Well . . . isn't that something," Enid said, seemingly surprised by Daisy's resurrection.

Daisy looked at the man in the doorway. Tall and lean with white-grey hair, his straight nose and blue eyes encased in a round, boyish face. "And you must be Jack," she said in wonderment. *My God, he's handsome*, she thought.

Jack smiled. He reached past Enid and grabbed Daisy's hand. "Yes . . . hello . . . Aunt Daisy." There was excitement in his voice. "You look absolutely wonderful."

He bent down and delivered a kiss to her cheek. Daisy's heart fluttered. She'd not anticipated being so overwhelmed with emotion upon seeing Jack.

"I had no idea you were doing so well," he continued. "We just got back from visiting Enid's sister in Boca."

"Stepsister," Enid icily corrected him.

"Did we miss your note?" Jack squinted.

The sun had risen above the trees and thrown a bright spotlight onto Jack's face. He raised his hand to block the sun's intensity, temporarily obliterating Daisy's view, denying her the opportunity to determine exactly whom Jack resembled. Still, Daisy's eyes remained on Jack. She wanted to hug him. To cry out with sheer delight. Any anger she held about the sale of her property fell away as Jack became her focus.

Jack apologized, the warmth in his voice denoting genuine regret. "I'd been meaning to stop by and visit, but those places, well . . . I can't really handle them," he said. "But Enid has kept me fully apprised. Now that you're well, I guess this is a chance to get to know each other," he said, winking.

Daisy was charmed. No other human being had ever had such an effect on her.

"So where are you staying?" Jack innocently asked, looking over at Enid. "You didn't tell me Daisy would be leaving The Village. What arrangements did you make? Is she renting in the Biltmore?"

"I've been visiting with two very fine men." Daisy glared at Enid. "To whom it seems you sold my home." Her anger instantly returned with a fury. And while Jack seemed perfectly calm, Enid looked like she wanted to melt into the walkway. "Now how exactly did that happen?" Daisy asked Enid. "I never gave permission to sell my home. I never would have allowed it," she said emphatically.

Jack glance over at Enid and then his aunt. "Why Aunt Daisy, you knew about the sale. Enid spoke with you. She told me. We thought you'd have to stay on permanently at The Village. Enid was just making sure you had adequate funds to afford the care. We sold the house to cover those future expenses."

"Is that what she was doing?" Daisy asked, her fists balled up at her side. Jack no longer had any power over her. She was shocked how quickly her feelings had shifted. He'd become the enemy.

"Yes," Jack answered. "You agreed."

Daisy stamped her foot. "I never agreed to sell my home. Never."

"You just don't remember," Jack said calmly. "No wonder. You were pretty sick. Enid discussed all the details with you. You clearly understood."

Daisy proudly raised her head. "Enid visited me once at the hospital and I was in no condition to make any decisions about my future."

"Oh no, Aunt Daisy, that isn't right. Enid was there quite a bit. She was very concerned."

"I've checked the visitor logs, Jack. Enid made only one visit to the hospital and only one visit to The Village to meet with the social worker to discuss discharge arrangements, which by the way, she never made. I had no idea my house had been sold. How could you," Daisy turned to Enid, "allow me to be discharged when I had no place to go? Who does such a thing?"

Jack turned to Enid. "What is she talking about?"

Daisy's eyes bulged as she formally accused Enid. "You sold my home right out from underneath me."

Jack pleaded with Enid. "Tell her she's wrong. Tell her she agreed."

Enid said nothing. Instead, she pushed past Jack and rushed back into the house, slamming the front door behind her.

* * *

Jack stood in the kitchen, arms folded, face set in a disapproving frown. "How could this have happened? You told me you talked with her."

Enid sat at the kitchen table, a glass of water in front of her. She struggled to gather her wits. How could she explain to Jack that Daisy's recovery had her baffled? That she had sold all the woman's possessions in anticipation of inheriting Daisy's estate? That her wild spending had been predicated on the thought that Daisy's money would soon be hers?

"I did talk with her," Enid insisted. She ran her hand over the glass table as if touching a clear solid surface could give truth to her lie. "She just doesn't remember."

Enid was unwilling to admit to the scope of her blunder; to explain that she'd misjudged Daisy's situation. Jumped to conclusions. Been caught up in the unexpected joy of plundering the spoils of Daisy's property. For the time being, it was her word against Daisy's. And who could possibly believe an old woman?

"It must be all the medication she was on. What other explanation can there be?" Jack surmised. If she agreed at the time, and now doesn't remember, you can't be held responsible. You only had her best interests at heart. She'll just have to understand. You did your best."

Enid saw no point in telling Jack the truth. That she'd concocted conversations with Daisy that had never happened. That she'd spoken of visits to the hospital and the rehab center when she was actually out shopping or enjoying a day at the spa. That she'd assumed Daisy was dying based on nothing more than intuition. That she'd never have lifted a finger to help Daisy if there wasn't money to be had.

"Circumstances change," Jack said. "It wasn't as if you intended to defraud her."

Enid nodded. "She seemed pretty angry."

"Oh yeah . . . she stormed off . . . that was one pissed-off old lady . . . but I do believe you were only doing what you thought was right."

Enid was grateful for Jack's sympathy, but she wasn't so sure she could forgive herself.

While Jack puttered outside in the garden, Enid tried to figure out what to do.

There must be a way to make this right, she thought, unable to come up with any reasonable solution that allowed her to save face.

She stared off in space, frightened, weighing her options. The truth loomed like an Arizona bobcat sunning itself by a swimming pool—scary, dangerous and unwanted.

She'd have to stick to her story—that Daisy knew and approved of the plans all along.

And then Enid's mind switched gears.

But really, it's Dr. Mueller's fault.

She remembered the physician sitting amid his stack of medical records. *He's the medical expert and even he wasn't sure she'd survive that superbug.*

Enid recalled her discussion with the social worker at The Village. *She said Daisy hadn't been responding to treatment and might have needed long-term care.*

That's it, she thought.

I was just following the recommendation of the professionals. Trying to cover all the bases to make sure she'd be able to pay for her care.

And just like that, Enid felt better.

* * *

Jack Lee had always needed a woman in his life to feel complete.

His childhood had been dominated by his mother Rose, an opinion-ated and disagreeable woman who was not fond of little boys. Jack's father, Jacob, spent his days on the road selling restaurant supplies. Jack had just turned ten when Jacob dropped dead of a heart attack, leaving Rose in the role of family breadwinner. Jack's two older sisters took charge of his daily care.

When Jack attended Queens College, he met Betsy in his freshman year, an attractive, energetic, and forceful brunette. At twenty-one, he earned a bachelor's degree, and married Betsy, moving out of his mother's house. By then, he was accustomed to taking orders from women.

Like Rose, Betsy had a formidable personality with the verbal agility of a prosecuting attorney, hot on the heels of a defendant's next vagary. Jack fell into step behind Betsy. He went along to get along. It was easier.

Betsy organized Jack's life. She maintained the couple's friendships and kept in touch with relatives, including Jack's family. Had Betsy lived, Jack would never have looked at another woman, but Betsy died of breast can-cer at age thirty-eight. With Betsy's death, Jack's main connection to the world was broken. After seventeen years of marriage, he was in freefall.

For two months, Jack rehashed the terrible twist of fate life had handed him. The loneliness was unbearable. Jack's sisters encouraged him to take time to grieve before he started to date, but Jack had no patience for emotional healing or self-discovery. He wanted his life back. He was desperate to put the memories of Betsy behind him and to shed the anguish of being a widower.

Meeting Enid had been a miracle.

Betsy's illness had left Jack with significant financial debt. Where some women might have looked at Jack as a financial burden, Enid saw a man who needed her guidance. Like Betsy, she was fully prepared to dictate how Jack would live his life, but unlike Betsy, she wasn't in love with Jack. For Enid, Jack was a means to an end. He was an available man who eased the social stigma of a woman alone. As far as Enid was concerned, her marriage to Jack was a perfect union. She was in control.

After six months of dating, they married. What had once been *Betsy and Jack* became *Enid and Jack.*

* * *

In the short time they'd been together, Anna had come to love having Henry around. Still, she firmly believed that the best place for the boy was with his family, and so, she arranged to meet Henry's mother at Starbucks near Paradise Valley Mall.

As she exited Highway 51 at Cactus Road, traveling east toward Scottsdale, she found herself feeling increasingly protective of Henry. Uncertain she was doing the right thing. She suppressed her desire to turn the car around and go home.

Henry's mother was waiting for Anna outside, sitting at a metallic green table. Her shoulder-length blond hair was cut in a youthful, Jennifer Aniston style, to frame her face. She wore a dark-grey Juicy Couture yoga outfit which seemed too informal for the occasion. Up close, Anna clocked Lena to be in her early-forties, though from a distance, she had seemed much younger.

There was a strong family resemblance. Something about the eyes, the shape of the face, and the way Henry had of squeezing his jaw when stressed. Anna recognized the facial expression, without considering what mood it suggested.

"You must be Lena," Anna said, excited to be meeting Henry's mother. She reached out to shake an unexpectedly cold and limp hand. "Can I get you a coffee?" she offered, wishing to be a good hostess.

Lena declined as she suspiciously eyed Anna.

Anna nervously pulled out the metal chair and sat down. She'd asked for the meeting and now, face-to-face with Henry's mother, wondered how to begin.

Lena took the initiative.

"You said you wanted to talk about Henry." Her tone was tinged with irritation. "Well here I am. So what's there to say in person that you couldn't have told me over the phone?"

"Henry's safe. He's staying with me."

"Yes, you already told me that." Lena's expression left little doubt that she disapproved of the stranger before her. "Now, what would a woman like you want with a teenage boy?"

Anna was taken aback. The tone of the question sounded almost predatory.

"You want money? Is that it?" she asked contemptuously. "You think I should be paying you for his support?" Lena folded her arms and leaned back in her chair, glaring at Anna.

"Not at all," Anna said, alarmed at the direction of the conversation. "That never even crossed my mind."

"Then what's the big mystery? Why did I *have to meet you*?"

"I thought it best if we knew each other . . ." Anna's voice trailed off, beginning to doubt her own good judgment.

Lena sighed. "I don't know what you're up to, but to be honest, Henry's welfare is of little concern to me. If Henry isn't interested in his parents and their feelings, well, there's little we're prepared to do for him."

"But he's only fifteen," Anna felt compelled to point out.

"Old enough to understand we won't have him in our home the way he is. We don't approve of the homosexual lifestyle. And since you like him so much, maybe you should keep him," she said sarcastically.

Anna was taken aback by Lena's harsh response. She felt totally misunderstood. "I realize this is a private family matter. I just thought you'd want to know where and how he's living."

"Do you have children?" Lena asked, breaking the flow of Anna's thought.

Anna shook her head, not sure where Lena was heading.

"Then you can't possibly understand our pain. My husband and I have a successful life. We're good people. We've always treated Henry well. We didn't deserve this. Having a defective child is something you'll probably never understand."

"Defective?" Anna gasped.

"He's not normal. The odd part is that Henry fooled us. We thought he was an average kid. There never was any clue he was one of *those gays*. He always had girls around and he played football. A very athletic kid . . . and then one day . . . Well, you probably know the rest. He's a liar. And he expects us to change how we feel when he's unwilling to change in any way."

Anna struggled to understand the intensity of Lena's anger. "But you have a moral and legal obligation . . ."

Lena finished Anna's sentence. ". . . not to a run away."

"Henry didn't tell me that he ran away."

"I wouldn't trust much of what Henry says if I were you."

"You're horrible," Anna said. "Really horrible."

"You asked me if I'm concerned about my son. Is my son concerned about me? Has he once asked about his parents? I'll give you the answer. No, he hasn't." Lena stood up, pushing her metal chair backward. It fell over with a crash. She made no attempt to pick it up. "You tell Henry we're glad he's getting on with his life. We wish him well. Now, if you'll excuse me, I have other things to do."

* * *

Bonnie came to cherish Thursday evenings. Single, and with no relationship in sight, dining with Charlie, Dave, and Daisy had become her touchstone, the one night she could count on for great food, terrific wine, and wonderful conversation. All Bonnie needed was to show up and enjoy.

"You're lucky," Bonnie confided to Daisy as the two waited in the living room, side-by-side on a white sofa, while the men were busy in the kitchen getting dinner ready. "This house is really filled with love."

Daisy smiled. "I adore them, but I'm afraid I'm imposing on their good nature. Dave is so unhappy at work. He shouldn't have to worry about entertaining an old lady in his home. I'm the dreaded house guest who shows up and refuses to leave."

"That's not true," Bonnie corrected her, turning to peer into Daisy's eyes. "I see the way they look at you. They don't feel that way at all."

"Perhaps, but the longer I stay here, the more I risk wearing out my welcome. This isn't my home any longer. I can't pretend it is."

A silence fell between the two women. Daisy seemed lost in thought. Bonnie could see the wheels spinning. "What are you thinking about?" she asked her friend.

Daisy waved her hand in a dismissive gesture.

"Oh, no," Bonnie pressed. "I really want to know."

Daisy looked off in the distance. "I was thinking I should have married. If I had, I wouldn't be in this position."

The years between the two women faded. Daisy was young again. Bonnie, her contemporary. They leaned in like girlfriends.

"There was this young man I was seeing . . . I was such a silly fool. Bob was handsome, athletic, and tall. He swept me off my feet. We kissed the first time on Valentine's Day. Odd, I haven't thought about that in years. I guess there are some people we're reluctant to remember."

Bonnie kept still. She dared not break the spell.

"If you were a good girl, you kissed a boy, went steady, and got married. It was all planned out. When I was in high school, most of my girlfriends knew who they'd marry. We were kids. All of us just kids."

"Were you a good girl?" Bonnie asked.

"I wasn't," Daisy admitted. "Oh, you'd never know it to look at me now. I was once young and beautiful. I could have had any boy. And I knew my way around the backseat of a car. I was liberated—ahead of my time. I enjoyed men. Most women back then didn't admit to it. And, after all, babies weren't being born because men were having sex by themselves. Women were interested, too. Oh, we can all be such hypocrites."

Bonnie couldn't imagine a lovely grandmother-type like Daisy as a sexual being, but then, she knew from her experience at The Village that sex was not the exclusive domain of the young.

"When I met Bob, I was so young. One thing led to another. No one talked about sex. I had no idea what was happening. Bob and I were alone, it was raining, and it happened. It was thrilling. And then, when I didn't get a visit from my friend, I nearly went out of my mind with fear. I'd just turned seventeen."

"At first, I was in denial. I pretended nothing was wrong. Then after a few weeks, I got up the courage to talk with Bob. He didn't believe it was his baby. He thought he was just one of many men. I was a tease and a flirt and he believed all my nonsense. He refused to marry me. So there I was, pregnant, and I couldn't have the baby."

Bonnie put her hand on Daisy's. "Oh my God, what did you do?"

"I tried to find a doctor to take care of it. I went down to the East Village but couldn't get the doctor to help. But he took pity on me and told me about someone who would. It was all very hush-hush. He gave me a phone number and made me swear not to tell where I'd gotten it. There was a seedy office, dirty floors, a man who looked at you like you had it coming. I felt so dirty and ashamed."

Bonnie remembered the abortion she'd had in her early twenties at Planned Parenthood. It was legal thanks to Roe v. Wade. The matter had been handled in a respectful and professional manner.

"I should have insisted Bob marry me," Daisy said with conviction. "But I was too ashamed at his reaction. I just shut down."

Together the two women sat in silence, Daisy unable to go on with her story . . . overcome by her memories.

"And now here I am, all these years later, reliving my youth." Daisy gave Bonnie a wry smile. "Learn from me. Don't procrastinate. Find a man. Have a family. Don't wind up an old lady living in someone else's house."

"But you're not alone," Bonnie countered. "You have people in your life who care about you. And besides, having a husband or children doesn't necessarily mean there'll be someone to look after you. Spouses die. Children live out of state. There are no guarantees in life. The only ones we have in the end are ourselves. We can't really rely on anyone else."

"Yes, I suppose that's true," Daisy sadly agreed.

"And you were the one who introduced me to Charlie and Dave. Without you, I'd have never have met them. That was a connection you made for me."

Daisy nodded, her eyes glowing brightly. "If I'd had a daughter, I would have liked her to be like you," she confided. "You're a competent and strong woman. You know how to take care of yourself. I had to learn those lessons through years of trial and error. But you seem to know it instinctually. You're amazing."

"Am I?" Bonnie wondered out loud. Only earlier in the day she too had been struggling with her choices. "You and I are actually a lot alike," Bonnie admitted. "I'm also alone in the world."

"I guess we all are," Daisy acknowledged, squeezing the younger woman's hand. "But every now and then we get lucky. We come across friends who distract us and make us feel honored and loved."

* * *

Harvey Lederman, Esquire, prided himself on being the most aggressive, offensive, in-your-face attorney money could buy. Abrupt, ill-mannered, and completely narcissistic, Harvey could no sooner sit patiently to learn the facts of a case than he could be bothered to remember the first and last name of a client. That was the work for his underlings who screened inquiries and recommended the cases that offered the best opportunity for a quick buck. And though Daisy's case was certainly not high profile, Harvey's team sensed the potential for some good publicity. There were lots of seniors in Arizona who ran the risk of being ripped off by family members. Daisy's case was a natural.

Once Daisy retained Harvey to represent her, the wheels were set in motion.

The following Monday, there was a knock on the Lees' door. A young Hispanic male asked for Jack Lee. When Jack identified himself, the young man pressed a letter into Jack's hand and fled.

"What the heck is this?" Jack muttered, examining the document. "Hey you," Jack yelled, but the youth had already jumped into his car and pulled out of the driveway. "*Daisy Ellen Lee v. Jack and Enid Lee*," Jack read aloud. "Enid," Jack hollered. "We're being sued."

"What?" Enid shouted as she headed towards him from the other end of the house. "What did you say?"

Jack slammed the front door. "We're being sued. My aunt is suing us."

Grabbing the paper out of Jack's hand, Enid examined the document. "This is ridiculous. How could she be suing us?"

"She's doing it," Jack said, closing his eyes as if to erase the last few moments while Enid excitedly paced back and forth in the hallway.

"She has no right," Enid fumed, gripping the document in her hand.

"I'm not so sure of that," Jack said, his jaw firmly set.

"How dare she sue us after all we've done?" Enid reiterated.

"You mean after all *you've* done," Jack said, clarifying Enid's responsibility. "This is all your fault."

"I won't listen," Enid said, covering her ears. "I did exactly what we discussed. Don't you dare pretend that you knew nothing about what I was doing? You're as much a part of this as I am. I was only acting in your best interest."

Jack tilted his head and gave Enid a suspicious look. "I thought you were acting in *Daisy's* best interest."

Enid's eyes flashed molten lava. "Sarcasm and attitude . . . that's all I get from you. I was only trying to be helpful," she shrieked.

"And just look what your meddling has done," Jack said, grabbing the subpoena from her hands and holding it up between them. "Well, here's to a job done *the Enid way.* This whole thing will cost us a pretty penny by the time Daisy is through with us."

"How dare you blame me? She's your rotten relative."

"And you're my rotten wife."

"Well, at least I'm not suing you, Jack," Enid snapped as she grabbed the subpoena back, crushed it into a tiny ball, and flung it at Jack's face, hitting his forehead.

"Nice . . . real nice," Jack said as the paper bomb bounced off his forehead and landed on the floor. "I think someone needs a time out."

And with that, Jack grabbed his keys from the hall table and headed out the door.

8

....

"It's done," Dave announced as he entered Charlie's office, papers scattered everywhere.

He stepped carefully amid the piles on the floor, lifting a thickly-bound Williams-Sonoma report from a brown leather chair and placing it on a nearby Chinese alter table, before falling backward into the seat. Hips low on the cushion, he rubbed his face as if awakening from a dream.

"I did it. I gave notice today. It's all over."

Charlie, seated in his desk chair, pivoted 180 degrees, breaking away from his laptop, and faced Dave with a look of astonishment. "Really?" He leaned forward, palms cupping his knees, excitement in his voice. "You did it? No kidding? You're free of that hellhole."

"I just couldn't take it," Dave said plaintively. "I never thought I'd actually throw in the towel but I couldn't do it anymore. I was just spinning my wheels. I couldn't stand working for that company another day."

Charlie's eyes lit up. "Wow. I was hoping you'd leave. I just thought it might take a few more months. Well good for you! You were absolutely wasting your time there. *That's such terrific news*," he said, bright and cheery. "Hallelujah. We should go out to Morton's or Ruth Chris's Steakhouse for dinner. Have a great meal to mark the occasion."

Charlie's reaction rubbed Dave the wrong way. He'd misread the moment. His glee seemed the height of insensitivity as Dave reeled from the gravity of his recent decision. He was not much in the mood to celebrate. "You don't have to be so damn happy about it," Dave moodily answered. "It doesn't exactly feel wonderful to quit a high-paying job. To decide at long last that Bremer was the wrong place for me."

"I didn't mean that," Charlie smiled benevolently. "I know this was a hard decision for you."

"That's right," Dave said adamantly. "Very hard."

"Well, it's all over now," Charlie said, shrugging his shoulders, as he eyed one of his color-coded maps lying on the floor. "This damn project is due on Friday and I still have to forecast sales for at least another twenty stores."

"I get it," Dave said, somewhat indignantly, getting to his feet. "I know you're busy."

Charlie's attention shifted back to Dave.

"Hey wait a minute. I didn't mean to cut you off." He waved at Dave to sit back down. "We both know that job *was* unsustainable." His words were now soft; his expression guarded. "You couldn't continue to work those hours with that kind of intensity, engage in all that stress, not sleep at night, and think it wasn't going to affect your health. We're not young men anymore."

Dave bristled at the mention of age. Though he knew Charlie was right, he didn't want to hear it. Not at that moment. Not on that day. And now he couldn't get Charlie's jubilant reaction to his sad news out of his mind. The joyous smile. The flash of those white teeth. *We aren't what we do*, Charlie had always said. But it didn't feel that way to Dave. He'd spent thirty years as a healthcare executive. That had been his primary identity. Now, who was he? What would he do? With his job gone, Dave feared he'd come to a dangerous crossroad, and mistakenly, taken the wrong path. He felt old. Older than a man in his mid-fifties.

Dave cracked his knuckles as Charlie went on about the importance of their relationship. That being together superseded any concerns about what either of them did for a living. But Dave was now suspicious of every word Charlie uttered. He studied Charlie's facial expression as if seeing him for the first time. *It's all so easy for Charlie to say. He's happy living in Phoenix. He's the one who pressed to buy the house. He is doing just fine.*

Dave suddenly felt trapped.

"Well, I'm truly glad it's over," Charlie enthused. "There are so many places I want to go. China. Vietnam. Thailand. There was no way we were going to be able to travel while you were employed."

Is that why Charlie wanted me to stop working? So that he could travel? Is that why I gave up my career?

Charlie squinted downward at a map lying on the floor. "Oh, that isn't right," he balked, shifting his focus back to the project before him. "I'm going to have to get this map redone. The cartographer incorrectly placed the retail site outside of the intended trade area. Crap. Okay. You're going to have to excuse me. I've got to take care of this now."

* * *

As Dave lay by the pool, newspaper spread across his lap, he was haunted by the memories of Bremer. He knew it might take time to get it out of his system . . . Daniel's screaming, Mossy's manipulations. He'd been certain the bottom-line financials were fixable. A hard road, but doable. He'd already made tremendous strides. But the real challenge wasn't the business, but the personalities of the players. He just wasn't being allowed to do the job. And now Dave thought about how his type A intensity had added fuel to the mix. He knew he couldn't change the culture of the organization. The only thing Dave had control over were his choices.

Maybe if I'd taken it more in stride. Chilled out. Not been so insistent on perfection. He closed his eyes and relived the confrontations with Daniel; how Daniel had resisted every suggestion before ultimately agreeing; how Mossy had blocked him from the start. It was all so pointless. *I was just spinning my wheels. Those people were freaking nuts. I had to get out of there. If only for my own sanity.*

Dave had to refocus his energies. *If I lay here, I'm just going to go crazy,* he thought as Charlie's voice called from the open sliding glass door. "Hey, if you're not doing anything, would you mind going to the bank and making a deposit for my business? And we need milk. How about stopping at Fry's and picking up a gallon?"

"Is that now my new role?" Dave shouted back, putting the newspaper aside, his mood deteriorating. "I've gone from executive to helpful housewife?"

Charlie stood in the doorway as if suspended in place. "Gee, I'm sorry. I didn't realize I was *imposing.* I thought we were here to help one another. Forgive me," he said, his voice full of attitude as he stepped back inside and started to close the sliding glass door.

Dave immediately reversed. "I'm sorry," he called out, quickly rising from the lounger. "I guess I'm just testy. Of course I'll do it. Just let me know what you need and I'll take care of it."

Charlie lingered at the door as Dave came inside. "Are you okay?" he asked.

"No," Dave admitted. "I'm not okay."

"Well why don't you occupy yourself with some of things we need to do around here?"

Dave bit his lower lip. *I guess that's my new role. Prepare meals, clean closets, gather clothing to donate for Salvation Army. And the garage, I could always clean that out.*

The garage was loaded from the move to Phoenix. Charlie and Dave had unpacked only what they'd immediately needed. Dave regretted the decision to work through the pile as soon as he'd started.

"If I'd known I'd find myself sorting through all this crap," Dave told Charlie, "I would have kept that damn job."

The more thought Dave gave to the process, the slower it went. He soon realized that the trick was to toss items quickly. If he thought too long about any one item, whether it might come in handy down the road, whether it was still useful, he became immobilized. For the first time in his life Dave understood the mindset of a hoarder.

He refused to allow such thinking to rule him.

Stacks of papers found their way to the recycle bin; old financial records shredded; outmoded electronics donated. It took dedication, but in the end, the garage was clean.

"I just can't imagine what I'm going to do with the rest of my time," Dave lamented on their evening walk with Timmy.

"Do you want another job?" Charlie asked as he tugged on Timmy's leash, uprooting the little poodle from a spot that had captured the dog's interest for far too long.

"I'm burnt out. If I go back to work, it's going to have to be outside of health care."

"Dave, you don't need to work. We've saved our money and invested well. We can live nicely without your working," Charlie said as Timmy sniffed a nearby bush, circled, and prepared to do his business.

"But then, what the heck am I going to do?"

"We live in Arizona. You can go hiking, biking, and horseback riding. Leisure activities! Take up golf," Charlie said. "Good boy, Timmy. Good boy . . . *hurry up*."

Dave watched Timmy scoot forward and then kick dirt over his deposit. "But what am I going to do for my mind?"

"There's the library. And think of all the non-profits that would love to have access to your experience." Charlie passed Dave a plastic bag. "Can you pick that up?" He nodded in the direction of Timmy's delivery.

Dave crouched down and grabbed Timmy's dropping, its warmth, permeating the plastic. *I can do anything I want*, he thought as he knotted the bag, overwhelmed by the sheer enormity of all his new, free time.

* * *

Dave struggled to sleep, waking up at two in the morning, tossing and turning, thinking about his life, the choices he'd made, before sitting up in bed, frustrated, unable to fall back to sleep.

"What's going on," Charlie asked, a light sleeper, and keenly awake. He turned on his side to face Dave. "Go back to bed. You need your rest."

Dave stated the obvious. "I can't sleep."

Charlie lifted his head and fluffed the end of his pillow before dropping the weight of his head back down and crushing the corner. "What's wrong now?" His tone was more exasperated than exhausted.

"I can't seem to turn my mind off. And now, it feels like there are a thousand tiny violin strings playing in my body."

"Violin strings? That's a new one." Charlie rubbed an eye.

"I think it's an anxiety attack."

"What's there to be anxious about?"

Dave vigorously shook his hands back and forth, fingers spread wide, in an effort to release the nervous energy. Timmy stood up, yawned, and repositioned himself into a crescent next to Charlie.

"I have no idea what I'm doing. I've always known what I'm doing. I've always made the most of every moment. Now I don't know what to do with myself."

"That's crazy," Charlie answered, sitting up next to Dave. "You've been so busy."

"Busy doing nothing," Dave answered.

"That's not true. Everything you're doing is important for our family."

"Charlie, there's no value to what I've been doing. Going to the supermarket every day. Picking up the dry cleaning. This is not a career."

"Yes, but you don't need to have a career any more. That isn't important."

"That's easy for you to say," Dave argued. "You still have your life. You still know who you are."

"Go back to sleep," Charlie pressed, rolling over. "It's late. This is no time to figure out the rest of your life. I have meetings in the morning."

✳ ✳ ✳

Daisy Ellen Lee had spent a lifetime adhering to the solemn belief that the best-kept secret is the one not shared. And so, for decades, Daisy had not spoken of her teen pregnancy. The only person she'd confided in, up until Bonnie, had been her brother Jacob. But then, she'd had no choice. She lived in Jacob's home and, sooner or later, Jacob and his wife Rose would come to learn of her condition. There was no way to hide it.

Ten years older than Daisy, Jacob was short in stature but big in heart. At five-foot-six, he had a full head of scruffy brown hair and a warm, friendly smile, befitting the job of a restaurant supply salesman who peddled pots and pans, cutlery, tablecloths, napkins, and anything that was needed to run a food-service business. The distinct scent of Brylcreem, which Jacob used daily to tame his unruly mop, came to mind whenever Daisy thought of her brother, the father of two toddlers the day Daisy, at age fourteen, moved into his home.

"My parents may be dead, but I know what they'd expect. As long as we can manage, she's staying with us," she overheard Jacob telling his wife as they both stood in the small galley kitchen of their Bronx apartment talking, a pot of lentil soup on the stove.

"But there's no room," Rose had pleaded, still a young, pretty woman, wearing a housedress, the fabric imprinted with tiny yellow and white flowers.

"Well then, we'll make room," Jacob answered simplistically, the matter already decided. "She can sleep on the sofa. And she'll be helpful around the house." Jacob lifted the lid of the soup pot and inhaled. The rich aroma of the beans filled the air. "You'll see. You'll come to rely on her."

But Daisy was an adolescent girl with a mind of her own. While her brother was on the road, traveling cross-country, weeks at a stretch, Daisy enjoyed her youth. She stayed out till all hours, driving Rose nearly out of her mind with worry.

"How about cleaning the kitchen?" Rose would ask as she diapered her youngest.

Daisy would have none of it. "I'm not a servant girl," she'd tell her sister-in-law. "I'll help, but only if I want to. Not because I have to."

But Daisy never seemed to want to.

And so the women co-existed, Daisy too resentful to be grateful for the roof over her head, Rose too intruded upon to appreciate Daisy's pain in not having a family or home to call her own. Clashes were frequent and heated. Upon returning home, Jacob would pick up immediately on the tension in the house and admonish his sister.

"You promised me you'd be kinder to Rose."

"I try," she'd answer, looking down, avoiding any eye contact. "I really do."

"Then try harder."

"But she's so mean to me," Daisy would insist, shamelessly exaggerating.

"She has a lot of responsibilities. One day when you have children, you'll understand. It's hard work raising a family."

Daisy listened politely to her brother, and silently swore she'd never be a hausfrau like Rose, stuck home all day with two babies to care for.

As Daisy matured into a beautiful young woman, she attracted her fair share of male attention. She reveled in her new-found power. But mostly, she loved the way her body felt when a man touched her; the warmth that flowed through her limbs; the urgency of her need. It was as natural as breathing.

Jacob was up on the roof of the six-story building one twilight, smoking, staring at the view of Yankee Stadium off in the distance, lights ablaze for an evening game, when Daisy joined him.

"It's beautiful up here," Jacob said, flicking the ashes off the tip of his cigarette, a pack of Kent's by his elbow. He leaned forward on the roof's ledge. "So quiet and peaceful."

"Less crowded," Daisy agreed as she breathed in the sweet summer air. A cool breeze, courtesy of the Harlem River, lifted her hair gently as she admired the flickering lights along Shakespeare Avenue that blended into the larger thoroughfare of Jerome Avenue, leading ultimately to Yankee Stadium.

"Sometimes," Jacob said, "I think there are just too many people in the world. Every day we fight for our small bit of space. The traffic, the crowds, it's all too much. And then I come home, and there we all are, squeezed together in that small apartment. Five of us . . ."

Daisy hadn't known how to break the news to her brother. Doing so obliquely seemed the easiest way. "Soon to be six," she interjected, staring off at the bright lights.

Jolted, Jacob faced his sister. The last of his cigarette burned his fingers before he dropped it to the rooftop. With a twist of his heel, he snuffed out the greyish orange remnant. "Oh no, Rose isn't pregnant again. Did she tell you?" Jacob's face had gone pale. Deep lines gathered about his eyes and mouth as he winced, seemingly in pain, a palm holding his forehead. "How are we going to manage with another mouth to feed?"

Daisy held his gaze. "It's not Rose."

A silence fell between the two siblings.

Back in the apartment, two toddlers underfoot, Rose refused to look at Daisy.

"This is unbelievable," she bristled at Jacob. "We can barely manage as it is. How could she have let this happen?"

"I didn't realize what I was doing," Daisy answered. "I wasn't thinking."

Rose grabbed Daisy's arm and pulled her forcefully into the bedroom, away from the front door and hallway where sound traveled to the neighbors. Jacob followed, lingering in the doorway.

"These things don't just happen," Rose insisted, placing a hand on Daisy's shoulder, and pushing her to sit down on the small bench at the vanity table. "You must have encouraged it. Why . . . you're nothing more than a common *slut*." She whispered the last word. "Thank God your parents are dead. This would have killed them."

"Rose," Jacob said sharply. "It's no good shaming her. What's the point? She already feels terrible. Harsh words aren't going to help."

"You've protected her for too long, Jacob. You've allowed her to take advantage of us. She thinks she's a little princess. Well, now see what comes from us being too kind to your sister. This is how she repays us."

"I want to die," Daisy admitted, tears gathering in her eyes.

"I don't doubt it," Rose continued. "You're almost a child yourself and unmarried. How is this supposed to work out?"

"I don't know," Daisy said, turning to look at herself in the mirror. And for the first time since she realized she was pregnant, Daisy cried. She cried in response to the anger and disappointment in Rose's eyes. She cried because she'd allowed herself to submit to a man without any thought of the consequences. But mostly, she cried because her hormones were raging, and crying was the only way she could possibly respond.

"Jacob, come in and shut that door," Rose ordered. "We don't need the neighbors listening in." Rose turned to Daisy. "Now stop that," she warned. "I'm not going to listen to you cry on top of everything else."

Daisy calmed herself.

Rose reviewed the possible solutions. The choices were limited. None offered a good outcome. "You're going to do what women have done since the beginning of time. You're going to face up to the situation."

"Rose, I can't. How am I going to take care of a baby?"

"There are ways," Rose answered. "We'll have to figure it out."

"I just can't believe this has happened," Daisy admitted.

Rose agreed. "No matter our differences, I always thought you were a smart girl. I thought you knew better than this."

Daisy's shame was powerful. She had been foolish and careless. She'd made an unalterable mistake. "How am I going to raise a child?" she repeated, terrified of the prospect of being pregnant.

Rose looked into the eyes of the frightened girl and sighed. "We'll take it one day at a time. Life works best when we don't get ahead of ourselves. Tomorrow will come soon enough."

Rose was right.

Things did take care of themselves. Daisy's pregnancy passed quietly. The baby was born. The world didn't collapse, and given time, the trauma slowly faded into a distant memory. What had once been so painful now seemed as if it had happened to someone else. To survive, Daisy disassociated from the experience. She left New York, never again to see Jacob or Rose or the beautiful baby boy that her brother raised and named Jack.

* * *

On Friday nights the neighborhood kids gathered in front of Anna Garrett's flickering neon sign, smoking cigarettes, telling jokes, and laughing much too loudly. As the noise escalated, Anna wasn't shy about reprimanding the teens.

"Go home," she'd shout from her kitchen window. "Don't make me call the police."

But idle threats didn't work.

With her hair in curlers, face covered in Pond's Cold Cream, the short, rotund psychic, dressed in a red terrycloth robe, would rush the lawn, wildly swinging a bat and shouting "Get out of here!"

She created quite a scene for the cars passing on 19th Avenue. The neighborhood kids laughed and scattered while passing motorists honked their horns seemingly in solidarity with the teenagers.

Henry, dressed in jeans and a black *Voice of Reason* tee shirt, was sitting on his bed reading James Redfield's *The Celestine Prophecy*, a book he'd pulled from Anna's bookcase when she stormed into the room without knocking. There was a bowl of raisins and nuts on the bedside table.

"Rotten kids," Anna lamented, furiously pacing back and forth. "Cigarette butts all over. They have no respect for private property."

"That's what kids do," Henry reminded her, folding down the edge of the page so as not to lose his place.

"But why on my property?" Anna complained as she noticed the book Henry was reading. "Oh my God. That's one of my favorite books. Very spiritual."

"Well, don't sound so surprised," Henry answered. "It's not like your shelves are lined with Faulkner, Dreiser, or Hemingway. There wasn't much to choose from that didn't have the words *journey*, *destiny*, or *souls* in the title."

Anna laughed. "I guess that's true."

Henry changed the subject. "Did you ever think maybe you bring all this attention on yourself?"

"Because of my new sign?" She spotted the bowl on the bedside table. She looked at Henry, raised her eyebrows, and nodded in the bowl's direction; he smiled offering his permission; she tipped the bowl, shaking some of the snack into the palm of her hand, and without hesitation, popped the entire treat into her mouth. "The neon is kind of bright," she agreed as she chewed.

"Sure, but have you looked in a mirror lately?" He gave her a good once-over. "You do look kind of nuts."

"I do?" she said, coughing on the salty treat as she turned to check out her reflection in the mirror on the wall. Her right hand caressed the back of her exposed neck, just below her hair curlers, while her left hand smoothed out a crease in her red robe. She continued to chew.

"Now come on," Henry continued. "If I didn't know you, I'd think you were a real loon."

Anna wasn't immune to her reflection in the mirror. For years, she'd tried to avoid looking too closely. After all, it was painful to be overweight. And though she'd hoped by ignoring her appearance, others might too, she still noticed people staring. She just considered them rude.

"I can't help it," Anna turned back to him. "I'm just a big-boned girl," she said, her hands on her hips, upset that Henry was critical of her appearance.

Henry laughed. "No, you're not. And if you were, no one, and I mean no one, is that big-boned." Henry reached into the bowl of peanuts and raisins and scooped up a handful.

"Okay, so I eat too much," she admitted. "Is that what you're trying to tell me?"

"And way too often," Henry pointed out, putting a peanut in his mouth and beginning to chew. "And you never exercise."

"You mean like jogging," Anna said sarcastically.

Henry stated the obvious. "Well, that *is* considered exercise."

"I don't need to run. That's why I own a car," she snapped. "Besides, can you imagine this," and Anna waved her hand from the top of her head down to her thighs, "running down the street?"

Henry squinted as if trying to picture it. "No, I can't quite see that."

"So, how am I supposed to exercise?"

"Have you ever heard of Jenny Craig or Weight Watchers? Maybe if you dropped some weight, you'd be able to move."

Anna had to admit that those names had crossed her mind.

"You know, losing weight at my age is no easy trick," she complained.

"Well, it seems to me that if you don't lose the weight now, you won't be able to later. You need to decide if you want to live the rest of your life carrying all that weight around."

"Yes, that is *my decision*," she retorted, hoping to end the conversation.

"Now don't get angry. I'm saying this for your own good," he said, giving Anna his best doe-eyed look.

Anna's heart melted. "And here I was under the delusion that *I* was helping *you*."

"How about we help each other," Henry suggested.

And just like that, something clicked for Anna, who understood the laws of the universe. Yes . . . she was destined to help Henry. All the signs had been there. But suppose Henry was also destined to help her?

"Okay, so maybe I need to make some changes."

"And you might want to think twice about your get-up. Those turbans and crazy outfits have to go," Henry blurted out.

"I don't know," she considered. "There's something about my look that matches my business. I think my headscarves add a certain kind of appeal and style."

"Only if you're doing readings from the asylum," Henry shot back.

"It's that bad, huh?"

"That bad," Henry confirmed.

"Okay. Okay," she conceded, reaching for another handful of peanuts and raisins.

Henry quickly pulled the bowl from the bed stand and held it close to his chest, out of her reach. "You know, I'm only saying this because I care about you. I don't want you to be the laughingstock of the neighborhood."

Anna was touched by Henry's sentiment. It had been a long time since anyone had spoken to her with such honesty. And though it was hard to hear that she needed to lose weight and change her look, she was willing to do it. *Henry only has my best interest at heart*, she reassured herself. That alone made her smile.

She walked over to Henry as if to give him a hug, arms outstretched. "All right then, tomorrow's a new day," she vowed just before grabbing the snack bowl out of his grasp. "But for tonight, I think it would be nice if you shared. It's a sign of good manners," she said haughtily, giggling at Henry's surprised reaction.

* * *

Bonnie desperately needed a cocktail after a long week working at The Village. She pushed her way into AZ88, a popular bar and restaurant in Old Town Scottsdale. People were already lined up outside, waiting for a table for dinner. It was only six-thirty on a Friday night and the bar was packed with young professionals.

Bonnie had done her best to freshen up. A spritz of Elizabeth Arden's Pretty, a brush through her hair, and some fresh lipstick would have to do. *Take me as I am*, she brazenly thought, unbuttoning the two top buttons of her favorite blue silk blouse, acutely aware that there were no immediate takers.

AZ88 offered high ceilings and well-placed wall sconces that focused light downward, creating an elegant, muted effect. A seat opened up at the bar and Bonnie slipped onto the backless black leather stool. She scanned the area. The mature men were talking intently with younger women. Much younger women.

The bartender took her order, a dry martini with a twist.

The thought of going home to an empty condo depressed her.

She remembered the older men who'd chased her in her youth. Mostly married, overweight, nervous, desperate little boys, unable to appreciate age-appropriate women. *It's sad*, she thought, eyeing a man in his early fifties leaning into a young woman who could have been his granddaughter.

She sipped her drink, a bit too quickly on an empty stomach. Within moments, reality shifted. A calm settled over her. Life became easier, the bar less intimidating. She noticed a young buck at the far end checking her out. Killer dimples and a cleft chin. *Hmmm*, she thought. He raised a glass in her direction. He winked.

He's twenty-five, if a day, she thought, her juices churning. *Life has come full circle. I'm now the older man.* Liquor eased her inhibitions. She might have looked away had she not been tipsy. Instead, she locked eyes with the stud, inviting him to approach.

A quick drink, a fast hook-up did scratch a certain itch.

"Hello. May I join you?" The man's voice came from behind.

Mr. Twenty-five was still staring in her direction. Swiveling, Bonnie spotted a familiar face. He wasn't one of the self-professed Lotharios who roamed the lounge. He had a kind face. A strong jaw line. Distinguished grey hair. She couldn't quite place him, but she knew she'd seen him before.

"Can I get you another martini?" he asked, his breath offering a hint of mint. His eyes sparkled when he smiled.

"All right," she said, knowing two drinks were her max. "Have we met before?" She couldn't help noticing his wedding band.

"I don't think so," he answered. He was trying not to stare at her chest.

"I know we've met," she said unsure of where or how.

A look of recognition crossed his face. "You like to dance."

Bonnie's eyes flashed. "You were that guy at that Republican thing."

Back at Bonnie's place, her bra on the floor, his pants on the back of a chair, her legs straddling his shoulders, she spied for the first time, between his loud cries of ecstasy, that there was an irregular crack running across the ceiling. *I've got to get that fixed,* she noted as his thrusting ended with a whimper.

* * *

Charlie was at a loss for words when Daisy broke the news that Saturday morning at breakfast. "I can't impose any longer." She buttered one-half of an English muffin that Charlie had toasted and delivered to the table. "It's wrong," she said, biting into the crunchy round treat.

"It's only wrong if we *wanted* you to leave," Dave countered, grabbing the other half of the English muffin Daisy left on the serving dish. He glanced at Charlie and pointed at the jam on the counter.

"You've both been so wonderful," Daisy said, her eyes watery, "but you need your privacy."

"Daisy, we've been all through this." Charlie said as he passed Dave the jar. "Dave and I want you to stay. We love having you here. The guestroom is on the other side of the house and this really is your place as much as ours."

"No, my darling, it isn't," Daisy corrected him, her hands flat on the table as if she was about to stand up to end the discussion. "It's a wonderful house, a beautiful house, but now it's *your* house. I love you both for thinking you want me here. You've been so kind. But I must get on with my life."

"I don't understand what that *means*," Charlie said, eyes wide open, gesturing at Dave to *say something*.

"I've been talking with a friend who has room for me. We can keep each other company. Now, I've made up my mind. I'm going to move."

Charlie frowned, realizing he'd run out of plausible arguments. The truth was that he'd come to rely on Daisy's gregarious presence. Since Dave had quit his job, he'd been talking less and less, as if he were a wind-up toy that had lost its tension. And as Dave grew increasingly sullen and distant, Charlie had tried to ignore his behavior, thinking he just needed time. If Dave had been hungry, Charlie would have fed him. If he'd been financially strapped, Charlie would have given him money. But Dave's sudden retirement hardly seemed to Charlie a problem that required addressing. Didn't everyone want to retire one day? And really, aside from his jeremiads, Dave had never been much of a talker. Mostly Charlie jabbered away while Dave listened. But Daisy loved a good conversation. And she had so much to say. There was hardly a topic on which she lacked an opinion.

Charlie fretted over Daisy's departure. "Well, I guess your mind is made up," he finally acknowledged. "We'll go along with whatever you decide. But that doesn't mean we won't miss you terribly."

* * *

Anna checked her reflection in the mirror. She couldn't remember the last time she'd been at a salon. It was a Saturday morning, her wet hair wrapped in a towel, and she was about to get a new look.

It was both exciting and terrifying.

Anna had made a habit of avoiding the mirror. When she did look at herself, she focused solely on her eyes, which were soft and warm. In this way, she managed to block everything else out.

Now, Arturo, the owner of the salon, busied himself behind her.

Anna feared Arturo's enthusiasm.

Tall, dark, and handsome, Arturo had immediately taken Anna under his wing. He loved makeovers, and after seeing her standing in the doorway of Chez La Fab, he knew she was long overdue for a look that would bring her into the 21st century. Clearly, her hair color—mousey grey—was all wrong. Such drabness washed out Anna's very pale skin tone.

Taking a deep breath, Anna hoped for the best as Arturo removed the towel and her long hair cascaded down her shoulders. She stared at her reflection and realized that anything Arturo did had to be an improvement. *Henry is right, I'm a mess,* she sadly thought.

When Anna emerged two hours later from Arturo's magic act, she looked years younger and her hair felt like silk. She couldn't stop running her fingers through the bob. It was pretty. Arturo had been right. Shorter was better. And the red highlights in her restored auburn locks shimmered beautifully in the desert sun.

Is everyone looking at me?

She floated down the interior promenade of Biltmore Fashion Park feeling amazing; a new woman. Passing Macy's window, she caught her reflection in the glass. She could see her new do. She gave her head a fast shake. The bouncy style did look fabulous. Then, her eyes drifted downward to her clothes.

It was time.

Entering Macy's, Anna froze in front of the first full-length mirror she encountered.

Oh no. She eyed her reflection. *This is going to be a lot harder than I thought. Well, here goes nothing.*

* * *

Daisy loved Charlie's French toast but ate only half a slice the Sunday morning that she moved out. *Nerves,* she thought, as she pushed what remained on her plate from one side to the other.

It had already been an unusual morning.

Charlie had behaved like a whirling dervish, traversing the kitchen in a rush of nervous energy. He pulled from the refrigerator a half-dozen eggs, rapidly broke each one into a red Pyrex mixing bowl, flung the shells into the InSinkErator, searched for vanilla in a cabinet by the sink before realizing he'd stored it in the pantry, hurried back to the refrigerator, pulled out a gallon of milk, flicked off the plastic cap with his thumb, gave the eggs a splash, and then whipped the liquid concoction into a frenzy with a wire whisk. Using his hands, he dragged bread through the batter while eyeing a pan of sizzling bacon on the stove, reaching over and poking it every now and then with a fork, while he delivered the saturated bread to a nearby Presto griddle. Once everything was underway, he rushed about pouring orange juice and coffee.

Daisy was exhausted just watching him.

Meanwhile Dave, sitting at the kitchen table with Daisy, had the newspaper open to the obituaries.

"Has anyone important died?" Daisy asked, hoping to draw Dave into conversation.

"No one I know," he muttered, voice almost imperceptible, head down, poring over what seemed to Daisy, every morbid detail.

Daisy's heart went out to him. He seemed lost. Exceptionally quiet. No longer tethered to a career and uncertain about his future. Daisy wondered if he regretted his decision. *Ah*, she thought, *all change is hard*.

"I know I have powdered sugar somewhere," Charlie said as he searched a kitchen cabinet.

"Charlie, please," Daisy coaxed. "Come sit down and eat before it gets cold."

"In a moment," Charlie said as the oven timer went off and he reached in and pulled out a square pan.

"My word," was all Daisy could muster as cinnamon rolls found their way to a cozy on the table. "I'm afraid, I haven't much of an appetite," she admitted. "And here you've gone to all this trouble . . ."

"I understand," Charlie said with a sorrowful smile as he slipped into his chair. "We're going to miss you terribly. I guess none of us has much of an appetite," he said eyeing Dave's clean plate. "It's a sad day."

Daisy nodded. She hadn't anticipated how hard it would be to leave Charlie and Dave.

"You mean you wouldn't give us our dog back?" Dave teased.

"Oh, I'd be willing. But Timmy may not want to leave me." Daisy said, raising her head with an air of noblesse oblige.

* * *

The three settled into Charlie's white Ford Explorer.

"I bet you're going to miss the Biltmore," Charlie said as he backed down the driveway.

"I am," Daisy acknowledged, looking out the backseat window. "The flowers, the trees, all the dogs in the neighborhood. It's just beautiful here. But most of all, I'm going to miss my time with you two."

They drove in silence through the development, passing the guard gate. As Charlie turned right onto 24th Street, he glanced in the rearview mirror and caught Daisy's eye. He wondered what she was truly thinking. After spending so many years in her home, now their home, the final goodbye must be bittersweet. "You okay back there?" he asked, turning onto Lincoln and heading toward Highway 51.

"I want to thank you both for being so welcoming," Daisy said. "I really don't know what I would have done without you. You're both such good men. Your mothers would be proud to know they raised such fine gentlemen."

Charlie and Dave exchanged glances. Neither mother had respected their relationship or been appreciative of their characters. Both had expected certain things from their sons—wives and children mostly—and in that regard Charlie and Dave had proven a disappointment.

A large gate off Northern Avenue welcomed them to the Casa Verdes Retirement Community, a complex of single-story, cream-colored attached patio homes, nestled beneath a mix of mature Arizona ash and ficus trees. Driving toward the back of the neighborhood on a winding road, they passed a large community swimming pool, tennis courts, and picnic tables placed amid green space, before reaching the *Havens*, one of the many subdivisions within the complex.

"I've got the luggage," Charlie said, slamming the trunk closed.

"This way," Daisy called out. "It's over here."

An older man waved from the open doorway of a corner unit. As they headed in his direction, they passed other front doors. One held a Christmas wreath, oddly out of place in the warm Phoenix sunshine. Another, a small, wooden sign, painted gunmetal-blue with white lettering that read *Welcome to Grandma's House.*

Daisy was the first to reach the open door. Dave and Charlie lagged behind.

"That must be the manager of the complex," Charlie said to Dave.

"I don't think so," answered Charlie. "He's kind of old to still be working."

The two seniors warmly embraced. And then, while still in each other's arms, they passionately kissed. Dave and Charlie stopped dead in their tracks.

"He's not the manager," Dave whispered to Charlie.

"If he is, that's a hell of greeting," Charlie answered.

Daisy waved them over.

"Dave and Charlie, this is my friend Lyle."

Charlie stared at the man who had his arm about Daisy's waist.

"Lyle and I met at The Village when I was in rehab. If it wasn't for Lyle . . . well, I'm not sure that I'd be walking today."

Dave was the first to break the silence. Leaning forward, he offered his hand. "It's so nice to meet you, Lyle. I'm Dave."

Lyle offered a warm smile. "Daisy has told me such good things about the two of you. It's so nice to finally meet you."

Charlie was dumbstruck. He stood open-mouthed until Dave poked him. "Charlie, this is Lyle." Dave pointed in the older man's direction.

Charlie cleared his throat. "Why yes, Lyle." Charlie blushed, beet-red.

He and Dave had been expecting to meet a woman and Daisy had done nothing to correct that expectation.

Lyle reached for one of the bags but Charlie waved him off, coming to life after standing nearly frozen in place. "I've got it," he said full of bluster. "Just tell me where to put it down."

Charlie followed Lyle through the front door which opened into a large living area with twelve foot ceilings. Paintings of cowboys and desert scenes, stacked two or three high on the wall, created a distinctive south-western decorative style that Charlie thought rather passé. At the center of the room sat an oversized, tan-leather pit couch, on what appeared to be an enormous Indian rug of red, gold and black. Matching oak tables, with metallic crossbars at the base, were placed about; Charlie noticed a large bronze sculpture of horses rearing on a table right behind the sofa. There was an open kitchen to the right with a skylight that brought natural light into the entire space. Down the hallway, past more paintings of Indians wearing decorative garb, Charlie came to the only bedroom in the tiny apartment. Charlie's face burned. The room held a queen-size bed covered by a simple white knitted blanket.

"You can put it down over there," Lyle pointed.

"Did you make enough room for me?" Daisy asked, suddenly appearing in the doorway. Dave stood behind her peeking in.

"I cleared out half of the closet and most of the dresser. I hope that'll be enough."

Charlie cleared his throat. "Dave, can I speak with you for a moment?"

Charlie excused himself and stepped outside onto the patio off of the bedroom. Dave followed.

Charlie lowered his voice. "Do you think this is okay? We don't know this man at all. Do you feel comfortable leaving her here?"

"I don't know. It's all happening kind of fast," Dave answered. "But she's an adult, and she seems to know the old guy. And he's very nice. Who are we to tell a woman in her seventies what she can and cannot do? After all, I don't think you'd like someone telling you what to do."

"I know, I know." Charlie nodded. "It just makes me nervous. Who's taking care of whom here? She's not a young woman. He looks older than God. I'm just not sure this is a great idea."

Daisy stepped out onto the patio.

Charlie and Dave fell silent.

"Before you two make any decisions about my life," she interrupted, "you should know my mind is made up."

Both men were startled.

"Damn! For an old gal you sure have excellent hearing," Dave said.

"Now, I don't want you to worry. We're going to be fine. In fact, Lyle and I are getting ready to take a walk. So, if you two mother hens will excuse us, we have places to go and people to meet."

Dave took the cue. "Okay." He leaned over and kissed Daisy on the cheek. "Have I told you today that I think you look lovely?"

"No, you haven't. And I'm still going for that walk."

"Say goodbye, Charlie," Dave prompted. "We should be heading out."

"Okay," Charlie said, "but Daisy, if you need anything, and I mean *anything*, promise you'll call."

"Yes, yes. My goodness, you two are worse than the nurses at The Village. Don't worry. I'll call."

With that Charlie and Dave took their leave. But the complex was large, and after two wrong turns, Charlie finally turned the car around and found the signs leading to the front of the development. Ahead, they glimpsed an old married couple. The woman had her arm linked in the man's. They walked slowly, talking, admiring the day and each other. It took a moment before Charlie realized it was Daisy and Lyle.

* * *

At the LA Fitness on 20th Street and Highland, Henry stood in the shower, the warm water cascading down his broad back. He'd been on the treadmill in the late afternoon when he first noticed an attractive guy in his early thirties. Henry had tried not to look at the dark-haired stranger with the five o'clock shadow and bulging biceps, but he couldn't seem to help himself. Repeatedly, he looked over, mesmerized by the deep-set, piercing dark eyes, and the powerful build. He looked like something out of *Men's Fitness*.

Henry was entranced.

The stranger offered Henry a flirtatious wink.

Henry looked away, too uncomfortable in his sexuality to make a direct connection, though his body immediately responded. There was a quickening of his pulse, a shallowness in his breath, and the sweet, tender sensation, growing between his legs.

Henry struggled to refocus.

He shifted his gaze to the overhead television screens. Talking heads on *ESPN*. A commentator on The Weather Channel. Then Henry glanced back over at his object of desire; their eyes again connected; another quick smile offered; and Henry again looked away.

Henry had been with other men. A counselor at camp. A boy in his neighborhood. And then living on the streets. It wasn't something he wanted to do. It was something he felt physically compelled to do.

At home, he'd heard his parents discuss homosexual perversion. They vilified the GLBT community, scoffed at gay marriage, and mocked those on television marching for gay rights. At puberty, physical pleasure had brought the realization of his sexual orientation. It had been a shameful secret he'd kept from his parents until he could no longer . . . the day they kicked him out.

Now, living with Anna, he kept his sexuality separate and apart from his home life. He'd learned his lesson. He couldn't trust adults. And though Anna had seemed supportive at the start, he didn't feel comfortable sharing his *other life* with her. After the trauma with his parents, he didn't believe any respectable adult could ever truly accept him.

He stepped off the treadmill, his body dripping with sweat. He glanced over at the stranger; his resistance down; his body yearning.

The stranger approached.

The conversation was awkward. Henry frequently looked away unable to hold the stranger's gaze. Nonetheless, he agreed to follow the man to his apartment in the Esplanade.

It was over in less than an hour.

Afterward, the stranger offered to buy Henry dinner. Henry declined. All Henry wanted to do was go back to the gym and shower. To get the stranger's scent off his body.

As Henry soaped up for the third time, he wondered, *how could something that felt so good feel so dirty?*

9

....

Daisy's lawsuit triggered a change in Enid's relationship with Jack.

Before the subpoena arrived, Jack had been her shadow; always near but mentally absent; distracted from any activity she was immersed in. He'd wait in the car while she ran into Walgreens or the dry cleaners, listening to talk radio, tuned into Rush Limbaugh, wondering why Enid insisted on Rush instead of NPR, but not changing the station. When she shopped at Saks or Nordstrom, he'd sit in a comfortable chair, off in the corner, alone, holding her purse. She'd catch him eyeing other women, and on occasion, confront him. "What are you doing?" she'd ask as he ogled some woman searching through a rack of dresses. "Just checking out the ladies," he'd innocently reply, a glint in his eye, adding, much to her disgust, "You know . . . I'm not dead yet."

But recently, Jack had started to complain about pain in his lower back. He claimed he had difficulty sitting for long stretches and so he stopped driving Enid, preferring to give his sore back a rest.

Instead, Jack joined LA Fitness.

"The chiropractor recommends vigorous exercise," he explained over dinner with Enid at Hulas. The doors of the restaurant, which had once been a full-service garage, were fully open, creating a modern/hip indoor/ outdoor space in which servers circulated about the candlelit tables. "Swimming should stretch my sore back muscles and eliminate the stiffness. And LA Fitness has a heated indoor pool."

Enid was glad something helped. She'd grown tired over their years together of Jack's many complaints about his minor health conditions. The ache in his trigger finger, the cramp in his leg from sitting too long, the itchy dry skin that had shown up with their move to the desert. As long as he was being proactive, and not complaining, she was all for any pursuit that kept him otherwise engaged.

So Jack began spending more and more time away from the house.

And just like that, any thought of Jack slipped from Enid's mind as she adapted pleasantly to a new routine. She went to Starbucks where she read the newspaper and sipped iced Hazelnut Macchiatos. She hadn't realized that having Jack by her side twenty-four-seven had been such a downer.

When his back heals, he'll be following me around again like a lost puppy, she sighed. *Underfoot and needy as ever.* She hated the thought. *Men are such babies.*

That afternoon Enid stopped at the Safeway on Camelback and 32nd Street to do some grocery shopping. As she pulled into a parking spot, she caught sight of a man wandering the lot, searching for his car. Enid chuckled. It wasn't hard to lose your car in a parking lot. It had certainly happened to her.

She took a moment to enjoy the show.

The man waved his keys in the air trying to locate the sound of the beeping vehicle. Enid had never been in quite that much difficulty. And then, the man started to cross the lot. He walked up and down the aisle one lane over from where she was parked. There was something familiar about his gait, the way he carried himself.

As he came closer, Enid recognized her husband.

It was a shock to see Jack out of context.

His grey hair looked great cut short. *He must have just gone to the barber,* she thought. His posture seemed to also have improved. But then, when was the last time she'd really looked at him? Mostly, she was too busy thinking about what she needed to do next, where she needed to be, what she wanted to say. Watching Jack, she realized he was still an attractive man. Somehow he looked different—better—better than she thought he had a right to look, considering his bad back. *He certainly seems to be moving well. He actually looks wonderful*, she thought. *The swimming must be agreeing with him.*

This alarmed her. She had no desire for Jack to trail after her again; she'd grown to enjoy her independence and appreciated her time alone. In fact, she felt free. They hadn't been intimate due to Jack's pain and stiffness, and she hadn't missed it; the clamminess of his sweaty body, his razor stubble scraping up against her neck, his fetid breath as he slid his weight on top of her. Not having sex with Jack had been one of the benefits of his bad back. She hoped his back wasn't *too* much better. As she watched him locate his car, she hoped against hope that their sex life had actually come to an end.

That was her grand wish.

Lost in thought, Enid failed to notice the red roses Jack carried.

Enid was allergic to roses.

* * *

When lawsuits play out, lawyers win big. Jack was learning the hard way that retaining a lawyer was an expensive proposition.

"Have you seen this?" Jack shoved the latest invoice from Harper Gaines, LLC, under Enid's nose. She was outside on the deck reading the newspaper.

Enid gave Jack a sour expression. "Can't you see I'm reading?" she said, grabbing the invoice from his hand. "This controversy over that Muslim community center in lower Manhattan is really awful. You'd think those people would have greater sensitivity after 9/11."

Jack paid no attention to what she said. He was not about to be distracted. "Your esteemed attorneys are charging us for conference calls at fifteen-minute intervals."

Enid scanned the three-thousand-dollar invoice. "Legal documents, filing and processing fees, copying— it's all here, Jack. This is more than conference calls."

"I don't care what it says. I see only the number three, followed by three zeros."

"And what would you like me to do about it?" she asked, exasperated, turning back to the newspaper.

"Speak to them. Negotiate the rates."

Enid closed the paper. "Don't be childish, Jack. We've already signed an agreement which outlined the fees."

"Well, we can't afford these bills." Jack stood before her as if expecting an immediate solution.

"There's no way around it. We're being sued and we need representation."

Jack raised an angry index finger. "I blame you for this," he said, pointing at her.

"Me?"

"Yes, you had to get involved."

"This is your fault, Jack," she snapped back.

"And how exactly do you figure that?" Jack's tone grew sharp.

"It's your family—your problem. You were the one who wrote that stupid note. You wanted to meet your aunt." Enid waved the invoice. "Consider this the price of that introduction."

"Oh, no. You don't get off that easily." Jack snatched the invoice out of Enid's hand. "This is about you," he said, holding the invoice up in the air as if she might misconstrue the nature of their argument. "All about you. Your greed. Your selfishness."

Enid stood up. "You ungrateful little boy," she sneered. "Will you ever grow up? Blaming me? You should look into your own heart. Maybe I didn't do everything correctly. Maybe I was too aggressive. But at least I tried. What did you do?" Enid made a circle with her thumb and index finger and held it up to Jack's face. "Nothing. Zip. Nada. Zilch. All you can do is complain after the fact. When it's too late to be of any help or do any good."

"You're a real bitch," Jack said, angry at her for playing on his weaknesses. His pronouncement came in the tone of a statement of fact more than an insult, as if he'd just learned that the sky is blue, the ocean is deep, and grass is green.

In an instant Enid's palm landed hard across Jack's cheek. The slap was loud enough to disturb nearby doves resting on the roofline of the townhouse just above the deck. The birds took to startled flight, wings flapping, as if a predator had been spotted.

"Screw you, Jack," Enid shouted, reaching for the sliding glass door and disappearing into the house, newspaper abandoned, and Jack's cheek smarting.

The blood pumped hard through Jack's veins as he replayed the encounter in his head. Unwilling to yield to Enid's assertion that he bore any blame, he decided to take matters into his own hands. He scheduled a meeting with their attorney.

"I want this to go away," Jack informed Fred Harper as he struggled to catch his breath, uncertain of Fred's reaction, hoping to keep his anxiety in check. "Settle the matter."

Fred, a stout man in his early sixties, looked at Jack with a mix of irritation and pity, as if too many cases, and too many difficult clients like Jack, had worn him out.

"No one enjoys this part of the process," Fred Harper said, running a thick hand over his bald head, "but I know Lederman. If we approach him now, he's going to smell blood in the water. It's too soon. Give it time. Lederman has a contingency case. The old lady has no money. Let Lederman spend his resources. Once he sees the expenses ratcheting up, he'll be more inclined to do the right thing and settle. If not, we'll threaten court action. He'll think twice before he lays out any more cash."

Jack listened impatiently. He refused to be cowed by the expensive office décor, the dark wood paneling, the impressive bookcase lined with leatherbound editions. Jack eyed Fred. "Okay, but how long will that take?"

"Well, Mr. Lee, that all depends."

Frustrated, Jack left the meeting unsatisfied.

If only I could talk to Daisy directly, he thought. *I bet I'd make more progress.*

* * *

In a building nearby, Daisy was in a meeting with Harvey Lederman.

"So glad you were able to come in today," Harvey began. "Can we get you any water, or coffee perhaps?"

Daisy held up the mini-bottle resting in her lap.

"Oh, I see we've got you covered," Lederman said. He searched his desk for something he'd apparently misplaced.

For a hotshot lawyer, and a relatively young one at that, Lederman seemed scattered and distracted. The notecard he was searching for was leaning against his coffee mug. After scanning it quickly, he looked at

Daisy with newly sympathetic eyes. She shifted anxiously in her chair. She hadn't been born yesterday. Clearly, she was just one of many anonymous clients to him. Lederman knew next to nothing about her or the lawsuit; one of his assistants had prepared the card as a snapshot review of the case's status.

At least she wasn't paying him out-of-pocket.

"Now, I know you're worried about the lawsuit," Lederman said, his voice unctuous and soft. "But I assure you we have everything perfectly under control. Papers have been filed. The wheels are turning. We're going to make your nephew pay for this horrible breach of faith."

"I'm not a young woman," Daisy said, "as you can see. How long do you think it might take for this whole matter to resolve?"

"Months. Maybe a year on the outside," Harvey acknowledged. "And we will keep you updated at every turn."

"I appreciate that," Daisy said. "It's just all the energy that this takes."

"I assure you, Ms. Lee, you're in good hands. This will require no more than your being present for a deposition, and then, as we approach the trial date, we can talk more about the next steps."

Daisy nodded. "I understand."

Harvey rose to his feet indicating that their brief meeting was over.

"You're doing an important thing," he said, escorting Daisy to the door. "Not every senior has the courage to sue a family member that has taken advantage. There are so many stories out there of parents being abused, estates squandered, and no one seems to do anything about it."

Well, Daisy thought. Maybe she wasn't invisible after all.

* * *

After Daisy left, Harvey turned to his receptionist. "Did you ever see such a sad look on a client's face? You'd think we were forcing her to litigate. When the time comes, she'll buckle at the first offer. I'll have to work hard to keep her motivated until we can manage our best deal."

"Yes, Mr. Lederman," the young woman answered as he walked past her into his office.

For Harvey Lederman, the timing of a settlement was critical. Rash behavior went against the grain. And though he settled the majority of his cases, he preferred to wait until after the deposition phase. That was his shining moment. Harvey only needed one afternoon to grill the defendants; to see their confused expressions; to hear their stuttering denials. He'd manipulate their words, throw their lies back in their faces, lies that would fill the air with the stench of larceny. He'd raise his voice, shouting at them like they were children. He'd glare with such contempt it would induce shame in Mother Teresa.

To Harvey, depositions were an aphrodisiac. Back at his desk, he rubbed his palms together and imagined the sweet pleasure of tearing into the Lees. He was certain Jack and Enid Lee would beg to settle. He leaned back in his chair and smiled. He loved being a lawyer. There was nothing like a ripe, juicy defendant to cut to pieces.

* * *

It was Anna's fourth appointment of the day and she was already struggling with her powers of concentration. The human condition was exhausting. Dead relatives, broken relationships, failed marriages, doomed careers—they all sapped her energy.

The stranger arrived at noon, a mature gentleman with the kind of grey hair that makes so many tanned men look exceptionally handsome.

It's not fair, Anna thought, eyeing the Chad Everett look-alike. *Men get so darn attractive as they age.*

He took a seat.

She felt an immediate change in her body chemistry; a tingling throughout her extremities. She sensed the presence of a female energy, a spirit eager to fulfill an obligation. A wrong had been done and this was the moment to make it right.

"Tell me your question," Anna asked the stranger. "Why are you here?"

The man glanced about the room as if the answer might be written on the walls. "I don't really know. I was just driving by, saw your sign, and felt a strange compulsion to come in. I have no idea what I'm doing here. Honestly, I don't even believe in any of this."

Anna ignored the comment. Negativity upset the vibration. Her talents were real. Innate. Undeniable. Today, with the spirit so near, it was her job to help the client understand why he'd chosen to access her gifts.

"You're here because of a woman," Anna began. "She's the one who has called you here today. Her desire to deliver a message to you is very strong. I smell lilacs. The scent is powerful. She must communicate with you."

The man seemed captivated by Anna's every word.

"She has a secret. She wants to share it now. Something you do not know but should. It has to do with a baby." Anna cleared her throat. "I see a baby being passed between two women. Does this have any meaning for you?"

"No," the man said uncertainly. "I don't have any children."

"One woman is begging for her baby back."

The man squinted as if looking into a bright light, clearly searching his memory for anything Anna's words might refer to. Then he shook his head. "I have no idea what you're talking about."

"The spirit of the woman who raised that baby is here now, in this room. She wants you to know that this was her mistake. The baby was not rightfully hers. She shouldn't have taken it."

"Okay . . ." the man said somewhat sarcastically, still unable to connect to the information in the reading.

"She's gone," Anna announced, as the energy receded. "We're alone now." She sat back, drained.

"That's nice—I guess," the man answered.

Anna fixed him with her eyes. "She came especially for you. It's important."

The man looked around as if expecting hidden cameras to pop out at any moment and surprise him. "This is a joke," he said. "Right?"

Anna bristled. "I'm a professional. I don't make jokes."

The man chuckled uncertainly. "A baby? What kind of cock-and-bull story is that? Is that the reading du jour? If I come back tomorrow, will there be a man whose name begins with T who'll have a message for me?"

Anna began to get angry; she took pride in her work and resented any implication that she was a con artist. "That message was for you and you alone. I'm sorry there wasn't more, but that was what the spirits wanted you to know today."

The man now laughed belligerently. "But it doesn't make any sense."

Anna wasn't surprised. Clients didn't always grasp the meaning, much less the importance, of a message as it was conveyed. This was certainly true when messages challenged expectations. Everyone wanted good news. Confirmation that they were loved, talented, intelligent, or had been the victim of a great wrong. Clients were especially grateful to hear stories that explained the reasons for their individual shortcomings. Personal responsibility be damned.

Anna gathered her wits. "Well, that's what I saw, and that's the message you're supposed to receive." And then Anna had a final flash of insight. Though she was annoyed at the man's rudeness, she needed to share this final part of the message. "One more thing," she said, certain that this would clarify the message for him. "That baby is you," she said with conviction. "The woman who raised you was not your biological mother."

The man exploded. "Don't be ridiculous. I should know who my mother was."

"Yes." Anna felt relieved. "That's it. You're the baby," she repeated, the vision finally making sense.

Clearly upset, the man got to his feet. "Ridiculous," he sputtered as he stormed out without paying. His final words: "The woman makes it up as she goes along."

That afternoon, Anna was reading reviews of her business on Yelp. Amid all the praise, she found a complaint, just posted, written by the man who had been in earlier. The word *fraud* appeared several times in his posting. It was signed *Jack Lee*.

Anna responded.

This Jack Lee has a lot of nerve. He never paid my fee and now he dares to complain about my professional services. From now on, I'm collecting my fee upfront. Thanks for the business lesson, Jack.

* * *

After Daisy moved in with Lyle, Charlie slipped back into his familiar routine. Much to Dave's chagrin, Charlie walked about the house in his briefs, showering late in the morning, sometimes not until mid-afternoon, often forgetting to shave. Dave too reverted to his old habit of farting and belching while watching television and to wearing old knock-around tee shirts that he'd rescued from the *donate pile* at the rear of their bedroom closet.

It was as if Daisy had never been in the house.

Timmy took ownership of the guestroom where Daisy had slept, cuddling among the decorative pillows on the bed, comforted by the remains of Daisy's scent. Daisy had been good to the little poodle, making certain he had plenty of between-meal snacks and belly rubs. Timmy, ever hopeful for Daisy's return, curled up into a neat crescent, head barely distinguishable from his bottom, gently snoring atop the softest pillow.

Though the rhythm of their life had been re-established, Dave sensed that Charlie missed Daisy's companionship. During dinner, he caught Charlie glancing at Daisy's chair, moping over his lost friend. Dave, however, was glad for the privacy. Though he loved Daisy, he appreciated things getting back to normal, and assumed, in reality, Charlie felt the same way.

He was in Charlie's office one afternoon, setting up Charlie's new Dell laptop, planted at Charlie's desk, when Charlie burst in, clearly agitated. "I just got off the phone with Daisy and I'm worried."

Dave had just slipped the installation disc into the CD tray. "This can't be that hard," he muttered, waiting for the first set of instructions to appear on the screen.

"I think we've made a mistake."

Dave looked up from the screen. "What mistake? I just started."

"About Daisy."

Dave refocused, irritated at the interruption. "Can't we talk about this later?"

Charlie's new screen beeped. Dave typed in the registration information.

"I just don't like her living over there with a stranger."

"He's obviously not a stranger," Dave said as he waited for the next laptop prompt.

"And he has all these health problems."

"Who doesn't?" Dave answered, waiting for the computer to connect to the house's wireless network.

"But do we really know anything about him?"

Dave sighed, entering the wireless password. "I don't think it's any of our business. Lyle seems nice enough. She chose to live with him. He has to be a good guy. At their age, they certainly know about the birds and bees."

"Please," Charlie said covering his ears, "let's not talk about old people and sex."

"You have to admit Lyle is charming. And she's a woman."

"A woman of a certain age," Charlie emphasized.

"What does her age have to do with it?" Dave wondered, searching for the cable to plug in the printer.

"If something happens to him, she won't be able to manage alone. We'll need to step in and help."

Dave couldn't believe his ears. He looked up from the screen. "Whoa. Who said we're taking on responsibility for Daisy? Where'd you get that?"

"Of course we are," Charlie countered. "I love that woman. She has no family. We're it."

"What about Jack and Enid? Have you forgotten about her nephew and his scheming wife?"

"Those two are incapable of taking care of anyone," Charlie insisted. "I refuse to allow them to have any further interaction with her."

"Wait a second." Dave stopped what he was doing and gave Charlie his complete attention. "I know you love her, and I love her too, but she's a grown woman and you're not her father. You're not her brother and you're not her son. You can't dictate who's in her life. That's her decision. And as for Lyle, maybe you just need to get to know him better."

"I really don't want to." Charlie was emphatic. "The guys a relic."

"Hey, none of us knows when our last day might be. It could happen like that." Dave snapped his fingers to emphasize his point. "Here today, gone tomorrow. The same is true for us, Charlie. We're not young. And even if we were, there are such things as car accidents, drive-by shootings, all forms of random mayhem that cross your path. Shit happens."

Charlie leaned against the desk, resting a hand on Dave's shoulder. "I know, but I worry about her."

"Well, worry less. She's been in this world seventy plus years and appears to be doing just fine. She found us. Now she has Lyle. It's great that we stay connected, but they're adults. You can't stop them from living together. And frankly, I don't think you should."

"I'm not looking to interfere. I just want to be sure she's okay."

"Honey." Dave's tone softened as he looked up into Charlie's eyes. "There's no way to know if *anyone* will be okay. All we can do is love her. There are no guarantees in life."

Charlie listened and nodded his head, but Dave knew he really didn't agree. To Charlie, love was more than being concerned about someone. Love was creating a safety shield to block out any potential for hurt, disappointment, and suffering. And as if to prove Dave's very thought, Charlie said, "I'll do whatever it takes to protect her." His eyes misted over.

"Hold on, cowboy," Dave warned. "Don't get all weak in the knees. Just make sure your devotion isn't the thing she needs protection from. She has a life. And like all lives, it has its ups and downs."

"I know," Charlie said. "I know."

"Do you?" Dave wondered.

"Yes, I do." Charlie responded with an edge. "I get it."

"Then just let them be. Give them a chance to settle in. Let them have their space."

"Of course," Charlie said. "I'll give them space."

But Dave could tell that even now the big buttinski was wondering when he'd next be over at Lyle's to check on Daisy. Dave patted Charlie on the thigh. "You're a sweet guy. Have I told you that lately?"

Charlie smiled, seemingly reassured.

Certain he'd said all he could about Daisy and Lyle, Dave changed his tune and pointed at the door. "Now get the hell out of here before I screw this computer up. Go ahead . . . out."

"Well, you're the expert," Charlie said, making his way to the door.

* * *

When Bonnie arrived at Daisy and Lyle's for lunch, her smile practically lit up the room.

Daisy watched as Bonnie gave Lyle a hug.

At first, she assumed Bonnie was just happy to see her and Lyle living together. But as she welcomed Bonnie into the apartment, her female intuition told her it was something more.

"Doesn't she seem different to you?" Daisy asked Lyle when Bonnie excused herself to use the restroom. Daisy fussed with the candy dish on the coffee table, unable to decide if it looked better centered or slightly off to the left.

"How so?" Lyle asked, shifting his position on the living room sofa. "I think we either need better cushions," his face twisted in an expression of discomfort, "or I need more padding on my ass."

"Oh . . ." was all Daisy could manage. "I wish you wouldn't talk like that," the giggle in her voice making it clear she was more amused than put off by Lyle's curmudgeonly ways. "No . . . there's something different. I can't quite put my finger on it."

She'd gone to a lot of trouble to make a lovely lunch of quiche and a salad. Good food and company always put a smile on Lyle's face, but Daisy doubted Bonnie's exuberance was all about lunch. It just had to be more.

"When you reach my age, there's little time for cat and mouse," Daisy said, pouring her guest a glass of ice tea as the three gathered about the kitchen table. "So, please forgive me for being so direct. Something's happened. I can tell. What's changed to make that pretty face light up like a Christmas tree?"

"Why there's nothing. I'm just happy to see you both." Bonnie said as she slipped off the brass napkin ring from the white cloth napkin. "How cute is this," she said, admiring the miniature cowboy boot that adorned the front of the decorative ring. "I love it."

Daisy shook her head. "No, it's more than that. I can tell. I know that inner glow."

"Now Daisy," Lyle interrupted, a slice of Edam balanced precariously on a Wheat Thin cracker held gingerly between his fingers. "Bonnie came over to eat lunch, not to be interrogated. We at least owe her a slice of cake before you start your cross-examination."

Daisy laughed and turned to Bonnie. "Isn't he the dearest man? He doesn't understand that we women know things men never can. They see the rainbow while we see all the colors of the spectrum."

Lyle objected, but Daisy waved him off.

"Love comes once or twice in a lifetime, if you're lucky. And if we're very lucky and good little children, more often." Daisy's eyes flashed in reverie. "I've been lucky." She winked at Bonnie. "How's your luck running?"

Bonnie blushed.

The jig was up.

Daisy waited. Lyle adjusted his focus from his plate to Bonnie's beaming face.

Bonnie finally relented. "Yes, okay, I think I'm in love."

"Think," Daisy exclaimed with excitement, "there is no *think* when you say *I'm in love.* You either are or you aren't. You don't *think* you like the taste of chocolate. You either do or you don't."

Bonnie laughed at Daisy's analogy. "Well, I'm not quite sure if this relationship has blossomed into love or whether I'm just grateful for the physical intimacy," she said. "But I'm happy. I'm truly happy."

"Well, cheers then." Daisy lifted her glass of ice tea. "Here's to a lovely lady beginning a lovely new adventure."

Lyle and Bonnie raised their ice teas and clinked.

"Perhaps this calls for a celebration with something a bit stronger," Lyle winked.

"It's only noon." Daisy pretended to be shocked. "What will our guest think of us?"

"She'll think we know how to live," Lyle answered, wandering off to find a bottle of sherry.

With Lyle out of earshot, Bonnie leaned in closer to Daisy and asked if she, too, was happy.

"He's a lovely man. I'm grateful to have found him. You know, my parents died young, and yet I can't help but wonder if they'd be shocked by their seventy-seven-year-old daughter living with a man out-of-wedlock. Isn't that silly? After all these years, I'd still like their approval."

"It's not silly. It's sweet."

"I just hope you find the happiness I've found with Lyle. And for all that jazz about sex being the most important thing, it's just as important to choose for kindness. You know, dear, in the end, kindness is really all that matters."

"Choose for kindness." Bonnie repeated Daisy's words as if memorizing the advice.

"Kindness," Daisy reiterated. "All the other things we assume are important when we're young get in the way of making good decisions. We want them to be handsome and strong. All that fades. I know now that if I had chosen for kindness, my life would have gone far more smoothly. It might have been a gentler, more satisfying ride."

"Do you regret many of the men who've been in your life?"

"I hate the word *regret*. It's a complete waste of time. What's the point of wishing things had turned out differently? Wisdom doesn't come from regret. Wisdom comes from making better choices."

"I've always struggled to understand why I'm alone," Bonnie admitted. "Therapy hasn't provided any answers and I've spent hours thinking about how I may have distanced myself from others. But no amount of reflection makes it any clearer."

"If you choose to love someone," Daisy said, "the action follows the thought. Did you ever notice that the more you focus on the negative the worse things get? It's the same with people. If you allow your mind to create your future, it will. Think good thoughts and good things happen."

"I don't know," Bonnie said. "That takes a real leap of faith."

"If you decide to love this man, you will love him. If you decide he's just someone you're passing time with, don't expect it to last. It's your choice how you approach the relationship. And how you approach the relationship will dictate where it goes."

* * *

After Henry's hook-up, he stopped going to the neighborhood gym. He was uncomfortable with the way the other men checked him out, afraid he was seen as an easy touch. Henry switched to a gym across town. He kept to himself. No connections, no conversation. If a guy made eye contact, Henry looked away. He swore he'd have no more trouble at LA Fitness.

But the urge to connect persisted.

He stumbled upon his next cruising spot by accident. Sitting with Anna at a picnic table in the park eating lunch, he noticed the comings and goings at a nearby restroom where a steady flow of men seemed to pass in and out, though the park itself was relatively quiet. At first Henry paid little attention, but then, a tall blond with broad shoulders, wearing a blue tank top and tight black workout shorts, caught his eye. Henry wet his lips as his mouth went dry.

As Anna nibbled on her carrot stick and discussed the virtues of Weight Watchers, he recognized a nervousness as the blonde scanned the area, walking in quickly and then out again, before finally disappearing back into the bathroom. Odd behavior for anyone needing to relieve themselves. Instinctively, Henry sensed something more was going on. So he excused himself in the middle of Anna's lecture on the high number of calories in bananas and grapes, two of her favorite fruits that ranked high on the glycemic index, and went to check out the restroom activity.

He quickly put two and two together.

"Are you okay?" Anna asked when he returned to the picnic table.

He nodded, pretending that everything was just fine, even though his mind repeatedly played through the scene of men of different ages and sizes, some dressed for the office, others in casual attire, standing about, leaning against the walls, smoking, checking each other out, one even nodding to Henry, seemingly inviting him to come closer. Unnerved by the discovery, and more than slightly titillated, Henry had backed off and exited. But he was intrigued. Intrigued enough to return the next day after school.

The fantasy of men available for such an easy connection had fueled his imagination. The lure was far too compelling to resist.

At first, he was sickened by the stench, and midway through an intimate moment with an Asian man who'd taken charge, pulling Henry into an empty stall, he pulled up his jeans, and despite protests from the kneeling stranger, made a hasty exit. By his second visit, he managed to suffer through the smell, pleasured by a Hispanic in a brown UPS outfit.

Men came and went. Henry stayed as long as necessary to get off. Unlike the gay men at the gym, the men who frequented the restroom were a closeted, clandestine bunch. Sex remained detached, impersonal, and if done quickly, discreet.

The last time Henry had visited the park restroom, the place was eerily quiet. No men loitering about, standing by the urinals or the sinks. Disappointed, Henry slipped into the center stall to wait. His pulse quickened as he became aware that he was not alone. There was a tap coming from the adjacent stall. Someone wanted to know if he was interested in making a connection.

Henry was interested.

Again, a tap.

Henry's brain worked double-time. The smell of urine was overpowering, but the enticing sexual graffiti spurred him on . . . large penises scratched into the metal stall, crude messages in ink . . . *for a blowjob call Jenna . . . Tim sucks great cock* . . . erotica created to inspire the lust in men.

Henry's heart pounded.

There was another tap.

The longer Henry waited, the more uncertain he became. He weighed his options. He could tap on the stall and the stranger would join him. Or he could leave.

And then he started to think. *Who was in the next stall? What did he look like? Would he be clean? Would he let Henry do the things he liked?*

Henry's excitement ebbed. An analytical mind was the number one turn-off. He left.

Later that day, watching *The Six O'Clock News* with Anna, the story broke. An undercover sting operation had nabbed fifteen men having sex in a public restroom. Henry watched as the station rolled film of the men being placed in patrol cars. Some shielded their faces while others hung their heads, looking down at the pavement. Henry recognized Mr. Blond Shoulders.

"Are you alright?" Anna asked, seeing Henry's shocked expression.

"Fine," Henry answered. "It's just so disgusting. Who would have sex in a public restroom?" he added sheepishly.

"Who indeed?" Anna replied shaking her head in disapproval.

10

....

By the time Anna's first letter reached Ernie, he and Maria had moved twice to escape the roaches that infested the rented rooms of Puerto Vallarta.

Ernie hated the filthy devils.

Two inches long with brown cellophane wings, the awful creatures were practically indestructible. Ernie's stomach flipped whenever he heard the sound of their crunching carcasses under his shoe. Antennae flickered, wings flapped; crushed, yet still alive, they skittered away. Given time, Ernie learned to be quick and efficient, to slide his foot across the floor at the same time that he applied a firm, downward pressure.

The bug mash made him gag.

With each subsequent move, Ernie worried about the forwarding of the mail. He was most eager to hear from Senator John McCain's office to whom he'd written twice for help. He believed in McCain. Surely the senior senator would see the injustice of Ernie's situation. After all, Ernie had been raised in the Phoenix school system. He'd been a Boy Scout, had a paper route, played baseball, and aced his classes. He'd graduated from ASU. That had to count for something. Surely McCain would support Ernie's plight. He would understand that America had been his home for nearly forty years. He'd speak out in Ernie's defense against the unfairness of his deportation. Ernie simply refused to accept any other reality.

And so Ernie waited to hear from the Senator's office. And that's when Anna's letter finally reached him.

Ernie was overwhelmed with emotion as he held the envelope in his hands. The postmark indicated it had been sent months earlier. Tears welled in his eyes. He had not been forgotten.

Anna wrote warmly about the events at home; the attorney she'd hired to help him; the petition with five hundred signatures that had been turned over to McCain's office; and about Henry moving into her home.

But Ernie wasn't soothed by Anna's letter.

The wound was still raw.

His anger stirred once again. *If it hadn't been for that kid, I'd still be in the United States.*

The irony tugged at his heart. It was all so unfair.

* * *

As the afternoon heat intensified, the tourists of Puerto Vallarta abandoned the crowded streets of the city in favor of its resorts and beaches. Ernie walked past the empty shops displaying the colorful oversized sombreros . . . the *I Love Tequila* tee shirts . . . the ancient Mexican warriors kilned of red pottery . . . all sporting hidden labels . . . *Made in China.*

He wore a white cotton dress shirt, sleeves rolled up, and carried a navy polyester sport coat, clothing purchased the day before at Walmart. Ernie was on his way to the Villa Allegra Resort. He'd secured an interview and, despite the heat, was determined to appear cool and mentally sharp. But his decision to walk, in order to save money, was working against him. Jacket folded neatly over his arm, he was sweating profusely.

The humidity was stifling.

Once at the resort, Ernie slipped into the men's room in the lobby. He grabbed a handful of paper towels from the dispenser, entered a stall, and latched the door. He removed his shirt. Perspiration had soaked through the stiff cotton fabric. He used the paper towels to wipe away the dampness from his chest and underarms. He sat on the toilet seat and waited until his body adjusted to the cool air-conditioning. He thought about the impending meeting. He anticipated the interview questions and practiced his answers. After five minutes, he put the damp shirt back on and buttoned it up, and then stepped out of the stall to comb his hair and secure a clip-on tie he'd carefully rolled up and stored in the inside pocket of the coat. Moisture gathered on his top lip as he slipped on the jacket.

He checked himself in the mirror.

He looked fine.

Though his interview was scheduled for two-thirty, Ernie waited till three o'clock before finally being invited to meet the director of human resources. A statuesque young woman in her late twenties greeted him. Her dark tailored suit was in notable contrast to his inexpensive Walmart apparel. Self-conscious, Ernie rubbed his hand on his pants before shaking her hand, hoping he wasn't too clammy to the touch.

After exchanging a few pleasantries about the weather, Ernie relaxed.

The interview began.

"Your English is excellent. I don't hear an accent at all," the young woman said, kindly gazing at Ernie.

Ernie shifted uncomfortably in his chair. "Thank you," he said, feeling completely disingenuous. *Of course I don't have an accent*, he thought, irritated by the very nature of the remark. *I was raised in America.*

"Tell me about your background in facilities management."

Ernie explained that for fifteen years he'd run his own handyman business and had worked in construction since he was in his twenties. Ten years of solid labor doing everything from fixing roofs to rebuilding kitchens.

But the young woman didn't appear to be listening. She'd become distracted by the paperwork on her desk. As he spoke, she paged through some documents. Ernie struggled to remain focused. Then she appeared to be doodling on his application form, scribbling something or other. Ernie was convinced the interview wasn't going well. His heart sank. He worried that she thought his experience was not up to the scope of the job.

He felt like an imposter.

As the interview started to wrap up, Ernie panicked. He decided to tell the woman about his immigration plight, his dependent mother, his need to work, and above all else, his aspirations to be successful. She looked up as he went through his personal story. He'd captured her attention. "I hope I've conveyed my sincere interest in the job," he added at the very end.

It was a pointer he'd practiced in the restroom.

The young woman stood.

Ernie stood.

She extended her hand and thanked him for coming.

He thanked her for her time.

And then she asked, much to his surprise and delight, if he might be available to start the following week.

* * *

Jack popped his second Pepcid. His heartburn had intensified. Lawsuits, marital problems, and a new affair had conspired to ruin his digestion.

"You okay, buddy?" The bartender read the look on Jack's face.

"Not really," Jack answered, glancing through the bar menu at Durant's. "I'll take a Scotch on the rocks. That should help."

Quietly, Jack warred with those who'd done him wrong. His bitterness knew no timeline. His anger with Daisy mingled with his anger at his mother. His irritation with Enid held echoes of the frustrations he'd faced in his first marriage to Betsy. The present and future merged as he downed his Scotch and felt sorry for himself.

Everyone was against him.

"Any lunch today?" the bartender asked.

"I'll have the Kobe sliders."

"Would you like another drink?"

"Sure, I'll have another," Jack answered, passing the glass to the bartender, still deep in thought about Daisy and the lawsuit.

How did she ever get a lawyer to take her case?

Earlier in the day, Jack had Googled Daisy's attorney. He was deemed a maverick in the press. Young, energetic, taking on cases that seemed to be long shots, but in actuality offered deep pockets for settlement. Jack winced at the headlines: *Homeless Man Hit by Train Claims City to Blame. Accused Arsonist Sues Shelter for Lock-out. Parents Point Finger at Hospital for Child's Bruises. Food Bank Sued for Distributing Tainted Food.*

Jack sipped his second Scotch as he wondered what Enid had actually told Daisy about the sale of her house and why Daisy couldn't seem to remember anything. Was it all the medication she'd been given in the hospital or was this the beginning of dementia? Would they ever be able to prove the conversation had taken place? Or would the entire matter ride solely on Daisy's testimony?

Jack felt a gentle buzz. The liquor was working. There was a growing confidence that no matter how bleak it all seemed, he'd somehow make it through.

Lederman's a fool to take her case.

Jack twisted his head sharply to the right; his neck cracked, a welcome release of tension.

Enid was only trying to do the right thing. Okay, so maybe she made a mess of it. Hey, who amongst us is perfect? Enid will just have to explain it to the court.

Jack smiled at the image of Enid on the witness stand.

With her clever wit and sharp tongue, I'd like to see Lederman try to take her down. He was certain Lederman had met his match in Enid. *Go head-to-head with my wife,* he threatened an imaginary Lederman. *She'll kick your ass. She'll make you eat worms.*

And then reality set in.

He thought about the cost of legal representation. The aggravation which was now affecting his marriage. The potential for his humiliation since he didn't handle their financial affairs. How would he be able to answer any of Lederman's questions about Daisy's property without appearing the fool?

I have to put an end to this, he finally decided, shoulders high and tight. *And now.*

The sliders arrived but Jack wasn't hungry. He skipped the protein, paid the check, and headed for the door.

Thirty minutes later, across from Harvey Lederman, Jack was intent on mediating directly. He had no appointment, but Lederman was only too glad to listen to his pitch.

To Lederman, Jack's disoriented whining was the music of Beethoven.

No, Lederman wouldn't settle the case without talking to his client. Yes, he'd accept a settlement offer but couldn't guarantee there wouldn't be a counter. No, he'd have to work directly with Jack's attorney, since that had been the standing arrangement.

By four o'clock that afternoon, defeated, Jack was back home and again into the Scotch.

How could financial ruin find him twice? First the 2008 economic crash had devastated his nest egg, and now, Lederman was prepared to take the rest. Jack could still see the attorney's face, animated, all smiles, his voice dripping with sarcasm and venom. He had practically swooned with excitement as he sized up his prey.

Visiting Lederman had been a mistake. It had been a long time since Jack had had so much to drink. A long time since he'd felt so foolish, the little boy who'd done something terribly wrong.

When Enid returned from her day of shopping, Jack was asleep on the living room sofa, feet up, shoes on, drool staining her favorite silk pillow.

"So you're back," Enid said, nudging him awake. "Looks like you've made yourself comfortable."

She picked up the empty bar glass from the coffee table.

"I do what I can," he groggily answered, slowly sitting up. Somewhat unsteady.

Enid sat next to him. "Look Jack, I've been thinking. There's no point in us turning on one another. We should be working together or that lawyer is going to clean us out."

Jack knew Enid was right.

"So Jack, let's bury the hatchet. We need one another to get through this. What do you say?"

Jack looked at her through the foggy eyes of three Scotches. *Why not? Why not make peace?*

That night, Jack had sex with Enid for the first time in weeks. As soon as they were done, Enid slipped off to the bathroom. Jack lay in bed staring at the ceiling.

The lovemaking had been unsatisfying; Enid had seemed tense and unhappy.

Jack thought of Bonnie. The subtle scent of her perfume as she pressed up against him. Her lips full and open, eager for his, as she ran her hand behind his neck, pulling him closer, demanding that he sublimate to her will. Had he not met Bonnie, he might have been able to make do, but now, he knew for sure he couldn't move ahead with Enid. On that point, he was very clear.

* * *

Daisy leafed through the pages of an old *Time* magazine. She'd already glanced through the issue twice in the last twenty minutes, too upset to concentrate.

What could I have possibly expected? It's not like we're kids.

She sighed. It was bound to happen. When you live with a man in his nineties, you're destined to visit the emergency room.

She looked about the crowded waiting area. Dingy walls, brash overhead fluorescent lighting. The windows looked as if they hadn't been cleaned in years. The linoleum floor, scratched and coming up in the corners, sorely needed to be replaced. The faded oak tables and sea-foam green chairs were relics from the 1970s.

She gave the décor a D . . . D for depressing.

A large Hispanic family dominated one corner of the room: a cocoa-skinned child with jet-black hair seated at a tiny table obediently attended to his coloring book; the raven-haired mother nearby in tee shirt and jeans, a worried expression; others anxiously gathering about; some sitting by the women; some outside by the glass sliding doors, talking and smoking, coming in and out as if on a vigil.

In the opposite corner, a middle-aged black man in worker's overalls sitting in a wheelchair, a nasty gash on his head, the front of his shirt blood-stained; a dark-skinned youth at his side, possibly his son, jeans barely reaching his waist, red boxers exposed, speaking softly to the man next to him.

Filling in the remaining space: a pregnant woman with a toddler pulling on her arm; the little girl clearly wanting to go home; an older man with a foam boot; a woman, possibly his wife, beside him.

People were arriving, approaching the sign-in desk, others occupying seats in the waiting room, family members and friends filling up the space, talking, milling about, leaning in and leaning over.

So many people . . . so many problems.

Daisy at once empathized with the young woman who sat at the desk.

It must be overwhelming to spend every day here. People all stressed out . . . families in crisis.

The desk clerk happened to look in Daisy's direction.

Daisy smiled, appreciative of the challenge the young woman faced: the unending line of the sick and injured. The stress of the human drama.

The expansion of time which seemed to linger endlessly, defying reason and sensibility.

And then, the clerk coldly glanced away, seeming to deliberately avoid eye contact with Daisy, turning her attention to the paperwork on her desk.

Daisy bristled, her attitude immediately turning.

Snotty little bitch. She could at least be pleasant.

But had Daisy wanted courtesy and pleasantness, she was in the wrong place. The hospital emergency room followed the triage rules of life and death. The sickest, most at risk, immediately passed through the metal doors that separated the healthcare workers from the public. It wasn't about politeness. It was about saving lives.

It had unnerved Daisy as Lyle had been whisked to the back without even registering. She'd watched others arrive, who appeared to be in far greater discomfort, but who had been allowed to remain in the waiting room with their relatives.

Why didn't I just lie and tell the clerk I was his wife?

She was too honest for her own good. She couldn't imagine telling a lie about something so important. But now, alone in the same chair for nearly three hours, her body ached. She could feel the pain moving up from her legs, to her hips, to her lower back.

"Ma'am, as soon as we hear something, we'll let you know," the clerk had snapped when Daisy had repeatedly asked about Lyle.

There was nothing to do but wait and hope that someone would eventually let her know that Lyle was okay, resting comfortably, so she could go home.

But no one did.

It was dinnertime. Her stomach growled.

There must be a place to eat here, she thought.

She followed the hall signs to the cafeteria. The institutional smell reminded her of The Village and she momentarily lost her appetite. She purchased a bowl of chicken broth, something light to tide her over. By the time she took her second spoonful of the tepid liquid she'd decided to call Charlie.

I hate to bother him, she thought, *but I need help.*

* * *

The answering machine picked up.

Charlie and Dave must be out to dinner.

She broke down as soon as she heard Charlie's voice on the recording. She hadn't realized until that very moment how desperately alone she felt.

At seven o'clock, Daisy got up the courage to ask the desk clerk about Lyle. There'd been a staff change and a new clerk sat behind the counter. "Are you a relative?" the girl asked, loudly popping her gum.

"Yes," Daisy said. "I'm his wife."

"Okay, take a seat and I'll see if there's an update," she said popping a bubble as she dialed the telephone.

Daisy sat down, resigned to wait still longer, scanning through the battered magazines spread out on the coffee table before her. In an issue of *AARP*, she noticed a picture of an attractive older woman with silver hair. Daisy had no idea that Lady Clairol could leave your hair so shiny and soft to the touch. *That has to be a pretty terrific product*, she thought, envying the woman's gorgeous mane. *I should try that.*

"Mrs. Fenton? Mrs. Fenton," a voice called out. A nurse in green scrubs stood before her. "Are you Mrs. Fenton?" The facial expression was a mix of irritation and concern.

"Yes, yes, that's me," Daisy stammered, jarred by her own bold-faced lie.

The nurse assumed Daisy was slightly deaf. She shouted, "Would you like to come back and see your husband? He's resting comfortably."

Startled, Daisy followed the woman through the security doors to a draped-off area at the far back corner of the emergency department. Lyle was asleep, hooked up to a series of electronic machines. Tubes were coming out of his nose. The nurse pulled a chair into the space and invited Daisy to sit down. Daisy was unable to tear her eyes away from Lyle. His skin was so pale. He looked so small.

"The doctor will be in shortly," the nurse said, pulling the curtain closed for privacy.

Daisy sat and waited. In that white space, isolated from the rest of the emergency department, she and Lyle seemed to float untethered, apart from the rest of humanity. For the first time that day, Daisy was afraid.

Dave looked up. "I guess we should get going soon."

"Look who has finally joined us," Charlie teased. "*Earth to Dave. Earth to Dave. Welcome back to the land of the living.* How about some breakfast first?"

"I know how he feels," Daisy said. "Change doesn't come without some emotional adjustment."

Dave directed his comment to Charlie. "Gosh, I'm going to miss this woman. She's so sympathetic. So understanding."

"That's because," Charlie snapped back with a big grin, "she doesn't have to live with you anymore."

"Now stop that, you two," Daisy admonished. "I know you're both teasing, but I don't like to hear it. Now, I'm all packed and ready to *go*." Her stomach flipped at the mere mention of leaving. Timmy responded enthusiastically, since *go* was part of Charlie's daily prompt . . . *let's go for a walk*. The sixteen-pound poodle became frantic, leaping and barking in a high-pitched screech. He'd been underfoot all morning, following Daisy's every move, seemingly aware that something was happening. The word *go* seemed to somehow clinch it.

"He knows you're leaving," Charlie said lifting the excited animal onto his lap, stroking his head. "He's afraid he might never see you again."

"He's just nervous. He wants to be sure I'm going to be okay," Daisy said, projecting her feelings onto her beloved Timmy.

"More likely, he wants to go outside," Dave countered, smirking behind his cup of coffee.

"No," Daisy repeated. "He loves me. That's all."

Dave rolled his eyes as Charlie provided long, firm strokes, calming Timmy down. Daisy reached over and scratched Timmy behind the ears.

"You've spoiled him," Dave said as Timmy stood up in an effort to get to Daisy's lap. Charlie held him firmly in place. "It's going to be hard to live with him once you're gone."

"Well, I'm just fifteen minutes away. He can visit. And I expect to see the two of you also."

"Hear that, Timmy?" Dave asked. The dog's ears perked up. "We're going to have someplace to drop you when we go out of town. Daisy will take care of you."

Daisy laughed. "If I do, you may not get him back," she warned.

She hated being afraid.

She silently prayed. *I hope it's not too late for an old woman to ask a favor*, she started. *It's been a long life, and I've had my share of men, but if you can let this one stick around a little longer, I'd be so grateful. He is such a dear. I know he isn't young, and I know it'll be a lot of work, but I'm willing to take care of him. So, if you see fit to let him live, I'd be ever so appreciative.*

Charlie suddenly slipped into the draped-off area.

Daisy jumped. "You nearly scared the life right out of me."

"I'm sorry," Charlie whispered, seeing Lyle was asleep. "Are you okay?"

"I'm doing better than Lyle," she answered. "But I'm exhausted. How did you get back here? They only let relatives in."

"I told them I was his son."

Daisy nodded. Leave it to Charlie to know the best thing to do. And to think it had taken her hours to finally make her way past security.

"Well, I'm waiting for the doctor to come by. I'm his wife."

"Mom," Charlie said lightheartedly. "That sounds so right."

Daisy laughed and the tension in her body eased. It was good to have Charlie with her. She felt blessed. She was glad she'd called him. And though she felt compelled to apologize for disturbing his evening, she wasn't sorry in the least. He was a warm, strong presence, and she needed him. She'd managed so far, but now everything would be better. Whatever might happen, Charlie would help. She wasn't alone.

* * *

Dave found Charlie sitting in the Family Waiting Area on the fifth floor of the hospital. The dimly lit space, set aside for quiet contemplation, possessed an inherent sadness, and just as the lampshades that had become soiled over the years, the room too seemed to have morphed from a pristine white to a smoky grey.

"How's Lyle doing?" Dave asked, his voice low, in deference to the setting.

Charlie sighed. He was sitting on a faded mauve sofa. Dave noticed a stain on the arm. "No change," he said.

Dave took a seat next to Charlie. "How's Daisy holding up?"

"She's pretty tired. She's been here all day. Lyle's still out of it. The doctor says he should be okay once the antibiotics kick in. It's pneumonia. He's lucky to be alive."

"Oh wow," was all Dave could manage.

Charlie rubbed his eyes. "How about we bring her home with us? I think she could use the rest."

"Absolutely," Dave answered without hesitation. "She can stay until Lyle gets out."

"We can switch off taking her to the hospital," Charlie suggested.

Side-by-side the two men sat and stared off into space. An elderly gentleman wandered into the waiting area, clearly lost. When he asked about the location of the nurse's desk, Charlie jumped up and pointed him in the right direction. "It's no problem," Charlie said, as the senior profusely thanked him for his kindness.

"Charlie, when I get to be Daisy's age, I want someone like you in my life," Dave said as Charlie sat back down.

"Hey, don't worry, Dave. I'll be there."

"Yeah, but you'll be too old to be of any help. I want someone young, like you are now."

Charlie smiled. "Dave, I'll always be young enough to take care of you."

"I'm not so sure. We're two men without children. One of us is going to wind up alone. There's no way around it."

"Now there's a happy thought."

"What are we going to do when that time comes?"

"I don't know," Charlie answered. "I'm not sure I want to think about that now."

"But we should think about it while we can still make plans."

"I suppose."

That night Daisy returned to the house with a small overnight bag. Timmy was so excited, he tinkled in the hallway. When Daisy retired to the guest bedroom, Timmy followed, close on her heels.

Charlie and Dave sat up sipping Dewar's.

"Nothing like Scotch to take the seams out of your pants," Dave joked, hoping to take the edge off of his fears about Lyle and Daisy.

"You're such a lightweight. Red wine would do the trick," Charlie mused, shifting the pillow on the sofa before dropping it onto the floor by his feet. "It's good to be home. I don't know how she did it. She was at that hospital for hours on end. I'm years younger and I'm exhausted."

"What do we do if Lyle dies?" Dave hated to ask the question but knew it was on both their minds.

"Well, let's not get ahead of ourselves," Charlie demurred. "Lyle may do just fine."

"But Charlie, you know as well as I do, Lyle won't be around forever."

"Neither will Daisy," Charlie pointed out, finishing up the golden liquor with one final gulp, as if to wash away his own sharp observation. Charlie stood up. "I'm going to go check on her. Make sure she's settling in."

"Leave her alone," Dave said. "Let her be."

Charlie ignored him. "I'll be right back," he said, heading down the hall to the guest room.

Dave felt the warmth of the Scotch doing its magic. He closed his eyes and leaned back into the sofa, his body relaxing. *God forbid Charlie dies first. I don't think I could manage.* It had been years since Dave had entertained such dark thoughts. Years since his first partner, Edward, had died. And yet, in any given moment, the memory was still fresh. Still terrifying.

It was 1990. New England Deaconess Hospital in Boston. Edward was participating in an experimental AIDS drug trial. Emaciated men, covered in purple lesions, populated the waiting room of the Infectious Disease Clinic. Dave tried not to stare, but he'd never seen so many sick young men in one place. Hollow eyes, frightened faces. No one spoke. Sadness permeated every corner of the clinic.

Back at the apartment they rented, Edward broke into tears. Dave was taken aback. He'd never seen Edward cry. Edward had always been defiant, certain he'd survive, but the waiting room of sick men had shaken his confidence. "I don't want to die. I don't," Edward sobbed, face buried in his hands. "This is so unfair. What did I do to deserve this? Why . . . ?"

Dave choked on his silence. What could he say to ease the anguish? The terrible tragedy that he was powerless to change. He had no words. No power, but to hold Edward. To love Edward until the very end.

"She seems fine," Charlie whispered, coming back into the room, and bringing Dave forward to the present. "I can hear her gently snoring."

The memory of Edward's suffering lingered. Dave had never truly let go of Edward. No matter how many years might pass, no matter how much he loved Charlie, Dave would always ache for the loss of Edward. A young man sacrificed to a virus that took no prisoners.

* * *

"Do I know you?" asked the guy standing behind Henry in line at Starbucks on Camelback and 16th Street. "You look familiar."

Henry, a complete coffee addict, had stopped in for a Caffé Misto after buying a pair of Nikes at the nearby Sports Authority. He'd almost walked out when he saw the long line, but then, at the last moment, decided to wait.

"No," Henry answered, awed by the guy's piercing blue eyes.

"Isn't your name Ben?" the young man pressed. "I know we've met."

"No," Henry blushed, momentarily looking away, attracted to the stranger. Not wishing to be rude, he quickly offered up, "My name's Henry."

"Henry? I guess I'm wrong. I don't know any Henrys." The guy extended his hand as the line moved forward. He was shorter than Henry at five-ten, with a stocky, powerful, athletic build. He wore his dark brown hair cropped close on the sides, a bit longer on top, combed straight back and off his forehead to reveal a broad brow. His eyes, deeply set, were a marked contrast to his olive complexion. "Anyway, it's nice to meet you, Henry. My name's Paul. Do you go to ASU?"

"No, I go to Central High," Henry said, shaking the stranger's hand.

"Wow. You look a lot older."

"Just big for my age, they tell me." Henry smiled.

And that's how the friendship began.

Paul invited Henry to join him at a small table. Together they sat, shooting the breeze. Paul shared that he'd been on the wrestling squad when he attended ASU, and after graduation, had taken a job at the Apple Store in Biltmore Fashion Park.

"I plan on getting an MBA," Paul said, "but I just need some time to chill out. This is my chance to be on my own and think about what I want to do next."

Henry, who tended to be shy, warmed to Paul's extroverted nature. Paul had no trouble flirting with the girls at the next table or talking with the firefighters who had stopped in to grab their cup of java. Paul was completely natural, spontaneous, and friendly. Comfortable in his own skin, his eyes seemed to be acutely observant, recording every subtle movement and mannerism of Henry's, a level of attention Henry found both flattering and exhilarating.

"Hey, I've been talking your ear off," Paul said. "It's a bad habit of mine."

Henry didn't mind. He was happy to listen.

"You work out a lot," Paul suddenly said. "I can tell." His eyes wandered to Henry's chest. "Me too. I think that may be why you look so much older. You're really developed for a kid. Let me see your biceps. Flex."

Henry became uncomfortable. "I don't think so. Not here."

"I want to see if you're bigger than me. Go on. No need to be shy. We're both guys."

Henry demurred, feeling uncomfortable with Paul's blatant interest in his physique. But Paul was not to be deterred. "Have you taken steroids?" he asked with a tone of judgement in his voice.

Henry shook his head.

"Stay away from the steroids," Paul warned. "They'll destroy your liver. It just isn't worth it."

Henry had seen the effect steroids on the male body. Some guys practically ballooned overnight. He thought it kind of hot.

Paul's eyes lit up. "We should work out together. I belong to Lifetime Fitness. Ever been there? It's a great club."

"I've read about it," Henry admitted.

"Sure. That would be great. My friends are so busy now, working, new careers. I bet you'd have more free time. Especially after three o'clock." Paul flashed a dazzling smile. "Hey I don't know if you have plans for later, but do you like football?"

"Sure," Henry said.

"I have an extra ticket to the Sun Devils tonight."

"I don't know," Henry said. "I really can't afford it."

"No problem," Paul said. "It's on me. Otherwise, the ticket goes to waste."

Henry became suddenly suspicious. "We don't even know each other. Why would you do that?"

Paul jerked his head back, apparently startled by Henry's question. "Hey, I'm just a nice guy," he said. "If you don't want to go, that's fine. If I'm bothering you . . ." and he made a move to get up.

Henry blushed. Paul did seem to be a good guy. A friendly guy. Someone with whom Henry could imagine spending time.

"I'm sorry," he said, reaching out to grab Paul's wrist. "I didn't mean to be rude. It's just that I don't have many friends . . ."

"Well, then it's time to make some, don't you think?" Paul flashed that smile again, and Henry's suspicions faded.

"Well if you're sure . . ."

"Like I said, why waste the ticket? And who wants to go to a football game alone? My friends are too busy and my girlfriend won't go with me. Susan hates football."

Henry looked warily into Paul's eyes. This beautiful man wanted to spend time with him. Why struggle?

"I'll pick you up and we'll ride together," Paul said.

"Well, okay," Henry conceded. "Count me in."

* * *

In the passenger seat of Paul's Mustang, Henry tried not to stare at Paul's powerful hands. "Great car," he finally said.

"When I graduated, I decided to treat myself. It's a lease."

Henry stretched his legs. "There's plenty of room."

Paul glanced over. "What are you driving?"

"I don't have a car. I just got my learner's permit."

"Oh wow. If you'd like, I can give you a couple of lessons."

"Really?" Henry could hardly believe his luck.

"Sure," Paul said, pulling off I-10 at University to make their way to the stadium. "I'm an only child. You're the perfect age for a kid brother." He turned and winked, telegraphing, *don't worry . . . I'll handle it.*

Henry was over the moon.

Seated high in the nose-bleed section, the two waited for kick-off.

"So, where are your parents?" Paul asked when Henry explained he lived with Anna.

"Around," Henry answered, unwilling to reveal too much.

"Why don't you live with your folks?"

"It's not convenient," Henry said.

Paul shrugged, signaling to Henry it was no big deal. But Henry couldn't help but wonder if his inability to address a simple question raised more suspicion than if he had answered the question directly. Still, Henry had no interest in tainting new friendships with his backstory. Not when he was on the verge of finally enjoying life. And while Henry concealed his true nature from Paul, he struggled with the intense attraction to his new friend. Henry wasn't quite sure whether it was Paul's good looks, attitude, or innate confidence that created the aphrodisiac.

Maybe it was all three.

Whatever it was, Henry was grateful to be in Paul's orbit.

The stadium was packed with fans. Young men and woman from the University crowded in for the kickoff. The air was electric, the excitement palpable.

"I do understand," Paul said, turning his radiant blue eyes on Henry. "I was an only child. My parents didn't want me. My dad used to beat the crap out of me. Especially when he was drunk. It sort of leaves you feeling lonely. And it's hard to talk to other people about. Everyone expects you to be happy. Sure I have a lot of friends. They cushion you from the loneliness. But it's like standing in a crowd. You don't want to be alone. But you are. You always are."

Henry didn't know what to say. Was Paul's story so different from his own?

Paul reached over and squeezed Henry's knee. His touch was electric. "Hey, no need for that worried look. You don't have to say anything. I'm okay. And you will be too. Guys like us have to stick together. Agreed?"

Henry nodded.

"I'll get us some beers," Paul said. "You wait here."

"I'm underage." Henry stated the obvious.

"No sweat. I got it covered."

"Are you sure?"

Paul flashed his pearly whites. "Hey, little bro, I can't be drinking alone."

* * *

Anna saw less and less of Henry as she became completely engaged in Weight Watchers, attending evening meetings and measuring every bite that went into her mouth. For a woman who'd always eaten whatever she wanted, Weight Watchers was a revelation. She'd assumed her size was a result of genetics, but now, she learned it had to do with portion control and calories. She took up walking, starting off with a mile every morning. As the weight melted off, Anna felt extreme pleasure at finally being in control. She loved the way she looked, even if she wasn't yet at her ideal body weight. For the first time in her life, her body wasn't the enemy. She was on the road to mastery.

＊ ＊ ＊

Henry reached for his phone. "Hello?"

"Hey, what are you doing?" Paul's voice boomed.

His homework was done and Anna was out for the evening. Henry had been reading the microwave instructions on the side of a Marie Callender's chicken pot pie. "Henry, I'd be truly grateful," Anna had said as she headed out the door, "if you'd eat the Marie Callender's in the freezer. I can't eat that anymore and I can't bear to throw it away." Henry had laughed. "Oh," Anna had sighed dramatically. "Marie Callender and Sara Lee. I'm losing my two best friends."

"How about if I pick you up and we grab dinner together?" Paul offered. "No reason for us both to eat alone."

"Okay, but this time, you have to let me pay," Henry insisted.

"Do you have any money?" Paul asked.

"A little," Henry answered, knowing full well his livelihood was based on Anna's generosity. She'd agreed to provide a weekly allowance if Henry maintained a B+ average.

"Okay, then . . . I'll stop by in thirty minutes. Where do you want to go?"

"We can walk over to Arby's. They have a great roast beef sandwich."

"I haven't eaten at Arby's since I left high school."

For Henry, Arby's was the limit of his pocketbook.

"Don't sweat it, little bro. If that's where you want to eat, that's good enough for me. I'll be by soon."

That night at dinner, Henry studied Paul's every gesture. The silly faces he made to emphasize the punchline of a joke. The way his eyes lit up when he shared stories about his friends. His serious tone when he discussed Susan.

"It's been an adjustment," Paul admitted. "You go to college and make all these friends, and then you get out into the real world and everyone goes their own separate way. No one has time any more. We sometimes still get together on Sundays to hang out, but during the week, it's every man for himself. Everyone's busy just trying to make a life."

"But college must be a blast," Henry said as he sipped his diet root beer.

"Yeah," Paul said sadly. "It was. But now, it's all over. Time to be an adult."

* * *

For years Ernie had been his own boss, coming and going as he pleased. But now, he worked for the Villa Allegra. The structured week proved to be an adjustment. And even when he wasn't working, he was still working.

In his new role as Director of Plant Operations, his cell phone rang at all hours. He was bombarded with questions, mostly from facilities and housekeeping, the two departments that ran twenty-four-seven. At first he was overwhelmed, but after a while he came to realize that the staff respected and needed him. That alone was enough to energize him at the beginning of every day.

Being new to the job, Ernie was the topic of conversation among the employees. They assumed he was American of Mexican descent since he was bilingual without a trace of a Mexican accent when he spoke English. And though he was warm and friendly, he projected a confidence that eluded many of the Mexican working-class. Head up, shoulders back, eyes forward—Ernie's posture spoke volumes to those who worked under him.

He was a man to be admired.

And so the young maids in housekeeping eyed Ernie with the intent of seducing him, but Ernie was too busy to take notice of such advances, and far too conscientious to ever engage inappropriately with employees.

Ernie was grateful for the job and dedicated to doing his best work.

He came to love every moment of the workday. Any thoughts of returning to the United States quickly evaporated as he busied himself moving with Maria into a modern, high-rise building, not far from the center of town.

Maria cringed when she first saw the floor-to-ceiling glass windows off of the living room that provided a gorgeous view of the ocean. Stepping behind Ernie, she said, "I don't know," about the sixth-floor apartment which boasted a chef's kitchen that opened onto a large living room-dining room. There were two bedrooms with private baths and a spacious terrace that overlooked the beach. "Aren't we awfully high up?"

"Yes," Ernie said. "Off of the street and away from the crowd. Isn't it peaceful?"

But Maria remained concerned. "Ernie, I don't like this apartment. Isn't there something on a lower floor?"

"Mama, don't be silly. This apartment's perfect."

"I'll never use that terrace," Maria pointed toward the sliding glass door off the living room. "Never."

"Then don't," Ernie snapped, realizing his mother was scared of heights. "The most important thing," he pointed out, "there are no cockroaches. And check out the thermostat. We have both central air and heat."

That night, Ernie slept well in the new air-conditioned quarters. He had his privacy in the spacious master bedroom and the sheets didn't stick to his back. And while Maria did complain about the vista, begging him to close the living room curtains so that she wouldn't get dizzy looking out, she finally had her own room.

Life was beginning to feel normal again.

* * *

Bonnie rushed to the phone on the first ring.

"Hello, pretty lady."

His voice warmed her.

"What are you doing?" he asked.

"Nothing," she said. "Just waiting for your call." She was happy to snuggle up on the sofa to the sound of his voice. "I wish you were here, next to me."

"Oh yeah, and if I were, what would you do?"

She blushed. "Come over and find out."

But he couldn't be with her. He wouldn't be able to see her until later in the week.

She could hardly wait.

The feeling of being connected to another was thrilling, intoxicating. *Too long*, she thought. *I've been alone too long.*

The outside world disappeared as they became the only two people who mattered.

* * *

Unlike Ernie, whose days were filled with people and challenge, Maria had nothing to keep her mind off her troubles. Having once escaped Mexico at a significant emotional cost, she now reveled in her contempt of it. And though circumstances had improved markedly with Ernie's new job, she resisted the sterile luxury his income now afforded. She wanted her old life back. She wanted to live in the United States again. She desperately yearned for Phoenix.

She missed her Volkswagen Beetle, the small apartment with its kitchenette, and, most of all, her dog. She missed the loudmouthed neighbors who hung around the complex drinking beer and complaining about Arizona politics. And like all people who wax nostalgic, she conveniently forgot the grit of the neighborhood, the challenge of earning a living without a Social Security number, and the employers who'd paid her under-the-table, below minimum wage. She forgot about Arizona's intolerance of foreigners and the governor's refusal to allow the undocumented to carry valid driver's licenses. She forgot about her fear of the police, a fear that extended to the fire department, physicians, anyone in a position of authority. She forgot because in Puerto Vallarta she saw Americans enjoying the privileged life of travel—laughing, drinking, and spending money—Americans who reminded her of Phoenix and the dreams she held dear. Dreams now lost to her.

With each passing day, America slipped further away. In its place, a gnawing panic that her life had been lost . . . wasted. Her efforts had been for nothing. With the struggle over, she'd become useless. She was a woman who needed a reason to get out of bed in the morning. A purpose.

Her feisty nature required she wrestle the world. The fight might be over, but her hands remained fisted.

She couldn't be happy. This was not what she'd planned. Here in Mexico, she felt isolated, alone in her high-rise apartment.

I'm an old woman, she thought, examining her hands, noticing the wrinkled skin and age spots. *I've outlived my purpose.*

Her eyes scanned the horizon.

What value is my life?

* * *

"What the devil is wrong with you?" Ernie asked Maria, arriving home from work, impatient at seeing her still wearing a robe. "You look exactly like you did when I left you this morning. Haven't you showered and dressed yet? God, you look so damn unhappy."

"Do I?" Maria answered. "I hadn't thought you noticed."

"I try not to," Ernie admitted as he slipped off his sport coat. "Gosh it's hot in here. Is the air conditioning out?"

"I turned the thermostat up," Maria admitted.

"To what?" Ernie checked the thermostat on the wall. "83?"

"Electricity is expensive. We don't need to be spending all that money."

"Look. We've talked about this. I can afford to pay for the air conditioning. I want the air on. We're not living in one room anymore. I make good money. You don't need to go without. You have everything you've ever wanted. A beautiful place to live. Money in your pocket. You can go anywhere in the city . . . do anything . . . and you choose to mope around here all day."

Angry, Maria snapped back. "Perdóname! It seems I'm spoiling your good time. Maybe you don't want your mother here? Maybe I should find someplace else to live."

Ernie cocked his head. "What the devil is wrong with you?"

Maria's eyes were damp. Her shoulders sagged. "I have no purpose," she quietly confessed. "I've struggled my whole life. I raised you in America and was proud of what I did. I worked, pushed myself. Now," she said as she looked about, "it all seems to have had no meaning. No one needs me. I cook. But you don't eat your meals here."

Ernie defended himself. "Not every night. I work late. But you can always join me at the resort."

"I've done that. I've sat alone while you run around, fixing whatever you fix."

Ernie shrugged. "I have to work. It puts a roof over our heads."

Maria lifted a three-inch potted cactus Ernie had brought home for her when they moved into the apartment. "I'm about as useful as this itty-bitty plant."

"I can't deal with this now." Ernie waved a hand in the air, signaling her to stop. "I'm exhausted. You just don't know when things are going well. You're so used to suffering . . . I think you actually miss it."

Maria bit her lower lip.

"It's been a long day. I'm going to take a shower," Ernie said as he slipped off his tie. "Hopefully when I come back out, you'll be in a better mood."

* * *

"Can I be of help?" Bonnie asked, joining Charlie in the kitchen. She held a glass of merlot in one hand and a sliver of brie on a toasted sesame cracker in the other. "God, I just love coming over here on Thursday nights. I can't tell you. And this cheese is just divine." She held the cracker high, exalting it one last time before popping it into her mouth.

"Trader Joe's," Charlie said as he tossed a fresh green salad loaded with cherry tomatoes, spinach and warm bacon. "You seem unusually happy," he observed while sprinkling bits of blue cheese into the salad.

"Do I?" The wine had taken affect. Bonnie did feel happy. Truly happy.

Charlie opened the oven door to inspect the roasted chicken. Wearing a pair of red oven mitts, he pulled the golden brown bird out and placed it on the counter. Small red potatoes, orange carrots and green celery hugged the pan. The scent of roasted garlic and thyme filled the air.

"Oh Charlie. It's absolutely gorgeous. You should take a picture."

Charlie stood back and admired the bird. "It's Daisy's favorite. With Lyle in the hospital, we've been doing all we can to get her to eat."

"You two are so thoughtful," Bonnie remarked. "Dave's in the living room with her going over what the doctor said today. He's so at ease with all the medical jargon."

"He's an old hand at that," Charlie answered. "Gay men who survived the AIDS crisis know how to navigate the healthcare system."

Bonnie sipped her wine. She'd heard about Edward. Dave had teared up when he had told her.

"And you. What's going on with you?" Charlie asked.

Perhaps it was the wine or the sudden desire to change the subject from death and illness, whatever the reason, Bonnie let it slip.

"I'm in love."

She hadn't expected to share her secret. The admission at first startled her . . . as if by merely saying so . . . something awful might happen to make it untrue. As if a more measured approach to the subject of love would be appropriate. And as when she told Daisy and Lyle, she instantly regretted her words.

"You almost seem ashamed," Charlie said. "You're blushing."

"At my age I didn't expect to fall in love. I thought that was for kids."

Charlie pulled a boxed Sara Lee cheesecake out of the refrigerator. "When it comes to matters of the heart," he said, "we're all teenagers. If the hormones are willing, we're always ready for another round."

Bonnie was beginning to believe.

"Sara Lee?" she observed. "I thought everything was homemade."

"Baking isn't my thing. And you know how much Dave loves dessert. I probably should take a class. So when do we meet your mystery man?" Charlie asked.

Bonnie stalled. "Well, I'm not sure. He has a busy schedule," she lied, knowing full well her new boyfriend was not quite suitable for introduction. "For the time being," she begged Charlie, "can we just keep this between the two of us? It's all so new. I'm not quite comfortable yet."

"Sure," Charlie agreed, counting out the dessert forks. "But I don't see why. It's kind of sweet."

Bonnie felt awful. She'd tried staying away from married guys, but they were everywhere. The singles landscape was booby-trapped with married men. And yet this time, it was different. There was a real connection. Something beyond just the physical.

She was certain he felt the same.

"I just hope he's good enough for you."

"Me too," she said, feeling trapped by Charlie's concern over her half-truth.

Why, she thought, *didn't I keep this to myself? Why did I have to open my big mouth?*

"Do you think this is the one?" Charlie asked as Dave came through the kitchen door.

"What am I missing?" Dave asked. "What's all this collusion about?"

"Bonnie's in love," Charlie said.

"Charlie!" Bonnie glared at him.

"Calm down," Charlie said. "There's nothing you tell me that Dave won't eventually know. We're partners. We discuss everything."

"Why are you keeping secrets from me?" Dave asked Bonnie. "I'm trustworthy."

Bonnie rolled her eyes.

"How long have you been seeing this new man?" Dave asked.

"Not long," Bonnie answered. Being non-committal with her responses now seemed like the best course.

"And you're already in love? That seems kind of fast. How well do you know each other?"

"I know all I need to," she assured Dave, uncomfortable with the tone that the conversation was taking. "He's sweet. He cares about me. He calls every night no matter where he is. He calls," she repeated as if in disbelief, "every night."

"Sounds serious," Charlie said, glaring at Dave. "Very serious."

"Just take it slow," Dave warned. "Don't get ahead of yourself."

"What kind of advice is that?" Charlie asked. "She's head over heels and you're telling her to take it slow. Come on, Dave. No one wants to hear that. She's in love. Let her enjoy it. Lord knows it doesn't happen every day."

"At least not to me," Bonnie added.

"Okay," Dave hugged her. "Okay, I'm happy for you."

"But remember," Charlie reminded her, "we want to meet him."

11

....

Harvey Lederman scared the hell out of Jack. But instead of backing off and leaving the matter of the lawsuit to his attorney to handle, Jack was determined to speak directly with Daisy. *I have to convince her to settle,* he thought, sipping his morning coffee. *It was an honest misunderstanding. No one meant her any harm. Maybe if I personally tell her how sorry we are, I can make her understand.*

Later that morning, as Jack's car approached the gate on his way out of the development, Sheila stepped out of the booth, her flaming red hair catching the bright morning sunlight.

She waved to him.

Jack came to a full stop and lowered his car window. "Well this is a pleasant surprise," he said bolstering all his charm. "Shouldn't you be over at Biltmore Greens? What brings you to our gate this fine morning?"

"Coverage issues," Sheila said, leaning on Jack's car window. "I did the night shift at Biltmore Greens and since I'm a flexible, single gal, living alone, I can easily pick up some morning overtime at the Terraces. I can't do it often, but every now and then, I can manage."

"Well good for you," Jack answered, a smile painted on his face.

"I saw your aunt yesterday over at Biltmore Greens. She told me Lyle was in the hospital." Sheila wore a concerned expression amid a sea of freckles.

Jack nodded. He had no intention of letting on that he knew nothing about his aunt or her life. Instead, he smiled and waited, hoping Sheila would back away so that he could get on with the rest of his day. But she didn't. Instead, she lingered, seemingly enjoying the opportunity to share confidences within the Lee family.

"It was so sweet of Dave and Charlie to invite Daisy to stay at their house. That must have been a huge weight off your mind to know she's with them. Those guys are the greatest."

Sheila's eyes invited Jack to agree. Her ears, which pinned her shoulder-length hair back from her face, seemed poised to hear some interesting tidbit of information. Jack was mystified. What could she possibly want him to say, this stranger who knew more about his aunt than he did?

He finally responded: "What time did you say you saw her?"

Jack had an idea forming in his mind.

"Early," Sheila confirmed. "But I think she's still over there. Charlie was heading out for a business meeting and Dave was on his way to the gym. I'm sure if you stopped by now, you'd catch her. Charlie and Dave have been switching off taking her to the hospital to visit with Lyle. Maybe you could take her today and give them a break."

"Great idea," Jack answered, certain that this would be the best time to speak with his aunt alone. He checked his watch. It was 9:40 a.m. "Can you give me the house number again? I always get lost in that neighborhood," Jack lied. "All those winding streets look alike to me."

Sheila scribbled the address down on a scrap of paper and handed it to Jack. "There you go," she said.

How proud she is to be helpful, Jack thought, as he worked to decipher her scrawl.

"Now you tell her that I'll be saying a prayer," she called to Jack as he took his leave, foot off the brake, rolling toward the front gate as it slowly opened.

He gave Sheila a big thumbs up.

Within minutes, Jack was parked in front of Daisy's old house—now Dave and Charlie's.

Please God, he thought, *let her be understanding.*

He walked up the path to the house, stood in front of the door, and considered what he might say. At last, he rang the doorbell and waited. He caught the movement of a curtain. Daisy looked out from a side window.

They locked eyes. She shook her head sideways and retreated, the curtain dropping back into place.

"Please, Aunt Daisy," Jack called out, ringing the bell again. "Please let me in. Please let me talk to you. This isn't fair," Jack pleaded. "Please open the door."

"Jack," she called from behind the door. "Go home."

"Aunt Daisy," he said calmly. "I want to talk with you. That's all. Please let me talk with you."

He waited. Time seemed to stand still as he took root on the doorstep. The air was fragrant with the smell of morning grass. A gentle breeze stirred the scent, reminding him of Michigan summers. A dove waddled nearby, seemingly calling out to its mate. Jack was astonished that the little guy would get so close. Then, at last, Daisy unlocked the door, opening it halfway. She stepped forward, tucked between the open door and the doorframe, her right hand holding onto the outside knob.

"Thank you," he said to the tiny woman who stood before him.

She looked tired, her eyes red and swollen as if she'd been crying. He hadn't realized till that moment her fragility. He thought of his mother Rose. She too had the capacity to manifest physical weakness despite fierce, inner strength. But Rose had been a manipulative woman, and he had no intention of being manipulated by Daisy.

"I understand you're upset," Daisy quietly acknowledged. "But you and Enid had no right to do what you did. It was wrong, Jack. And you shouldn't be here."

"I'm not leaving until we talk this through." Jack's voice was determined, forgetting that she'd only opened the door at his bequest.

"I'm not inviting you in, Jack. There's nothing more to say."

"We did nothing wrong," Jack practically whimpered, as if the truth demanded that he insist on his innocence.

"Jack," Daisy said in astonishment. "It *was* wrong."

His tone telegraphed his exasperation. "We did everything we knew to take care of you and make sure you'd be okay. Enid went out of her way to help you. She paid your bills . . . visited you at the hospital and in rehab. Aunt Daisy, if it hadn't been for us, you'd have been all alone."

"Perhaps," Daisy conceded, "but it didn't warrant you stealing. Who gave you permission to sell my home? And where are my belongings, Jack? What happened to all my lovely things? Where are they?"

"We did the best we could at the time," Jack defended. "You were completely out of it. The doctors didn't give us much hope. We were only trying to secure your future. No one can say that we didn't have your best intentions."

Daisy took a deep breath. "Jack, I don't have the energy to teach a man your age about decency. And I'm too old to fight."

"Yes, but you're not too old to sue me."

"Jack, by now you should know the difference between right and wrong. Sadly, you don't," and with that Daisy made a motion with her hand for Jack to leave because she was closing the door.

He ignored her.

"I want you to drop the lawsuit. Please, Aunt Daisy. Please."

"That isn't happening, Jack. Now get off this porch before I'm forced to call the police."

Jack wanted to grab Daisy and shake some sense into her. He wanted to punch the wall out of frustration. But most of all, he wanted her to understand that he was innocent. He'd done nothing wrong. Instead, he turned and walked away, cursing the old woman under his breath.

* * *

Daisy had no intention of making amends with Jack, and yet she couldn't help but be moved by his plea. He was clearly in distress, and despite the wrong done to her, she had no desire to see him suffer. Had things been different, she'd have welcomed him warmly, eager for the opportunity to know Jack the man. But as things stood, she was afraid. Afraid of the intense emotions Jack had stirred within her. Her anguish ran far deeper than the recent loss of her home. After so many years, she'd thought herself immune to such intense emotional pain. Now she realized there was no such thing as immunity in life. Immunity was a sham.

She was seventeen again . . . the day her baby was born.

All babies are beautiful, but to Daisy, hers was exceptional.

She held her newborn, carefully counting fingers and toes, inspecting tiny nails, admiring the shape of his head. She was relieved her baby was healthy. She couldn't help but be a little proud she'd produced a boy. The sweet scent of talcum powder and baby breath were in the air. His eyes struggled to focus as she gently supported his head in the crook of her elbow. He drooled when she held him close.

"Mrs. Lee." The nurse appeared. "It's time to take your baby back to the nursery. We're going to get him ready to go home."

Rose entered the room.

Daisy squeezed her eyes shut.

Not Rose.

Why did Rose have to ruin her reverie?

Why couldn't she edit Rose out?

But there was no use in even trying. Traumas couldn't be corrected by wishful thinking.

"He's beautiful," Rose said, pulling up a chair. She wore a black felt pillbox hat with satin trim. It was Rose's only hat. The one she wore for all occasions. Daisy had never fully appreciated its simplicity, both formal and severe. "You know you can't keep him."

Daisy blinked hard. "But we agreed. I'm to raise my baby."

Rose's mouth was a gash upon her face. Her eyes, determined, hard, unwavering. "Don't be foolish, Daisy. You have no means of support."

"Jacob said he'd help me. Jacob promised."

"Jacob and I have decided to raise the baby," Rose said firmly. "You're going away."

"What are you talking about?" Daisy asked in a growing panic. The room spun like a funhouse ride as she struggled to catch her bearings.

"This is for you." Rose placed an envelope in Daisy's lap. "Jacob and I have pulled together some money. It's not a lot, but enough for a few weeks."

Daisy's heart raced. "And what if I don't agree?"

"You know in your heart this is the best thing for the baby."

"I don't believe my brother agreed to this," Daisy cried. "My brother would never do something like this to me."

"Do you see your brother here?" Rose asked. The pitch of her voice had changed; anger in her tone. "Do you think he's hiding under the bed? He couldn't face you. Now pull yourself together. We've agreed to raise your baby, but we're done trying to raise you. You're on your own."

"But what will I do?" Daisy asked, reminded of the day she first moved in with Jacob and Rose, how lost she'd felt, how afraid she was of the future.

"You'll go somewhere new and start over," Rose suggested. "Get a job. Build a life. If you can figure out how to make a baby, you can figure out how to make your way in the world. Only next time, try not to get pregnant."

* * *

Henry was jealous.

He couldn't help himself.

Though Paul made time to see Henry during the week, on the weekends, Paul was often tied up with Susan or hanging out with his other buddies. And Henry didn't fit in with the older crowd. At Paul's apartment, where his friends gathered on Sundays, Henry occupied a space in the corner of the living room. While the others clowned around, passing weed, drinking beer, Henry struggled to hide his passion for Paul and his growing contempt for the others. The more time he spent with the group, the angrier Henry became. He'd shut down, stop talking. Paul's friends ignored him. Most would have preferred he just go home.

"I think you need a hit," said Jerry.

Jerry loved weed. If there was grass to be had, Jerry was busy buying, rolling, and smoking it.

Henry wasn't interested. "No, thanks."

"Take it," Jerry ordered. "It'll chill you right out. Go on . . ."

Henry took a drag.

"Hold it," Jerry directed once Henry inhaled. "Wait . . . wait . . . wait. Okay."

Henry exhaled.

"One more time," Jerry commanded.

Henry did as he was told. When he went to take a third hit, Jerry pulled the joint back. "You've had enough," he said, moving to the other side of the room.

As the grass took effect, Henry focused on Paul.

Sitting on the floor, back against the sofa, Paul exuded the magnetism of a natural leader, someone who reveled in telling others which movies to see, foods to eat, and books to read. He projected an all-knowing, air of confidence as he held court. The others in the room, less certain of themselves, deferred to Paul. They appeared to welcome someone who had all the answers.

Stoned, Henry's heart swelled as raw lust mixed with adoration. Frightened by the intensity of his feelings, he got up to leave.

Paul noticed.

"Hey, where are you going?"

"I've got to get home," Henry lied, looking down to avoid being trapped by Paul's blue eyes.

"I'll drive you," Paul offered, hand on Henry's arm.

Henry wanted to cry. "No, you have your friends here. I'll manage," he said, heading out the door, tears rolling down his cheeks.

* * *

Daisy Ellen Lee wasn't afraid of death. It was the act of dying that scared her. She didn't want to experience a slow painful exit which required a lot of medication and lingering. She wanted death to come quickly, pain- lessly, and without a lot of fanfare.

These were her thoughts as she watched Lyle regain his vitality.

It had been a long hospital stretch. Ten days. When Lyle was finally released, Daisy's energy was tapped. She napped in the afternoon, a practice she'd long frowned upon. But now she was exhausted by three o'clock. She needed to rest.

At home, Lyle slept on and off all day, getting out of bed only for meals. His color was coming back but Daisy was keenly aware that he was no longer sure on his feet. He used a cane to steady himself. Daisy took his arm and guided him slowly along. They pretended nothing had changed. But they both knew better.

Charlie checked in regularly, stopping by unannounced to see how things were progressing. Daisy could see the concern in his eyes. It scared her. She wasn't ready to let go of Lyle though she certainly understood no one lives forever. It just didn't seem fair. They'd only just found each other.

And though Daisy adored Charlie, she didn't want to be the old woman he worried about. She wasn't quite ready for that role. She still thought herself vigorous and energetic, regardless of Lyle's condition. She still wanted so much out of life. She had her health, and if she couldn't have Lyle, she wanted her freedom and independence. She wanted to be able to hop on a plane and head off to Europe, leaving her cares behind. She wanted to sit in a Parisian café enjoying a glass of cabernet. Shop antiques in Hyde Park. Sail the blue waters of the Greek isles, filling herself with moussaka and tomato salad. She still had so many things left to do. Caring for Lyle was a wake-up call. Time is short. Life is limited. Do it now, or forever regret the missed opportunity.

She wanted more than she could possibly handle.

Under the pressure of Lyle's illness, her body too, was beginning to give out. She could feel it. For Lyle's sake, she pretended to be upbeat, but in reality, every morning, there was the ache of another day notched on her joints. Pains appeared in places she hadn't even been aware of before. Her third toe on her left foot. Her thumb on her right hand. *If only everything didn't ache so much*, she thought. *I can bear anything but this nagging pain.* She rubbed her hands together. *How come Lyle never complains? How does he manage?*

That night, Charlie brought in Panda Express for dinner. He and Daisy sat together in the kitchen working on the chow mein, a single portion large enough to feed a family of three. Lyle was still fast asleep. Daisy had thought to wake him but decided to leave him be. It had been awhile since she'd been alone with Charlie. It was good to sit quietly with him. His presence was a comfort.

"A penny for your thoughts," Charlie asked as he picked at a tiny green pea with his chopsticks.

She shook her head no, afraid to talk. Afraid that whatever she'd say would be maudlin. Afraid that if she gave voice to her real fears, they'd all come true. Charlie was too sweet, too kind, and she didn't want to frighten him.

Dear Charlie, she thought, *I can't share what's running through my head. These are the troubles of old age. Fears you needn't bother with now.*

And so they sat together in silence. Daisy, grateful to Charlie for not prodding her to talk. It was the greatest gift he could have offered, moral support without the need for revelation.

* * *

Older people can have an incredible tenacity, and, as it turned out, that was certainly true in Lyle's case. When he'd first been hospitalized, Daisy had thought, *this might be the end*. But after a few days in Daisy's care, Lyle began to blossom. His strength gradually returned as did the joy in his eyes.

The cane he'd used rested in the corner of the bedroom as he became determined to make every second count. And that meant Daisy had to keep up with him as they went out to movies, restaurants, and resumed their regular afternoon walks.

"It's like being reborn," Lyle explained to her. "I can feel the energy surging through my limbs. I've absolutely never felt better. You'd think I'd be scared by all this vitality. But I'm not. I don't know why I feel so darn energetic, and frankly, I don't care. I'm just glad I do. It feels so natural."

"But you need to pace yourself," Daisy warned. "You're not a youngster."

"I know my time is running out. Obviously it is. I'm not a fool. But I don't care. There. I said it. I don't care and I'm not afraid, Daisy. I'm not afraid," Lyle repeated, surprised to hear himself say the words that perfectly mirrored his thoughts. "I've been afraid before, but now I'm beginning to feel like it all goes on. Death is not the end."

"I don't like this conversation," Daisy protested. "Let's change the subject to something more pleasant."

"No, Daisy. It's important for you to hear me. I have a sense of inner peace. Something I've never felt in all my decades of living. Perhaps it's a knowledge that it's all wrapping up. No more struggle. No more want. I can't quite put my finger on it." He laughed at the absurdity of his explanation. "What could it be that a man my age doesn't know yet?"

"Tell me," Daisy said. "I'm listening."

Lyle sighed. "Another day, another week, another month . . . that would be nice, but really, what's the point? If you haven't lived your life by now, then shame on you. What more could I possibly want? I feel so blessed to be with you. I hope it lasts, but I know that nothing really does. It can't. We're not meant to be static. If we were, we'd experience our existence in a bubble, protected."

Daisy reached for Lyle's hand. "I'm just so grateful we're together. I don't want us to be parted."

"Well, neither do I, but it's inevitable. And when I'm gone, I want you to embrace life. Let Charlie, Dave, and Bonnie help you. Don't be too proud. And if you decide to forgive Jack, that's okay too."

Daisy nodded her head. She'd heard what Lyle was telling her.

Lyle perked up. "Okay, enough of this dreary talk. Let's have a cocktail. How about a Manhattan?"

Daisy knew a drink wouldn't mix well with Lyle's medications. He was already on five scripts and she had enough trouble keeping them straight. She had no intention of allowing him a drink.

"But I want a drink," Lyle insisted. "And frankly, I don't give a damn about those medications. I'm going to be on those pills for the rest of my life, however long or short that might be, so I'm going to do what I want. I think you should join me. It'll take the edge off."

That night they drank Manhattans and played old Benny Goodman records. They laughed about the past and even laughed about the future. The alcohol eased Daisy's fears and worries. For the first time since Lyle had been hospitalized, they had fun.

Lyle nibbled on her neck while they danced. She touched him lovingly, remembering the wild passion of former lovers, grateful her current love affair was far more grounded. She closed her eyes as they swayed to "Sentimental Journey." It was divine to be in his arms. The tension in her body eased with each passing note. Her breath deepened. And then he led her down the hallway to the bedroom.

* * *

"Ladies and gentleman," Ernie began, "if I could have your attention."

All of Ernie's staff had gathered in the cafeteria ten minutes ahead of morning break as he'd asked them to.

"I've received some troubling news from management." Ernie held up the memo. "I think it's important to share this information with you. The Mexican government has stepped up its crackdown on the drug cartels. The United States, in response, has issued a travel warning to American tourists. Now we haven't seen any violence in Puerto Vallarta, but we need to be concerned about the impact on our guests. We're in the hospitality industry and it's our job to calm any fears they may have. A smile, a warm greeting can help ease uncertainty. Finally, I'd like you all to know how much I value working with you. Therefore, I'm requesting that when you come and go from the workplace, you travel in groups. These are uncertain times and just because we haven't seen any violence doesn't mean we won't. My primary concern remains your safety."

* * *

The next day, outside the local market, a beggar with jet-black hair in blue jeans and a dirty tee shirt approached Maria. White plastic cup in hand, he blocked her as she shifted first to the right, and then to the left, in an attempt to pass. His determination was unshakeable.

"Get away from me," Maria growled. "I'm not giving you a damn thing. You should be ashamed taking money from a woman."

The young man glared at her but held his ground. A gentle breeze offered the scent of the unbathed stranger. Maria turned her head and waved a hand in front of her nose as if by doing so she could make the man disappear. But he stood, unspeaking, pushing his cup again toward her. She pushed it away.

He'd pressed her and now she was angry.

"How old are you?" she demanded, her irritation piqued. "You look able-bodied. You should get a job."

The man did not answer. He stepped aside, withdrawing from Maria's outrage. A little girl, four or five, dressed in a ragged pink top, dingy yellow shorts, and worn sandals that exposed her filthy feet, had been sitting on the sidewalk near the entrance to the store. She ran up and threw her arms about the man's waist in a protective gesture of love. Her tiny innocent heart-shaped face was smudged with dirt, her hair was as black as soot. She offered a smile to Maria, as if to excuse the boldness of the man to whom she now clung and to make another silent request to fill his cup. Maria looked into the child's dark eyes. She remembered her father. A memory she'd spent a lifetime trying to forget. Maria reached into her purse where she found a few spare coins to drop into the cup.

In the market, flies darted in and out of the produce. She examined the head lettuce. It was brown around the edges. The tomatoes were over-ripe and the avocados too expensive. Finding fresh affordable produce in the city was a fool's mission. Only the Walmart on the outskirts of town offered anything near the shopping experience in America. And even the Walmart was filthy by American standards.

Wandering the narrow aisles of the local store, she saw a prominent display for El Jimador tequila.

The ghosts were gathering and circling.

She stopped and stared at the brown glass bottle, examining the label as if about to make a purchase. Her thoughts drifted to the past.

It had been dusk on an exceptionally hot day when she'd decided to leave Mexico. The sun's departure from the sky had allowed a hint of a cool breeze to pass through the open windows of her rented rooms. It was humid and her clothes clung uncomfortably, sticking to her as she had stuck tenaciously to her marriage. Juan had been drinking all day. He kept a bottle of El Jimador in the house. It had become a nasty habit. They'd been married seven years by then. The first few had been happy, but financial troubles have a way of depleting love. Juan, a day laborer, struggled to find work. The bar became his second home when jobs were in short supply. Maria tired of watching him squander the family's meager resources on booze.

Frustrations mounted. In a drunken haze, Juan's anger turned violent.

"You'll never touch me again," she swore, a kitchen knife in her hand for protection against the man she loved. He'd once promised salvation from the poverty of her youth. But their life together had taken another turn. A darker turn.

"Put that knife down." Juan staggered closer. "You don't have the guts." He was right.

After wrestling the knife away, he beat her. The bruises on her face and body served as potent reminders that she had to get away. She made plans. She gave up her wedding ring.

"This isn't enough," Jorge the mule told her as he examined the gold band with the eye of a disappointed jeweler. "It's not even fourteen carat," he said. He thrust the ring back into the palm of her hand. "I can't help you."

"You have to," she pleaded. "I have nothing else to offer."

Jorge came closer. The stench of his foul breath, a mixture of cigars and burnt coffee, caught in her nostrils. "Well then, this will have to do," he said, slipping his callused hand inside her blouse and cupping her breast.

Maria withdrew, disgusted by the man's familiarity.

"Do you want to cross the border?" Beads of sweat gathered on his forehead as he awaited her answer.

She nodded.

"Well then, you'll do as I say."

A week later, she and her boy, along with ten strangers, hid in the pitch blackness of a delivery truck crammed with fruits and vegetables. The intensity of the Sonoran heat threatened to suffocate the group. Few survived the crossing.

Once in the United States, Jorge had plans for Maria.

"I have arranged a job for you."

Maria straightened her posture. "I don't want anything more to do with you," she said defiantly. "I will get my own job."

In a flash, he flipped her around, holding a knife to her throat. "Do you think I brought you over here out of the kindness of my heart, you stupid girl?" he said, pressing the metal to her skin. "You'll do as I say or I'll kill you right where you stand and drop you into a canal."

She gasped for air.

"Don't test me," he warned.

Maria did what she had to in order to survive. She tricked in an East Valley brothel until one Thursday, on a brutally hot July day, she developed a toothache. She pleaded with Jorge to see a dentist. He reluctantly agreed. "But when you get back, I expect you to do a full day."

That afternoon the brothel was raided. Jorge and the others were rounded up and deported. As Maria turned down Vermont Avenue, she could see the police barricade ahead. Without missing a beat, she made a U-turn, and walked toward freedom.

* * *

Enid wrote the monthly check to Harper Gaines, LLC. Had her pen been a dagger, she'd have happily cut the throats of all the partners of the firm who were now bleeding her dry. She'd been caught in her own machinations, and as she struggled with that reality, she refused to fully accept the truth – that her avarice had brought this trouble upon herself.

Enid closed the checkbook. She was in a take-no-prisoners mood.

I hate you, Jack, she thought, as if he were responsible for the poor decisions she'd made.

It was easier to blame Jack.

It had always been that way.

At nine years old, living in her family's duplex on Park Avenue in Manhattan she'd once had the finest of everything—beautiful dresses from the seventh floor of Miss Bonwit Jr. at Bonwit Teller, dolls of every shape and size, and a private school education. And still, she hid in her bedroom. Content to be alone. Surrounded by her possessions.

"Enid," her father sternly called. "Come down here."

"Coming, Papa." Enid deliberately dawdled, examining the mysterious eyes of her stuffed teddy bear from FAO Schwartz. Her mother had recently purchased it for her before going into the hospital.

"Enid." Her father stood in the doorway, a dignified man with just the slightest touch of gray at his temples. "Didn't you hear me call for you?"

"I'm sorry, Papa." The little girl rushed to her father's side, taking his hand in hers.

"Were you daydreaming again?" he asked in a disapproving tone as he glanced down at his daughter.

"I guess," the little girl answered, her voice muffled in the fabric of his blue serge suit as she pressed her face into the sleeve of his jacket.

"It's time to go to the hospital," he said, pulling her away to examine his coat. "Enid, I wish you wouldn't drool on me. You've stained my suit."

"Papa, I don't want to go," she said, tugging on his hand, wrestling her father's attention away from his jacket.

"But your mother wants to see you."

"Please, Papa, not today. It's Saturday. I want to stay in my room and play. We've seen Momma every night this week."

Enid's eyes pleaded for a reprieve.

Her father softened. "You know you'll be here alone. Both the cook and maid have the July 4th holiday weekend off."

"I know, Papa."

He knelt down before her, pulling her into his arms. "Okay, my darling. Today will be your day. You get to stay home."

"Oh Papa, thank you," Enid murmured.

"But make sure you don't open the front door while I'm gone."

"I won't," Enid said, pleased and happy with her power to get what she wanted.

"I'll be back later then."

"Send my love to Momma," Enid said, locking the door behind her father.

It was nice to finally be alone. Instead of retreating to her bedroom, Enid wandered the empty rooms of the apartment, enjoying the sudden freedom to be anywhere and everywhere. Entering the study, she climbed into her father's favorite wingback chair. She looked about, imagining the world from her father's vantage point. The deep red mahogany paneling shimmered in the morning sun. Leatherbound medical texts lined the wall and mixed with the great works of Shakespeare, Chaucer, and Dickens. Enid was proud to be the daughter of such an important man. One of the leading physicians in New York City, he sat on two hospitals boards and served as the departmental chair for Obstetrics & Gynecology at Roosevelt Hospital. He even had an office in Harlem where he provided free care to the needy. His credentials were most impressive.

Enid was fast asleep in the study when her father returned home four hours later. She awoke groggily to find him kneeling before the wingback chair.

"Enid," he said as he gently touched the child's knee. Her father watched as she rubbed her eyes. "I've some news."

The little girl sat up and gave him her full attention.

"Your little brother's in heaven."

Enid's heart stopped. She knew all about heaven. When someone went to heaven, they were never seen again. That's what had happened to her pet hamster, Mr. Jeepers.

"And because Momma loved him so much . . ." He looked down, averting his eyes from his daughter's ". . . she didn't want him to be alone. So . . ." Her father's voice got very soft. "Momma has gone to heaven too."

"But she loved me," Enid cried. "She loved me."

"Now, we're going to have to be very brave," her father said. "It's going to be just you and me."

But Enid couldn't stop crying. "I should have gone to the hospital. I should have been there. If Momma had seen me, she'd never have left. Never," Enid sobbed.

Her father stood. "Enid, stop it," he said, his voice weary. "You need to be a big girl now."

"If she loved me, she would have stayed. Why didn't she love me?" Enid cried.

"Enid, I can't cope with this today," her father said rubbing his brow. "Now I've tried my best to explain the disastrous events of the day. I can't bear this outburst."

"Why didn't she love me?" Enid again asked, increasingly confused, overwhelmed by the devastating loss.

"Because you're a spoiled and selfish little girl," her father blurted out as he withdrew, leaving his daughter distraught.

That night Enid ripped the eyes off her teddy bear. "It's your fault I wasn't with Momma," she said as the black marbles rolled across the floor. "You're the one to blame."

* * *

Jack had just woken up and stumbled into the kitchen for a cup of coffee when he ran into Enid on her way out. "I'll meet you tonight at 6:00 p.m. for dinner at Durant's," Enid said. "I left a note on the counter." Jack nodded, grateful for her impending absence.

Peter Gaines of Harper Gaines, LLC, called midmorning.

"Jack, any chance I can speak to Enid?"

"She's at the hairdresser's," Jack answered. "Anything I can do to help?"

"I want to get a copies of the account statements for the money Enid is holding for Ms. Lee. I need the statement with the opening balance as well as any follow-up statements, documenting all of the transactions through the last bill paid."

"Gee." Jack was caught off guard. "Enid handles all that paperwork. I'm not sure I'd even know where to look."

"She told me it was in a Wells Fargo checking account."

Jack scratched his head. "Are you sure? That isn't where we bank. We're Bank of America folks."

"Okay, well then, maybe I made a mistake. Either way, I need to see those statements. Can you drop them off at my office later today?"

"Sure. I'll get them. No problem," he said, wondering where he should look first.

In the top drawer of Enid's desk, Jack found the Bank of America checkbook. The checks displayed both Jack and Enid's names and their home address. Just beneath that checkbook was another from Wells Fargo. The register revealed the account had been opened with a balance of close to five hundred thousand dollars. Jack assumed that represented the proceeds from the sale of Daisy's home and other belongings. And then he noticed that only Enid's name appeared on the checks. Jack scanned the details of the Wells Fargo register. The log documented checks written to physicians, the hospital, and The Village, along with payments to Macy's, Nordstrom's and other in-store credit cards that Jack did not have in his wallet, including an American Express that ran about five hundred dollars a month.

This can't be right, he thought flipping through the register. *She said she was only paying Daisy's bills.*

Like a man waking from a long, deep sleep, Jack became acutely aware of his wife's outrageous lie. He couldn't believe Enid could be so duplicitous.

I must have been deaf, dumb, and blind not to see her true nature.

His stomach twisted in to a knot. Enid as *the bad wife* was a new concept. It lent sudden credence to his cheating with Bonnie, but mostly, it allowed Jack to truly sidestep any responsibility for the damage done to his aunt.

Suddenly all the pieces of the puzzle that was Enid, fell into place.

It was good to have a scapegoat.

* * *

Jack arrived late. The hostess directed him to the rear of the restaurant. His eyes slowly adjusted to the subdued lighting. *Dark restaurants,* he thought. *Enid's all about dark restaurants.*

"You're lucky I'm still here," Enid said as Jack approached. "I've been waiting twenty minutes."

Jack slid into the crescent booth upholstered in dark brown leather. Enid sat in the middle, looking out onto the restaurant. "Hello to you too," he answered, eyeing the half-empty martini glass in her hand. "When did you start drinking?"

"What time is it?"

"I'd say it's time for you to slow down," Jack answered, knowing that Enid wasn't much of a drinker. A glass of red wine was her limit before she became silly.

In defiance Enid finished what remained in her glass in one fast gulp.

The waiter approached. "Can I get you a drink, sir?"

"I'll have the same as the lady."

"Make that two," Enid added.

Jack sat back and crossed his arms. "Whoa. We're on a bit of a toot." He examined her face, wondering what this was all about. "So how was your day?" he asked innocently enough.

"I had my hair colored and my nails done." She waved a manicured hand. "And I did a little shopping. Nordstrom's had a sale." She touched a corner of the dinner napkin to her mouth to catch a bit of spittle that had escaped.

"Nordstrom's," Jack said. "Pretty fancy shopping. What was the damage?"

She dismissively rolled her eyes. "I just picked up some shoes and perfume."

"Tell me how we can afford that with all of our legal expenses?" He leaned forward, head cocked to one side. "Isn't that a bit rich?"

The waiter placed two vodka martinis on the table.

Enid lifted the drink to her lips. "I've always managed our money," she said somewhat defiantly. "I certainly don't need advice from you."

"I see." Jack glared at her, thinking he deserved her contempt. For it was true. He had always acquiesced to her.

Enid smirked. "Better drink up. You don't want to fall behind."

Jack sipped his drink and watched as Enid downed her second martini. He was seeing her with fresh eyes.

"I've been thinking," he started nonchalantly, hoping to startle her, "maybe we should return all the money you embezzled from Daisy and then we can settle this whole legal matter."

Enid took a breath. "Embezzled?" she said, her eyes the size of saucers. "Where did you come up with that?"

Jack was awed at her pretense of innocence. The way she projected a bold confidence in the face of her deceit.

Jack rang a finger over the top of his glass. "I'm on to you," he said, fixing his eyes on the woman who'd ruled his life for so many years. "I know about the private checking account with Wells Fargo."

"You don't know a thing," she said indignantly. And even though she needed to slide around to the end of the booth to exit, she suddenly started to rise from the center of the table seemingly intent on leaving. Jack grabbed her by the arm and pulled her back down. The liquor made it easier to manage her.

"I know it all," he said as he downed his drink, one hand on her arm, keeping her firmly in place. He wondered if she'd ever own up to the truth. "So why did you do it?"

Enid wrestled her arm away. In the tumult, she'd slipped backward, and being a small woman, partially disappeared into the booth, landing on her side, struggling to get back up into a vertical position. Once righted, she adjusted her blouse. "Why did I ever marry a man with no money? I should have known better," she said, the liquor releasing her inhibitions. "I was a fool."

Jack felt the sting of the accusation. It was as if she'd slapped him across the face. He'd grown tired of her complaining about money. Tired of being a failure in her eyes.

"Enid, I did my best to support you. Why wasn't that ever enough?"

Enid's voice dripped with venom. "Maybe that was okay for Betsy. She was a woman of such simple taste. Sweet *Betsy.*"

Jack's temper flared. "I'm sick of your nasty comments about Betsy. Have you looked at yourself in the mirror? You're mean, Enid. Mean to the bone."

Heads in the restaurant turned as Jack and Enid's voices escalated.

"This lawsuit is your doing," Jack snarled. "I have that checkbook. So get this through your thick skull. You're not keeping one penny. If we have to repay every last dime you've spent, we'll do it. That woman's money is going to be turned over to her. Your high-flying lifestyle ends now. And if you don't like it . . . *I suggest you go get a job.*"

Jack pushed hard against the table as he slipped out of the booth. Glasses rattled.

"Up yours," Enid screamed.

Jack stopped and turned to make direct eye contact. "You can drop dead for all I care," he said loud enough for everyone in the room to hear before walking out.

*　*　*

Bonnie had wanted to try something different. "Let's go to Durant's," she'd suggested. "They have one of those three-course dinner specials. The change should be fun."

And so the three friends found themselves in a booth sipping cocktails.

"Great table," Dave pointed out. "Nice and quiet."

Bonnie nodded in agreement. "I love this place. It's so classy. These highbacked booths make it so cozy and private. It's like being in your own cocoon."

"Very *Mad Men*," Charlie agreed, swirling the maraschino cherry in his Manhattan. "You can almost imagine Donald Draper coming in here."

"I love him," Bonnie admitted, "except for all that smoking. I could never be with a man who smoked." She sipped her Lemon Drop martini.

"He's handsome," Charlie said. "But he's not my type."

"Right," Dave added, a classic vodka martini before him. "He's straight."

"That's not it," Charlie argued. "I didn't like how Don Draper reacted when that closeted art director was fired because he refused to have sex with the client."

"Do you think that stuff really happened back then?" Bonnie asked.

"Plenty of people lost their jobs out of ignorance and fear," Dave answered. "Gays and lesbians who worked for the government during the McCarthy era. And how many teachers found themselves out of work because they were deemed unfit?"

"Not just teachers," Dave added. "Gay people were pariahs, frightened into the shadows. Even in America today, you can still be fired for being gay. There's no job protection."

Bonnie had really never thought about it. "What a terrible way to live," she said, for the first time considering what it might be like to have to hide in the world. "No one should have to keep their true nature, or who they love, a secret." As the words left her mouth, she realized they applied to her own relationship.

"I agree. Just imagine living your life hiding, pretending you're some- one you're not. We both did it," Dave said, "before we came out. And even then, our families were difficult. Charlie, do you remember the time . . ." But before Dave could finish his sentence a commotion broke out nearby. Dave stopped talking.

"Oh my God," Bonnie said, straining her neck to look behind her. "What's going on? Is someone having a fight?" She thought she heard a familiar voice.

"That would be two very loud someones," Charlie corrected, strug- gling to see over the top of the booth.

"Get down." Dave tugged on Charlie's arm. "Stay out of it. It sounds nasty."

Slightly off balance, Charlie plopped back down.

The three friends listened intently to the heated exchange, smirking as if they had scored front row seats to a performance of *Les Misérables*.

Bonnie whispered. "Oh my God . . . she's shrieking."

"No shit," Charlie added.

"This is terrible," Dave complained. "They're ruining everyone's eve- ning. If people are going to fight, they should have the common courtesy to stay home."

"Shush," Charlie said. "I think I just heard a glass break."

"Don't exaggerate," Dave said as a man stormed past the table.

Charlie caught sight of the man's face as he passed.

Bonnie had only seen the back of his head, but his distinctive gait was familiar. She practically leapt out of the booth. "Oh my God," she said.

"What is it?" Dave asked.

"What is it?" Charlie echoed.

"That man. . . ." Bonnie stuttered.

"Jack Lee?" Charlie asked, sipping his Manhattan. "Do you know him?"

"He's the guy—the guy I've been seeing."

Charlie coughed hard, his drink going down the wrong pipe.

Dave patted him on the back. "Take it easy," he said as Charlie regained his composure.

"You're seeing Jack Lee?" Charlie asked in disbelief. "The guy who sold us Daisy's house?"

"He's a realtor?" Bonnie said in shock.

"No. He's Daisy's nightmare of a nephew," Charlie explained.

"Oh my God. How could I have not connected the two?"

"Maybe you weren't exactly discussing family lineage at the time," Charlie said, giving Bonnie a sideways glance. "*And they say men think with their dicks.*"

"And he's married," Dave confirmed.

Bonnie blushed.

"But then, you already knew that, didn't you? Well, we'd better have another cocktail," Dave said, calling the waiter over.

"I knew he was married," Bonnie admitted, her voice trembling.

"Well," Dave said, "look on the bright side. He probably won't be for long."

Charlie shot Dave a dirty look.

"And we certainly don't need to meet him," Dave added. "We already know him."

"We know him alright," Charlie agreed, "the miserable skunk."

* * *

It was an amazing desert sunset, the sky scorched a pinkish-orange, as Henry and Paul swam laps in tandem. They'd snuck into the Biltmore resort with little trouble and had gone directly to a pool hidden toward the rear of the property.

It was midweek and the resort was quiet.

Henry was the first out of the water. Dripping wet, he felt chilly even in the warmth of early evening. Paul looked on, clinging to the side of the pool. "I can see those goose bumps from here," he laughed. "How can you be so cold? It must still be ninety degrees out."

Henry dropped into a lounge chair as the moisture on his body slowly evaporated in the warm night air, the sensation, like the gentle beating of butterfly wings upon his damp skin. Paul swam two more laps, stopping just below the ledge by Henry's lounger. With a great whoosh,

Paul lifted himself up and out of the water, hands planted firmly on the ledge, shoulders flexed forward, chest concave, water splattering from his impressive form, deluging the flagstone as he gracefully twisted about to sit squarely on the pool's edge. Henry stared at the musculature of Paul's back, memorizing every nook and valley, wanting to reach out and touch the deep crevice that bisected his torso.

Oblivious to Henry's thoughts, Paul turned and winked, as if to tele-graph his pleasure that they were together sharing the secluded setting. Henry, shy and self-conscious, shifted his gaze to a terrace above and beyond Paul's head, off in the distant background. The terrace was safe territory. No one could get turned on looking at a piece of cement jutting out from a Frank Lloyd Wright-inspired building.

"You're right. It's cold with that light breeze," Paul acknowledged. "Hey, what are you looking at?" He turned about, the light of dusk disappearing as darkness fell. "I don't see anyone up there."

Henry stretched out on the lounger. Music drifted from the hotel. Burt Bacharach. "The Girl from Ipanema." Henry admired the bright, flicker-ing stars, painted upon the dark Sonoran sky.

Paul rose and took a folded white towel from a nearby lounge chair and dried himself. Henry's body twitched as Paul ran the towel up and down his legs, over his abdomen, and then across his back, shaking it from side-to-side. Henry yearned to wrap himself tightly in the towel, pull Paul close and kiss him. He wanted to lie, legs entwined, hands exploring each other, making love for the first time. Instead, Henry tilted his head back, took a deep breath, and tried to ignore the man who had become his obsession.

Paul laid down on the adjacent lounge chair. "Is everything okay?" he asked.

"Fine," Henry answered, his heart trembling.

Paul closed his eyes.

Henry turned to admire Paul's chiseled face in the moonlight. The familiar warmth was building—an overwhelming desire to be close; to touch; to taste; to be a part of this man. The growing want between his legs. Desperate. Needy. He struggled with the urge, but so near to Paul, all he could think about was sex. How his lips might feel on Paul's neck. How perfectly Paul would fit between Henry's legs as he straddled his chest.

"Whoa," Paul said, opening his eyes and spotting Henry's building girth. "It looks like someone needs a release."

Henry's baggy bathing suit failed to hide his erection.

"We're alone," Paul teased. "Pull it out and have a go at it. Hey, I think I just might join you."

Henry's heart stopped. "You wouldn't mind?"

"Why should I mind?" Paul asked, looking around to see if anyone was coming. "We're men. Sometimes we need to do what we need to do."

12

....

After the big blow-up with Enid at the restaurant, Jack moved into the second bedroom.

They occupied the same house, but essentially lived as roommates. In the mornings, Jack enjoyed his paper by the pool. In the afternoons, he went to the gym, swam, and returned home for a nap. And though he'd tried to reach Bonnie, he'd been unable to, leaving message after message, confused by her sudden absence. He spent a great deal of time alone, walking the golf course, going to the movies, aware of the many couples that appeared everywhere.

Then, three nights in a row, Jack dreamt about Anna's little bungalow on 19th Avenue.

The first two nights, he awoke with vague recollections of his encounter with the psychic—impressions he couldn't quite put together: his urgent desire to turn in upon seeing Anna's red neon sign, the bright yellow of the room where he'd had his reading, the deep purple headscarf Anna had worn at the session. But on the third night, he remembered Anna had offered a message. *Perhaps that message was important*, Jack thought, momentarily suspending all disbelief as he struggled to recall what Anna had said. But it was no use. Whatever it was, he'd long ago forgotten. *How ridiculous*, Jack thought, annoyed at his faulty memory. *Psychics can't really communicate with the dead. That's all mumbo jumbo made up to feed on the weak.*

And yet Jack's desire to obtain another reading became unshakeable.

Swimming laps in the LA Fitness pool, he suddenly conjured Anna's face. The luminescent dark brown eyes seemed to look right through him. The wry smile held a great secret, worth his time and money. Distracted, Jack turned at just the last moment before striking his head against the pool wall. Startled by the near miss, he hung on the edge, breathing hard, wiping the water from his eyes. *What the heck*, he thought, gasping for air.

In the locker room, out of his wet bathing suit, a towel wrapped about his waist, he took a seat in front of his locker. *That's it*, he thought, unnerved by the experience. *I'm going to have to go back and see that woman.*

* * *

Anna was in the rock garden behind her house, assuming the pose for her morning meditation. Legs crossed, back straight, she breathed slowly in and out. The purity of her breath eased the tension in her muscles. She imagined herself walking on a beach. The waves breaking on the shore, sea gulls calling overhead, a gentle breeze upon her face. She continued to relax, going ever deeper into her ritual as a female energy made its presence known. Anna tried to ignore the interruption, but the entity persisted. Distracted, she acquiesced, slowly coming out of her reverie, gently returning to her rock garden, keenly aware that the entity offered a message for a man who'd be visiting. A man whom Anna had read before.

Anna took three deep breaths.

She now had clarity about the troubled soul . . . the man who'd walked in off the street and stormed out following his initial reading. She remembered his angry glare and how he'd mocked her gift. Worse, he'd stiffed her. Why the entity brought this man to mind, she had no idea. *All things to be revealed in time*, she thought, having complete faith in spirit to guide her.

Later that morning, her doorbell rang. She peered out at him from a side panel of glass. *Ah, there you are*, she thought, spotting the man with the miserable scowl. *Just as expected.*

"May I come in?" the man asked as he stood on her front steps. "I'd really like to talk with you."

Anna hesitated. He wasn't dangerous, that she could sense. But he had acted rather like a bully at their first meeting. "You need to give me your word that you'll be on your best behavior. No more outbursts," she shouted through the door.

"So you remember me," the man sheepishly acknowledged.

"Oh . . . I remember you," she confirmed. "Now, I need your word."

"Why yes," the man agreed, turning red. "Of course."

Anna opened the door and directed the stranger inside.

"That'll be fifty dollars," she said, seated across the table, hands folded, unwilling to proceed until her fee was paid upfront.

"Fifty?" He pulled out his wallet. "The last time it was thirty-five." He counted the bills and placed them on the table.

"Great," Anna said as she took the cash. "That covers the first session. Fifteen dollars for the late fee. Now you can give me another thirty-five for today."

The man's eyes bulged. "What? Are you kidding? I don't have that kind of cash on me."

"I take credit cards," she said firmly, daring him to object.

He tossed a Discover card on the table.

She picked up the card and read the name. "Jack Lee," she said aloud. "Well Mr. Lee, I only take Visa or MasterCard." She tossed the card back at him.

He searched his wallet.

"I sense your hostility," Anna said, quite matter-of-factly. "It really doesn't help."

"But eighty-five dollars does?" Jack snapped as he handed Anna a MasterCard.

Anna ignored the remark, swiping the card through her credit card processor. As she stared him down, her intuitive powers kicked in. She gasped, in surprised elation, at the glorious bright-orange incandescence of his soul. She was instantly reminded that all God's children are divine spirits comprised of bits of God energy.

"Are you okay?" he asked as the little machine printed out the slip to be signed.

Anna stared at him, covering her mouth with her hand, overwhelmed by a sudden joy. "Just fine," she said with reverence. "Would you like a receipt?" The sweetness in her voice was disproportionate to the transaction.

"No, that's not necessary," Jack answered, seemingly flustered, looking at her oddly. "Well I suppose we should get on with this," he said, checking his watch, "You might rip off other people with your hocus pocus, but not Jack Lee. I'm timing you."

* * *

Anna took three deep breaths. The energy about her was strong. A dominant female was nearby, pressing to come through. Anna relaxed, signaling that the entity could come nearer. Two more deep breaths and the words appeared magically in her consciousness. The tone, a sharp, staccato. The thoughts, hurried and fast.

"The woman you called mother, is here," Anna finally said.

Jack sat directly across from her. He straightened before leaning slightly forward.

"She wants your forgiveness."

Jack exhaled. His eyebrows arched. "Forgiveness for what?"

Anna understood it was a test. Jack wanted to be sure that what she sensed wasn't smoke and mirrors. Hooey cooked up by a scam artist. Anna waited for the answers. All she needed to do was be open to the messages.

"She says she didn't treat you well. She broke your self-confidence. She spoke to you in such a way that made you question yourself. You felt small and insignificant. Stupid."

Jack's breath caught in his throat just as he was about to speak. He tried again. "What else does she say?"

Anna thought carefully before she shared the next message. It seemed harsh. She waited to see if it might be repeated. And it was.

"She should have loved you. She apologizes for that. But she lacked the capacity. She now knows how awful she was. How she failed you."

Jack took a breath.

"And she wants you to know that it was her fault . . . not yours."

Jack appeared speechless. The color left his face.

"But there is still hope for you. Hope that you will find the love you need. It is near to you now."

"Bonnie?" Jack said. "Does she mean Bonnie?" Jack was jubilant. His face lit up brighter than Anna's neon sign. "I knew it!" He raised a fist in the air. "I just knew Bonnie was the one."

Anna blinked as the spirit pulled back. She'd not heard the name Bonnie. She'd sensed the message was about an older woman. A mother figure perhaps. But Jack appeared elated. And so Anna decided to let it go. No sense rocking the boat when there was a happy customer to be had.

* * *

"Your mother's been in an accident," was all Pablo the doorman had said when Ernie took the call. Ernie had just completed the final inspection on the air conditioning system at Cabo Los Gatos, the newest restaurant at the Villa Allegra Resort. The project had been completed on deadline, but the momentary pleasure of a job well-done was lost forever as Ernie frantically raced to the front of the resort to grab a cab.

Within two blocks of the apartment house, traffic came to a complete stop.

"Damn," Ernie shouted at the driver, "what's going on up there?"

"I don't know," the man said. "It's not usually this busy."

Ernie tossed one hundred pesos on the front seat and jumped out. He rushed past the crowd of tourists that had gathered. The entrance to his building was cordoned off with yellow tape.

"No one allowed past this point," a burly policeman ordered, his hand in the air.

Ernie rushed forward. "I have to get through," he shouted, lifting the yellow tape to slip underneath.

"No one is allowed beyond this point," the policeman repeated.

But Ernie ignored the warning, attempting to rush the officer. The policeman delivered a hard jab with his elbow to Ernie's midsection, knocking him off his feet. Grabbing his gut, Ernie slowly got up. "But I'm the son," he yelled, surprised at the raw emotion in his voice. "She's my mother."

The scuffle attracted the attention of Pablo who was talking to a detective nearby. He recognized Ernie. Within moments, Ernie was on the other side of the tape, slightly bent from the impact to his stomach, sweat rolling down his forehead.

"Sanchez," the detective said, hand out, formally, introducing himself. A thick, barrel-chested man, he stood before Ernie with the presence of a linebacker, strong, solid, and determined. "I'm in charge of this investigation. Do you have any idea why she jumped?" he asked.

"Jumped?" Ernie repeated, unable to believe his ears. "Are you sure it's my mother and not someone else?"

"Jesus. Didn't anyone tell you? She jumped. A neighbor caught sight of her as she went over."

Ernie shook his head in disbelief. "I don't believe it. It's not possible. It's just not possible."

"There can be no other explanation," Sanchez said callously.

Ernie couldn't imagine Maria dead, much less that she'd taken her own life.

"You'll need to go to the morgue and identify the body. Think you can do that?"

Ernie blinked.

"Good enough," Sanchez said, turning away. "We'll be in touch," he called out as he walked toward a group of reporters.

* * *

The poolside encounter with Paul had been innocent enough, but soon, the two were regularly jerking off together. Paul arranged the time and secured the adult videos. They met at Paul's apartment. It was always planned and always secretive. And while Henry fantasized about touching Paul, Paul maintained a strict physical distance. They might be in the same room, doing the same thing, but Paul's eyes remained glued on the video.

Henry continued to hang out with Paul's group on Sunday which included Paul's girlfriend Susan, a social worker with Maricopa County.

"Henry," she called out perched atop Paul's lap, "Admit it. You have a little crush on me, don't you?" She giggled, her long shapely legs kicking back and forth in a pair of tight Daisy Dukes that offered but a hint of her womanly charms. A pink halter top emphasized her slim waist and delicate breasts. Her skin, tan and glowing, offset her green eyes and blond hair.

Henry thought her the prototype of feminine beauty.

"He can't help himself," Paul agreed, all smiles, stroking her hair.

"He's always staring," the blonde laughed, rubbing her forehead against Paul's, her hand resting on his bicep. She turned to wink at Henry. "It's a good thing he's your friend," she said admiring Henry and teasing Paul.

"He's just a kid," Paul pointed out to her, seemingly shocked. "Cradle robber."

Susan laughed. "Well, it's hard to remember he's so much younger. He looks the same age as your other friends."

"But he isn't," Paul said affirmatively.

She gave Paul a gentle kiss on the lips. "You're such a good guy taking a kid like Henry under your wing. Not many men would do that. I really like him," she said, looking over at Henry and eyeing him seductively.

"Me too," answered Paul, giving Henry a big thumbs up.

At night, Henry tossed and turned, fantasizing about being with Paul. Spending the nights in Paul's arms, safe, secure, and cared for. And though he recognized the limitations of their friendship, the desire in Henry remained.

* * *

"So tell me about school," Anna asked at breakfast as she wrapped a tuna fish sandwich in tin foil. "You've been so quiet lately. Shut up in your room. Is everything okay?"

"Nothing to tell. Just studying," Henry replied, checking out the back of the Rice Krispies box as he ate his cereal. He had no intention of answering Anna's question. Instead, he searched for a distraction. Anything to refocus the conversation. "Wow! I didn't know Snap, Crackle, and Pop were the names of the cereal elves."

He sounded every bit his age . . . innocent and full of wonder.

Anna laughed at the observation. "I thought everyone knew that."

Cereal gone, Henry brought the bowl to his lips to gulp down what remained of the milk.

"Henry, use your spoon," Anna said sharply.

"Sorry." Henry blushed at Anna's reaction to his poor table manners.

Anna washed off an apple. "I'm concerned Henry. Last night when I came in from my Weight Watcher's meeting, I tried to talk with you, but you were so distracted. Henry, we should be able to talk about anything. After all, that's what friends do and we're friends. Aren't we?"

Henry leapt up from his seat. He desperately wanted to get away. "Sure, Anna. We're friends."

He hoped if he agreed with her, she'd drop the subject.

Anna's expression turned serious. "Is it drugs Henry? Are you doing drugs? Are you hooked on something? Do we need to get you into rehab? Tell me the truth." Her expression set. Her glare fixed.

Surprised at the absurdity of her deduction, Henry laughed. "Really?" he said, a big grin on his face. "Is that what you're thinking?"

"I'm worried. And as long as you're living in my house, I need to know what's going on. I'm responsible for you. We should be talking more."

Henry kissed her on the cheek. "I can't now. I've got class in thirty minutes. Maybe later. I have to run." He grabbed his bookbag, forgetting the lunch Anna had prepared, and rushed out the door.

* * *

Anna was convinced something was up.

Hoping to summon help from her angels, she took a seat at the kitchen table and closed her eyes. Secure within her home, she was suddenly in a terrifying free-fall from a great height. She pressed her palms firmly on the table to stabilize herself, re-establishing her brain's connection with reality. After a few minutes, the horrible dizziness stopped. She secured her balance.

That had nothing to do with Henry, she thought, shaken to the core as she opened her eyes and her stomach settled. *What in heaven's name was that?*

* * *

Daisy stood at the kitchen sink, washing the last of the lunch dishes, looking out the window onto the courtyard, as Lyle sat nearby at the kitchen table reading the newspaper. A lush ficus, thick with greenery, provided shade for a family of grey doves gathered about the base. The chicks, not yet three inches tall, hopped about as the mature birds nestled in the summer grass.

Daisy counted four babies.

As she twisted the sponge around a water glass, her left thumb ached. The stiffness, a bit of arthritis, had crept up on her. With the last glass washed and rinsed, she let the warm water run and gently massaged her thumb. In a moment the ache subsided. *The secret to a happy life she mused . . . a little warmth to ease your pain.*

It was good being with Lyle.

She'd passed the harried days of his recovery acclimating to the rituals established as two people cohabitate. They'd come to an understanding of the best time to go to bed, when to eat, and most importantly, rules on using a shared bathroom. She preferred to take a long hot tub before bed. He urinated frequently at night, getting up two or three times. Each made way for the other. She made certain the floor by the tub was dry so that he wouldn't accidently slip as he passed by. He plugged in a nightlight by the toilet so that he might improve his aim.

She hadn't forgotten the joys of physical pleasure, but now, such endeavors came slowly, deliberately, and after much consideration, with care and patience. She relished being held, gently drifting off to sleep in the comfort of a man's arms. She enjoyed being wanted, but still found herself jumping in surprise when a hand reached across the bed to touch her. It would take more time to truly surrender to such intimacies.

"Those damn Cardinals will be the death of me," Lyle railed, in the midst of reading the *Arizona Republic.*

Startled, Daisy rushed from the sink to shut the sliding glass door to the patio. "They're just doves. It's silly to get so upset over birds."

Lyle looked up in astonishment. "I'm talking about the Arizona Cardinals, the football team."

"Oh." Daisy managed a smile as she dried her hands with a red dish towel.

Lyle chuckled. "How can you live in Arizona and know nothing about the Cardinals?"

"Do you know the difference between Dior and Chanel?" she quizzed him.

Lyle scratched his large bald head. He had no clue.

"See, there are just some things you know and I don't, and vice versa."

"I suppose," Lyle agreed, letting out a yawn.

"How about a nap?" Daisy suggested.

She'd taken to studying Lyle's every move. Becoming accustomed to his highs and lows. Understanding when his energy waned. She'd memorized the way the left side of his mouth curled upward when he smiled, the timbre and breath of his laugh, even the bright twinkle in his green eyes when he thought something was particularly amusing.

If her watchful gaze alone could keep him strong and healthy, he'd live another twenty years.

"Oh, I'm not tired," Lyle protested, despite clear evidence to the contrary. "I hate taking naps. Plenty of time for resting when I'm dead."

"Well, I'm kind of tired. How about we both go lie down? You can just keep me company."

"I don't know."

"You can hold my hand," she teased, hoping he'd change his mind.

"How about rubbing my back instead?" he asked, shifting about.

"Okay, you got it. A fast back rub and then maybe we'll close our eyes for thirty minutes or so."

Leading Lyle to the bedroom, Daisy noticed his unsteady gait. "Use the wall to help yourself balance," she instructed as he weaved side-to-side.

"I can manage," he answered stubbornly, unwilling to acknowledge any problem.

"I don't understand why you can't use the wall for support."

"I don't need to," he barked. "Now stop it. I'm just fine. Don't make me into an invalid."

"Okay, Superman," Daisy countered, aware that her hovering was having the opposite effect than she'd intended. "I apologize. You're right."

"Gosh, I hate it when you baby me," he complained, lowering himself onto the edge of the bed.

Daisy kneeled to untie his shoes.

"You know," he smirked, "it isn't good for my independence to feel as if I am being cared for by a nurse's aide."

"I know," she agreed. "Now lie down, roll over, and I'll rub your back."

They both giggled at the sternness of her orders as Lyle did as he was told.

Daisy massaged his lower back with gentle light strokes. "There we are. Just relax."

"I'm sorry, Daisy. I didn't mean to be harsh."

She shifted her attention to the back of his neck. She could feel the tightness easing. "No need to apologize."

"You've been so wonderful and I have this sharp temper."

"It's just frustration. It's hard getting old."

"I think I'm well past *getting old*," he joked. "I'm now *sincerely old*."

She smiled. "Well, at the very least, *clearly old*."

He countered. "Mostly *severely old*."

"But not *really merely old*?"

"But always *dearly old*."

"Thank you Wizard of Oz," she laughed. It was good to laugh. "Well, it doesn't matter. We're just lucky to have each other. Thank God for that."

"Daisy," Lyle's voice became serious. "I'm truly grateful you've moved in. You're a wonderful, amazing woman. I hope you know that."

"Thank you," Daisy said as Lyle's voice grew lighter. Within seconds, she heard the gentle snoring of a man who'd released all tension to the universe.

Daisy, you're an amazing woman was music to her ears. She'd waited a lifetime to hear a man say in a gentle, loving manner, that she was, what she had always hoped to be—*an amazing woman.*

* * *

At Culver's for lunch, in a booth crowded with Paul's friends, Henry sat with one shoulder up against Paul, the other crushed against the wall.

When the shakes and burgers finally arrived, Henry was barely able to eat. Overwhelmed by Paul's musk, Henry felt lightheaded, his body on fire. His erection, unwanted and embarrassing, pressed against his zipper, and though he wanted to, he resisted the urge to rearrange his cock, wary of touching himself. His longing, so powerful; he feared melting into a puddle of lust and running off onto the sticky floor.

Thereafter, Henry avoided Paul. He reasoned there was no point in the constant temptation; little pleasure in the carnal torture.

* * *

Without Paul, Henry was lighter, easier to be around . . . less moody. Anna realized her concerns about drugs were unfounded. She breathed a sigh of relief. Though she still didn't know the intimate details of Henry's inner life, she was grateful he appeared to be back on track.

And when she looked in the mirror, it was obvious the impact Henry had had on her life. She'd dropped sixty pounds, changed her hair, and tossed her old wardrobe. Now when people looked at her, they saw a confident woman. There was no need to hide in a costume that kept others at arm's length. The neighborhood kids who once teased her now waved hello. She was no longer the crazy lady.

* * *

Ernie couldn't stop wondering about Maria's last moments. Her state of mind. The terror she must have endured falling six stories to her death. He struggled to remember their last conversation, but drew a blank. He blamed himself for being distracted at work; for being so intent on making a better life that in the end, he'd lost his mother.

Reminders of Maria were everywhere. In the faces of women who worked in housekeeping at the resort—women who lacked a formal education but who had families to support and so they stripped beds, cleaned toilets, and vacuumed rooms. Some were young mothers, others widows; all had obligations beyond themselves. Ernie understood the bonds that existed in Mexican families, the powerful commitment of one generation to another. Maria had been the one constant in Ernie's tumultuous life, a woman who'd shown her son that courage knew no bounds and maternal instinct trumped fear.

With Maria gone, Ernie's appetite waned. Getting out of bed became a challenge. During the day, exhausted, he resisted the urge to nap, opting to drink cup after cup of coffee as he sank into a deep depression. Even breathing seemed like a chore. A terrible effort which required conscious thought.

I just need to get through the day . . . Ernie thought as he spotted Elena, manager of housekeeping, making a beeline toward him. A short, stocky woman, with rich black hair, Ernie thought Elena was excellent at her job. Intermittently he spot checked her paperwork, following behind as she did her daily inspections. Her dark brown eyes didn't miss much.

Chipped floor tiles, dirty walls, windows with broken seals. She had an excellent eye for detail.

"We need to talk," Elena said, pulling him into an empty room. "Have you signed my budget request? You said last week you'd look over the paperwork and approve it. I need to get it over to Human Resources so that I can post the jobs. Now you know it takes time to interview and hire and I'm already running short-staffed. We talked about it last week, and I'm still waiting. And while I'm waiting, we're paying overtime."

Ernie sighed. "It must be on my desk." He rubbed his brow in an effort to clear the fog. He honestly couldn't recall seeing the request. But then his desk was piled with papers and he hadn't been able to sort through it all. His head felt achy and heavy. He opened his eyes wide and closed them tightly in an effort to awaken from his stupor. All he wanted to do was lie down.

"I'm sorry, but I can't wait," Elena insisted, hands on her hips. "Yesterday alone, I personally cleaned fifteen rooms. Now, you are not paying me to clean rooms," she said, her tone sharp, her manner, mocking.

Ernie nodded. "Okay. Okay. I'll take care of it today," he promised, eager to get away from her.

She reached out and touched his arm. "I know this is a difficult time for you," she said tenderly, "But you should know we all care about you. And we need the old Ernie back."

Ernie nodded in a half-hearted attempt to appear connected.

"If you'd like to talk, I'd be glad to listen," she offered. "You're the best thing about working here. Everyone thinks you're terrific. You show people respect, you listen, you're the reason so many of us put in the extra effort."

Ernie smiled faintly. He needed to reserve his energy for an upcoming team meeting later in the day.

"But now you're disappearing. I feel as if . . . ." Elena stopped midsentence, weighing her words. "You don't want to be here anymore. You don't care about the resort or the staff. It doesn't feel good. We're all very aware of it."

Ernie was caught off-guard. It was hard to hear he was undermining his employees.

"I'm sorry," he said. The sadness in his voice barely registered in his quiet response. "Yes, of course. I'll be more mindful of my mood."

"That's all I ask," Elena said as she headed off down the hall. "That, and your approval to post those jobs. Don't forget."

* * *

After the incident in the restaurant, Bonnie abruptly severed her relationship with Jack. She'd known Jack was a married man. That was no surprise. But she hadn't known he was Daisy's nephew, the one responsible for looting Daisy's property. Thereafter, she refused to take his calls which triggered the arrival of flowers to her office. Vases of red roses with cards that read *I miss you . . . What happened? . . . You mean the world to me . . . Please give me another chance.*

She thought a face-to-face meeting might be the kinder way to end the relationship. Lunch, she assumed, was a safe bet. It was time-limited and in a public place. What she hadn't counted on was how she'd feel when she finally saw Jack. How her heart would race when he smiled at her. How her breathing would alter when he came near. How against her better judgment, she'd let him kiss her on the lips before he sat down.

"Thank you for agreeing to see me," Jack said, as he settled into the corner table. "It's been hell not being with you."

Jack talked about the mistakes he'd made in his life. He discussed his marriage, his disappointments, and how things had turned sour. He talked about Bonnie and how often he thought of her and why he hoped they could at least remain friends.

Bonnie found herself unable to eat. She managed a few bites of her BLT, but was grateful when the waiter finally cleared the plate away.

Together they sat. Thirty minutes stretched in to an hour. The surrounding tables turned over as lunchtime customers came and went.

The waiter asked if they were interested in dessert. Bonnie ordered coffee, knowing it was too late in the day for her to be taking in caffeine. But she didn't care. She'd have gladly ordered a second lunch if it meant spending more time with Jack.

As she sipped her coffee, Jack continued to talk. He explained the mess with Daisy. He swore he'd had no knowledge of it. Enid had been completely responsible. And he vowed to make it right.

After two hours, they left the restaurant, she in her Toyota Camry, he in his Audi convertible. They drove directly to the Valley Ho, a landmark hotel in Scottsdale, and checked in.

* * *

Dave adjusted the pace on the elliptical machine from 8 to 9. The sweat poured down his back as he hit the twenty-minute mark. Sinatra was in the midst of "Day In, Day Out." Dave's head bopped in sync with the Nelson Riddle Orchestra as his legs rhythmically kept pace. He was one of Sinatra's back-up dancers in Vegas, hands swinging to the left and then the right. Dave wore a black tuxedo as he moved across the hardwood floor, smiling at the audience. Old Blue Eyes winked in his direction.

And then the elliptical shifted to cool down.

Four times a week for an hour, Dave realized his dreams of musical stardom at LA Fitness. He'd danced with the young Debbie Reynolds on the MGM sound stage of *Singing in the Rain*; been a part of the Mack & Mabel cast album; appeared in Sondheim's *Follies*. Sometimes he was the star, sometimes the up-and-comer. LA Fitness was his escape from life's stresses and disappointments. It was magic. It was fantasy. It was therapeutic. And it motivated Dave to stay the course of his workouts.

Back in the locker room, Dave welcomed an eyeful of young buck. However it was the older men who tended to parade *au natural* with extended bellies, droopy butts, and legs loaded with blue varicose veins. *This is the reality of aging*, Dave thought, catching sight of a man in his seventies as he passed by to weigh himself on the locker room scale. *Beauty comes . . . beauty goes . . . and somehow . . . we manage.*

And though Dave admired the golden oldies who came to the gym in defiance of nature, he nonetheless wished they'd cover up. Aging was difficult enough without having to see upcoming previews.

* * *

At six-foot-two, dark, swarthy, and handsome, Curt Dawson was originally from Omaha. He moved to New York City at sixteen to model, but instead, became the lover of a famous New York City fashion designer. The relationship lasted less than two years. When things didn't pan out in

New York, he applied and got into Arizona State University. He completed two semesters before dropping out.

Over the years his body had transformed from slender to muscular. Now he was thirty-six and his jet-black hair had recently started to grey at the temples, causing Curt to worry about getting older.

Curt had mostly covered his living expenses working as a bartender, putting in the usual late night and weekend hours. But lately he found the going tough. Standing for hours on end was a challenge. And even though he had a second line of work, supplementing his income as an escort through a popular Internet site, at $250 a pop, the money was decent but certainly not enough to live on.

As Curt examined his reflection in the gym mirror he decided he'd need a permanent relationship to shelter him from an uncertain future that was beginning to terrify him. He needed a daddy. A sweet and loving sugar daddy.

* * *

As the economy improved, Charlie's business prospered. America seemed to be turning a corner, not quite out of the recession, but on its way toward recovery. Americans were slowly returning to the shopping malls and Charlie was back in demand as a retail guru. So hectic was Charlie's schedule, that in one week alone he might travel to meet clients in Dallas, Minneapolis, and Los Angeles, before returning home to Phoenix. With each passing week, the cities and itineraries changed. Dave gave up trying to remember where Charlie was at any given moment. When friends called and asked for Charlie's whereabouts, Dave confessed he wasn't really sure. All Dave knew was when Charlie left, and the day of his expected return. The rest of Charlie's travel schedule was a blur.

With Charlie increasingly away, Dave grew closer to Bonnie. The two friends spoke often on the phone, and, on Thursdays, continued to meet for dinner. Seated at Hula's Restaurant, the conversation turned to Jack. Bonnie had mentioned that she and Jack were going away for a weekend to Flagstaff.

Dave sipped his vodka on the rocks. "You know I think you're wonderful," he eased his way into the conversation, "but I'm really uncomfortable hearing about Jack."

Bonnie hardly seemed surprised. "If it's because of Daisy, he's explained that to me. He said it was all Enid's doing. And I believe him," she said emphatically. "He's a sweet man."

The waiter interrupted their conversation, placing before Dave a turkey burger, and Bonnie, the fish of the day.

Dave pondered his next words carefully. "Bonnie, I don't know how you can trust a man who cheats. What good is his word if he is lying to his wife? How can you believe him?"

Dave detested cheaters. And while he was willing to cut Bonnie slack for her part in the fling, he was unwilling to give Jack an inch. The thought of a married man being deceptive made him angry.

"But it's all over between them. The marriage is dead. They don't even sleep together."

Dave pointed out the obvious. "That's what he says."

"Well, I believe him."

Dave reached across the table and squeezed Bonnie's hand. "I just hope you're right. I hope that marriage is over and everything that he says is true. I don't want to see you get hurt. You deserve a man who is able to fully commit. I just don't see Jack as that guy."

Bonnie's face registered disappointment. "I never realized you were so judgmental." She poked at her salmon with her fork.

Silence fell between the two friends.

Over the years, Dave had made exceptions for friends who were cheaters, blaming their behavior on some fault in their current relationship. But in each case, Dave eventually lost respect for the person and the friendship inevitably waned. There was no getting around it. Dave believed cheating to be a major character flaw. And when Dave whined about these lost friendships, Charlie often reminded him: *Some friends are here for a season, others, a lifetime. So if you love someone, and want them in your life, you probably need to lighten up, enjoy what they bring to the party, and accept them for who they are.*

Dave rethought his position. "I'm sorry," he offered.

Bonnie wiped her mouth with a napkin. She didn't appear ready to forgive him. "Friends don't judge. Not unless they themselves are perfect." She glared at Dave. "Are you perfect?"

Dave swallowed hard. "I guess no one is perfect," he answered, wondering why he'd deliberately hurt her feelings. "Okay." He reversed course. "Tell me what's been going on. I'm all ears."

* * *

On Tuesday nights, Dave and Bonnie brought in dinner to Lyle and Daisy. Lyle's health scare was now behind them, and for the moment all was peaceful.

Dave enjoyed the company of the two seniors. He loved listening to them discuss their lives, the challenges they'd faced, and their past relationships. There were moments of true pathos when Dave realized that smiles often camouflaged painful memories of loved ones long gone. Dave admired how the two had weathered the storms of life and emerged triumphant. If ever there was a lesson to be learned about adapting, Lyle and Daisy were the two who could teach it.

Before dinner, sitting in the living room, Lyle showed off his collection of old sheet music.

"We both play the piano," Daisy explained.

"Though not very well," added Lyle.

"Yes, but well enough . . ."

"I loved Alice Fay," Lyle admitted, holding up the sheet music from *Alexander's Ragtime Band*. "She was so beautiful. I remember seeing her on stage at the Loew's Grand in New York. What a wonderful girl."

"He had a thing for blondes," Daisy informed Dave and Bonnie.

"She had such a great voice. Sad she isn't remembered today."

"Who is?" Daisy answered. "Think of all the famous people from our day. Estes Kefauver. Adlai Stevenson . . . Steven Boyd, Elke Sommer. Once the journey's over, no matter how famous you are, given time, you're forgotten."

Dave interjected, "Unless you die young and troubled. James Dean and Marilyn Monroe are immortal."

"Oh but what a price to be remembered," Daisy murmured, sadly shaking her head. "Who wants to die before you even know who you are?"

Lyle agreed. "That's a complete waste. Why, it takes a lifetime to know yourself and understand why you're even here."

Dave's ears perked up. "Do you ever really know yourself?" he asked, curious to hear the response.

Lyle gave Dave a serious look. "Well, I'm pretty sure I do. I wasn't certain until I turned eighty. Imagine it taking so many years to figure it out."

"So who are you?" Dave pushed.

Lyle laughed. "Someone who needed a long lifetime to discover the true value of kindness. You see, I'm a slow learner. I needed more time than most to learn to *love thy neighbor*."

"That sounds like religion."

"I've never believed in religion. Those are institutions. I don't think any man has the right to stand between you and the universe as the divine interpreter, though plenty of people seem to value that kind of assistance. It's what's in your heart. You'll know by your reaction to others. How you behave speaks volumes about who you are. Determine if that's the person you want to be, and then, if you don't like what you're feeling, make a change. Every day we get to choose who we want to be. When you find the response that feels best, you've found your true self."

"It's an innate knowing," Daisy added, "of right and wrong and having the courage, no matter what others do and say, to be who you are. That isn't always easy. What sometimes plays in our culture as *right*, isn't necessarily so. We've had a lifetime to learn that lesson."

Lyle agreed. "When you're young, you take it all in . . . the things society tells you, messages from your family, and you follow along, without much thought. There are plenty of adults our age who live their lives according to the expectations of their youth. But to have a good life, you need to understand what's right for you. You need to be selfish. You need to be a critical thinker. For instance, if Daisy and I had followed the dictates of our youth, we wouldn't be living together," Lyle said. "We'd be married."

"Dear Lord!" Daisy raised her hands in the air evoking a laugh from Bonnie and Dave.

"Thanks a lot," Lyle snapped back.

"But what about the legal protections that marriage offers?" Dave asked. "All the thousands of benefits that Charlie and I don't have that come with a legitimate marriage."

"You're still young," Lyle conceded. "For Daisy and me, that's all super-fluous. We have no illusions that we have a long-term future." Lyle reached over and placed his hand on Daisy's. "A few more months would be nice."

"You two will have many years together," Bonnie insisted.

"No." Lyle threw Daisy a wink. "I think not. But whatever time we do have, it will be grand."

Daisy became teary. "Now how did we get on this topic? We started off on Alice Faye and now we're at the cemetery."

Lyle placed his arm around her shoulder and pulled her close. "I guess that's what happens when you hang out with an old man," he said, letting out a guffaw. "The scenery can change mighty quickly."

* * *

In bed that night, Daisy sat up reading the newspaper while Lyle laid on his side, eyes closed, quietly resting, waiting for Daisy to turn off the reading light.

It was their habit to go to bed by nine o'clock, though Daisy tended to read till ten. He didn't mind her reading a book, which she often did, but the newspaper seemed too much. And though he might fall asleep with her reading light on, he knew, with the paper folding this way and that, he'd never drop off.

"Anything good in there," he asked impatiently, annoyed by the crin-kling of the pages as she flipped through the paper, the sound, finger nails on a chalkboard, driving him crazy.

"Just the usual," she answered. "Mayhem, violence, destruction. Your typical day."

"Oh good," he said, adjusting his head on the pillow. "I wouldn't want to think we'd missed anything really important."

"There's a lot of coverage about gay marriage. There must be five or six articles in the paper about it. Whether the Supreme Court will take up the matter. It'll be interesting to see if that ever becomes a reality in America."

"Why not?" Lyle answered, rolling onto his back. "We have a black president."

"I never thought I'd see that in my lifetime," Daisy agreed.

"Me neither. Thank God we live in a country where anything is possible."

Daisy changed the subject. "What did you think about what Dave said about marriage?"

"You mean about the benefits?" Lyle asked, sitting up and sliding backward so that he leaned against the headboard, Daisy at his side.

Her reading glasses slid down her nose as she looked his way. The paper fell into her lap. "Oh now look what I've done. You're wide-awake. I should have turned out the light so you could get your rest."

"Too late. I'm up," he wearily responded. Pointing at the paper spread wide on her lap, "That wrapping paper party you've been holding, did it."

Daisy giggled. "Sorry." She lifted the paper, dropping it to the floor by her side.

"So what's this about marriage?" he asked, eyes focused upon her.

"I don't know," she started, removing her reading glasses and depositing them on the bedside table. "If it's good enough for the young people, why not us? What makes us so different?"

"Well, for one," he pointed out, "we're not having children."

"Neither are Dave and Charlie," she quickly added.

"True," he said. "But have we really committed to a life together?"

"Haven't we?" she asked, looking about. "Are you planning on dating anyone else? Please let me know now," she said lightheartedly, "before I wind up with an STD."

He grinned. "A *salty turkey dinner*?"

She rolled her eyes as she did whenever his jokes landed flat.

"Is marriage really that important to you?" he asked, somberly, approaching the subject from another angle. "What if something happens and I wind up in a nursing home? It happened before. It can happen again. And what if I'm unable to come home again? Would you really want to be responsible for me? Isn't that asking too much?"

She scrunched up her face. "How's that any different from now? Do you think I'd just suddenly disappear on you?"

"But you wouldn't be committed financially. Tied down. I wouldn't want you to feel obligated."

"Nonsense," she said.

"So you want to get married?" he asked, concerned that perhaps he was the one who really didn't want to be financially responsible *for her*.

"I wouldn't exactly say that," she answered, tentatively. "I just think it's interesting how quickly we dismiss it."

"Oh," he said, sliding back down into a horizontal position and rolling away from her, "I thought you were serious. How about getting some sleep. It's late."

"Sure," Daisy said, turning off the lights.

But that night, sleep was difficult. Lyle was frequently awakened, disturbed by Daisy's tossing and turning, her inability to settle in. He too felt uneasy, as if something had changed in their relationship. A stressor had been added. A new expectation that he wasn't quite prepared to negotiate.

* * *

Elena's words haunted Ernie. He feared the very job that had kept him sane was now slipping from his grasp. He struggled to concentrate, as if he'd been anesthetized, rendering his mind useless. And when he did sleep, Maria appeared in his dreams, frightened, searching for him. Ernie would awaken in a sweat, certain his mother was alive, just in the next room. Then reality would set in and he once again remembered.

I can't go on much longer like this, he thought. *I have to know what really happened. I have to know!*

His thoughts drifted to Anna, the heavy-set psychic dressed like a pirate, chasing the neighborhood children. He envisioned the crazy scarves wrapped around her head. He saw the red neon sign advertising her services.

He was certain Anna was the right person to help him.

* * *

In Phoenix, Anna became distracted.

During a reading with Mrs. Hartsover, she sensed the intrusion of an energy working to get her attention. She ignored the source. It wasn't uncommon for competing spirits to demand her time. And then, while recommending that Mrs. Hartsover schedule an annual physical so that a doctor might find the cancer Anna sensed was growing in her colon, Anna shrieked. She was once again in a free-fall, struggling to maintain her balance as the room slipped away. Mrs. Hartsover, horrified, rushed to Anna's side, kneeling by her chair. "Is that my Morty?" Mrs. Hartsover demanded to know.

Mrs. Hartsover had been eager to connect with her dead husband. They'd been married some forty years, though the marriage had unofficially ended in their fifth year together with the birth of their only son, Stevie. After that, Mrs. Hartsover directed all her attention to the child, ignoring her husband. As Stevie grew, so did Mrs. Hartsover's intense interest in everything he did. When Stevie turned thirty-seven, Morty died. A year later, Stevie cut off all contact with his mother.

"Is that Morty?" Mrs. Hartsover asked again, her voice filled with wonder. "Did he hurt you?"

Anna was unsure how to respond. Could Morty be the reason for her dizziness? Over the years she'd sensed what it was like to suffer any number of deaths. Had Morty fallen off the roof? Out a window? Was Morty responsible for her streak of dizzy spells?

"Morty could get very physical," Mrs. Hartsover warned. "You better watch him. Once, we were fighting and he pulled on my arm. *Pulled on my arm*," she repeated indignantly at the mere memory. "I had bruises for two weeks."

Anna could only imagine the brute force Morty must have mustered. Her third eye revealed a slight, gentle man. A meek soul. Only such a spirit could tolerate the overbearing Mrs. Hartsover for so many years.

"You listen to me, Morty Hartsover," Anna's client yelled. "You keep your hands to yourself or so help me ..." Mrs. Hartsover's raised her fist in the air, convinced that Anna had connected with her ever-elusive, bookish, and sadly absent Morty. All five foot two inches of him.

* * *

Curt checked his reflection in the mirror. A black Nike shirt hugged his chest, revealing a powerful physique. No doubt about it. He was still hot.

"Hey Curt," a trainer called out as Curt made his way to a free bench by the weights.

Curt nodded but didn't stop to talk. Lifting was serious business. No time for idle chit chat.

Grabbing two forty-pound weights, Curt positioned himself for seated flies. Shoulders and traps flexed as he listened to "Telephone" by Lady Gaga on his iPod. He stared into the mirror, the veins in his forehead bulging on the tenth rep. He transitioned to lighter weights, repeating the same exercise. By the time he was down to twenty-five pounders, the muscles in his shoulders burned. Endorphins flooded his body. The pleasurable sensation confirmed it had been a good set.

It was noontime and the place was getting crowded.

* * *

When Dave hopped on the elliptical, the treadmill in front was occupied by a slightly overweight redheaded woman wearing purple leotards. Her saddlebags stretched the shimmering fabric tight across her ass. Each step threatened to rip the tights asunder. Moisture gathered at her butt crack. Dave tried to focus elsewhere, but the dampness of her booty, much like the Grand Canyon or Niagara Falls, became the great American landscape. Too compelling to ignore.

Within minutes, she finished her routine, and Dave thanked his lucky stars. An athletic man assumed her spot. Dave marveled at the broad back that tapered down to a narrow waist. The firm bottom seemed the perfect balance to the powerfully chiseled legs.

Wow, Dave thought. *Impressive.*

* * *

Curt jogged lightly on the treadmill before ramping up the speed. For the next twenty minutes he pounded away; a stallion in full gallop. He then slowed for a fifteen-minute cool-down. Soaked to the skin, he reached for a towel to wipe his face, perspiration stinging his eyes.

"Call me," said a short, pock-faced little man who crossed in front of him. The man held up an outstretched index finger and thumb simulating a mock phone. Curt nodded in the man's direction. He made a mental note to call. Cash was king and the guy was a great tipper. *I'll just close my eyes*, Curt thought, remembering with a wince the last time they'd been together.

* * *

Dave finished his workout and headed to the water fountain. An old man hobbled by, his metallic cane creating a clicking on the tiled floor. As the cool water washed over Dave's dry throat, the old guy limped past the treadmills heading toward the locker room. *Dear lord*, Dave thought. *The guy's barely able to walk . . . but he's still at the gym . . . engaged in an activity that has long ceased to be helpful in any way.*

* * *

Curt took a swig from his Gatorade. He spotted a gentleman in his seventies, cane supporting a heavily bandaged knee. It suddenly all seemed so exhausting . . . the workouts, the diet . . . the endless attention to his appearance. The fear that, no matter what he did, it was slipping out of his control.

* * *

Dave checked out the aerobics class underway in the glass-enclosed studio. Everyone was so young. So energetic. He'd thought about taking the class but was concerned it would be too hard on his joints. *That's all I need*, Dave thought, *an injury that limits my ability to work out.*

He made his way to the locker room.

* * *

Now that's a good-looking man, Curt thought as he spotted a gray-haired guy passing by. *Love that distinguished, mature look. And he's in fine shape. He must be fiftyish*, he thought, checking out the guy's box as he passed. *Yeah, I could easily fall in love with that.*

Curt bailed on the last five minutes of his cool-down.

* * *

Dave was washing his hands when he caught sight of a handsome, tanned stranger, heading his way. Jet-black hair framed the taut angular face. An aquiline nose, perfectly straight, balanced the high cheekbones. Dave realized it was the guy in front of him on the treadmill. Intimidated, he looked away and reached for a paper towel. It took concentration to hold his ground as the hunk saddled up to the adjacent sink. Unable to resist, Dave snuck a peek at the guy's basket. When Dave glanced up, the guy caught Dave's eye in the mirror and winked.

Dave blushed.

"So how was your workout?" the stranger asked.

"Good," Dave responded, surprised to be talking to anyone so amazing-looking at the gym.

"Looks like you're here a lot." The guy glanced over and eyed Dave's chest.

"Four times a week." Dave answered, uncomfortably aware of the swelling between his legs.

"You've got a great body for a man your age."

"Thank you . . . I think," Dave said, slightly flustered. "Well, I've got to get going." He backed away, drying his hands with the paper towel.

"By the way, my name's Curt."

Dave stepped forward to clasp the extended hand. "Dave," he barely managed to get out.

"Nice to meet you, Dave." Curt shot Dave a killer smile. "See you around."

13

....

Jack tripped over his shoe. It was 5:00 a.m., still dark out, and he didn't want to wake Bonnie. But he had to leave. Though he and Enid were no longer sharing a bed, he didn't want to explain why he hadn't come home.

Oh, I am in for it now, he thought, searching the floor for his underwear. He'd have to concoct a story.

His mind raced through various scenarios. He'd gotten drunk and slept in the car; been mugged and spent the evening at the police station; had heart palpitations and went to an Emergency Room. *Yes, heart palpitations,* he thought. *That one is plausible. I didn't call because they took my cell phone away.*

Jack hated to lie. He wasn't very good at it. He tended to turn bright red and provide too many details as he rambled on, desperate to cover his tracks.

I need to make it believable. Where was I when it happened? What time was it? What was I doing? Endless questions came to mind as he created answers, all the while concerned about an ugly confrontation.

Finally dressed, he sat on the edge of the bed. "You're so beautiful in the morning," he whispered as Bonnie half-smiled, coming out of a peaceful sleep. "I have to go. I'll call you later."

"No, don't go," she reached for him as he started to pull away, grabbing his arm. "Stay. Have breakfast with me."

"I can't."

But he wanted to. He wanted to so much it scared him.

"I've got to go," he said, his mind sifting through the series of lies he'd have to tell.

* * *

Bonnie watched as Jack withdrew. She rolled onto her side and pulled the covers in tightly under her chin. The bed was warm as she relaxed, ready to drift back to sleep. Then she heard the bedroom door close. It was the familiar sound of a man leaving; making his way back to a life in which she held no place.

Why am I always attracted to unavailable men?

Alone again, she tossed and turned. Her mind too busy to rest.

I'm not getting any younger. How many more chances will I have to find love?

Without a man in her life, she'd had no expectations. No highs, no lows. But now with Jack, she once again was free to hope and dream. To reimagine her existence.

I don't want to be alone she thought, awake and upset. *I need more.*

She yearned for true love. Whether that was Jack or someone else, she wasn't sure. But she wanted more . . . more than Jack appeared to be prepared to offer.

* * *

Henry pretended everything was fine when Paul cornered him outside of Starbucks.

"Where have you been?" Paul wanted to know. "I've left you message after message. Why haven't you returned my calls?" He was chewing gum.

Henry eluded the question. "I just got caught up in things."

Paul grabbed Henry by the collar and pulled him close. In a soft voice he said: "I missed hanging out with you. Is something wrong? Talk to me." There was a scent of spearmint on his breath.

"No," Henry lied, uncomfortably off-balance as he leaned into Paul, unwilling to struggle in a public place to escape Paul's grasp.

Paul squinted and focused his gaze. He blew a giant bubble that extended from his mouth to the tip of Henry's nose, before popping. He sucked the gum back in his mouth. "Well, don't ever do that again." he said, releasing his grip. "I was worried about you."

Henry smiled nervously. He was flattered by Paul's attention and thrilled by the sheer physical force Paul had undertaken to pursue the friendship. Moreover, Paul's sweet breath, had left him feeling giddy.

"Come on back to my house and we can catch up. I'll order in pizza and we can chill."

The old fear crept back in. Henry didn't want to be alone with Paul . . . to desire him . . . to ache for his touch. "I better not," Henry stalled. "I've got to study."

"Don't be lame," Paul admonished. "You can study at my house. We'll play video games. I just got *Call of Duty.*"

There was no point in denying Paul. Henry didn't have the temperament to stand up to him. When Paul was near, Henry was awkward, unsure, easily persuaded. Whatever Paul wanted, Paul got. There could be no other way. And so Henry relented.

On the way to Paul's house, they talked about the future. Paul's future.

"Susan and I are thinking of living together," Paul shared.

Henry pretended to be happy for him. "Do you love her?" He was afraid to hear the answer.

"Love? Yeah, I guess I do."

"How do you know?"

"When I'm around her, I want to touch her all the time. And I always want to be with her. She's constantly in my thoughts. If that's love, then I suppose I love her."

At some level, Henry was relieved. He might continue to long for Paul, but now he knew Paul was out of reach. Henry could relax. There would be no more monkey business. No more risk of Henry showing his true feelings. And yet, Henry couldn't help but wish he was Susan . . . to know the joy of being the object of Paul's affection.

Back at Paul's house, Henry sat on the floor of the living room and did his geometry homework while Paul sat on the sofa videogaming. Opening an oak box on the coffee table, Paul retrieved a metal cigarette case. He showed the contents to Henry. "Want some?" he asked.

"No, I've got a few more problems to solve," Henry half-protested.

"Don't be such an old fart," Paul teased, flicking a red BIC lighter embossed with the word *Stud.* The tip of the joint burned bright as Paul inhaled, holding the smoke in his lungs. He took two more hits and passed the joint to Henry, shouting "and now it's time for *Call of Duty*."

* * *

That night, alone in his bedroom, Henry covered his face, but he couldn't block out the memory of his afternoon with Paul. After losing at the video game, Paul had slipped in a porn video. Stoned, Henry was unable to control himself. As Paul laid back on the sofa watching the girl-on-girl action, Henry positioned himself between Paul's legs. Paul's eyes remained glued to the screen as Henry unzipped Paul's pants. When it was over, Henry tried to kiss Paul.

"Knock that off," Paul said, pushing Henry away. "I'm not like you."

The words burned in Henry's ears. Now Paul knew his secret. No more pretending to be just buds, chilling and doing their thing. The stakes had suddenly gotten higher.

Henry was confused. "If you're not gay, then what just happened?"

"Nothing," Paul answered as he hopped up and zipped up his fly.

"Then what was that all about?"

"That was just a release of tension. Nothing more. I didn't touch you," Paul said tucking in his shirt. "And I never will."

Humiliated, Henry had to ask the next question. "Then why'd you let me?"

"I knew you wanted it. You gay guys are all alike. You love straight guys."

"Straight. You think you're straight," Henry heard himself say, tears gathering in his eyes. "You're not straight," he pronounced, mustering his courage. "But you are an asshole."

"Hey, I'm not the one with no friends or family," Paul said matter-of-factly.

"No. You're just a closet case."

"You better go home little boy," Paul said, pulling Henry toward the door. "Your work here is done."

* * *

Anna spotted Henry in the backyard lying under her orange tree. She knew teenagers were a breed unto their own, and still, she wanted to know what was troubling him. "Are you okay?" she asked, wandering over. "Is everything alright?"

"Yeah, sure," Henry said, squinting up to look at her.

She examined one of the buds coming up. "I think we're going to have a lot of oranges this year. You like oranges, don't you Henry?"

"Sure," he said.

"It's a wonderful thing about nature. We have these terrible monsoons in July and August that blow through Phoenix. Awful windstorms that you'd think would bring every tree down. And yet our trees survive. They stand tall and continue to bloom."

If he wants to talk, I'm here, she thought. *No need to push him. He deserves his privacy. I need to respect that.*

"Enjoy my tree," she said, turning back toward the house. "Dinner's in ten minutes."

"Anna." Henry sat up, rubbing his hands together, bits of dirt and grass falling away. "I'm not really very hungry. I had something on the way home and if it's okay with you, I think I'll pass on dinner."

Anna was startled. Not eating was serious. "Well okay. As long as you already ate."

I can't push him to tell me what's going on. But she desperately wanted to know.

Later in the evening, Anna brought up a tray with a peanut butter sandwich and a glass of chocolate milk. Henry grabbed it through the half-opened door.

Anna decided to let Henry be.

Whatever was the matter, she trusted he'd find his way to her.

* * *

Alone in his room, Henry sat on the floor leaning up against the wall. He looked about and realized that everything, the bed he slept in, pictures on the wall, desk where he did his homework, curtains on the window, roof over his head, all belonged to somebody else.

The sting of his parents' rejection rushed back.

You'll never have a happy life. You'll never have a family. No one will ever love you.

Henry hid his face in his hands. He wondered if perhaps his folks had been right all along.

* * *

At breakfast, Anna offered a suggestion. "We need a holiday," she said as she measured out a half-cup of All-Bran. "Someplace with a pool and gambling. Someplace fun."

"You know I can't afford that," Henry answered.

"You don't have to," Anna said, smiling. "I'm going to foot the entire trip and we're going to have a blast."

"Really?" Henry said, a hint of excitement in his voice.

She had it already planned. "Sure . . . we both need to get out of here for a few days and Palm Springs is only a four-hour drive."

"Palm Springs. I thought you meant Vegas."

"There's gambling in Palm Springs. And Vegas isn't somewhere you go to get away from it all. It's where you go to find it. Palm Springs," Anna said, slowly savoring the sound. "Now that is quiet and relaxing."

"Sounds boring."

"No, it'll be a gas."

"A gas? Is that a real expression?" he asked, rolling his eyes.

"It'll be fun. Now let me see what kind of arrangements I can pull together. You go and pack."

The next morning, as the car approached the Verrado Way exit on Interstate 10 heading west, Henry relaxed. He was out of Paul's orbit at last. The next four hours they listened to *STARS* on Sirius. In Blythe they grabbed a coffee at Starbucks. As Anna had promised, that afternoon they found themselves enjoying the pool at the Riviera Hotel on Palm Canyon Drive. The world looked different on the California side of the desert. It only took an ice tea, the *USA Today* crossword puzzle, and two gorgeous hunks from LA sitting across the way to make Henry realize that his worries about Paul, Phoenix, and an embarrassing sexual encounter, were now well behind him.

"Is this the same sun as the one in Phoenix?" Henry asked.

"Of course," Anna responded.

"I don't know. It feels a whole lot warmer."

"That's because we're in Palm Springs. Everything feels better in Palm Springs."

* * *

The Riviera Hotel, an iconic midcentury modern resort, offered a poolside patio café where patrons dined outdoors. It was there where Anna and Henry started their mornings. Anna drinking coffee while Henry scanned the Palm Springs magazine. Two breakfast plates before them. Henry's waffle, long gone. A strip of bacon in his hand. Anna's poached egg on toast, half-eaten.

"Check this out." Henry showed her the page. "They have a tram that takes you to the top of the mountain. Pretty cool. We should do that."

"Count me out," Anna answered breezily. "You know I'm afraid of heights. But why don't you go without me?"

"Oh, I don't think so. It wouldn't be any fun alone."

"You really should," Anna said, aware of a sudden dizziness.

"Are you okay?" Henry asked. "You look like you've just seen a ghost." The irony of the statement, lost on him.

"Oh God," she cried, dropping her coffee cup, the sound of china shattering on the cement patio.

A waitress rushed over as Anna threw herself face-down, grabbing the edge of the tabletop, silverware flying, a water glass toppling over, as Henry watched helplessly.

"Is she having a seizure? Is she epileptic?" the young woman asked Henry as she crouched by Anna's side.

"Not that I'm aware," Henry answered.

"Ma'am, are you okay? Do we need to call an ambulance?"

Anna was slowly coming out of it. She lifted her face up and blinked, blushing over the fuss being made. Egg yolk covered her neck. "No, I'm fine . . . really."

"Ma'am, you're certainly not fine," the waitress said.

Anna slowly sat up. "I've been having these terrible dizzy spells," she admitted, her blouse stained yellow from her breakfast. "They come on quite suddenly."

"You should see a doctor," the waitress suggested, using a clean napkin dipped in water to help Anna clean off the mess on her clothes.

"I probably should," Anna agreed.

* * *

"Are you sure you're going to be okay?" Henry asked, uncertain what to do.

Anna was in bed, the curtains pulled tight to block out the sun. She had a cold wash cloth on her forehead. "You go ahead to the pool. And make sure you order yourself some lunch at noon. Just sign it to the room. I'll be fine. And please don't worry about me. Just go and have some fun."

"You're going to be hungry by then. Should I bring something back? A hot dog? A cola?"

"Please, Henry," Anna croaked, hand in the air, "let's not talk about food. If I'm hungry, I'll order room service. Now go enjoy yourself. I'll sleep a bit and be fine."

With a cheap pair of CVS sunglasses perched atop his head, Henry clopped along in his flip-flops, sporting a psychedelic *Hey Man* Jerry Garcia tank top paired with a knee-length, blue Hawaiian-style bathing suit purchased at the Palm Springs Gay Mart. The bathing suit reached just above his knees, and had so much material, Henry wondered if it might pull him under should it actually get wet.

He found an open lounge chair and dropped his knapsack down. Usually loaded with schoolbooks, the knapsack carried the morning newspaper, a copy of *Tess of the D'Urbervilles*, a bottle of water, and sunscreen lotion.

Nearby, two older men in matching blue and red Speedos that barely covered their privates, shared shade under a large white umbrella. The red Speedo guy smiled at Henry. Henry offered a meek "hello" before pulling off his top and sitting down on the edge of the lounge chair. He momentarily closed his eyes, feeling the warmth of the sun flood over his body. Even with his eyes closed, the intense sunshine seemed to peek through.

"Excuse me," the gentleman in the red Speedo called out. He wore a closely clipped crew cut and looked to be in need of a shave. His face, both weathered and tough, seemed in direct contrast with his kind and inviting smile. His arms, covered in tattoos, barely attracted attention away from the thick pelt of grey hair on his abdomen and chest. "Would you like some sunscreen? We have this wonderful stuff, SolBar. It's greaseless. You really should use something to protect your skin."

The man next to him in the blue Speedo sat up. "You'll have to excuse Bart," he said, lifting his sunglasses. He was a large barrel-chested man who reminded Henry of his dad. "He's always trying to warn others of the dangers of the sun. He's had a bout with skin cancer so he's like that ex-smoker who wants everyone to quit."

Henry offered a crooked smiled. "Well, I do have something." He pulled out an orange plastic tube of Banana Boat from his satchel.

"Well, good for you," Mr. Crewcut beamed. "By the way. My name is Bart, and this is my partner, Joel. We've been together thirty-five years. Isn't that something? Thirty-five years."

Henry nodded. "Wow."

"I know," Bart said. "When you find the right person, it's easy." Bart reached for Joel's hand.

"Well," Joel added, "It's all about communication. There are lots of pretty faces and beautiful bodies, but at the end of the day, home is where Bart is."

Henry had never considered he could have a long-term relationship with a man. One night with Paul would be miracle enough.

* * *

Anna's dizzy spells continued to get worse.

Back in Phoenix, she scheduled an appointment with a neurologist. The expensive MRI failed to uncover a brain tumor, blood clot, or blockage of any sort. The neurologist recommended an ophthalmologist. The ophthalmologist confirmed there was no apparent physical reason for the dizzy spells. Her vision was perfectly fine. Had she considered dizziness and nausea might be symptoms of migraines? He recommended an internist. The internist prescribed Fioricet. "It's not uncommon for women your age to have migraines," the doctor said. *How sexist*, Anna thought, eyeing the free vial of sample medication she'd never take, convinced it would only dull her senses and block her ability to channel.

Poisoning herself didn't seem like the answer.

And so the terrible sensation continued to haunt her, two or three times a day. At night, as she drifted off to sleep, she might experience another free-fall. Startled, she'd spend the next few hours lying on the carpet by her bed, taking great comfort in the solid floor beneath her.

As the days passed, she became increasingly phobic.

Afraid to leave the house, she peered out at the world behind locked windows and doors. She worried about poisons in her food. Mad Cow Disease. Salmonella. She feared rats had invaded her flat roof and were searching for a way into the house. She anticipated a speeding car on 19th Avenue would jump the curb and drive through her kitchen. For the first time in her life, her fears ruled and she simply gave into the terror.

She cut back on her schedule, refusing to see anyone who wasn't an established client.

She tried meditating, assuming the lotus position, hands turned up, resting on her knees. She took deep rhythmic breaths, quieting her mind. She felt the energy surging through the top of her palms as her spirit guides replenished and cleansed her aura.

But the dizziness returned.

Brace yourself, she thought, gritting her teeth as she entered another dreaded free-fall, her head spinning, the room losing focus, as the floor once again became the ceiling.

* * *

And then Anna remembered Emily.

Emily had been Anna's psychic mentor in her youth. It had been forever since they'd last spoken. Anna wasn't even sure Emily was still alive until she did a Google search. Emily's name popped right up, and much to Anna's surprise, she lived in the same Maryvale home that Anna remembered. Within the hour, Anna called and scheduled a time to visit.

Maryvale in its heyday had been one of the first planned suburban communities in metropolitan Phoenix. Built in the 1950s, the simple three-bedroom, two-bath homes were part of America's post-war boom. Emily's house, Anna remembered, had been a pink cinder-block ranch with a lovely white picket fence. As she drove on Camelback, heading west, she wondered if the house was still that same lovely pastel color.

Entering Emily's neighborhood, Anna noticed that many of the houses had thick black iron bars on the windows. Roofs, decks and front steps, all looked to be in need of repair. Ugly wire fences with *Beware of Dog* signs seemed to be everywhere.

Anna spotted Emily's house. It had retained its pink color, although what had been a bright happy shade had faded significantly with the years. A small sign, prominently displayed on the lawn warned of an alarm system. Anna looked at the house, read the sign, and glanced about the neighborhood, worried about the safety of her car.

An elderly woman clad in a yellow housecoat answered the front door. At age eighty-five, Emily lived alone. She wore no make-up; her long white hair pulled back in to a ponytail. Somewhat unkempt, Anna barely recognized her old friend.

Emily's eyes sparkled as she welcomed Anna. "It's been such a long time. Please come in, dear."

Anna stepped out of the bright sunshine into the dark house. From the smell alone, there had to be a cat or two, or four, hiding somewhere, perhaps under the ratty-looking sofa in the living room.

Anna followed the older woman to the kitchen. A kettle for tea was on the stove. Turning the burner to high, Emily invited Anna to sit down at the kitchen table.

"I wish I had something to offer you to eat, but I hadn't had a chance to get to the store."

It broke Anna's heart to see what had become of the woman she so fondly remembered. "Oh, I'm fine. No apologies. I really don't need the calories," Anna confided, hoping to make light of the awkward moment.

"Do you remember the first time we met?" Emily asked as she gathered two tea cups and matching plates from the cupboard. "It was at the Metro North Bookstore. You were having those dreams? Am I right?"

Anna nodded. "Yes, a lot of bad dreams. Mostly horrible deaths."

"It's ironic that this is what brings you back to me again."

"But these are not dreams. It's something else."

Reaching for Anna's hand, Emily closed her eyes. "Ah yes, you're awake. But you're channeling. You're channeling an entity who very much wants your help."

Anna shook her head in agreement.

"The entity is scaring you. It doesn't mean to. It's just taking you through the last moments of its life to get your attention. It's a female energy."

Anna had sensed it was female. She was grateful for the confirmation.

"But how can I help her? How can I let her know that I understand how she died and I don't want to re-experience it over and over?"

"You must go where she wants you to go. You must find who she's trying to connect you with."

"But how? I have no idea who she is or who she's looking for."

"Ah, but you do," Emily confirmed as the teakettle whistled.

"Who is it? A client? A friend? A relative? Who?"

"I can't tell you that," Emily said, pouring the hot water through the tea sifter.

"Then what can you tell me?"

Emily took a seat at the table next to Anna. It was absolutely quiet. With a palm on her forehead, she closed her eyes. Anna waited. "Her name is Maria. She wants you to connect with her son. His name begins with an E."

Anna drew a blank. *Maria? A man whose name begins with an E?* None of it sounded familiar.

"It'll come to you. Just focus on the man's name. Give it time and it will all become clear."

"But those dizzy spells. Oh, I don't think I can go on much longer with all of that."

"You won't have to. Just focus," Emily assured her. "Think on whose name it could be. She's very persistent. She'll eventually give you the name or she'll lead you to some clue that will help you know who it is."

Anna sipped the hot tea. A mild dampness broke across her brow. The room suddenly cooled. Anna felt refreshed.

Emily burned incense in an ashtray to clear Anna's chakra. The thick scent stuck in Anna's throat and made her cough. She never had cared for the smell. *Perhaps that's the odor I'd mistaken for cats*, she thought as an orange-striped tabby jumped on top of the table, nearly knocking Anna's mug of tea to the floor.

"Matilda!" Emily called out. "Off the table."

The tabby gracefully leapt away.

"Oh dear," Emily apologized. "She knows better. The others would never do that."

"The others?" Anna asked.

"Three others. They're too scared to come out. They're hiding . . ."

". . . Under the sofa in the living room."

"Why yes, dear. You're as sharp as ever," Emily declared.

* * *

"We're getting so old," Dave said as he passed through the bedroom on the way to the master bathroom.

Charlie was in bed, a book in his lap, Timmy curled up by his side.

"It's only nine o'clock."

"Are you tired?" Charlie called out, his reading glasses sliding down his nose.

"Of course, I am," Dave said, popping his head around the door, looking back in the bedroom. "Just look out the window! *It's dark out.*"

They both laughed.

In the bathroom, Dave stepped out of his shorts and pulled off his tee shirt. He examined his face in the mirror. Gentle lines gathered at the corners of his eyes. For a man in his fifties he still looked damn good, but instead of seeing the glass half-full, all he could focus on was the ravages of time.

"I think we may need to get rid of all the mirrors in this house," Dave called out as he pulled on some loose skin under his chin.

"Sounds like someone is having a *very late* midlife crisis," Charlie answered, turning a page of his book. "How would you get ready for bed without a mirror?"

Dave studied his reflection. His eyes were slightly bloodshot. He'd checked it out with his optometrist, but there was no explanation for it. Just another sign of the body's aging process. He applied facial scrub from Clinique for Men, turned on the water, and vigorously washed. "I won't need to look at myself," he called out, "to brush my teeth or wash my face. And when my last hair falls out, I won't need a comb."

"That'll be the day," Charlie laughed as Timmy stood up, shook, and resettled into a tight ball. "I can't imagine you without a mirror."

"Do you remember," Dave said, pulling the blanket back and climbing into bed, "when the whites of your eyes were actually white? I was at the dentist and they suggested I whiten my teeth. I kept thinking, *sure, but won't it make my eyes just look even redder?*"

Charlie turned another page. "Stop exaggerating."

"I don't know," Dave said, hopping out of bed. "When did this all happen? When did we get so old? Sometimes, it's like I'm looking in a funhouse mirror."

"You used to have a career. People who work for a living don't have time to worry about such nonsense."

"Look at this," Dave said. He pushed his stomach out some three inches and then miraculously sucked it back in. "I could do before and after photos for weight loss supplements."

"There's a new career," Charlie said. "Maybe then you wouldn't be so focused on yourself."

"I bet they'd pay good money for my photos."

"Yes, that's just what advertisers want . . . some old man posing with his shirt off."

"Old man . . ." The words stung. "I guess I am an old man."

"You could be someone's grandfather," Charlie clarified, a smile crossing his face.

"Ouch."

"It's true. You're a grandpa. Face it . . . grandpa." Charlie laughed.

Timmy lifted his head.

"Grandpa, huh?" Dave pulled his boxer shorts up above his waist and just below his nipples.

Timmy sat up and let out a subdued cry.

"I haven't seen you here before sonny boy," Dave teased Charlie. "When did you move into this nursing home? How about a little smooch?"

Charlie howled. "Do you think you could do something about that old face?"

"If you don't want to look at it," Dave teased, "maybe you should sit on it."

Charlie nudged Timmy off the bed. The poodle walked into his crate. "Good idea," he said, pulling back the covers for Dave to slide in next to him.

* * *

Lyle loved Costco's roasted chicken. Dave thought it too salty, but to an aging palate like Lyle's, it was the perfect shock to the taste buds. So that Tuesday night Charlie and Dave brought in a prepared Costco's chicken, much to Lyle's delight.

"This chicken is so darn good." Lyle smacked his lips.

"Such table manners," Daisy said. "And your hands, just look at them, covered in grease."

Lyle laughed, licking his fingers.

Daisy moaned. "I give up. That's disgusting."

"Now, you listen to me, woman," Lyle said, directing his words to Charlie and Dave. "This is my home and I will lick my fingers if I want to. Besides, that's a compliment to the cook. Don't you know that?"

"Oh you . . . I guess you really can't teach an old dog new tricks. Just look at you," Daisy said, pretending to be mortified.

Lyle took a second helping of mashed potatoes. Charlie had carved the bird and limited his and Dave's portion to a small sliver of breast. He wanted Daisy and Lyle to have enough chicken for a second meal.

"Please take some more," Daisy implored.

"We're fine," Dave said looking over at Charlie. "We've had plenty."

"Don't you men know it pays to have a little extra weight? What would have happened to poor Lyle if he hadn't had a little extra meat on his bones when he went into the hospital?"

"We're just trying to maintain our target weight," Dave explained. "A fist size of protein is all we're allowed."

"At my age," Lyle said, "there's no such thing as target weight. They expect you to be dead."

Daisy gave Lyle a withering look. "Well then, how about some pie? Wouldn't that be nice? I have a fresh apple pie."

The rule of fist-size didn't apply when it came to desserts.

Daisy passed out huge portions of warm pie topped with gobs of Cool Whip. The white fluffy stuff defied melting. Charlie couldn't help wonder what it looked like flowing through his arteries.

"We'll split a piece," Dave suggested.

"Not in my house. Now don't insult me." Daisy assumed a cross manner much like a grade school teacher correcting her two young students.

"Okay," Dave said, capitulating. "But this means we're going to have to limit the number of times we eat here if you can't accommodate our eating habits."

"Oh no," Daisy gasped. "Okay. You can split it."

But it was too late. Charlie had already eaten his way through most of the serving.

Dave gave Charlie a surprised look. "You pig."

"Well," Charlie explained, "I thought I'd do you a favor. I know you wanted to stay away from sweets, so I wolfed it down."

"Right," Dave answered. "Sure."

"I'm just being a loving partner."

The four laughed.

Together they sat and drank coffee. Daisy doled out second helpings of the pie. No one objected.

"I'm so glad you two are here," Lyle said. "Moments like this are so special. Being with friends," and Lyle turned to Daisy, "and someone whom you truly love. If I had my life to live over again, I'd have laughed more."

"Well, there wasn't a lot to laugh about when we were growing up. The Depression, World War II, the Red Scare. And the 1950s were a stifling time," Daisy reminisced. "Duck and cover."

Lyle agreed. "The 60s weren't so great either. All that unrest. And I voted for Nixon the first time he ran."

"Oh my God," Daisy shouted, "and I sleep with you?"

Lyle smiled. "Hey, I was too busy getting divorced, remarried, and divorced again to understand what was happening. He was as uptight as I was. I felt sorry for the guy."

"Daisy," Dave asked. "Who were you involved with while Lyle was busy at the altar?"

"Oh, wouldn't you like to know?"

All eyes turned Daisy's way.

"I would." Dave leaned forward like a little boy waiting to be told a secret.

Daisy adjusted her posture, sitting straighter, her head held high. "I was seeing a big car executive from Detroit. He came to Phoenix twice a month. He was quite well-to-do."

"Were you his mistress?"

"I don't like that word. I was his . . . friend."

"Naughty girl," Lyle teased.

"I loved him," Daisy volunteered to the surprise of the three. She paused. Her voice took on a petulant tone. "I hoped he'd leave his wife. But that didn't happen. I wasted ten years before I realized we'd never marry. And marriage was important back then. Everyone was married. If you weren't married, people assumed there was something wrong with you. I was miserable, but I also admired him for keeping his vows. I just wish he'd been kinder. He should've told me we'd never be truly together. But then, I suppose, the truth was right in front of my eyes. I was just unwilling to see it."

Lyle lovingly placed his hand on top of Daisy's.

"Whatever happened to him?" Charlie asked, curious as to the fate of Daisy's lost love. "Did he stay married?"

"He died suddenly," Daisy replied. "Years before his time. Too much stress and probably not enough love in his life. They found him in the office, dead of a heart attack. He was only fifty-two years old . . . younger than the two of you."

Dave clutched his chest. "I hate that story. It's such a waste to die in the office."

Daisy nodded in agreement. "I always wondered if he would've left his wife had he known he'd die so young. Would he have continued to stay married, just for the sake of appearances? Maybe leaving her would have extended his life."

"That's what we did back then," Lyle added. "We didn't go to therapists and talk out our problems. We muddled through. Most of us were unconscious. We worked, came home, and did the best we could."

Daisy sighed. "Things are better today. The old rules are gone. We have legal abortions, couples living together outside of marriage, and really, who doesn't know someone who is gay? These all used to be causes for such shame and derision. People were so isolated by their problems. I don't know about you, Lyle, but I like it better this way."

"It gives you faith, doesn't it?" Lyle looked at Daisy affectionately.

"Yes," Daisy agreed. "So many people complain about the collapse of American values, whatever that means. I say, good riddance. Time to try something new. The hippies had it right. Don't trust anyone over thirty. They're too set in their ways. Their vision is narrowed."

"Life," Lyle said, "is about change. You change, you survive. Look at us. We're still here because we know how to go with the flow. Anything else kills you."

"I'll try to remember that when I get to be your age," Dave remarked.

"Remember it now," Lyle corrected. "Live it now. It's the rigid who break. The flexible ones persevere. And try to be as loving as you can. I've seen anger kill too many of us. Mean-spirited bitter people get to the graveyard first."

Charlie sat quietly digesting Lyle's words, sipping what remained of his coffee, and feeling profoundly grateful that he and Dave knew Daisy and Lyle.

"Today's a good day," Daisy said interrupting the silence. "Anyone want more pie?"

"No, no," Charlie protested, hands in the air. "We couldn't."

But it was too late. Daisy had sliced another wedge and hoisted it on Charlie's plate. "Just a little more . . . it's good for you," she announced with such strong conviction that Charlie truly believed, at that very moment, she was absolutely right.

* * *

Ernie went over it again in his mind.

There was no way his tiny mother, barely five feet tall, had leapt to her death from the terrace. He was certain. Not only was she terrified of heights but she would have needed a chair to get over the five-foot railing. No chair had been found on the terrace. Nothing on which she could have stood to boost herself up and over. Ernie was certain she hadn't jumped. It was physically impossible.

"Not you again!" Detective Sanchez said spotting Ernie in the doorway. He took a last sip of his coffee. "You're not going to let this go, are you?"

"I can't," Ernie confessed, walking into the tiny office and collapsing into the chair by Sanchez's desk. "This thing is eating me up. I can't sleep. I can't work."

"Maybe you need some sleeping pills. The Mercado on the corner sells them."

"I don't want pills. I want to know who killed my mother."

Sanchez leaned back in his chair. His desk was a mess. Papers scattered everywhere. A red plastic Coke cup with a straw, a yellow legal pad covered in chicken scratches that Ernie assumed passed for handwriting. He looked incredulous. "You said she was depressed. Why is this so hard for you to believe she committed suicide? The neighbor saw it. Why would a witness lie?"

Ernie could only shake his head in denial. "My mother was a small woman. She couldn't have scaled that railing."

"I told you," Sanchez said, still leaning back, fingers rubbing his temple. "She pulled herself up and over. There's no great mystery. Someone who wants to die, always finds a way."

"She didn't have that kind of physical strength."

"There was no sign of a forced entry," Sanchez reminded him. "No sign of a struggle."

"She wouldn't have killed herself. There has to be more."

Sanchez stood up. "Look, I know how you feel. It's your mother. But I don't have time to sit here and go over this again. I'm sorry. You're not the only case in Puerto Vallarta."

Ernie slowly stood up. "I know . . ." he said, swallowing the words.

"How about," Sanchez offered, "we grab lunch somewhere on the street? It's almost noon. I have to head over to the beach. We can talk on the way."

"You'd do that?"

"Hey, you got to eat. I got to eat. Come on. Let's get out of here."

Ernie followed Sanchez out the door. They walked two blocks to a nearby park. There, Sanchez bought tacos off a pushcart and sat down at one of the park tables. "Best damn tacos in PV," he said as he shoved the crunchy mess into his mouth.

Ernie sat and stared as his lunch. Flies circled.

"Tell me you're not going to eat that," the detective said.

"I'm not much for eating."

"Are you kidding? That's a Taco Supreme. You haven't lived till you've tried one of these. Go ahead, take a bite. I'm not telling you a thing till you taste that taco. It's the least you can do after someone buys you lunch."

In the next twenty minutes, Ernie discovered the address of the witness who'd told police she'd seen Maria. It was a small bit of evidence that Sanchez let slip.

That evening, Ernie stood at the door of the apartment and pretended he was a building inspector. Annoyed by the intrusion, the woman failed to recognize him in his borrowed overalls, blue worker's hat, and dark glasses. But then, Carmen, a voluptuous sales agent who sold timeshares at Villa Allegra through a third-party real estate company, had never paid Ernie much attention.

As Ernie finished the final inspection of the new HVAC unit at the Villa Allegra Resort on the day Maria died, Carmen, the strikingly attractive blond in her late twenties, who favored short, tight skirts, and five-inch heels, had sat but a few feet away from Ernie with an older couple, poised to close on a timeshare unit. Her gorgeous legs were hard to miss. And even harder to forget.

* * *

Bonnie made up her mind.

The relationship with Jack was going nowhere and she wasn't getting any younger. She'd already spent too many years alone. If she ever hoped to be in a committed relationship it would have to be with someone who was free to be with her.

And that simply wasn't Jack.

His slipping in and out of her life had become too difficult. One minute there, loving her, the next, gone. The void in his wake was unbearable.

Jack left message after message, but Bonnie refused to return the calls. It was bad enough she missed him so terribly, but then to hear him begging—well, it broke her heart.

And so she returned to the quiet rhythm of her life before meeting Jack. Her career was once again her central focus, but now, she no longer accepted its dull limitations. She trusted that her heart would mend and in so doing, she might eventually meet a man with whom she could share her life.

She gathered strength as she observed the struggles of others seeking to mend. Mrs. Adelman's torn Achilles; Mrs. Blumstein's knee repair; Mr. Gleason's recent hip replacement. When she looked into their eyes, she wondered if she had the same inner strength to fight for a better, happier life. Only time would tell, but she was willing to give it a start.

* * *

At midnight, a Honda Civic pulled up to the back of the Little Tortilla Shop on Avenida Americano.

Wild chickens roamed the dusty streets of dilapidated tin shacks covered in angry graffiti. A heavy smell stained the air. It was a mixture of raw sewage, body odor, and rotting animal carcasses.

The inhabitant of the vehicle stepped out of the car and snorted hard. He spat out a wad of phlegm, hoping to get the awful smell out of his nose. Instead, he'd cleared his sinuses allowing for a better whiff of the horrible stench that stifled the neighborhood.

He winced.

He hated it here. He had good reason. He'd been born and raised only a few blocks away. A childhood spent barefoot in a one-room cinder-block house with a dirt floor. He could hardly wait to get back in his car and escape.

Why do we have to meet here?

It had been years since he'd left. He vowed he'd go anywhere, do anything, be anyone, only not here in this place. Never here in this place. And yet he stood once again in the same filth. The darkness of the night invited him to crawl back to his impoverished youth—a drunken father; the whore he called mother. It made him viscerally ill to think of it.

Lighting a Camel, he inhaled deeply. The smell of tobacco was a welcome relief. The act of smoking relaxed him. It hadn't been easy to escape this place. Most did not. But he'd been lucky. And he was still alive.

Alive to enjoy all his life offered.

He thought of his wife and children; two boys and a girl; happy and healthy, well-educated, well fed. What would they think if they could see him here? He'd never told them where he came from. He was too ashamed and too grateful to have left it all behind. He wanted no memories of this place, and yet, there he stood, smoking a second cigarette and waiting for his contact.

He was eager to leave, but not yet. Not until he had what he'd come for.

A black sedan pulled up, creating a cloud of dust.

He turned his back and cursed. *Goddammit,* he muttered as he shielded his eyes.

A tall broad-chested man, dressed like an advertisement for Ralph Lauren, with boots and a Stetson cowboy hat, stepped out of the car. He turned and came forward. "Sanchez," he called out as the two men clasped hands in greeting. "How are you?"

"Fine," Sanchez replied, knowing full well that the man had no interest in making polite conversation. They were there to do business, and so, the faster they got to it, the faster he could get the out of this hellhole.

"Good. This week, we need to get rid of any evidence on those killings by the beach. Can you make that happen?"

He knew there was only one answer. "Sure."

"Good."

The envelope passed hands.

"See you next week."

The meeting was over and they parted ways. The sedan headed back to town. Sanchez waited ten minutes and then followed at a safe distance.

That night he took a hot shower before getting into bed. The soapy water killed the scent of the neighborhood but only his wife's radiant black hair could get the smell out of his nose.

14

....

Henry turned toward the wall and hid his face with the palm of his hand. *Shit*, he thought, a geometry book opened to isosceles triangles, *this is my goddamn Starbucks. What the hell is he doing here?*

It had been Henry's habit on Mondays and Fridays to stop at 16th and Glendale on his way home from school, buy a coffee, sit at a high-top, and do homework. A treat to ease the start of the school week; a celebration to mark the end.

I can't believe it, he grimaced, head slightly turned, peaking through the spread of his fingers as Paul approached the counter. *He doesn't live around here. What's the deal?*

And then Paul spotted him.

"Hey, look at you." His voice bright . . . head tilted at a sharp angle. "Where have you been? I haven't seen you in forever."

Henry was speechless.

Paul's hand reached for Henry's shoulder and gave it a friendly squeeze. "You look good, little bro."

Henry's breath caught in his throat as Paul's touch released a rush of electrical charges through his body.

Paul studied his face. "I'm going to grab a bottled water. You want anything?"

Henry held up his Venti. He muttered, "I'm good."

"Okay then," Paul said, heading to the counter . . . his posture cocky . . . his attitude entitled.

Henry's heart raced. He'd deliberately avoided Paul. Not taken his calls. Not answered his text messages. After their last encounter, he'd had enough.

Henry's eyes followed Paul's every move. He watched as Paul paid for a bottled water, and then returned with a big smile and a wink. Paul lifted Henry's book bag off the chair and placed it on the floor. He then sat down, sliding the chair over so that he could be closer to Henry.

"So what have you been up to? It's been awhile since we last connected. Fill me in," he said as he twisted the cap off of his Pellegrino and brought it to his lips for a long swig.

Henry cut to the chase. "What are you doing here?" he asked. "You could have gotten water at any mini-mart? What's this all about?"

Paul appeared taken aback. "The same reason you are. I wanted something to drink, I was passing by, and I thought I'd stop in." His voice light and innocent.

Henry eyed Paul suspiciously.

Paul wiped his mouth with the back of his sleeve. "Okay, I missed you," he finally admitted, looking away as he fingered the label on the green bottle. "I should have never spoken to you the way I did. I'm truly sorry about that." His tone, somber and quiet, he once again returned his gaze to Henry. His blue eyes pierced Henry's armor. "You have to forgive me for being such an asshole. It won't happen again."

Henry had no words. His lips had gone dry.

"I know I don't deserve a second chance, but hey, I'm not such a bad guy. And I really do care about you." His expression was warm and generous. His tone, sincere. "We're still friends, aren't we?"

Paul waited for Henry's response.

Henry smiled timidly. He didn't want to be angry with Paul. If Paul was willing to make the effort, Henry wanted to smooth it all over. And so Henry nodded, not so much in agreement, but in an effort to keep up his end of the conversation.

Paul leaned forward and placed a hand on Henry's knee. He whispered seductively, "I know the other day you were just helping a buddy out. I get that. There's nothing to be ashamed of. No regrets. We both know the score. It's not a big deal."

Henry said nothing.

Paul checked his watch. "Hey, I got to get going. I'm meeting up with Susan for dinner. I'll call you later."

Henry relaxed once Paul was out of sight.

He couldn't deny the two shared a special connection; a feeling of belonging that went beyond friendship. He no longer cared that Paul had treated him badly or might do so again. He'd come to expect to be treated badly. That had started with his parents and been reinforced by scores of disinterested adults who had turned their backs when he was living on the streets and begging for money. He'd come to understand that in the scheme of life, he didn't matter much. And even though Anna had defied his expectations of adult behavior, Henry was afraid to trust in that difference. If she changed her mind, he risked losing the very roof over his head, and so, as a survival tactic, he compartmentalized his relationships, making certain Anna knew nothing about Paul.

* * *

Curt Devlon was used to being stared at.

In Safeway, women made eye contact when he was grocery shopping. In Walgreen's, the ladies waiting for their scripts glanced his way as he passed. At Scottsdale Fashion Square, females of all ages ogled him. Once, he'd even caught an elderly woman with a walker checking him out.

Men also noticed Curt.

Gay men, alone or in pairs, did double takes. Sometimes, men passed twice or three times when he was at Macy's just so they could get another look. In Banana Republic, Curt had had to brush off an overzealous salesman who tried to push his way into his changing room.

The staring, the touching, the leering, all went along with being beautiful.

Even straight guys had a thing for Curt. He'd spent many an hour with a dutiful husband. Right off the top he could think of a chiropractor, handymen, security guard, UPS driver, and a cop or two who had made it into his club of straight studs looking for hot man-on-man action.

In Curt's world, no man was off-limits and everyone was ready.

That is, until he met Dave.

Dave was different.

Dave wasn't a player. Never had been, never would be.

To Curt, such men didn't exist. Anyone could be had. Time and again his experience bore that out. But Dave remained aloof, uninterested, and in many ways, seemingly oblivious to Curt's intentions.

To Curt it was maddening.

He'd have to turn up the heat.

* * *

Anna spied the postmark in her stack of mail. Pushing aside the other letters, she tore open the one from Mexico.

Dear Anna,

Recently my mother died and I've been unable to make peace with her passing. I'm hoping you might be able to help. As you now, I can't visit the United States, but perhaps, you might travel to Puerto Vallarta. I work for a resort and can secure your accommodations. I will reimburse you for the flight in addition to any other fees you might charge. And I have talked with our activities director. She is certain we can sign up guests for whom you can provide private readings. That might make it a lucrative travel opportunity.

Please seriously consider coming. I'd be grateful for your help.

Affectionately,

Ernie Gonzales

Oh my God, Anna thought. *A man whose name begins with an E.* "Henry," she called to the back of the house.

Henry poked his head outside the door of his room. "I'm studying, Anna. What do you need?"

"Have you ever seen the ocean? Been to a beach?"

Henry's face lit up. "I've seen pictures. It looks amazing. But why are you asking? Where are you thinking of going now?"

"Mexico," Anna quietly purred, knowing full well that Henry had lived his entire life in Arizona, and so Tempe Town Lake was the closet he'd ever come to a body of water, and that didn't really count since it was man-made. "Mexico," she squealed with excitement. "How about it? Would you go with me to Mexico?"

"Your dime, school break," Henry answered, "I'm there."

"Good. Or should I say bueno."

"Bueno," Henry agreed. "Muy bueno."

* * *

Daisy was wide-awake by 5:30 am. She pulled on a pair of yellow leggings over her pink spandex. An iridescent yellow top completed the outfit. Lyle, who'd been awake a good thirty minutes, was sitting on the sofa reading the morning paper. He wore black running shorts paired with a tee shirt that read *Equality Arizona*, a gift from Charlie and Dave. Daisy checked Lyle's black Nikes. Velcro flaps were secured. Hand in hand, they left the apartment and headed out in the darkness to greet the Arizona morning.

The pair walked along the pathways of Casa Verde just as the automatic sprinklers completed their morning cycle. It was still dark when they stopped to watch two white doves bathe at the base of a eucalyptus tree, their wings illuminated by a nearby street lamp. Tiny heads bobbed in and out of the puddle as water splashed down their feathered backs. The distinct scent of orange blossoms filled the morning air.

"This is the best time of the day," Daisy said, breaking the silence.

Lyle agreed. "And just look at the lovely blooms of the purple bougainvillea. Truly beautiful."

"It is beautiful," Daisy inhaled deeply as the first rays of pink light shattered the darkness, promising a brilliant morning sunrise. "Let's get married," she heard herself say as if suddenly possessed by an alien life force. It had not been her intention to propose to Lyle. Not that morning, not any morning. The idea of marriage had once seemed absurd, and yet, surrounded by the beauty of nature, she now wanted to be married.

"*You want to marry me?*" Lyle sounded surprised.

Daisy blushed. She'd never been a traditional kind of gal and marriage was certainly traditional. But at that moment, much to her astonishment, she had a desperate need to secure her future.

"I know it seems foolish," Daisy said, giving Lyle a sidelong glance. It was like finding religion at the end of one's life. She wanted it, no matter how absurd, and she knew Lyle was her last chance. "Don't you want to marry me?" she asked, her voice trembling, unwilling to relinquish her destiny to chance.

She looked like a young girl, uncertain of herself and her feelings.

"Of course, I do," Lyle answered. "I'd be honored. If marriage is important to you, we'll marry. I'll marry you wherever and whenever you want. The sooner the better."

"Okay then," she said, smiling as they continued on their walk, proud of herself for speaking her truth.

They stopped to admire the yellow flowers of a desert cactus. Such flowering in the desert comes and goes quickly, often within twenty-four hours. The majestic blooms, fully opened, carpeted the dry, spikey cactus, offering the promise of new life.

The sun shone brightly over the eastern horizon as Daisy and Lyle rounded the final block, heading back to the apartment. They passed a long green hedge. Strolling in silence, Daisy walked ahead. A gentle peace came over her. She could feel the tension in her body ease. It would be a good day. She'd call Dave and Charlie. They'd help her figure out the details of the wedding. She was lucky to have such good friends. They'd be happy to hear the news.

Lost in her thoughts, it took her but a moment to realize that Lyle was no longer behind her. She'd heard a disturbance and assumed it was a bird nestling in a nearby bush, flapping its wings to prepare to take flight. But when she looked back, she instantly realized her error.

* * *

Bonnie pulled Charlie and Dave aside at the funeral home.

"We have a problem," she confided. "I checked the lease on the apartment. The unit is in Lyle's name only and of course there's this huge waiting list. According to the manager, Daisy's an illegal tenant. In other words, Lyle should have added her name to the lease when she moved in. But since he didn't, she has no rights at all. They've agreed to allow her to stay through the end of the month. Thank God Lyle died on the 5th. Had he died on the 27th, she'd have to immediately vacate."

Dave shook his head in disbelief. "I had no idea they could put you out so fast."

"Well, they can," Bonnie responded.

"What should we do?" Charlie asked.

"Can she move back in with the two of you? At least until we figure something else out."

"Of course," Charlie answered without a moment's hesitation.

"Great," Bonnie said looking at Dave and then Charlie. "I hope she isn't resistant."

"Me too," Charlie agreed. "But what other choice does she have?"

"You know, if you think about it," Dave chimed in, "even if you love the people, there's a real loss of personal dignity when you're forced to live in someone else's space."

"Better to be with people you love than living on the street," Bonnie pointed out.

"Or with those who are paid to care about you," Charlie added.

"Now wait a minute," Bonnie said sharply. "There are lots of great places out there that care for the elderly. It's not easy work. The pay leaves a lot to be desired. But there are caring, well-intentioned people who do the job every day."

"But they're still strangers," Charlie pointed out.

Dave interjected. "Hey, wait, what are we talking about? Daisy doesn't need care. She's perfectly capable on her own," he said, getting between the two. "I think we've gotten off-topic."

Charlie nodded. "Yes, but she isn't getting any younger. How long should someone her age live alone?"

No one had an answer.

Bonnie finally said, "Isn't is a bit ageist to assume that just because you're a senior you have to live with other seniors?"

"I suppose," Dave answered. "But the real challenge isn't where to go when you're healthy. It's when you get sick and don't have family. Who will take care of you? And if you can't live on your own, that's not the time to make those decisions. So timing seems to be kind of critical. You need to pick a place where you can live independently and if the need arises, you can just move down the hall."

Bonnie nodded. "I don't have children. Who's going to take care of me when I need help?"

"Or us?" Charlie said as he looked at Dave. "We're healthy now, but what happens in the next ten or fifteen years?

"You don't have to be eighty. Have you seen the obits?" Dave said. "Fifty-eight, sixty-two, sixty-three, sixty-five. Not everyone dies in their eighties. I read somewhere that nearly 80 percent of a person's lifetime healthcare expenditures happen during the last two years of their life. We're kidding ourselves if we don't think this could happen to us. We could very well wind up in Daisy's situation. Or worse."

Silence fell over the three. Bonnie stared off into the distance, depressed by the conversation. Dave rubbed his brow. Charlie sat down on a nearby chair with a thump.

Bonnie finally spoke.

"Okay. It's settled. She's moving in with the two of you."

* * *

Just because Bonnie had stopped seeing Jack didn't mean she'd stopped thinking of him. And so, when Bonnie spotted Jack off in the distance at Lyle's funeral, standing alone under the shade of an Arizona ash tree, her impulse was to go to him. She was proud that Jack's common decency had trumped his anger over the lawsuit.

"Look over there," she whispered to Charlie, pointing her chin in the direction where Jack stood. "See, he's not such a bad guy after all."

Charlie looked but said nothing.

She persisted. "He came. That should mean something. He probably feels terrible."

"He should feel terrible," Charlie mumbled. "He's an awful person."

"No," she silently mouthed despite Charlie's dismissive glare.

She temporarily conceded the point. It was neither the time nor place for such a discussion as they stood beneath the hot desert sun at Lyle's gravesite. Bonnie next to Charlie—Daisy between Charlie and Dave. The minister said a few quick prayers but Bonnie barely heard a word. Her gaze was fixed upon Jack. He wore a simple blue sport coat over a pair of khakis. Casually dressed, yet smart. A pair of black sunglasses concealed his eyes.

He nodded to her.

She nodded back.

The casket was slowly lowered, and once settled into its final resting place, Bonnie followed Charlie and Dave's lead, tossing a small shovel of dirt on top. The hollow sound of gravel hitting the casket frightened her. Eager to leave, she nudged Charlie. Charlie ignored her. It was only then that she realized Daisy was staring mournfully into the grave, glued to the very spot.

* * *

The cemetery was the last place on earth Jack wanted to be. He felt no better about cemeteries than he did about nursing homes. As far as he was concerned, both places were warehouses for the dead.

As Jack looked about the cluster of headstones, he couldn't help but think about his marriage to Enid.

That too was dead.

He'd never met Lyle. He'd no clue about the wonderful man in the pine box. His only reason to attend was to garner favor with Daisy in the hope that she might see him and soften about settling the lawsuit.

But Jack doubted Daisy even knew he was there.

From his vantage point, she appeared to be in a stupor; a frail paper doll held up on both ends by Charlie and Dave. At the gravesite, her eyes remained on the casket. She never once looked in his direction.

Jack regretted coming. Even at a distance, he sensed Daisy's profound pain. *It must be unbearable*, he thought, touched by her plight. *She must feel as if she's lost everything.*

And still, with the lawsuit on, he felt trapped in an adversarial position.

Standing amid the sea of headstones, Jack thought of Bonnie. There had been a real spark between them. It seemed foolish not to see her now. The cemetery offered a vivid reminder that no one lives forever.

Later that afternoon, Jack pulled out his cell phone. The muscles in his stomach tightened and his call went straight to voicemail. "Bonnie, we need to talk. Let's not throw away what we have together. Life is so short. Please call me. Jack."

* * *

Sanchez shut his office door. His fan had inexplicably stopped working. He silently cursed the stifling heat, feeling a sudden crush of claustrophobia as he prepared to review the Gonzales file.

Lunch had not settled well.

A chicken and black bean burrito was fighting its way back up. As he turned the pages of the file, he repeatedly burped. He felt like a blowfish, filling with gas, his stomach extending ever forward, his mouth, opening and closing as he gasped for air. Hoping the sensation would ease, he ignored the discomfort. By the time he reached the fingerprint analysis which documented a match on the terrace door, he reached into his desk drawer for a roll of Tums. He popped off two chewables using the tip of his thumb.

The videotape from the building's lobby security camera had been kept in a clear plastic bag. Sanchez held the bag up to examine its contents. He'd viewed the evidence the day before, aware that it had caught the images of two men. He thought about Ernie. He liked Ernie. It was too bad. Too bad that Ernie had lost his mother. Too bad that he had to destroy the evidence. And too bad that his intense acid reflux felt as if he'd swallowed a flamethrower.

* * *

The day after the funeral, Charlie met Bonnie and Daisy at The Veranda Cafeteria. Charlie wasn't a fan of cafeteria-style dining, tray in hand, waiting in a line to select pre-made items, but Bonnie had insisted they take Daisy to her favorite lunch spot.

"It's just a meal," Bonnie rolled her eyes, aware of Charlie's finicky nature.

Dave had said he'd meet them later, driving separately so that he could go to the gym first and then run errands.

Daisy sat at a corner table at the rear of the dining room as Bonnie pushed along two trays; one for herself and one for Daisy. Charlie, stood motionless, uncertain what to select, holding up the line as the place began to get busy with the lunch crowd.

The special was pastrami, and though Charlie loved pastrami, the sight of the pre-sliced meat lying in a greasy pan made him queasy.

"Do you honestly think everything in a restaurant is made from scratch the moment you order it?" Bonnie scolded him. "Well, it isn't. If you ever worked in a kitchen, you'd never eat out again."

A grey-haired gentleman with a white chef's coat rang up Charlie's meatloaf, mashed potatoes and succotash. "That'll be six dollars and thirty-five cents."

"Really?" Charlie glanced at the tray before him. "Including the cola and roll?"

The cashier smiled warmly. "That's right. Today's drink is free. The bread comes with the entrée."

"Sweet," Charlie said, counting out the money and handing it over. "I think this just might be my new favorite place."

Charlie crossed the busy dining room examining the choices of the other patrons. *Wow, you could save a lot of money eating here*, he thought as he spied the plates loaded with open-faced sandwiches covered in thick cream sauces, salads topped with croutons and bottle-style dressing, and baked potatoes loaded with butter and sour cream.

He set his tray down across from Bonnie. She'd selected the pot roast. Daisy sat to Bonnie's left and was picking at a plate of stuffed cabbage with her fork.

Bonnie scanned Charlie's tray.

"You were supposed to get the desserts?"

"Oh crap," Charlie said, getting to his feet. "I just got so caught up in all those entrée choices. I'll go back and see what they have."

"No," Daisy said, her hand signaling for him to sit down. "Enjoy your lunch. I don't need dessert. I'm not even hungry."

"You have to eat," Bonnie insisted. "You need to keep up your strength."

"Why?" Daisy asked, her voice hopeless. "For what purpose?"

Bonnie sighed. She looked at Charlie.

He knew he was supposed to say something, anything, but words failed him. There was no point in taking anything Daisy said literally. No point in repeating how important she was to them. Daisy was in no mood to hear it. Bonnie had said she'd seen this before at The Village. The relationship between two seniors is interrupted by death. The one who remains suffers terrible pangs of loneliness. It would take time for Daisy to adjust. Just how long was anyone's guess . . . but Bonnie had confidence Daisy would rebound.

She had to.

Charlie picked at his meatloaf.

"Honey," Bonnie said to Daisy, "you know we're here for you. You're not alone. You know that."

It sounded like a question . . . though intended as a statement of fact.

"I wish I were dead," Daisy blurted out, tears welling.

Charlie grabbed at the pickle on Bonnie's plate. He hated when women cried. It made him anxious.

Daisy looked over at Charlie. Tears rolled down her cheeks. "What am I going to do? How am I going to start all over again?"

Charlie wasn't quite sure what to say. He felt helpless.

Bonnie retrieved a packet of Kleenex from her purse. The two women huddled together on their side of the table, Bonnie with an arm gently extended around Daisy's shoulders, Daisy using the tissue to blot her eyes, Charlie nervously shoveling mashed potatoes into his mouth.

"We have a few ideas, right, Charlie?" Bonnie said.

Charlie nodded. He picked through Daisy's French fries, savoring the salty crunch.

"We think you should move back in with Charlie and Dave. At least until you figure out what you want to do."

"I don't know," Daisy sobbed.

Charlie swiped a Parker Roll from Bonnie's tray, slathered it with butter, and in three bites it was gone.

"Charlie?" Bonnie glared at him. "Tell Daisy what we agreed to."

Both women gazed in Charlie's direction as he punctured an over-cooked carrot with his fork and popped it in his mouth. The soft, orange vegetable seemed to instantly implode, its mushy center more water than substance. *Where's Dave?* Charlie thought as he swallowed. *Dave should've been here by now.* "Well," Charlie began, wiping his mouth with a napkin, "Dave and I . . . I mean . . . Dave and me . . . we think you shouldn't be alone. We want you to come and stay with us."

"Oh, but I couldn't," Daisy responded, her face contorted in sheer misery. "I've already imposed on your good nature. It's too much to ask."

"Well," Charlie said, "we're not really asking . . . we're wanting." It sounded awkward as soon as Charlie said it. "I mean, we'd be honored to have you."

"There, you see?" Bonnie beamed, winking at Charlie to acknowledge a job well done. "You adore Charlie and Dave. You've lived with them before. Where else can you go and know the house will be absolutely immaculate? And you're comfortable with them. It's perfect. It's like going home again."

* * *

Daisy listened as the two tried to convince her.

Going home again . . . could that ever be possible? My possessions are gone. I have no money. Jack won't ever speak to me again. Lyle is gone. Could anything ever be as it was?

Daisy hardly knew what to say.

"For now, just think about it," Bonnie said.

Daisy promised she would, although she was fairly certain her decision was already made. She wouldn't go live with Charlie and Dave. Nor would she live with Bonnie or anyone else. She was tired of living. The pain and anguish of life was okay for the young, but she was too old. Her joints ached at the very thought of another day.

No, she'd made up her mind. For the moment, she'd appear conciliatory. It was only polite. After all, Bonnie and Charlie had been so kind. There was no need to worry them further since there was absolutely nothing they could do to stop her.

The next step was hers to take.

* * *

Dave never made it to The Veranda Cafeteria.

Following lunch, Charlie stopped to pick up a few groceries and so later that day, standing in the kitchen, putting the groceries away, he filled Dave in on the conversation with Daisy, and, of course, about the price of the meatloaf.

"Forget about the meatloaf," Dave said impatiently as Charlie slid a box of Cheerios into the pantry. "Tell me about Daisy. *What did she say?*"

Charlie held a bag of navel oranges. "She mostly cried. And you know how I get when women cry. I shut right down." He opened the bag and placed the oranges in a decorative bowl.

Yes, Dave thought, *I know how you get.*

"I was just hoping you'd miraculously show up and save the day. Hey," Charlie asked, "where were you?"

"At the gym," Dave answered, sidetracking the truth. "It was packed. I couldn't get on the treadmill so I waited at the juice bar. And then after I did my thing, I was really sore so I went to the sauna. By the time I showered and dressed, I was sure you guys had finished with lunch. I'd no idea it would be a really big scene and you'd still be there."

Charlie nodded. "Yeah, a really big scene."

"Well I'm glad she'll be staying with us."

"Me too."

Dave grabbed the newspaper from the kitchen counter. "If you don't mind, I'm going to read."

"Be sure to check out the obituaries," Charlie said. "Lyle made the paper."

Dave immediately turned to the section, He scanned the three pages. "Where?"

"Top left."

Dave looked again. He turned the page.

Charlie leaned over and pointed to an obit of a man who appeared to be in his late twenties. "Right there."

Dave couldn't believe his eyes. The photo was of a young, handsome man, his head posed at a sharp angle, looking up and off into the distance. He was instantly able to detect the elderly gentleman that he'd come to know as Lyle, even though the hairline had long since receded and the face was fuller, but the very essence of the man, his bold eyes and firm chin, were the same. "Holy crap. He was gorgeous."

"Gorgeous!" Charlie agreed.

"Who'd have guessed?"

"I know, that's what I thought."

"Did Daisy choose that photo?" Dave asked.

"No. Lyle made the plans ahead of time with the mortuary. He provided the obit and the photo."

Dave looked Charlie square in the eye. "When I die, promise me, that you'll use a picture of me when I was ten years old."

"What?" Charlie protested. "That's morbid."

"It's an obit. It's supposed to be morbid."

"Not ten. That's terrible."

"It's something they do here," Dave insisted.

"No, it isn't. A picture in your twenties is a lot different than a picture of a child."

"I don't see the difference. A man in his nineties has a photo at twenty. C'mon. And look at all these people." Dave pointed across the pages. "You can tell who was loved. No one who loves you would use a photo like this." Dave pointed at a woman wearing a bandana to cover her bald head. The woman glared up from the page, a breathing tube sticking out of her nose. "She must have been a real bitch to score that photo."

Charlie winced. "If she wasn't dead, that photo would kill her."

"If you use a picture of me at ten, everyone will read the obit. And I was such a beautiful child," Dave reminisced. "That should be the picture."

"It's all about you, isn't it?" Charlie shook his head.

"I'm dead, aren't I? It should be about me."

"Lord," was all that Charlie could manage to say.

Dave had given it a lot of thought. "You start off as a baby, bald and wrinkled. You blossom into youth and then you spend the rest of your life heading toward total decay."

"Now there's the positive Dave I've come to know and love," Charlie chuckled. "Lighten up. It's not as bad as all that."

"Oh, I think it is. My grandmother used to say, *you're born with the face God gave you . . . you wind up with the face you deserve.*"

Charlie smiled. "I love that line."

"Yes . . . but . . . it makes you the responsible party for being so damn ugly."

"Okay, enough." Charlie said. "Read the damn obit."

Dave turned his attention away from the photo of the young dapper Lyle to read the content of the obit Lyle had prepared.

Lyle Fenton was jubilantly welcomed into the arms of his Savior. Born in Oshkosh, Wisconsin, on January 9, 1918, his mother Mary Ellis was a talented artist and his father William Fenton was a cowboy who worked the ranches of the Southwest. His parents shaped his love and respect for the desert landscape of the American cowboy. Lyle exhibited enormous talent as a child. In his early twenties, he studied with many famous artists of the twentieth century, notably Edward Cucuel, Gordon Grant, and Maynard Dixon. In 1941, Lyle entered the Armed Forces as a private, serving his country proudly during World War II. He landed on Omaha Beach where he survived the onslaught and high death toll of Able Company. Upon discharge, he married Henrietta Longview. The marriage lasted three months. His marriage to his second wife, Agnes Tuller, ended in divorce after three years. His third wife, Evelyn Drescott, died in childbirth. Lyle won many awards and was recognized internationally for his artistic talents. Today his early works hang in the Heard Museum. He is a member of the prestigious Cowboy Artists of America.

"Holy crap," Dave said. "Are you kidding me?"

"I know. We spent all that time with him and had no idea who he was."

"We never asked."

"We were so preoccupied with Daisy."

"And all the artwork in the apartment," Dave recalled. "You'd have thought that might have been a clue."

"The walls were covered. But who looks at cowboy art? To me it's like painting on velvet. I just thought it was an Arizona thing. I never realized *he was the artist.*"

"I can't believe it," Dave reiterated.

"What did you think of the rest of it?" Charlie asked. "*Jubilantly welcomed into the arms of his Savior.*"

"Very sexy."

Charlie agreed. "Oh yeah, I loved that."

"It's so much better than Emmy Lou's." Dave pointed to an obit lower down on the page. "*She's gone home to meet her maker. Gone home* sounds like she did something wrong."

Charlie laughed.

Dave continued. "Hey listen, if you want to know what really yanks my chain, why is it that obituaries never reveal how the person died? That's the main point. It seems to me that if someone died in a car accident, it would serve the rest of us well to know that *he refused to wear a seat belt and subsequently died of his injuries.* Or, *she drank Diet Cola in excess until her colon exploded causing death by sepsis.* Or, *he didn't believe in vac-*

cinations and died of the flu. Something useful should come out of these narratives. And is it really important to mention the names of parents long gone? Why not tell us how the person died? That's the point after all. They are dead."

"I get it," Charlie acquiesced, changing the subject. "So tell me again. Why didn't you show at lunch?"

"I told you . . . I was running late," Dave answered, annoyed at having to repeat an untruth. His attention drifted. He thought of his afternoon with Curt and was instantly aroused.

Charlie shot Dave a quizzical look.

Dave shifted the conversation. "And what did you say you ate?"

"The meatloaf," Charlie repeated, going into great detail as he again recapped the menu.

* * *

Anna marveled at her accommodations at Villa Allegra. Ernie had secured a second-floor two-bedroom suite with an eat-in kitchen. The terrace overlooked a magnificent negative edge pool that faced the ocean. With the patio door opened, she could hear the surf. *This is all just too lovely*, she thought, shoving a bottle of Coppertone into an enormous canvas bag already overloaded with a beach towel that read *Ain't Vacations a Beach.* "Are you coming?" she called to Henry, who had planted himself in front of the widescreen LED television mounted on the wall in his bedroom.

"I'll meet you downstairs," Henry said. "I can't get over this picture. It's so clear."

"Henry, you can watch television anytime. Don't you want to go to the pool? See the ocean? Enjoy the sun?"

"Sure . . . you go ahead. I'll be right down."

Anna couldn't imagine being any happier. With the pleasures of the resort before her and Henry in tow, life offered a new excitement. The nagging dizziness had disappeared. For the first time in weeks, she felt free and energized. It was a relief to feel well again.

Anna settled into a padded recliner by the pool. She pulled out the paperback she'd picked up at the airport. On the cover was a pirate with deep, chiseled features, a killer five o'clock shadow, and flowing, shoulder-length black hair. He stood on the edge of a cliff, his expression dark and brooding, a torn shirt revealing a massive chest that seemed to beckon forth all maidens in need of protection.

Anna was ignited by his torrid sexuality.

She scanned the back cover. The reviews promised a thrilling read. For *twenty-one dollars*, she thought, *they better provide his home address so I can find and marry him.*

She looked again at the front cover, drinking in every hyper-masculine detail of her dream lover. She decided that his picture alone was worth the price of the book.

* * *

Henry joined Anna in the adjacent lounge chair. He, too, was preoccupied. He'd spotted a blond hunk poolside playing with his little son. The three-year-old was running back and forth, flapping his water wings, preparing to jump in. The father laughed and grabbed the little boy, lifting him high in the air and swinging him around. It was a sweet moment. Henry watched from behind his dark Arizona shades.

"Ernie's joining us for dinner tonight," Anna said, offhandedly, turning to look at Henry. She lowered her chin to her chest. The knock-off Armani sunglasses she'd purchased at Walgreens slid down her nose to reveal her big brown eyes.

"Maybe you should have dinner without me," Henry suggested.

"No, you have to come. I want to show you off."

"I don't know . . ."

"You could offer him an apology."

"I'm not sure an apology will have much meaning."

Anna pushed. "You'll never know unless you try. And perhaps, you'll feel better."

Henry resisted. "He really wants to see *you*. I think you two need privacy."

Henry's eye returned to Mr. Blond Dad. With his son in tow, he'd walked over to the cocktail bar. The female bartender tossed her hair and laughed before handing the man a plastic cup of water which he handed to his son. Even from a distance, Henry could see the well-chiseled muscles in the man's back as he leaned on the bar and appeared to be flirting with the bartender.

A grey sparrow landed near the little boy who screamed with delight. He chased the tiny bird as it hopped toward the edge of the pool before taking flight.

The kid pulled off his water wings.

Henry sat up.

The kid kneeled at the edge of the pool and looked down into the water.

Anna was talking. "Come to dinner with Ernie. I don't ask you to do many things, but this one, I'm asking you to do."

He heard her as mostly background noise. "Okay, whatever," he answered, eyes glued on the little boy.

"I looked at the menu online," Anna continued, "and the restaurant looks fabulous. Open-air dining with a Mexican flare. I was thinking about the grilled halibut . . ."

The father, still engaged in a discussion with the bartender, was oblivious to his son's whereabouts as the little boy leaped into the water with a shriek of delight and immediately disappeared. In an instant, Henry was out of his lounge chair and in the pool, swimming hard toward the deep end. He sharply descended to retrieve the little towhead, dragging the limp child to the surface. As Henry lifted the boy to the edge of the pool, the father realized what had happened, dropped the drink, and rushed over. In a matter of moments the father was performing CPR. A small crowd gathered and collectively held its breath.

Anna froze as she watched the action from her lounge chair.

The father pumped on his child's chest. Water shot out of the little boy's mouth followed by an enormous shriek as the kid screamed bloody murder. The tension in the father's face melted away as he grabbed his son in his arms and hugged him.

"Oh my God, you saved that boy!" Anna said as Henry wandered back. "I saw the whole thing. You're amazing. I've never seen anything like that in my life."

Henry had acted on pure instinct. He'd seen the child in trouble and responded. It wasn't until the little boy was out of the water and safe that Henry realized what had transpired.

"I can't believe it myself," he said, drying himself off with a towel. "I guess that's what they call *paying it forward*. After all," and he stopped what he was doing to catch Anna's eye, "you saved my life." For the first time since coming to live with Anna, Henry acknowledged the enormity of her deed. "I don't know what I would have done if it weren't for you."

Anna's eyes glistened. She was proud. Proud of Henry and proud of herself.

"Thank goodness the father was so good looking," Anna teased, "Otherwise you might have missed that opportunity."

"Busted," Henry sang out, aware that Anna had been on to him.

"I guess being gay has its advantages," Anna acknowledged. "You can check out hot men and save little boys at the same time."

"Hey, I sound like a gay superhero."

Anna didn't hesitate for a moment. "Yes. That you are, my darling, and always will be."

* * *

Anna caught sight of Ernie as he wandered among the hotel guests at the pool. She'd taken a fast dip to cool off from the midafternoon sun and remained slightly submerged in the warm water as Ernie wound his way through the sea of vacationers greased up with suntan lotion, lying prone in their lounge chairs, desperate to catch a healthy glow as the prized souvenir of a week in Mexico.

Maybe it was the bright sun, or perhaps it was the Mai Tai Anna had had with lunch, but Ernie looked different. Thinner. Certainly darker. And very, very sexy. The white slacks and white shirt made his bronzed skin pop. The graying at his temples was most becoming and more prominent since the last time she'd seen him.

She climbed out of the pool and called his name, waving as he passed nearby. The last time he'd seen her, she looked different.

"You didn't recognize me, did you?" she teased, noticing his surprised expression.

He stared at her in the wet bathing suit. Water dripped from her hair, droplets falling upon her ample bosom. "No," he admitted as she toweled off her legs.

"Well, it's me," she smiled, tossing her hair back and giving it a final shake.

Standing before him she felt like every inch a woman. Vulnerable, sensuous, eager to please.

"Is the room to your liking?" he asked, his eyes taking her in.

"It's wonderful. Everything about this place is wonderful." She slipped on her flip flops. "Is there somewhere we can go to talk?"

"Let's walk along the beach."

Together, they strolled along the sand. Ernie removed his shoes and socks and rolled up the bottom of his pants. The tide nipped at their feet. They came upon one of the resort's daybeds used for couple massages. Anna and Ernie sat next to one another. The gossamer canopy offered muted shade from the hot sun.

Anna couldn't remember ever feeling so comfortable with a man.

"I've been anxious to see you," Ernie confessed, his distress palpable. "Ever since my mother died, I've haven't been myself. I can't sleep. I can't work. I can't think. The police say she committed suicide. I don't believe that. Knowing my mother, it just doesn't make sense. She struggled all her life. She was a fighter."

"How was she adjusting to the move to Puerto Vallarta?"

"Not well," Ernie admitted. "It'd been difficult for her."

"Did she ever speak of suicide?"

"No. Never." Ernie glanced away. "But I was so busy, working all those hours. I'm afraid, I wasn't paying much attention. I hadn't been a very good son . . ."

"Nonsense," Anna interrupted. "I don't believe that for a moment. You're a good man. You can't blame yourself."

"That's kind of you to say. But I do feel responsible. I should have been with her."

"To protect her?"

"Yes," Ernie said. "I'm certain she was murdered."

"Do you have any proof?" Anna asked, sounding more like a detective than a psychic.

"No," Ernie admitted. "But it must be true."

Anna's pulse quickened. The conversation with Ernie was familiar; the beach, his clothing, the sound of the waves crashing against the shore. It was déjà vu. She recognized the moment as being pivotal. But why it was important, she wasn't quite sure.

Ernie filled in the details of his childhood. Clearly, she'd only known Ernie superficially in Phoenix. *Ernie, when you're done painting, take a look at the doorbell. There's something wrong with the chimes. And before you leave, check the drain in the sink. I have a leak. And Ernie, don't forget about the gutters. They need to be cleaned before the start of monsoon season.* Their relationship had been based purely on business, the conversation limited to the job at hand, when Ernie could do it, and the price. They occupied the same space but didn't know each other. She had always been eager for him to finish up and leave before another client arrived. Now she wondered if that had been her way of avoiding feeling uncomfortable alone in the house with an attractive man.

As Ernie recounted the details of the last few months, his eyes darted about, as if watching his life unwind on a screen that only he had access to, private and personal. "And then I thought of you," he said. "I remembered all the things you seemed to know."

"Well, I'm glad you reached out," Anna admitted, uncomfortable that his memory might include what she used to look like. She pulled her knees in close, wrapping her arms about her legs as she changed the subject. "This is such a beautiful place."

Ernie looked about as if seeing Puerto Vallarta for the first time. "It is."

"I'm glad you invited me."

He smiled. "Well, I'm afraid we're going to make you work awfully hard for that room. Our activity coordinator has a number of clients lined up for you to meet. You're going to have a pretty full schedule this week. I hope it won't be too overwhelming."

"I'll manage," Anna said taking a deep breath as the ocean breeze gently caressed her face.

* * *

Ernie agreed to meet Anna in her suite before dinner for their first session together. Eager to get started, he wasn't exactly sure what to expect. He knew he'd be seeing Henry, something he had hoped to avoid. But Anna had been insistent. When they'd sat together on the beach, she'd filled him in on Henry's background and progress. Ernie listened politely.

He looked off in the distance, waiting for his chance to change the focus of the discussion. But that chance didn't come.

"You're quiet," Anna probed. "You're silence is damning. You're still angry."

"I don't know what to say," Ernie said. "Had you asked me, I'd have told you not to bring him here. But you didn't ask."

"He's just a teen," she said, defending Henry. "A lost and frightened teen."

Ernie was indignant at the prospect of facing the youth again. "And what does that have to do with me?"

Anna gave him a crooked smile. "For you, nothing at all. But for Henry, it means a lot. You're an adult. You've made peace with the world. Henry still struggles. Oh, he doesn't talk to me about all the things going on in his head, but I can see. He's sensitive. He spends most of his time alone. What happened must weigh heavily on his soul. How is he supposed to move on with his life after he's ruined yours?" She arched her eyebrow. "Why would you want him to hold on to that?"

Regardless of what Ernie felt toward Henry, he admired Anna's spirit. When she spoke of Henry, her face lit up. It was as if she was speaking of her own flesh and blood. Her very own child. Someone whom she loved dearly.

At the agreed upon hour, Ernie rang the bell of the suite and hoped for the best. Anna greeted him at the door. Standing off in the corner of the room was the figure of a young man Ernie barely recognized. The last time they'd seen each other, Henry's dark hair was long, pulled back in a ponytail. His clothes, rough and torn. He'd looked threatening, a figure larger than the shy teenager before him now.

Ernie nodded at Henry. Henry nodded back.

"Henry. Isn't there something you wanted to say?" Anna asked. She tilted her head in Henry's direction.

"I owe you an apology," Henry blurted out. "I'm truly sorry for my actions that night. It was stupid."

"I've been through hell," Ernie said, eyeing the nervous teen.

"I know." Henry looked down. "Anna told me. I know it was my fault. And there's nothing I can do or say to make it right."

Ernie locked eyes with Anna. He sensed the warmth in her steady gaze. Perhaps it was time to let go of his anger. To release the outrage he felt over the police mistaking him for Anna's assailant. There were laws in place which spurred such prejudices that had nothing to do with the teen. An innocent traffic stop would have generated the same outcome. Perhaps Henry was no more responsible for his problems then he was responsible for his illegal status. He took a deep breath. Perhaps his deportation wasn't truly Henry's fault.

"Okay kid," Ernie conceded. "Okay."

* * *

With the apology out of the way, Henry excused himself and headed out the door. Ernie joined Anna on the sofa, handing her a handkerchief of Maria's. Anna had asked for a personal item to summon Maria's energy. The linen was embroidered with little red and pink roses and held the faintest scent of perfume. As Anna touched the cloth, she sensed the familiar dizziness. She closed her eyes and took three consecutive deep breaths, trying her best to focus. She instinctively clenched her teeth and prepared for the worst.

"There's a female energy. A strong female energy," she announced. Her eye's bobbed in their sockets as the visions started.

Ernie could hardly contain his excitement. "That must be my mother. Is it my mother?"

Anna didn't answer. She was fully adrift in channeling. There were flashes of a terrace. She hadn't seen the terrace before. A pair of strong arms wrapped around her torso. She was instantly filled with dread. She held her breath, realizing for the first time since the dizzy spells had started months ago that someone was indeed with Maria at the time of her death. A man. And then, another set of hands grabbed Anna by the legs.

There were two men.

Anna struggled against the two intruders. Her heart raced with sheer terror. Two men were swinging her roughly. One by the legs. One by the arms. They were going to toss her over the terrace railing. Anna heard, *Uno, dos, tres*, as she swung back and forth, helpless to free herself.

Maria screamed.

Anna screamed.

And then it was over.

* * *

Anna tried to compose herself.

"Are you okay?" Ernie filled a bar glass with water. "Here, drink this."

Anna did as she was told. But the dizziness lingered.

"What happened?" he asked, sitting next to her on the sofa.

She hesitated. She wanted to spare Ernie the pain of his mother's final moments. "My head . . . the room is still spinning."

Ernie persisted. "Tell me. And don't leave anything out. I want to know. Tell me."

Anna had no option but to speak her truth. "Your mother was thrown off the terrace." As soon as the words left her lips, she regretted them.

Ernie leapt to his feet. "Dear God. Why? Who would have done such a thing?" He paced the room. "They told me all along it was a suicide. From the very beginning. Sanchez insisted."

"It wasn't a suicide," Anna confirmed. "I felt hands around her waist; hands on her legs. Your mother didn't jump."

15

....

Charlie sensed something wasn't quite right at home. There was a breach growing in his relationship with Dave, a tension that he attributed to Dave's decision to retire.

They'd always been a goal-oriented couple. Two successful careers had been the cornerstone of their shared vision of a life which included frequent travel, dining out, and spending time with friends. Now, Dave seemed anxious and uneasy, unwilling to do much of anything. Charlie assumed that given time, Dave would get over himself, come around, and begin to enjoy retirement. And so Charlie did his best to ignore Dave, thinking that by doing so he'd be giving Dave time and space to adjust.

Together, they sat on the sofa in their family room, Dave with a big glass bowl of microwave popcorn resting in his lap, Charlie stretched out, his feet up on the coffee table. A burnt buttery smell hung in the air. Timmy lay between them, his back legs touching Charlie's thigh, his eyes focused on Dave's hand, watching for stray kernels.

Charlie scrolled through the cable guide. "It's Monday night. Where the hell is *The Bachelorette*?"

"You just passed it," Dave said, reaching into the bowl.

Charlie backed up on the guide. The screen opened to ABC. He muted the sound in anticipation of the start of the program. "We still have fifteen minutes," he said, in case Dave hadn't noticed the time. "You're really quiet tonight? What's up?" Charlie adjusted his position to face Dave. "And are you planning on sharing that popcorn?"

Dave offered the bowl up. Timmy sniffed the bottom as it passed overhead.

"Tell me . . ." Charlie said, picking through the bowl for the crunchy, denser kernels.

Dave gave Charlie a wide-eyed look. "There's nothing to tell."

Charlie shifted again, bouncing the bowl. Stray kernels landed on the poodle's back. Timmy jerked about to gobble up the snack. "You've been acting so strange."

"Just being me," Dave mumbled as he rubbed Timmy's haunches. Timmy readjusted to face Dave. Dave slipped his hand into the dog's mouth, initiating play. Timmy gummed Dave, flipping onto his back, front paws swiping at Dave's hands.

Charlie unmuted the sound. "There's something wrong. I can tell. I wish you'd just spit it out. It isn't about our moving to Phoenix?"

Dave exhaled.

Charlie muted the sound again, turning back to Dave. Dave's face was a frozen mask, revealing nothing. They'd been together for years. Charlie knew every expression. But this face he could not read. This face was different.

"Tell me," Charlie demanded to know. "Is it living in Phoenix? Is that the problem?"

Dave words came fast and hard. "I just wish I'd never taken that damn job. That company totally screwed with my head. I thought I'd work five more years before I retired. Now I'm not sure what the hell to do. I don't want to go back to work. I'm totally burnt out. But I don't want to sit around all day either."

Dave's face was a mask of sheer disgust.

"Hey," Charlie said, soothingly. "It's not your fault it didn't work out. It was a brave decision to take a new job. And from where I'm sitting, you saved yourself years of hell retiring early. Most men would have stayed. Most men would have dropped dead from the stress and aggravation. You took care of yourself. You valued your life as being more important than just a job."

"I know. I know," Dave acknowledged. "But I'd have preferred to wrap up my career on a happy note."

Charlie exhaled. "Then maybe you never would have retired."

Dave conceded the point. "Maybe not."

"Well, I don't know what you're upset about then. I wish it was me. I'd like to get off this merry-go-round . . ."

"For a week maybe."

"No . . ."

"Then do it," Dave dared Charlie. "Give up your career. Say *no* to National Public Radio and the *Wall Street Journal* when they call for your insight into the changing retail market. Turn Fox Business down when they want to discuss the future of mall development in America. Tell your clients you can't take their calls any longer. You're too busy. You've retired."

A moment of silence passed between them.

Charlie scratched his forehead. "Wow. You're really angry."

"Do you know what happens to a man when he gives up his career?"

Charlie hardly knew what to say. Dave appeared to be on a roll.

"He loses his grounding. There's a thrashing about as you try to figure out what you're going to do with the rest of your life. You look around for any distraction to anchor you. You're desperate to recapture what you've lost."

"And what exactly have you lost?" Charlie wanted to know.

"Your youth. Your vitality. Your purpose. Your importance in the world. No one needs you anymore. No one wants you. What you have to say doesn't matter."

Charlie sat straight up. "Now, you're exaggerating. You know you're loved. We," Charlie said stroking Timmy's head, "care about you."

"It's not about caring. It's about being useful. There's a void to be filled. You want to feel alive again."

"Okay. So you miss working. You're frustrated. You've been put out to pasture too soon. Is that it?"

"Now you're beginning to get it." Dave got to his feet. "You think I'm supposed to be happy. But I'm not. I'm more confused than ever," he said stomping out of the room.

＊ ＊ ＊

Daisy rummaged through Lyle's medicine cabinet, lining up the bottles on the bathroom countertop. Tylenol with Codeine #3 for an aching back, Percocet for an abscessed tooth, Oxytocin for a painful hip. Combined with a glass or two of Scotch, she thought there were enough. No more worry about where to move, how to live, or who to turn to for help. Soon all of life's challenges would be well behind her. *And good riddance*, she thought. Now the end would come at her choosing. She'd be in control.

She gently touched each of the vials. She wondered what would happen once she'd taken the pills. Would she float toward the ceiling? Would a white light envelop her in love? Would she see dead relatives? Or would everything simply go black?

Would it be painful?

She thought about the time when she was a young girl and nearly drowned. She'd gone with her brother to Rockaway Beach to escape a hot New York City summer. Wading out in the water, she'd been caught in a powerful riptide. Unable to breathe, she'd started to panic until a lifeguard pulled her to safety.

Would she experience the same hysteria as she did that day?

If only she could be sure about what might happen next.

She believed her soul eternal. It was a truth that spoke to her from the very core of her being. And so, she expected that after death she'd continue on in a different state, much like water evaporates to become mist while still retaining its essence.

She recoiled.

If my soul is eternal, then what can really be the point of killing myself? There can be no real escape. What if this is just another one of life's lessons? What if I'm supposed to struggle? What if there's more for me to yet experience?

Confused, she silently prayed. *Help me, God, to make the right decision. I'm tired. I need guidance. I need reassurance. I need your help.*

In the stillness of the moment, Daisy became keenly aware of her good health. She remembered the days at The Village, the desperation at being dependent. How she'd longed to be well again, living life on her own terms. She looked about the small apartment. All the beautiful things Lyle had collected over his lifetime. She realized Lyle had saved her. He'd been an important part of the healing process, instrumental in giving her a second chance at life. And now, healthy and capable of managing her own affairs, it would be wrong to throw it away. It would be a disservice to Lyle's memory.

The longer she stared at the pills, the greater was her commitment to live.

She'd go forward alone. She'd been alone before. She'd do it again.

And then she had another insight.

She wasn't truly alone. She had friends. People whom she loved. Dave and Charlie who treated her with such kindness and concern. Bonnie, a friendship so special that she was able to share her feelings without fear of judgment. Jack, too, came to mind. She'd loved Jack from the moment he was born. He'd never been far from her thoughts. Giving him up had been the hardest thing she'd ever done. She couldn't change the past, but perhaps she could affect the future.

Lyle was gone. That was the sad reality. But she was still alive.

She'd regroup and start over again.

* * *

As Jack and Enid's marriage fell apart, Enid began a new relationship, one that required little commitment beyond showing up twice a week. It had started innocently enough. The first time they met, they were complete strangers. For him, she was but one of many women he serviced. But to Enid, he was heaven-sent. An angel of mercy. Her special man.

His name was Carlos and he worked at the Massage Envy on Camelback.

Their sessions lasted fifty minutes. There was no penetration. No touching of private parts. Carlos never removed one article of clothing, and even if he had, Enid was lying face down and wouldn't have known.

Those fifty minutes were all about her. And that's exactly how she liked it.

Carlos worked wonders to ease Enid's tension. She could face any challenge with Daisy, Jack, and the pending lawsuit, as long as she had Carlos. His firm shoulder massage was divine. The way he worked out the knots in her lower back, pure magic. When he placed his giant mitts on her, and gently pressed in small circular motions, Enid would have gone anywhere with him, though she wouldn't have recognized him in the light of day. At $59 a session, with a monthly membership, Carlos was the best buy in town, and Enid knew it.

* * *

After meeting with Anna, Ernie slept soundly, his mood markedly improved. The staff at Villa Allegra noticed the change in his demeanor.

Gossip spread quickly.

She's his ex-wife. She's in from Phoenix and that's their son.

She's an old girlfriend. He's still in love with her. He wants her back. He's wooing her.

She's his sister. That's his nephew. They're the only family he has left.

She's his former fiancée and that's her cousin. They had a falling out before he left the States. She's here to patch it up. He's going to propose again. You'll see. They'll be engaged before the week is out.

None of it was true, but like all good stories started by well-intentioned people, the rumors were infused with a sweetness and hopefulness that lifted everyone's spirits. The staff wanted Ernie to be happy. It made coming to work exciting.

And so Ernie's employees banded together, in unspoken agreement, to make sure that Ernie and his entourage had the chance to achieve all that the employees wished for them. And whenever so many people focus their unified energies to create an atmosphere of love, the recipients of such attention are bound to benefit from the generosity of spirit.

Anna seemed happier than ever before, Ernie increasingly attentive. The two smiled at each other the way those who share a secret tend to do.

And as love filled the air, Henry became increasingly alarmed.

He wasn't quite ready to relinquish his Anna.

* * *

Bonnie agreed to meet Charlie for lunch at Christo's on 7th Street. The invitation had been very last minute. Charlie had sounded strange on the phone. Stressed. Bonnie couldn't imagine what the matter was. Things had gone so smoothly with Daisy. She'd moved into Charlie and Dave's, and unlike all matters that people fret endlessly about, the transition had gone off without a hitch. Daisy not only seemed glad to move back in, she had embraced the idea. Bonnie had been present at the dinner the first night when they were all together. Charlie had toasted to new beginnings. They'd clinked glasses. Everyone was all smiles as they sat in Dave and Charlie's kitchen eating cake, drinking wine, and getting tipsy. It had been a silly, fun evening.

And then the call from Charlie.

Bonnie checked her watch. She'd been doing paperwork all morning. Care plans needed to be updated, medical records reviewed, invoices processed. She rarely ate lunch out during the week, preferring to nuke a Lean Cuisine. On the rare occasion when she did go out, she typically grabbed a sandwich at Subway. It was never a fancy lunch like the one planned at Christo's.

She eyed the pile of paperwork in front of her.

I should never have agreed, she thought, annoyed at herself for giving in so easily. She winced. *Whatever I don't get done today, I'll have to take home tonight.*

Charlie was seated at a corner table when she arrived.

She cut her way through the elegant dining room with its crisp white tablecloths, sparkling wine glasses, and fresh baskets of hot Italian bread. Her eyes glanced about at the beautifully prepared dishes. Chicken marsala, veal parmigiana, pasta carbonara. The smell of tomato sauce and fresh basil filled the air. A waiter passed by with a tray of entrees. Her nose captured a whiff of eggplant parmesan and chicken genovese. Her mouth watered. Her tummy rumbled.

"Hello handsome," she said in a lighthearted manner as she approached Charlie's table.

He stood up and took her hand. She offered her cheek and he kissed it.

"Thanks so much for coming," he said. "I really appreciate it."

As she took her seat, the waiter appeared and asked if she wanted a drink. Noticing the worried expression on Charlie's face, she was tempted to order a merlot. But it was a workday. She ordered an iced tea.

They discussed the weather. They both agreed a temperature of 105 was manageable for the summer in Phoenix. Above 105, even long-term residents fled to Flagstaff. They talked of 7th Street and the difficulty of making a left turn during rush hour.

They perused the menu. Bonnie told Charlie about her favorite dishes and what she wished she could try if she wasn't ordering the chicken piccata, which of course she had to, because it was her favorite in the Valley.

By the time the waiter returned to take their order, Charlie seemed fine. Perhaps she'd misread him. Picked up on a passing mood. *We all have them*, she thought. *He's allowed.*

When she told Charlie about Mr. Denton who had turned one-hundred the previous Monday and couldn't find his dentures to eat his lobster dinner, Charlie laughed. In fact, throughout their conversation, Charlie laughed in all the right places.

"I love this restaurant," she confided, savoring each bite. "You have to try the piccata." She cut off a small piece and placed it on Charlie's bread plate. "It just melts in your mouth."

Charlie's eyes brightened considerably as he chewed on the tender chicken, infused with a tart, lemony, buttery flavor. "Just delicious," he agreed.

"So tell me," she finally asked, "how's Daisy doing?"

"Fine," Charlie said. "She makes everything so easy. The other day we awoke to this marvelous breakfast. Cinnamon rolls from scratch. I've scolded her a thousand times that we didn't invite her to be the live-in maid, but she has lots of energy, and Dave and I agree that if it gives her pleasure to do things around the house, and it really does seem to, why not? It's like having your mother around, but so much nicer. Daisy doesn't tell you what you don't want to hear."

"Did your mother do that?" Bonnie had never heard Charlie talk about his mother.

"Sure. But all negative messages were delivered under the heading of *for your own good*. Like the time she tried to convince me that if I wanted to be an artist, I needed to be a commercial artist because they can earn a living. I hated commercial art. I was terrible at it. But that didn't stop her. In the end, I lost my interest in art altogether. Why do you suppose mothers tell their children what they should do with their lives? My mother wasn't an artist. What the hell did she know about being an artist?"

"I'm sure she meant well."

"Meant well?" Charlie shook his head. "I'm not sure what that even means. I could never figure her out. The woman is dead some twenty-five years and I'm still thinking about what she said. It's ridiculous the power we give these people. When I reached fifty, it occurred to me that my mother was trying to tell me what to do when she was only thirty-five. She spoke with such authority, I assumed her immensely knowledgeable. Now I realize she had no idea what she was talking about. *Maybe my dreams* were worthy."

Bonnie touched Charlie's arm. "They still are, Charlie."

"Are they?" he said, nudging his empty plate away. "I don't know."

"Sure they are. If you want to paint or draw or sketch or sculpt, whatever an artist does, it's not too late to do it."

Charlie's eyes took on a far-away look. "My mother used to say you can't teach an old dog new tricks."

"Ridiculous," Bonnie said, as she took Charlie's bread plate and offered him the last of her chicken. Charlie waved his hand as if to decline, but Bonnie was not deterred. She pushed the plate toward him. "Grandma Moses didn't start painting till she was in her sixties. As long as you're breathing, and have the desire, you can do anything you want. I work with older people and I know it's true. Just the other day a woman of seventy-two confessed she didn't feel a day over sixteen. Her body was seventy-two, but her mind was still agile and young. She reads two books a week, loves science fiction, and thinks Ray Bradbury is the best."

"I guess I could take art classes," Charlie said as he chewed.

"Sure you could." Bonnie offered a warm smile.

"And I kind of need the distraction now," Charlie tossed out.

Bonnie immediately reacted.

"What are you talking about?"

She'd lost the flow of the conversation. If things were good with Daisy, and Charlie wanted to paint . . .

Charlie took a deep breath. "Well, that's really why I wanted to have lunch with you."

As the waiter cleared the table, Bonnie checked her watch. She had barely ten minutes left before she needed to head back to the office. Why would Charlie wait so long when he knew she had to get back to work?

Bonnie braced herself. "So what's going on?"

Charlie's eyes welled up. "It's Dave."

"Is he sick?" she asked. He'd looked fine the last time they were all together.

"No, it's not that." Charlie folded his hands, fingers interlocking. His thumbs nervously rubbed together.

"Then what can possibly be wrong?" she asked, growing impatient with the drama.

Charlie took a breath and let out a sigh. "He's seeing someone else."

"Another man?" Bonnie tried to maintain a neutral expression. It was difficult.

"Yes."

Bonnie couldn't believe her ears. "How long has this been going on?" she asked.

"I don't know." Charlie chewed his lips.

"Are you sure? That doesn't sound like Dave. I can't believe he'd be seeing someone else." Bonnie glanced at her phone. She really had to get back.

Charlie leaned into Bonnie, assuming the posture of a conspirator. "It's true. I got a call the other day. Some man said he was seeing Dave and then hung up."

Bonnie thought about her own indiscretions. She'd never left a message for another man's wife. It was just too tacky. "It could be a phony phone call or someone who's angry with Dave. Have you asked Dave about it?"

Charlie cradled his arms. "I can't. I had a feeling something was going on. Now I know it's true."

"How can you know?" Bonnie asked.

"He's been so damn moody," Charlie explained. "Whenever I talk to him, he snaps. It's like we've had this fight . . . and I somehow missed it. I know he's had trouble adjusting to not working, but he's so damn angry all the time. I feel like I've done something terrible to disappoint him . . . and all I've been is just me. Nothing different. Just me."

* * *

Minutes passed like hours as Bonnie listened to Charlie go on and on about Dave. She squirmed when he talked about their sex life. She nervously played with her bracelet, rotating it about her wrist when Charlie confessed he could have been more spontaneous in bed. Some things, she thought, were best left for a discussion with a good therapist.

She held her breath when he talked about the challenges they'd faced in their years together. Year one, year seven, year fourteen. For two men who Bonnie thought so well-suited to each other, those seemed like a lot of years when things weren't working well for them as a couple.

As Charlie continued, she started to rethink her relationship with Jack.

Who needs all this drama? First you're in love, then there's problem after problem. If Charlie and Dave can't make it work, what hope do I have with Jack?

"I just don't know whether to confront him or not," Charlie finally said. "I'm not sure I want to know the truth."

Bonnie understood only too well. She hadn't gotten to be single by avoiding awkward conversations. Too often she'd pushed, prodded, and ripped the fresh scabs off her relationships. She'd over-analyzed, over-verbalized, and sent many a man running for the hills to escape rehashing old issues. She hid her need to control behind a sincere wish to understand. In the end, none of it had helped. She didn't ever understand. And where had all those heart-to-heart discussions gotten her? Sitting in a restaurant with a gay man, listening to his problems. A gay man who had a long-term relationship she admired.

Charlie started to cry.

Bonnie refocused. She reminded herself that this was not about her. It was about Charlie and Dave. Even so, she wondered what the heck she and Jack were doing getting back together. Still, so many of the problems Charlie discussed were linked to male ego. Whose career dominates? Who makes more money? Issues that didn't play into her relationship with Jack. She was annoyed about Jack farting in public, much too loud for her to pretend she didn't hear it. And the length of his grey nose hairs. Dear God, she needed a weed whacker to keep those babies in check. And she hated the standing pools of urine around the toilet. Did the man ever hit the bowl? She thought of Charlie and Dave's toilet. She'd bet anything that toilet was spotless. Everything else in the house was spotless. How did they manage to keep it looking so clean and tidy? How often did they have a maid service? Maybe she should get that person's name and number.

Charlie finally stopped talking. "What do you think?" he suddenly asked.

Bonnie panicked. She'd been lost in her own thoughts. She opened her mouth slightly and shrugged her shoulders unable to come up with a response.

Charlie nodded his head in agreement. "It's hard to know what to do."

She wished she was back in the office. The chicken piccata was beginning to repeat.

"I think I'm going to let it ride. Pretend I have no idea. Let it run its course until it peters out. I think that's best," Charlie decided. "Thank you so much for listening to me. I don't know what I would have done without your help."

"I really did nothing," Bonnie said modestly.

Truer words had never been uttered.

* * *

The terrible dizziness that had plagued Anna in Phoenix took hold again in Puerto Vallarta. The unnerving imbalance shifted the axis of the room without warning, creating an alternative fun-house version of the world. Anna took to her bed, curtains drawn, and passed on meals.

"But you have to eat something," Henry insisted, standing nearby.

Lying face-down on the bed, she grasped the mattress as if it had been transformed into a bucking bronco and her only course, to hold on for dear life. "I can't keep anything down." Her voice was barely a whisper.

"We should call a doctor."

"I've been that route, Henry. It's no use." She curled into a fetal position, clutching the covers close to her face.

"Then what can we do?"

"I don't know," Anna said. "Maybe I can sleep this off. Why don't you go out and enjoy the day. I'm sure I'll feel better later. Go ahead," she insisted, her hand in the air waving him away. "Go."

In a panic, Henry headed out of the darkened room. The bright Mexican sun nearly blinded him as he made his way to the lobby of the resort. A young woman behind the counter seemed to recognize him as he approached. Or was she just being friendly? Henry was uncertain but grateful for her welcoming smile.

"Can you tell me where I can find Ernie Gonzales?"

Ernie was making his daily rounds with the housekeeping crew when Henry tracked him down. "There's something wrong," Henry began, oblivious to the two housekeepers huddled in a discussion with Ernie. "I'm worried about Anna. She's very ill."

Henry read Ernie's reaction. He was irritated at being interrupted. Irritated by Henry's very presence. Still, Henry persisted. "I'm sorry," he said, a tear escaping, feeling totally overwhelmed. "I'm sorry for everything," he blurted out a second time before completely letting go and starting to cry.

Ernie nodded to the two young women who took their cue and stepped away. He placed a hand on Henry's shoulder and gently guided him over to the open door of an unoccupied suite.

"Now, what's this all about?" Ernie said in a hushed tone of concern.

"I know you don't like me," Henry sobbed. "I know I did a terrible thing to you. But I was so frightened and confused. I was out of my mind that night. You must forgive me."

The iciness in Ernie's eyes softened. "Okay, take a breath," he said, as his hand rubbed Henry's back.

"I don't want you to hate me," Henry whimpered. "Sometimes I wish the cops had just killed me that night. Came into the house and shot me dead."

Ernie bit his lower lip. "Now let's not be dramatic."

"I know I've ruined your life," Henry said, desperately sorry, desperately in need of reassurance.

"Kid, does it look like my life is over?" Ernie answered. "I've got everything I ever wanted. I doubt I'd be doing half as well in the States. Hey, you didn't ruin my life. We can let go of that line now. I love my life. Whatever went down is over. It's history." Ernie gave Henry's shoulder a shake. "I promise you. I'm holding no grudges."

Henry felt lighter. He came back to himself. He remembered Anna.

"It started last night. I don't know what to do to help her. She's so ill."

"Are you sure it's not just a headache?"

"She's been throwing up," Henry said, touching his stomach, imagining Anna's cramps and nausea.

"The water's purified. It can't be gastrointestinal," Ernie said matter-of-factly.

"It's extreme dizziness. She had it in Phoenix, but not quite this severe. I'm really worried. I've never seen her this ill."

"Okay." Ernie gently squeezed Henry's shoulder. "You did the right thing finding me. Whatever it is, we'll figure it out."

* * *

Henry gently knocked on Anna's bedroom door. "Anna, are you up? May I come in? I have Ernie with me."

Together they entered Anna's dark room.

Anna lifted her head to see Ernie and Henry standing side-by-side. She'd hoped to mend the tension between the two of them. She hadn't anticipated that her dizziness would do the trick.

"Are you okay?" Ernie asked sitting on the edge of the bed.

"I've felt better," Anna said, her brow covered in perspiration.

"Henry," Ernie said. "Go grab a washcloth from the bathroom and run it under some cold water. Wring it out and then bring it back here."

Henry did as Ernie asked. Ernie applied the cool compress to Anna's forehead and held her hand.

"This trip has been difficult for you," Ernie acknowledged.

"Oh no," Anna mildly protested. "It wasn't until last night when the dizziness started. I guess I haven't been much help to you."

"Oh, but you have," Ernie assured her. "My depression is gone."

"Really?" she said, surprised at his shift. "Well, I'm glad. But I'm afraid I'm going to have to go back to Phoenix. My condition has gotten a lot worse. I've never felt this sick for so long."

"But," Henry said, "You had these same symptoms back in the States."

"Yes," she acknowledged.

"Before you agreed to come to Mexico?" Ernie asked.

Denial was useless. Anna knew that once she agreed to the trip, she had felt better.

"Then there's no guarantee," Ernie continued, "that those spells will ease if you go back home."

Anna nodded. There was no use fighting. She could see the concerned look in Henry's eyes. She'd frightened him. And Ernie was still desperate for answers.

"Anna, you have to finish this," Henry said.

"I wish there was more I could do," she said, slowly sitting up.

"You seem to be feeling better now," Ernie noticed.

"Why yes," Anna said. "I do feel a bit better."

Ernie crossed the room and opened the curtains. Morning light flooded the room. "Well enough to eat?"

"I think so," Anna answered, amazed at her quick recovery.

"Why do you suppose the dizziness comes and goes?" Ernie asked.

Anna wasn't certain what Ernie was getting at.

Ernie stated the obvious. "There's more to know. Maria has more to tell you. She wants you to continue."

"Ernie, listen to me," Anna said with great sympathy. "There are some things we will never know. What happened to your mother might be one of them."

"Maybe if I took you to the apartment. If we stood together on the terrace we might learn something new."

A chill ran down Anna's spine. She hadn't anticipated Ernie would ask her to go to the very place from which Maria had fallen. "I don't think I can," she said, frightened at the prospect.

Henry kneeled by her side. "Ernie's right. You're already feeling better. That's because Ernie's here. I know it."

"Not you, too," Anna lamented.

"Of course you can do it," Ernie assured her. "It'll be perfectly safe. I'll be there."

"No, I can't," Anna said. "You don't understand the intensity of what I'm feeling."

"You must," Ernie implored.

She was terrified. But the connection they shared was strong. There was no denying Ernie had become extremely important to her. She looked into his beautiful brown eyes and prayed it would be worth it in the end.

* * *

Charlie pretended not to notice Dave's long absences during the day. He kept silent and went about his daily business, speaking with clients, drafting reports, granting interviews with the press about the economy's slow but steady recovery. In the evening, watching television, Dave by his side, Timmy curled up asleep between them, Charlie was confident everything would be fine. He just needed to be patient and let Dave figure it out. They'd managed through so many challenges together, surely this too would pass.

* * *

Dave, unaware that Charlie was on to him, did his best to cover his tracks. He refused to shower at Curt's place, fearful that a different soap might raise Charlie's suspicions. Instead, he returned to the gym to shower, which allowed him to say with veracity that he'd actually been there, even on the days when he'd skipped his workout. And though Dave continued to vigorously lift weights, much of his time spent sweating was done at Curt's apartment.

Dave felt enormous relief as his libido kicked into high gear. He'd worried about getting old . . . losing interest in sex . . . the quality of his orgasms before Curt had been far less intense. Charlie had explained it as a byproduct of aging. *All men experience such variations,* he'd said. But when Dave was with Curt, it was different. The guilt of cheating combined with the lust for a younger man had proved a powerful aphrodisiac. His orgasms were mind-blowing. He screamed out when he climaxed, a spontaneous reaction to an explosive inevitability.

Dave now understood why men in committed relationships strayed. It wasn't about emotional needs. It was a fear that their virility was slipping away. The magic fix to an aging libido is easily found in the arms of a younger partner. Curt was Dave's way of upping the stimuli.

And so the affair progressed.

* * *

Jack waited patiently for Enid to return home. He turned on the television and settled into the living room sofa. *Judge Judy* was on. Jack snickered as the defendant, a woman who refused to take responsibility for a mishap with her car, squirmed under Judge Judy's intense questioning. Jack wished the good judge could take a crack at Enid. But then, Judy, an equal opportunity steamroller, suddenly turned on the plaintiff. Jack quickly dismissed the idea.

Then he heard the garage door go up.

He gritted his teeth.

This was bound to be messy.

"Jack, is that you?" Enid called out, tossing her purse on the kitchen counter. "I didn't expect you to be home."

Jack turned off the television.

"It's me," Jack answered.

Enid came into the room. "Well stranger . . . I trust you've been taking good care of yourself."

Jack stood up. "I've been getting by," he admitted.

"And to what do I owe the honor?"

"I think it's time we came to an understanding. I don't want to hurt you, Enid, but I don't want to be married any longer."

"You mean you don't want to be married to me."

Jack nodded.

"So, you've decided it's time to cut the apron strings." Her tone was sarcastic, her words dripping with venom. "After all we've meant to each other?"

"We both know that since we moved to Arizona our marriage hasn't been the same."

"Yes, that's true. But while you've been doing whatever it is you do, I was taking care of your aunt."

"Enid, let's leave her out of this."

"I see." Enid sat down on the sofa. "Jack, there's no incentive for me to divorce you."

Jack was stunned. "What do you mean?"

"I'm perfectly happy to go on playing house. I kind of like it. I come and go as I please. We sleep in separate quarters. All in all, it's the kind of marriage I always dreamed of."

Jack was stupefied. "You can't mean that."

"Oh, I do. And Jack, let's not forget there's still a lawsuit. I wouldn't even consider divorce till that's over. And it might take years to work through the courts."

"Yes, it might," Jack agreed.

He'd hoped to be able to do this without threats but it seemed that Enid was going to play hardball. Jack braced himself. He was ready to drop the next bomb. He only hoped Enid would believe him.

"Well then Enid. I hope you're prepared to deplete the rest of your precious trust fund to pay for your little misdeed."

Enid glared at Jack. "What do you mean?"

"I'm filing documents with the court confirming that you swindled my aunt out of her property. And Enid, I think that just might be a crime."

"You wouldn't dare."

"Oh yes, I would," he bluffed "Your signature is on every check. We can easily pull bank statements exposing where much of the money went from that private checking account. Your fingerprints are everywhere."

Enid smiled ruefully. "No good deed goes unpunished. You were a loser when I married you. Now you're a complete asshole."

Her insults no longer cut. He had the edge.

"One more thing," he added. "In addition to that divorce, you're going to cash out that bank account and hand a check over to Daisy. It's her money."

"Well, it's not all there. I've had some expenses."

"In exchange for the divorce, and the trouble Daisy has gone through, I'll be making restitution. You'll be free to move on."

"Will that be in writing?"

"I'll have my attorney draw up the documents. He'll include it with the settlement papers requesting dismissal of the lawsuit."

"Great. Than we can put this house on the market because I'm going back to Michigan," she said indignantly. "I've had enough of your little experiment in the Southwest."

Together they sat absorbing the end of their marriage.

Enid finally rose to her feet. "Well, I guess there's nothing more to say then."

Jack smiled. "Goodbye would be nice."

* * *

Anna was certain meeting Ernie at his apartment was a bad idea. But against her better judgment, she relented. Riding the elevator to the sixth floor, she thought through her possible reactions. She might feel absolutely nothing. Or she might experience severe dizziness. Either way, she'd given her word to Ernie and she was determined to see it through.

I just don't want to throw up in front of him, she thought as she stepped off the elevator and caught her reflection in the hall's full-length mirror. She turned sideways. She wore her hair up and away from her face. A white summer dress she'd bought at T.J. Maxx hugged her curves in all the right places.

She made her way down the hallway.

Even though she was officially working, it felt more like a first date.

Don't be so silly, she told herself as she approached Ernie's door and reached for the buzzer. *Well, here we go. Try to stay calm. Just keep breathing. You'll be fine.*

Ernie's smile lit up the doorway. He wore a pair of white jeans with an untucked black linen shirt opened at the collar that offered Anna a peek at his hairy chest.

The apartment was magnificent.

A wall of windows afforded a stunning view of the ocean. Anna hadn't expected it to be so grand. The kitchen had the latest in appointments, including stainless steel appliances and black granite countertops. Grey marble floors ran throughout the unit giving the apartment a clean contemporary feel. The furniture was post-modern, done in grey and white tones.

Anna scanned the room. Seeing the white couch, she made a mental note. *Head toward the kitchen if you need to pitch.*

Ernie grabbed her hand and pulled her into the foyer. Immediately her legs felt like weights; her stomach knotted. Was she picking up on spiritual energy or was she just nervous about seeing Ernie?

"I'm so glad you're here," Ernie said, with the sincerity of a schoolboy. "I've poured us each a glass of cabernet. In about thirty minutes the sun will start to set and the view from the terrace is absolutely fabulous."

Anna passed on the wine. "I couldn't," she explained. "Liquor clouds my receptivity. I need to have a clear head. No stimulants or depressants."

Ernie took the glass away. "Sorry. I didn't realize . . ."

"Oh, don't give it another thought," she said, admiring the graying at his temples. "How could you know?"

She took a seat on the sofa.

"Do you sense anything yet?" he asked, taking a seat next to her.

She was transfixed by his sheer presence. "No, not yet," she said, slightly faint as she gazed into his dark eyes. *He's so sexy,* she thought, glad to be in his home so near him . . . spiritual energy be damned.

"Are you sure?" he asked again, sounding disappointed. "I was hoping that here you might feel differently."

She shifted nervously, struggling to maintain her composure. Her task was to see what she could learn about Maria, and yet, she was bombarded by images of their lovemaking.

"Still nothing?" he asked.

"Nothing," she lied, imagining his body pressed close to hers, his tongue exploring her mouth. "Nothing at all," she repeated, blushing with intense physical delight.

"How about if we go out on the terrace?" he suggested.

She was horrified at the mere suggestion. "Ernie, I'm terribly afraid of heights. If it's all the same to you, I'd prefer to stay right here."

"I'll be with you," Ernie assured her. "Nothing can happen. If you'd like, you can hold on to me."

The terrace suddenly became a more interesting prospect.

He stood and reached for her hand. She slowly rose.

"But it's so high up. Oh, I couldn't even manage one step out there."

She followed him, hand-in-hand, as he approached the terrace door.

"I can't, Ernie, really."

He opened the sliding glass door.

She took a step back.

He went behind her and wrapped one arm about her waist. She pressed her back to his chest. She could feel the strength of his body against the smallness of her frame.

"Come on now. I won't let anything happen to you," he said, his voice soft and seductive.

In tandem they approached the threshold. She took the first step out. He followed directly behind. Once on the terrace, she slipped to his right side, leaning hard against the glass door. He remained at her side, arm wrapped about her waist.

"No," she sighed with relief. "I feel nothing."

"Give it a minute," he suggested.

They stood and waited. Anna could hear the seabirds whooping and hollering in the distance. Terrified, she refused to allow her eye to follow the rise and fall of their aerial dynamics against the setting sun. Then she firmly said, "No. There's nothing coming through. Nothing at all."

"How about if you were to touch the railing?"

Anna nodded in the direction of the railing. Her hands were firmly planted on the glass behind her. "You mean over there?"

"Yes. Come on now. We've come this far. I'll hold you."

"Oh, I can't. I can't," she pleaded.

"It's just a few steps to the rail. Turn toward me," he cajoled. "I'll hold you in my arms. I promise, you'll be fine. Nothing can happen."

Like a child she obeyed.

He held her tightly. Her head rested on his chest; her senses spinning with desire. In unison they took a small step sideways toward the railing.

"Wait," she cried out. "Give me a minute. I need a moment to adjust."

"Okay. You tell me when."

Anna took a breath.

Though she was frightened, it was wonderful to be in Ernie's arms. Being close to him was worth the risk.

"Okay, I'm ready."

Again another small sideways step.

"Take a breath," he commanded. "Are you ready?"

Together, another step.

Anna slowly reached her hand out. Shaking, she gripped the handrail. Electric waves bounced through her body. Her knees buckled.

Ernie held her up.

The images flashed. A woman pleading. *No, Juan, no. Let me go. Don't do this.*

Anna too struggled in Ernie's arms, fully absorbed in the experience. Ernie held her fast as she twisted and turned.

The transmission was perfect.

Let me go. Let me go.

Maria's voice.

You bitch. That was my son you took. My son!

A man's voice. His hands thick and deeply veined.

Let me go, she screamed, struggling, her arms pinned to her side.

No one can help you now, the man promised as he held her tight in his grip.

Stop it, she cried out, *you're hurting me.*

You'll pay for all those years. The man's voice determined.

Haven't I already paid? Have you no heart? Maria's words echoed in Anna's ears.

It's too late for that, the man insisted. *Enrique, grab her legs.*

Anna felt another pair of hands about her legs as she was lifted off the ground.

Maria's voice hit a shrill note . . . the guttural sound of a struggling animal.

Open the terrace door, Enrique. We need to get rid of this trash.

Don't, she begged. *I'll do anything you ask.*

Too late, the man answered. *You'll soon be dead. And the dead can't help anyone.*

No, no. Don't.

You should have thought of that the night you left with my son.

Dear God!

Enrique, on the count of three.

Stop, I am begging you. Please . . .

* * *

Anna let out a bloodcurdling scream.

Ernie struggled to hold on to her. "You're safe. I have you," he repeated.

But Anna couldn't be comforted. Her arms thrashed about as she tried to get away. Ernie held tight. Finally, she stopped fighting, going completely limp. He lifted her up and carried her inside to the safety of the living room where he placed her on the sofa. He rushed to the kitchen and poured her a glass of water. She was mumbling something or other he couldn't quite understand. He placed the glass on the cocktail table, kneeling by her side to rub her hands in his.

"Anna, Anna," he called. "You're okay. I'm here. You're okay. I'm so sorry. I should never have taken you out on the terrace. I'm so sorry. This is all my fault."

Anna slowly came to. She opened her eyes, taking fast sips from the glass Ernie offered.

"Ernie, this is water," she said, disappointed in Ernie's choice of liquids. "Don't you have anything stronger?"

Ernie took the glass. "But I thought you didn't drink when you're channeling."

"To hell with that," Anna said.

Ernie poured a glass of Chivas Regal. "Drink it slowly," he warned.

She did as she was told, sipping the golden fluid. The warmth of the liquor ignited her throat. She relaxed.

"So what did you see?" Ernie asked, standing over her. "Tell me everything."

Anna hesitated. There was no way to sugarcoat the pronouncement. "Ernie, you were right. She was murdered."

Ernie kneeled before her, head in his hands. "I knew it."

"I'm sorry," Anna said, sitting up, wanting to comfort him.

Ernie looked up. His eyes flashed rage. "But who did it. Why?"

Anna thought carefully. Should she tell Ernie everything she'd heard and seen? What would be the point of upsetting him about events he had no power to change?

"Tell me," she asked, "what do you know about your father?"

"My father?" Ernie asked.

"Yes. Did your mother ever speak of him? Do you have any photos of him?"

"No. He died when I was a baby. A car accident."

"Ernie, I don't think that's true."

"It's true," he insisted. "My mother wouldn't have lied to me. That's one thing that I am sure of. She'd never have lied. Why would she?"

Anna backed off. She tried a different tactic.

"Did your mother ever speak of her family? Where she came from? Do you still have relatives in Mexico?"

"I have no idea," Ernie admitted. "If she did, I don't recall, or I wasn't listening. When she was deported, she took a room in Nogales. If she had family, wouldn't she have gone to them?"

Anna wasn't surprised. Most families within a generation lost sight of their history. A single mother, distracted by the struggles of living in a new country, must have been solely focused on the future.

"But how does this tie into my mother's death?" Ernie asked.

Anna wanted to tell Ernie all she'd heard. She wanted to tell him she suspected his father had committed the murder. But she couldn't be certain. Her vision, no matter how clear, required too much of a leap of faith. Without proof, it was merely speculation.

* * *

Jack stood in front of Charlie and Dave's door weighing his options. He wanted to make peace with Daisy. He'd given it a great deal of thought.

On one hand, there was the protracted legal case and all it entailed. On the other, recognition of the harm he and Enid had done to Daisy's personal property. Either way, it was going to be an expensive end. He was tired of fighting his conscience. Only one choice allowed him to move forward with dignity. He'd have to apologize.

Jack swallowed his pride and rang the bell.

Charlie answered the door.

Jack had practiced what he'd say to Daisy, but seeing Charlie before him, he was caught off guard. An awkward hello escaped his lips followed by, "Is my aunt here?"

Charlie showed Jack to the living room.

Bonnie had intervened, prepping Daisy for Jack's visit. After their last encounter, Jack was concerned that Daisy might turn him away at the door. He'd asked Bonnie to smooth the way. To let Daisy know that he'd had a change of heart. That he wanted to make restitution.

Daisy looked frail sitting alone on the sofa. Her hair had gone a silvery grey. She looked older than Jack remembered, her shoulders slightly hunched forward.

"Please, sit down," she said, patting the sofa.

Jack joined her, uneasy and uncertain how to start.

Think before you speak. He rubbed his palms together nervously and wondered how to begin. As he focused his attention on her, he sensed an unspoken kindness, a willingness to hear him out, which he'd not noticed before. Could he ever be so understanding if the tables were turned? Could he ever forgive someone who'd done what he and Enid had done to her?

"Thank you for agreeing to see me, Aunt Daisy," he started. "First, I want to say how sorry I am about Lyle. I didn't know him, but I'm sure he was a lovely man."

Daisy's eyes moistened.

"I know I've behaved badly. My only excuse is that I've never been very good with hospitals. They scare me. So in the beginning, I didn't really understand what had happened. Why I didn't understand . . . well . . . we don't need to go into that today. Let's just say, I misjudged Enid's intentions. If I had I been visiting you, I might have known better. But now I do understand. So the time has come to take responsibility. We've done you a great wrong," Jack continued. "I'm prepared to return every penny we've taken. For starters I have this Wells Fargo check." Jack reached into his shirt pocket and withdrew the folded check with Enid's signature. "It represents what's left of the money in the account Enid opened. I'm going to have to pay you back on a monthly basis the funds that are missing, but I promise I will. As for your many possessions, I'm afraid it's too late to do much about that besides tell you how genuinely sorry I am. Enid will return what is rightfully yours. There are dishes and some furniture. We'll be sure to get that to you."

He took a breath. Daisy appeared to be sitting straighter, more alert than when he'd first come into the room. She held the check in her hand without even looking at it. The color had returned to her face. The corners of her mouth had turned up. She was clearly pleased.

He continued on. "We wiped you out. You have nothing . . ."

The words caught in his throat as he realized the enormity of the deed. He'd never acknowledged it out loud before. He bit down on his lower lip till he thought it might bleed. He felt the fool to have wreaked such havoc on someone under the guise of kindness.

She placed her hand on his. "You'll make it right," she said, her eyes signaling appreciation for the awkwardness of his circumstance.

"I will," he responded, vowing in his heart to correct his misdeeds.

"The most important thing is that we're together. We're still family. That's what matters now."

Jack heard Daisy's words but didn't understand. To him, they were still essentially strangers.

"And Jack, as for the lawsuit, I'm going to drop it."

Jack breathed a sigh of relief. "Thank you, Aunt Daisy. Thank you so much. That's a big weight off my shoulders."

"I'm sorry it got so messy between us," she confessed.

"My fault," he said. "I should've paid attention to what Enid was doing. I've relied too much on the women in my life to manage my affairs. I have to start making my own decisions. I'm not a youngster and I should know better. I just hope it's not too late."

"Well, you've taken care of this matter, so you obviously have a good head on your shoulders," Daisy offered. "Why is it that you don't trust your own judgment?"

Jack had no answer. It had always been easier to let the women in his life take charge. "I guess I've made a mess of my life," he answered, overwhelmed by regret.

"Nonsense," Daisy said. "You've had a successful career as a teacher. What could be more valuable than teaching children?"

Jack nodded. That was true.

"Jack, I know it's not my place," Daisy said, "but you still have a lot of life ahead of you. I know it can seem overwhelming, but you can still be your own man. It's possible."

And for a brief moment, Jack had clarity. He saw the path ahead. A life with Bonnie. It seemed so obvious he wondered why he hadn't realized it before.

"Yes, you're right, Aunt Daisy. I see that now. I really do."

* * *

Bonnie emerged from the office of attorney Arnold Feldstein. She'd found his business card rummaging through Lyle's documents. While Dave and Charlie had been busy packing Lyle's paintings, books, and furniture to move into storage, Bonnie had taken it upon herself to rifle through Lyle's desk drawers. In the third drawer on the left, she found an envelope marked: *To be Opened upon My Death.*

"When it rains it pours," Charlie responded to the good news as the three friends gathered about the boxes in Lyle's living room. "Besides the contents of the apartment, how much money did he leave her in his will?"

Bonnie had written the amount down on a small slip of paper. She'd never seen so many zeros. "Just over two million dollars," she said, shock in her voice.

"Dear Lord," Charlie responded. "And with the settlement check from Jack . . . I guess she's set."

Dave stated the obvious. "She won't have to worry about money again."

"I'm glad. She's been through an awful lot," Charlie said. "I can't wait to see her face when she hears the news."

"And she and Jack are now spending more time together," Bonnie observed. "It's really kind of sweet."

"It must be that special connection she had with her brother," Charlie added. "She told me how much she adored Jacob when she was a girl."

Bonnie smiled. She wondered if Charlie would be surprised to learn the truth. After all, if Daisy hadn't told Charlie about Jack, Bonnie didn't think it was her place to break a confidence.

But she wanted to.

She desperately wanted to.

16

....

Bonnie arrived at Dave and Charlie's back door at the agreed-upon time. "Does she suspect anything?" she asked, looking around the kitchen at the balloons and flowers.

"Not a thing," Dave answered. "Did you bring the champagne?"

"Right here." Bonnie handed over a shopping bag from AJ's Fine Food.

"What's all this?" Dave asked. He lifted the bag up and down in a bicep curl like a weight at the gym.

"I got a little carried away," Bonnie admitted. "I picked up a few appetizers. Some Brie, Edam, rice crackers and," she practically squealed, "caviar." Looking about she asked, "Where's Charlie?"

"Walking the dog. He'll be back in a minute."

"And Daisy?"

"She's lying down. The move has been a terrible strain. But somehow I think that this might make it all better."

Dave laid out the cheeses on a cutting board while Bonnie iced the bottle of brut in a bucket Dave dug out from the rear of the hall closet. "Yes," he called out pulling a tub of Philadelphia from the refrigerator. "We have cream cheese for the caviar."

Charlie came in the back door with Timmy. "Oh, this looks great. Are we all set?"

"Ready to go," Bonnie answered giving him a quick peck on the cheek. "Hey, the door isn't closed."

The back door had been acting strangely. Lately, it had been failing to catch; the tongue and doorjamb were slightly misaligned.

"It just needs a nudge," Charlie said giving the door a push. "There," he said as it clicked into place.

"Okay," Dave said, checking the last flute for water spots. "We're all set. I'll go get her."

* * *

Daisy was shocked when she learned of the inheritance.

"Here's to a very special lady," Bonnie toasted, her flute of champagne high in the air.

"Here, here," Charlie and Dave echoed.

Daisy raised her glass. "And here's to Lyle. Wherever he is, I want to thank him for his kindness. He never let on for a moment that I was in his will." A tear escaped and rolled down her cheek. She wiped it away with the back of her hand.

"To Lyle," Bonnie repeated, placing an arm about Daisy's shoulders, giving her a gentle hug.

There was a clinking of raised glasses, the sipping of champagne, and a wonderful feeling of comradery. Dave offered Daisy a travel-size Kleenex from the kitchen drawer which she happily accepted. Charlie picked up Timmy who'd begun to whine, seemingly begging for a treat, but instead, received a kiss on the head from Daisy. Dave passed out crackers with the delicate black caviar resting on a light spread of cream cheese. Everyone agreed it was delicious.

"It's an odd feeling," Daisy said, dabbing at her eyes. "I'm now an independent lady. I can do anything."

"That's right," Bonnie said, refilling her flute. "You can buy a new car. Travel. You can see Hawaii and Europe."

"You can even move into one of those really upscale senior communities they're always advertising in the paper," Dave added.

Charlie balked. "Oh no, you don't. You're not moving out again."

Daisy answered, slightly tipsy. "I don't want to be a third wheel."

"Nonsense," Charlie said, eyeing Dave. "We don't want her to go, do we Dave? She's family."

Dave blushed. He recanted. "Sure. Charlie's right," he said as he filled his empty glass.

But Daisy knew better. "Well, let's just say I'll stay put for the time-being. I have to admit I've gotten pretty used to being with the two of you. But if I'm a burden, you just have to kick me to the street. After all, I can manage for myself now. Why, I can even move into one of those fabulous casitas on the grounds of the Biltmore Hotel, maid service included," Daisy laughed, her fingers dancing through the fluffy hair atop Timmy's head as Charlie cradled the poodle in his arms. "And Timmy, they accept pets. What do you think? How would you like to go on vacation with me?"

The little dog raised his head, ears perked, and glanced about the four as if to answer, before letting out a big yawn.

* * *

Jack signed the paperwork to initiate the divorce process with Enid the same week the lawsuit with Daisy was settled. This eliminated any of the old excuses Bonnie had in moving the relationship forward. And yet Bonnie created new obstacles. She questioned whether the relationship had progressed too quickly. Did it make more sense to slow things down to ensure they really belonged together? And wouldn't it be best for Jack to live alone, after being married so many years, before jumping into another commitment?

Jack was caught off-guard. He couldn't see any reason why they should live apart. He loved her. She said she loved him. All he wanted was to be with her.

"I can't understand her apprehension," Jack complained to Daisy. "You know her as well as anyone. Why would she be dragging her feet?"

He'd stopped by for a cup of coffee but had ultimately succumbed to a slice of Daisy's freshly baked pound cake. He broke off a small piece of the buttery treat and popped it into his mouth.

Daisy opened a jar of blackberry preserves. "You should try a little on the cake. It's delicious."

Jack ignored the offer. "Aunt Daisy, what do you think?"

Daisy's index finger circled the top of her coffee cup. "I'm not sure I'm the best person to ask. You and I are only starting to get to know each other. And I don't want to betray Bonnie's confidence."

Jack pressed. "It's just that you know her so well . . . I thought you might be able to give me some insight."

No," she said, shaking her head. "It would simply be wrong."

But Jack was not to be dissuaded. "Now come on, Aunt Daisy. Bonnie's no fool. She knows you're going to give me advice."

Daisy straightened her back. "Jack, I'd never interfere . . ."

"Well, it seems to me," Jack continued, "that you're my aunt. And if anyone deserves your loyalty . . . well . . . that person should be me."

"Oh Jack," Daisy said dismissively as she placed an elbow on the table, her cheek resting in the palm of her hand. "I'm not choosing sides."

Jack lifted his coffee cup. "Aunt Daisy, I need your insight. You've got to help."

Daisy exhaled. "Jack, I hardly know what to say."

"Aunt Daisy . . ." Jack intoned.

"Well," she tentatively began, "Bonnie's lived her entire adult life as an independent, career-driven woman. So why not take it slow? Maybe she's the one who needs time to adjust; to be more confident in the relationship. If you love her, let her have the time. She's not going anywhere. And in six months or so, she should be ready to move forward. And you'll both be the better for it."

"But I don't have six months," Jack said, his shoulders arched forward. "I need someone now. I need to move on with my life. I need to get out of that house."

"Jack, you can move into an apartment with a short-term lease. You can see Bonnie as much as you want and still have your own place. A little time apart will convince her that what you two have is permanent. Don't push. Women don't like to be pushed. It isn't sexy."

Jack struggled to understand Daisy's advice. "The real problem is," he ultimately concluded, "I need her more than she needs me."

"Oh Jack. What a thing to say. Why put it in those terms? Two people who love each other both have needs. Why make it about whose need is greater?"

Jack gobbled down the last bit of cake on his plate. Crumbs stuck to the corners of his mouth. Daisy raised her napkin and motioned to him. Jack took the hint and wiped his mouth. Daisy sliced another piece of pound cake and placed it on Jack's plate.

"I know it sounds silly," Jack admitted. "A man my age should be able to manage on his own. But I just can't be alone. I can't. I need someone. I need . . ."

Daisy completed the sentence. ". . . A woman to take care of you?"

"Yes," he admitted.

"Would any woman do?" Daisy asked.

"I love her," Jack answered. "I do."

"Yes, but do you love her enough to make a real life with her? Do you love her enough so that she can remain her own person? Jack, those are two important questions. Bonnie has a career. She's not Enid. You'll have to manage on your own while she works. Have you considered that?"

"I know," Jack acknowledged with a firm nod.

"Have you thought about the age difference? She's not going to retire for quite a few years. Can you manage with a younger wife who maintains a career? A woman who may have other concerns besides your immediate happiness?"

"I don't know," Jack honestly admitted. "I'll cross that bridge when I get to it. All I know is that I need her now. Life is short. I might be one of those poor shmucks who dies young."

Daisy frowned. "Jack, that won't happen."

"You never know."

"Oh, Jack, you're not going to die in the next six months."

Jack shifted course. "I guess Bonnie doesn't really love me. I'm not surprised. I seem to have this issue with women. My first wife died on me. Enid never loved me. Even my own mother didn't love me."

Daisy's sympathetic expression transformed to shock at Jack's admission. "Jack, that simply can't be," she insisted. "You're being absurd."

But Jack held fast. "Even when I was a kid, I always knew it. Mothers are supposed to love their children. My mother loved my sisters. But she never loved me."

Daisy shifted uncomfortably. "Now Jack, how could you possibly know that?"

"She barely touched me, unless it was to slap my face or pinch my arm. That's how I was raised. There was nothing kind or gentle about her. I used to think it was my fault that she hated me. But how can a child warrant so much animosity?"

Daisy stirred her half-empty cup of coffee with ferocity. "I'm sure your mother loved you," she said with certainty, the spoon clanking loudly against the china. "Perhaps just not in a way obvious to a little boy."

"No," he said firmly, jaw set, eyes fixed, irritated at needing to further defend an awful truth. "She didn't love me. On that point, I'm very clear. And I'm the one who should know."

Much to Jack's surprise, Daisy seemed visibly agitated. Somehow, he'd upset her, but he couldn't quite understand how or why.

* * *

Daisy knew the realities of men and women.

She knew a woman could be widowed for decades managing quite well while a man could barely tolerate being alone a few weeks.

Daisy had seen it happen time and again. A spouse of thirty years, barely cold in the grave, and the widower eagerly jumps into the next marriage. Daisy had assumed men behaved this way in a desperate attempt to escape grief. But after listening to Jack, she wondered if the real reason might be emotional maturity. Unfortunately, this thought occurred to her at the very moment she'd been upset by Jack's observations on his childhood. Could it be possible? Was her child emotionally starved by the very family that had insisted on raising him? The idea shook her to the core, leaving her short-tempered and agitated.

"Are you okay?" he asked. "You've become awfully quiet."

She took a breath. "I'm fine," she lied.

Jack picked up the conversation where it had left off: "So Aunt Daisy, what about Bonnie? How can I get her to let me move in?"

Daisy bit her bottom lip. She didn't want to hear any more about Bonnie. She was consumed with anger over the injustice of her child being treated like an outsider. The years melted away as her rage flared. "Well, Jack," her tone sharp, her words cutting, "perhaps if you'd invested more time with a quality woman like Bonnie, you'd have avoided marrying someone like Enid."

She regretted those words as soon as they flew out of her mouth.

"That's pretty low," Jack said sitting back in his chair. "Maybe, I'm talking to the wrong person. Maybe you don't think Bonnie and I belong together."

She hadn't planned on lashing out at Jack, the very person with whom she was trying to build a relationship. But the visit had turned into an emotional melee. She ran a hand across her brow, certain that the past was closing in on her. "Jack, forgive me. I'm a foolish woman. I have no business offering advice. Who am I to tell you what to do? After all . . . this is all my fault."

"Your fault?"

"Yes, I should have . . ." Daisy uttered, unable to complete the sentence. Her mind was going a hundred miles an hour. Was this the time to tell Jack she was his birth mother? That his experience with Rose was her fault . . . that Rose had resented her. Was there ever a good time to make such an admission? And what good could come of it now? Surely he'd never forgive her. If only she hadn't been pressured. If only the world hadn't been so hard on unwed mothers. If only she'd been stronger. ". . . I should have . . ."

"You had nothing to do with it, Aunt Daisy."

She'd so many good reasons to give Jack up. Excellent reasons which at the time made perfect sense. Now, in the twilight of her life, Daisy wished she hadn't yielded to societal pressures. "Oh Jack . . ." was all she could manage as she started to cry.

She'd thought after Lyle's funeral she'd never cry again . . . but she hadn't anticipated this conversation.

The look in Jack's eyes softened. "Aunt Daisy, please don't." He grabbed her hand, holding it in his own.

Daisy wiped her eyes with a napkin. *I owe Jack the truth. But how can I tell him the truth? How do I explain that I'm a coward?* "You and Bonnie will be fine," she sniffled, sidestepping Jack's birth. "She loves you very much."

"Are you sure she does?" he asked, his troubled expression transformed to joy.

Daisy nodded. Her words seemed to resonate with Jack. Of everything she could have said, or should have said, confirming Bonnie's love, was all that truly mattered.

* * *

Sanchez waited in his accustomed spot. He'd destroyed the evidence as he was directed to do. Why this particular case was important, he had no idea. He'd decided years ago when he started to work for the organization that it was better not to ask questions. And yet he couldn't help but feel sorry for Ernie. He envied the devotion and respect he felt toward his mother. He wondered what Maria must have done to warrant such a violent end. For a moment, he even felt genuine remorse. But then his job was not to think. He was just a cog in the bigger wheel. Trying to get by. Trying to live the best as he knew how.

He lit a cigarette.

The noise of the neighborhood, a cacophony of sounds, subtly clarified as he waited for his contact. There was backfire from a gang of motorcycles. Two dogs barking. The scurrying of rats as they sifted through a garbage container. Off in the distance, a man and woman were fighting, their words punctuated by the insistent screams of crying children.

He was reminded of his childhood. And he wondered for the first time since he'd left the neighborhood if he'd ever truly escaped. Would it always be a part of him, waiting to pull him back into the abyss of endless poverty?

He took a deep drag, spitting out a bit of the tobacco from his unfiltered Camel that had lodged on his lip. He checked his watch. It was ten o'clock. His contact was late.

He shrugged.

Though he was irritated at being kept waiting, there was nothing he could do about it. And then off in the distance, he spotted the familiar headlights. The high beams of a black sedan practically blinded him.

He stepped into the street, taking his last drag. The smoke left his lips and curled upward. He flipped the butt into the dirt. He raised an arm and waved as the beams made contact. He squinted a bit before covering his eyes to shield himself from the brightness. He thought about his drive home. The wife waiting for him. His son's upcoming soccer game. He couldn't wait to get back to his family. And then, as if in slow motion, he bounced off of the hood of the sedan, thrown some twenty feet into the air, before he landed hard, broken on the ground.

A rat scampered by as he lost consciousness.

* * *

Jack rented a small furnished apartment on Indian School and 24th Street. The Hacienda, a pink adobe one-story building, offered twelve units laid out around the pool. In the Phoenix of the 1960s, the Hacienda had been a desirable address with proximity to the Biltmore, located on the bus line, and with the feel of a small luxury motel. But with the advance of time, the property had changed hands and the present landlord had failed to update the units. A single window air conditioner cooled two rooms of faded green shag carpeting; the living area included a beat-up beige sofa, an oak table with two matching chairs, and a galley kitchen hidden behind two folding doors; the bedroom was dominated by a queen bed and dresser, and on the lone end table, a lamp with a busted white shade that hung slightly to the right.

Jack was grateful for the cheap weekly rate but hoped his current address would be only temporary. He spent his days going to LA Fitness, meeting with his attorney, stopping in at the library to read the newspaper, and taking short drives to Bonnie's place of business to join her for lunch.

Most nights, he returned to the Hacienda alone. It was demoralizing to enter the small apartment with its smell of wet dog. Jack comforted himself with the notion that it was but a brief adventure; a moment in his life, bound to quickly pass. Surely Bonnie needed him as much as he needed her. This couldn't go on much longer; living in a run-down, third-rate rental unit, while she lived in a beautiful condo. She'd have to break down eventually and let him move in. It was only a matter of time. He was sure of it.

* * *

Charlie focused his energy on creating a wonderful home environment for Dave. He bought new sheets and pillowcases, had the carpets cleaned, and most importantly, signed up for cooking classes with Williams-Sonoma at Scottsdale Fashion Mall. Dave loved desserts and so Charlie was determined to learn how to make the most delectable treats. The plan: fight for Dave with an arsenal of homemade brownies, cheesecakes, napoleons and éclairs. He might not be able to compete in the bedroom with a boy toy, but in the kitchen, he was determined to take the gold medal.

Daisy appeared in the doorway. Charlie was at the stove stirring a pot of chocolate pudding with a large wooden spoon.

"I thought you were on a conference call," she said, as she inspected a Gala apple sitting in a ceramic bowl on the counter.

Charlie hadn't confided in Daisy about Dave. But he sensed she knew something was up since Dave seemed to be gone most of the day and had even started to go to the gym in the evening.

"What are you doing?" she asked, washing the apple off under the faucet before wrapping it in a white napkin.

"I'm saving my relationship," Charlie answered tersely. "You must have noticed by now that Dave is missing-in-action. I've tried to ignore it." He continued to stir the hot pot waiting for the milk and pudding to boil. "Somethings up. So, I'm handling it."

"Oh Charlie. You don't suspect he's fooling around. I can't believe that."

Charlie was in no mood to rehash the stranger's phone call or his suspicions. "No man over fifty wants to be sweating it out in the gym to keep up with a young boyfriend," Charlie confided to Daisy. "I'm going to load him with calories. By the time I'm done with his skinny ass, he'll be lucky if he fits thru the doorway."

Daisy picked up the empty box of Jello pudding. She examined the cover. "So after taking all those fancy baking classes, you're making pudding out of a box?"

"I wanted something fast for tonight," Charlie said defensively. "It's been so busy at work. I don't have a lot of time to play around. This seemed quick and easy. Pudding sets in a few hours. And Dave loves pudding."

Daisy offered a nervous laugh. "But Charlie, if you think something's going on, wouldn't it be better to talk with Dave?"

"I don't want to put him on the spot. And I don't want to accuse him. No, I think this is a far better way to deal with the problem. Woo Dave with food. Use his sweet tooth as his undoing. Bet on the banana cream pie and chocolate mousse to win the day."

Daisy shook her head in disapproval. She managed an "Oh Charlie."

"I don't want to hurt him," Charlie vowed. "I just want him back. And if that means he gets a little flabby, that's fine with me."

Daisy took a bite of the apple. "Well, I guess you know what you're doing."

A realist, Charlie had mostly done his crying in private. He might have been smiling and laughing on the outside, but on the inside, he was deeply disappointed in Dave. He'd thought that he was made of finer stuff.

"So, I'm making his favorite. A chocolate pudding pie with graham cracker crust, topped with whipped cream. Dave has no self-control when it comes to chocolate pudding and graham cracker. He can eat half of it in one sitting. Tonight, he definitely will be staying home."

"Now how can you guarantee that?" Daisy wanted to know.

"Dave has trouble handling milk product," Charlie explained. "He's not lactose intolerant, but he gets pretty gassy from too much pudding. I guarantee he's going to have at least two pieces, if not three. If he goes anywhere, it will be straight to the bathroom."

That night, Charlie served Dave a third piece of pie.

"I really shouldn't," Dave protested. "I've had enough."

Charlie leaned in and kissed Dave on the forehead. "You can afford it. Look at you. You're gorgeous. You have the body of an Adonis."

As Dave polished the plate clean, Charlie observed a change in Dave's expression as he tugged at the waistband of his pants.

"Are you okay?" Charlie asked, amused by Dave's sudden discomfort.

"I think the pie's beginning to talk back. There's some rumbling going on down below."

"Do you need a glass of water?"

"No, I think I just need to sit a bit and relax."

"Sure," Charlie agreed, "whatever."

And just as Charlie predicted, Dave didn't go out.

* * *

Henry left Mexico without Anna. He had to get back to school, and though he was reluctant to leave, Anna promised to follow soon after her work with Ernie was done. Together they stood at the front of the resort, saying their goodbyes, the cabbie placing Henry's bag in the trunk.

"Now here's two hundred dollars," Anna said, putting the wad of rolled twenties into Henry's hand.

"Anna, I don't know about this . . ." Henry responded, uncomfortable leaving her behind.

"Stop," Anna interrupted him. "You're a good kid. I know that. I have every faith in you. Take care of the house, and if any messages have been left on the answering machine, return them for me. I should be back in the next week or so."

Henry's left eyelid twitched as he slipped the money into his front pocket. Even though Anna would soon be following, he felt horrible pangs of abandonment. He'd struggled through lunch, barely able to eat his burger, as he watched Anna, her auburn hair loosely falling about her shoulders, nibble on a shrimp salad, not a care in the world. Her colorful summer dress of orange, yellow, and white daisies, luminescent against her rich tan, enhanced her immense vitality. Henry hadn't realized until that very moment how much he'd come to rely on her. How very dear she was to him. His stomach clenched at the very thought of leaving her.

"Now don't you worry," Anna said. "You'll be just fine. You've got your passport. And you have nothing to declare at customs." The tone of her voice, assertive and confident. "Just follow the signs to the taxi stand when you exit the terminal. Now make sure you have the house keys."

"They're in my backpack," Henry replied.

"Check," Anna insisted.

Henry unzipped the front pocket and looked inside. "Got 'em."

"Now are you sure you're going to be okay?" she asked.

He stared into her brown eyes. He wanted to confess that he wasn't so very sure. He'd no doubt that he could manage the flight back to Phoenix. That part was easy. There'd be lots of people around. But it was being back in Phoenix that triggered his fears. He'd already spent too many hours in his young life alone after his parents had tossed him out. Their hostile words echoing over and over; the default tapes of his troubled mind. *You're worthless. You're damaged and can't be fixed. Your life will never amount to anything*. He'd struggled with the negative messages, hoping one day, they'd be gone for good. But the words were never far away. Always lurking . . . waiting to resurface.

Now, as he looked at Anna, waves of rejection swept over him.

He'd somehow failed.

The cab driver, a short, dark-skinned man, with a face like a plump eggplant, offered a toothy grin as he opened the passenger-side door for Henry. Henry nodded in the man's direction, acknowledging the kindness, even though he wasn't quite ready to leave.

"Are you sure you're going to be okay without me?" he asked, desperate for any sign that she still needed him.

"I should be asking you that question," she laughed, pulling him into a tight hug. "I'll be just fine. Now you take care of yourself and make sure you pick up the mail from the post office. And don't forget about taking out the garbage. It starts to smell after a day or two."

"I'll remember," he said, keenly aware that Anna appeared happy, almost excited to see him go. "How long do you think you'll be?"

Her eyes shone brightly. "I can't imagine more than a week or two."

"Something's happened," Henry guessed aloud. "What is it?"

"Henry," Anna admonished, "you're going to miss your flight standing around here and asking me all sorts of questions. I already told you about Ernie and his mother."

"No, it isn't that," Henry probed. "It's something else."

She blushed. "There's nothing else to tell. My goodness. The way you're acting, it's like you're the psychic in the family."

* * *

Once Henry was gone, Anna packed her things and moved into Ernie's place. And though she felt a twinge of guilt about not being totally honest with Henry about her burgeoning relationship, she remained convinced that whatever might happen, it was solely her business. After all, she was an adult, and adults aren't required to consult with teenagers regarding their behavior, even if she suspected that her behavior was akin to that of a teenager . . . impulsive . . . and without regard to her responsibilities as Henry's guardian.

That night, she and Ernie walked along the beach. She hadn't cohabitated with a man before, and though the arrangement was purely temporary, it presented concerns. She wasn't sure what to expect. Would there be a routine to follow? Would they go out to dinner or cook? Were they going to be having sex in the evening or would that happen in the morning before Ernie went to work? Would she need to slip out of bed before he awoke and brush her teeth so that she was prepared?

Anna had no idea.

"I'm not sure what I'm doing," she admitted as they stopped and stood together at the shoreline, watching the sun setting in the distance, its yellow edge barely touching the horizon.

"You're taking a walk after dinner," Ernie answered. He reached for her hand, bringing it up to his mouth for a gentle kiss. "Watch as the colors change. First yellow, then gold, and if we're lucky, a burnt orange."

Anna squeezed his hand in return and smiled. She'd been too oblique. "No, I mean with us. What am I doing here?"

"You're here to help me," he answered as the tide drifted high on the shore, cool water rolling over their bare feet.

Anna let out a tiny yelp, simultaneously lifting each foot up, attempting to rescue her pedicure from the salty Pacific. Ernie's eyes registered amusement. She released his hand. Was she moving too fast? Were her feelings growing more intense than his? Was she being a fool?

"Is that all this is?" she reluctantly asked.

He beckoned her closer.

She leaned in for a hug.

His arms enveloped her small frame. The bronze skin on his neck exuded a masculine scent of pine. She wanted to nuzzle her nose there. Memorize the moment.

She pulled slightly back, now looking into his eyes. She was helpless before him, passion aflame, weak and hopelessly his. "I'm not sure I can be of any real help," she admitted, exploring his face for signs of a negative reaction. "We're too involved. I'm not sure I can remain objective."

She hadn't expounded on the details of her vision on the terrace; she'd failed to mention anything about Ernie's father. The man was clearly dangerous and she was afraid that if Ernie knew the truth, he'd personally seek justice. And Anna couldn't risk anything happening to Ernie. If she had proof, hard evidence, then that was a matter for the police to handle. But she had nothing beyond the voices and flashes of imagery to explain Maria's death.

Anna wondered what secrets Maria had taken to her grave.

Ernie pulled her close, gently turning her about to face the setting sun. He now stood behind her, arms wrapped over her shoulders as she nestled her head against his chest. "Look at nature's beauty," he said. "If you continue talking, you'll miss the best part."

The sun had nearly completed its triumphant slide. Orange and yellow spurs, like 4th of July rockets, brilliantly illuminated a sliver of the horizon.

"I'm not sure what this all means," she finally said. "I'm not sure what we're doing."

"Does it have to mean anything?" he asked, turning her about for the return walk home.

"It's all happening so fast," she said. "While you're working during the day, what shall I do?"

"You'll do what everyone else does. You'll go to the beach and enjoy the ocean. And then, when I come home, we'll have a light meal, and then *we'll be together.*"

"*Together?*" There was a lustful hint in her voice.

"Yes," he said, slipping his arm about her waist.

And as if on cue, she stopped walking and turned toward him. He bent down and took her in his arms, kissing her passionately, his tongue ardently connecting with hers. There was no doubt about it. She'd be able to sleep late tomorrow morning. There would be no need to get out of bed to brush her teeth. Whatever was going to happen was certainly going to be happening at night.

* * *

Back in Phoenix, Henry adjusted the thermostat. Seventy-five at night when he was home, eighty-five during the day while he was out.

He remembered to empty the kitchen garbage when the stench from the Kentucky Fried Chicken alerted him to the need.

He opened the mail, texting Anna about bills coming due.

At her request, he overnighted her checkbook to Ernie's home address.

He now realized she was no longer at the resort and why she'd stayed in Mexico. He felt suddenly foolish, as if he should have known right from the beginning that Anna was staying behind to be with Ernie. He'd sensed the sparks between them but hadn't actually thought Anna would abandon him for Ernie.

That he hadn't foreseen.

School remained a lonely place. He walked the corridors feeling invisible.

To all outward appearances, he was a tall, handsome, confident kid. But the truth was quite different. He'd been aloof at the start of the school year, maintaining a careful distance from the other students. He'd even been deliberately unfriendly. It wasn't because he was cocky or arrogant, though he suspected that some might perceive that to be so. He remained alone as a protective mechanism. He had a secret and he didn't trust the others. He had learned from his parents what he could and could not share, and being too uncertain about his ability to lie, isolated himself, opting to eat alone, study alone, and to all outward appearances, experience school alone. And though he at times wanted to connect with the other kids, make friends, it had become impossible for him to do so. He couldn't break the pattern. And so he gave into the loneliness, increasingly spending his time at Starbucks where he could be with others but still remain apart. And while he completed his homework at a corner table, an iced coffee within reach, he relished the sense of community among the gathering of strangers.

* * *

"Nice tan. How were the beaches?"

The familiar voice caught Henry by surprise. He'd been in the midst of solving a geometry problem involving an isosceles triangle. It took but a moment before he realized the question was directed at him. When he looked up, he saw Paul's handsome face.

"I spent most of my time at the pool," he answered, wondering why Paul had tracked him down. "What are you doing here?"

"Looking for you." Paul said. "I bet you have some amazing tan lines," he whispered, a provocative glint in his eyes. "How about stopping by my place and we'll check it out."

The offer was direct and brazen. Henry shut his book. "That's a weird thing for a straight guy to say. Are you sure you're not gay?"

"What is it with you and labels?" Paul said, pulling up a chair. There was just the tiniest hint of stubble on his chin.

"Why would I go anywhere with you? You've been a complete asshole." Paul tilted his head as if he didn't understand. "Me. Come on now."

"You're . . . entitled," Henry answered, proud to define Paul's behavior in one word. "Like you think you have it coming."

"Hey," Paul postured, leaning on the table with both elbows, his face cradled in his hands. "I just appreciate what you know how to do. That's all. You like it, I like it. What's the harm?"

"I don't like it," Henry lied. "And it's not happening again."

"Okay," Paul leaned back in the chair. "That's fine with me. Susan is all over me."

"Good," Henry replied. "Just so we're clear."

Paul raised his hands in the air. "We're clear. We're clear. Don't give it another thought."

"Good," Henry said, satisfied that he'd made his point.

"But that doesn't mean we can't hang out," Paul said.

Henry thought about it for a moment. It didn't seem to be a good idea.

"Now come on," Paul coaxed. "We're still friends, little bro."

"Don't call me that."

"Look, I'm sorry," Paul said, much to Henry's surprise. "I didn't mean to hurt your feelings. How about you let me make it up to you? *Notre Dame* is playing at noon tomorrow. Some friends are coming over to watch. We can catch it together."

Henry hedged. "I don't know. It's my first Saturday back and I have a lot to do."

"Don't be such a pussy. Why would you want to be alone?"

Henry reconsidered. He didn't want to spend the day alone. He'd been dreading the thought of a lonely weekend. "Okay," Henry relented. "I'll be there. Your place at noon."

* * *

Daisy used pillows to prop herself up in bed. She pulled the lamp on the adjacent end table closer to get a better look at the newspaper. In a busy world dominated by the Internet, email, and cell phones, the *Arizona Republic* remained the one opportunity for Daisy to delve past the sound bites of the day and into the details of the news. Without a newspaper, Daisy wondered how the average American could possibly know what was going on in the world.

As she turned to the obit section, her heart sank. Faces of her contemporaries stared back at her. So many people her age and younger were now gone. They'd lived and shared her life experiences. The crushing pain of the Depression. The horror of Hitler and the necessity of World War II. The absurdity of the Korean War. The Cold War. McCarthyism. Vietnam. The assassinations. Nixon. The second Bush administration and the invasion of Iraq. With the 2008 financial meltdown, history seemed destined to repeat itself. Had Americans learned nothing? Could there be no learning curve?

Live long enough, everything changes . . . and nothing changes. The old guard dies off . . . the young grow old . . . closed minds fail to see the mistakes of the past. What we don't know, Daisy surmised, *we're destined to repeat.*

Daisy thought about her family and the mistakes she'd made. The sister-in-law she despised. The brother she adored. The newborn she'd given up.

Why had she succumbed to the morals of the day? Why had she not known better? Why had she lacked the backbone to be true to herself? Would she have behaved differently if she'd been older—twenty-one, twenty-five, thirty?

Daisy suspected it wasn't her youth or lack of maturity that had driven her poor decision-making.

It was fear.

Fear had been the great motivator when Jack was born. And as Daisy read "Dear Abby," fear seemed to be the universal emotion at the heart of so many letters.

Fear seemed to explain the actions of Jan Brewer, John McCain, and Joe Arpaio. Fear of people they didn't know or understand. Fear of opening their hearts. Fear of the financial implications of helping others. Fear that there wasn't enough for everyone.

Daisy was reminded of Franklin Delano Roosevelt when he said, "The only thing we have to fear is fear itself."

Fear had ruled Daisy like an unbreakable genetic code. She'd passed her fear on to Jack who had spent a lifetime giving his power away to the women in his life.

Daisy wondered how different life might have been had she faced her fears.

Instead of being the distant aunt, a burden, a responsibility, she'd have been the treasured mother to an adoring son.

But that was all fantasy.

She now realized that Jack was destined to struggle. To live in the shadow of the women in his life. If life was about facing one's fears, Jack had not learned the lesson. Had Daisy known this truth when she was younger, she'd have been braver. Done what she must to raise her son to be fearless.

Daisy closed the newspaper and turned off the lights. It was time to rest. She was tired. It had been an exhausting evening.

* * *

Henry showed up at Paul's apartment on Saturday carrying a large bottle of Pepsi purchased at 7-Eleven. Although Henry had no true interest in organized sports, its obsession with statistics and athletic prowess, he appreciated how it brought men together. And for that, he was grateful. It had been a quiet week without Anna. Alone, he'd struggled with his own thoughts. Any excuse to spend time with others . . . watching great-looking athletes overtly sexualized in tight-fitting uniforms . . . was a good excuse.

"Door's open," Paul called out when Henry rang the bell.

Henry peeked his head in. The place was empty. Nobody on the sofa, though the widescreen television mounted on the wall was tuned into the pre-game festivities. The camera scanned a tailgate party of rowdy friends drinking beer, eating hot dogs and hamburgers, and having a raucous good time.

"Come on in," Paul said, as Henry tentatively stepped inside.

Paul wore a Cardinals jersey with the red and yellow cardinal logo. Henry wondered why the small bird had such a nasty glint in its eyes. *It looks more like an angry woodpecker*, Henry thought.

Paul took the soda out of Henry's hands. "Make yourself comfortable," he said, directing Henry to the sofa. "The other guys should be here soon. I'll grab us some beers. Help yourself to some snacks."

A large bowl of tortilla chips dominated the coffee table. Guacamole and onion dip were nearby.

"Chips 'n dip are good," Henry said mostly to himself, as he sat down on the sofa, eyeing the bowl. He reached for a chip and scooped up a wad of green avocado. The concoction hung tentatively on the chip's edge just long enough for Henry to catch it in his open mouth.

Henry leaned back and relaxed. The dark grey sofa was soft and cushy. Paul had purchased the furniture at IKEA. Contemporary in style, but inexpensive. Designed to appeal to those who like midcentury modern.

Watching the pre-game opener, Henry was amused at the adolescent behavior of the sportscasters. Good ole boys, ex-athletes, fiercely masculine, focused on other fiercely masculine men. Film highlights from earlier games in the week: athletes crying over incomplete plays, hugging at completed passes, and the all-too-evident slapping of rear ends. To Henry, it all seemed so gay.

Paul came back into the room. He handed Henry an icy cold Michelob. Then sat down.

Henry pretended to listen to the announcers as they reviewed the team's current strengths and weaknesses. But all he could focus on was Paul. He remembered their last encounter. The shame he felt. The way Paul had seduced him without any intention of reciprocating. Henry was determined that would not happen again. He was not about to service Paul, no matter how hot he looked in his Cardinals football jersey.

"You know, it's not happening," Henry said as he sipped his beer. "So if that's your intention, give it up."

Paul took a handful of chips. "What are you talking about?" he asked as he crunched away.

"You know." Henry eyed Paul suspiciously. "You know what I'm talking about."

"Don't make more of it than it was," Paul wisecracked.

Henry's face burned red. "Fine. I'm out of here," he said, standing up. "You're an asshole."

Paul reached for Henry's arm and pulled him back down to the sofa. "Okay, okay. Don't go. Just chill out. I do have friends coming by. They're just running late. They'll be here soon."

Henry heard a car pull up. He relaxed. "Okay, I'll stay."

Parked in front of the house was a 1987 red GTO. It sported a personalized license plate: BIGMAN. The owner of the car was Drew Allen, the lineman who played for the ASU Sun Devils.

Henry had never seen Drew Allen up close. The guy was a monster with a 52-inch chest, huge arms, and the posture of an angry black bear getting ready to charge. Drew walked in as if he owned the place. He looked at Henry and smiled. Henry had never seen such huge white teeth.

Suddenly, Henry was glad he'd stuck around.

"You guys don't know each other," Paul stated the obvious.

Drew reached out his hand to Henry. "Hey, little buddy."

Henry's hand disappeared in Drew's giant mitt.

"How much have I missed?" Drew asked, dropping onto the sofa, legs spread wide for Henry to sneak a peek.

"Nothing really," Paul answered. "It's first and ten."

Paul passed a beer to Drew.

Drew guzzled it down, wiping his mouth with the back of his hand. "I'll take another."

Paul placed three more beers on the coffee table.

"I better go grab some more beer." Paul said, jumping up to grab his car keys off a nearby tabletop.

Henry spotted Paul winking at Drew as he left.

"I'll be back," Paul said as he headed out the door.

* * *

The crowds were cheering, but to Henry it had all just become background noise. Drew looked over at Henry, seemingly sizing him up. "You're a good-looking guy" he said, much to Henry's surprise. Drew drank his third beer as he slipped slowly down, shifting his hips forward with his head coming to rest at the top of the back of the sofa. With his eyes closed he whispered, "I'm so damn horny."

Henry's heart raced and his mouth went dry. He admired the big man's approach. There was no doubt what was happening. Drew was coming on to him. Henry licked his lips. Paul had just left and Henry had no idea when Paul's other friends might be arriving. There was the familiar sense of urgency rising in Henry's loins. A sweet itch that begged to be scratched.

"Haven't had any in a while." Drew said, hand drifting over to his crotch as he looked at Henry. Heavy-lidded green hazel eyes offered permission. "Think you might be able to help me out," he asked, giving Henry a wink.

* * *

While Drew was in the bathroom, washing up, Henry was in the kitchen gargling with Diet Coke. It was an unusual choice, but readily at hand, out on the counter. The sweetness of the cola combined with the carbonation was a refreshing relief.

Henry checked his watch.

Paul had been gone an hour. No one else had shown up since Paul had left.

Good thing, Henry thought. *I wouldn't have answered the door anyway.*

He washed his hands using dishwashing detergent and smiled, remembering Drew with his pants about his ankles. *I better give him my number,* Henry reasoned, drying his hands off with a paper towel. *Otherwise, he won't know how to reach me.*

He imagined the two of them together. Attending ASU games, dining out, making love. He saw himself curled up in bed on a Sunday morning. Drew beside him. Utter contentment.

On his way back to the living room, he peered into the hall mirror. All was well. Nothing on his clothes. Nothing in his hair. *Good*, Henry thought, gleeful about his recent conquest.

It was halftime. The voices of the commentators blended with the music of the marching band to create a cacophony of sound.

There was a flush in the hall bath. Drew appeared. He looked uncomfortable, hurried. Eyes down, he was tucking his shirt into his jeans. Henry watched as he struggled to retrieve the keys from his pants pocket.

"I got to run," Drew said, not making eye contact with Henry. "Where the heck is Paul?"

The front door opened.

Paul was back.

"You done?" Paul asked Drew.

"Oh yeah," Drew responded.

"That's one-fifty," Paul said, hand extended.

Drew reached into his pants and withdrew his wallet. "One-fifty, huh?"

"Yeah, one-fifty. Don't pretend you didn't know."

"Here you go." The big guy handed over the cash.

"Great. Let me know if you need anything else," Paul said.

"What's going on?" Henry demanded to know as Drew walked passed him.

"Just a friendly transaction," Paul answered.

"Thanks, Paul. That was great," Drew called out as he made his way to the door.

Henry's heart sank. The interaction with Drew had been prearranged. It hadn't been a spontaneous moment. "What's going on?" Henry demanded to know, his body rigid.

Paul reached for the remote and turned off the television before picking up the dip and heading for the kitchen. Henry's mouth hung open as Paul crossed the room.

"What's going on," Henry now shouted, following close behind Paul. "What just happened?"

The refrigerator door was open. A gallon of milk and three apples occupied the top shelf. Otherwise, the refrigerator was empty. "Don't make such a big deal," Paul said as he placed the dip on an empty shelf. "You enjoyed yourself. Drew enjoyed himself. No harm."

"Where's your food?" Henry asked, distracted by the empty refrigerator.

Paul ignored the question, returning to the living room.

Henry opened the freezer. It too was empty.

He opened the kitchen cabinets. Except for a few plastic plates and cups, there was a box of Cheerios, a can of tuna, a box of graham crackers.

"Where's your food?" he called out again, startled at the discovery.

He'd been over to Paul's house before. He'd been to parties. There had always seemed to be plenty to eat. Party buckets from Kentucky Fried Chicken or boxes of Domino's Pizza. But Henry had never gone into the kitchen. He'd never looked in the refrigerator or opened the cabinets. Why would he?

He confronted Paul in the living room.

"I've been short lately," Paul answered.

"Then how are you paying your rent?" Henry insisted to know.

"I have some money saved from Apple. Not much."

"But your car? The furniture?" Henry looked about. "All of this?"

"The car is leased," Paul explained. "My Dad pays for it. My folks divorced when I was twelve. My Dad is a successful surgeon, so he runs the car through his company."

Henry realized there was a lot he didn't know about Paul. Certainly nothing about his family life. He'd never thought to ask. "And the rest," Henry said glancing about.

"My Dad's one very guilty guy."

"And the money Drew just handed you. What the hell was that about?"

"A new business venture," Paul offered. "I've been recruiting talent."

"Like hell," Henry yelled, grabbing for Paul who quickly sidestepped Henry's lunge. "That's my money. Give me my money."

Paul's eyes became narrow slits. His brow arched and his mouth transformed into a sinister grin. He resembled a lizard, tongue readied to snatch at its prey. "You should be grateful to me. That lady you live with has dumped your ass. I'm all you've got. And what you did this afternoon beats the hell out of working at Walmart. At least you'll be making real money with me."

Henry was suddenly frightened. He'd been kicked to the street before. Surely Anna wouldn't abandon him. That seemed impossible to imagine. "What are you talking about?" he asked, bewildered at the turn of events. "Anna's coming back."

"Is she?" Paul sneered.

Henry didn't know what to say.

"At least this way," Paul explained in a calm tone, "we're both helping each other out. And you won't be the only kid. The city of Phoenix has plenty of runaways who need a hand."

Henry was dumbstruck.

"Don't make such a big deal out of it," Paul said in a cavalier tone. "It's just sex. You do it for free. Why not make a little cash on the side."

"And here I thought you were my friend," Henry answered as a wave of depression settled over him. "That you cared about me."

"I do. Would I be asking just anyone? Let's face it . . . you like it . . . and you're good at it," Paul beamed. "It's probably the only thing you'll ever be really good at," he said so matter-of-factly that Henry accepted it as a truth. "Some guys want it. You like to do it. What's the harm? And this is something we can be partners in. Think about it," Paul said with wonder and excitement. "You and I working together. Wouldn't that be great?"

Henry was bewildered. Is this what Paul had in mind all along? Is this why Paul had befriended him? Had he been such an easy touch?

And then he got angry.

Blind anger.

"No way. No freaking way. Give me that money," he shouted as he rammed Paul with the full weight of his body. Paul fell backward onto the sofa, Henry on top of him.

"Hey," Paul barked, wrapping one arm about Henry's neck and pulling him into a tight chokehold as he flipped Henry onto his back, pulling him down to the floor.

"I want that money," Henry shouted, arms flailing, unable to get a grip on Paul to free himself from the headlock.

"Chill out," Paul warned, as he pressed one side of Henry's face into the carpet. "Calm down before you get hurt." Paul's large hand covered the back of Henry's head like he was maneuvering a basketball. "You know I can beat the shit out of you if I wanted."

Henry struggled, but was unable to free himself. "Let go," he grunted between loud snorts.

Paul held Henry's head down firmly. Reaching about was impossible. After a few minutes, Henry finally relented.

"There you go. That's better." Paul slowly lifted his hand off of Henry's head, eventually standing up and straightening his shirt. Henry remained flat on the floor panting for breath. "I'm sorry you made me do that, little bro," Paul said. "But you were freaking out of control. I hope I didn't hurt you." He laid six twenties down on the carpet by Henry's face. "That's yours."

Henry looked up at Paul. His big, blue eyes assumed the familiar warmth that had captivated Henry from the start of their acquaintance.

"You know I really do care about you," Paul said. "I only have your best interests at heart."

Henry slowly sat up.

"Sure, I do," Paul said, helping Henry to his feet. "You're really important to me. We shouldn't be fighting." Paul's voice softened, taking on the same tone he used when talking to Susan. "I'm really sorry," he said in a near whisper. "I truly am."

And before Henry had a moment to think, Paul pulled Henry close, and wrapped his arms about him. Henry's body relaxed as the tension between them slowly melted away.

* * *

Though Charlie had confided in Daisy and Bonnie about his suspicions regarding Dave, he didn't want to wear out his friendships by complaining. So, with Bonnie's encouragement, Charlie located a therapist, Howard Elston, and made an appointment.

Elston, a spry, energetic man in his mid-seventies, stood just five foot three. A tiny gray goatee adorned his moon-shaped face. The gentle lines about the mouth and eyes hinted at a wisdom born of age and seasoned by intellect. Dressed in a crisp white button-down shirt and tan slacks, Elston vibrated with kinetic energy.

Charlie instantly liked the older gentleman.

Elston offered Charlie a seat on a weathered, cracked, brown leather sofa. Slowly, the sofa cushion gave way as Charlie settled, sinking ever deeper, seemingly caught in a quicksand of fabric and coils, until he finally came to rest in the imprint left by so many others who had visited Elston through the years.

Elston hoisted himself into a nearby cane-back oak swivel chair that Charlie assumed to be an antique. "So tell me about your goal for therapy," Elston inquired, reaching for a yellow notepad and slipping on a pair of tortoise-shell glasses, the lenses so smudged that Charlie wondered how he could see.

"Goal? Do I need a goal?" Charlie asked, surprised at the question.

The older man beamed enthusiastically. His head rocked from side-to-side as he explained, "If you don't have a goal, why are you here? What are we doing? And how will you know whether this process has been successful?"

"Oh. That makes sense," Charlie answered.

Elston's eyes flashed an impish twinkle. "Unless of course you want to come for months on end and spend a lot of money." His eyeglasses slid down his nose. With the help of an index finger, he pushed the glasses back up.

Charlie rubbed his hands together. "Well, I'd like to come to terms with aging."

Elston retrieved a pen from his shirt pocket. He started to take notes. "Yes, getting older can be challenging."

Charlie sighed. "And I suppose I need to make some decisions about my relationship."

"Good, good," Elston chimed, head tilted down, looking over the top of his eyeglasses. "What kind of decisions?" His glasses slid down his nose.

Charlie paused. He blinked. "Whether to stay."

"Oh. Okay, then. Why don't we start there?" Elston suggested, pushing his eyeglasses back up.

Over the course of the next fifty minutes Charlie shared his fears about Dave, the decisions he'd made about the relationship, and Dave's cheating. Elston listened politely, nodding every now and then, periodically interjecting, asking for further clarification or repeating what Charlie had just told him. Charlie came to understand Elston was actively listening. Charlie managed the discussion, but Elston mirrored it back, helping Charlie to solidify his thoughts. At the end of their first session together, nothing had been resolved, but Charlie felt he had greater clarity on the situation.

* * *

On the other side of town, Dave was stepping into his black Nike gym shorts.

"Where are you going?" Curt asked, splayed naked on the bed, a single white sheet tangled about his legs. "Come back and lie down," he said, patting the side Dave had just vacated. "We still have time."

"I can't," Dave said, searching for his left sneaker. "I need to get home."

Curt sat up on his elbows, pecs popping. "You're not going home. You're going back to the gym to shower."

"That's right," Dave said as he finally located the sneaker near the end of the bed and slipped it on.

Curt scowled.

Dave ignored it. He looked at himself in Curt's dresser mirror. He had bed head from rolling around and falling asleep. He needed to shampoo.

"Boy, you're a cold one," Curt said.

Dave pretended he didn't hear him. He slipped his gym shirt over his head. The orange Nike logo jumped out against the dark blue nylon. Dave checked the stitching. Was the shirt on inside out? *No*, he thought, lifting the tee shirt up from his stomach and inverting it. *It's on right.*

"And I thought I was a pretty cool customer," Curt added.

Dave looked over, impatient with a lot of conversation while he was getting dressed to leave. He checked his cell phone. He wanted to be home at five. It was four. "Okay . . . what are you talking about?"

Curt sat fully up in bed, sliding back until he leaned against the headboard. He pulled the white sheet up to cover his crotch. He opened the drawer of the side table and pulled out a pack of Marlboros, a book of matches, and an ashtray.

"What are you doing?" Dave said. "You don't smoke."

Curt lifted a cigarette out of the pack and gently tapped the tip on the edge of the bedside table. He lit up, inhaling deeply. Dave stared as Curt exhaled. Smoke gathered about his head.

"That's disgusting," Dave bristled. "That shit will kill you." He grabbed the cigarette from between Curt's fingers and headed to the bathroom to flush it down the toilet.

When he returned, Curt was still in bed, his arms crossed, with a big smile on his face. "See," Curt said, his perfect teeth displayed like a row of white Chiclets, "you do care about me."

Dave had no clue how to respond.

"You might even love me," Curt offered in a sing-song voice.

Dave struggled with the moment. At some level, he feared Curt might be right. He'd allowed a dalliance to go on far too long. And like any bad habit, change wasn't easy. What had started as an indiscretion had progressed to three afternoons a week. What had been a passing fling was now a physical need. Curt had reignited Dave's sex drive. Dave felt helpless to end the relationship.

"This is more than just getting off," Curt repeated. "We should be seeing each other on the weekends too."

Dave's stomach knotted. He was afraid Charlie would find out. "I can't," Dave said.

But Curt wouldn't take no for an answer. He pressed. "We can go to lunch, see a movie. We can be together outside of the gym and my apartment."

Dave shook his head. "Charlie usually makes plans."

"Screw Charlie," Curt said, as his eyes darted about the room. "He could drop dead for all I care."

"Don't speak like that about Charlie," Dave said.

"I don't get it," Curt answered. "I spend the afternoons with you, and you spend the weekends with him. I do the heavy lifting, and he gets to sit back and enjoy you whenever he wants. You two don't even have sex anymore."

"I don't want to talk about this. I've got to get going." Dave held his keys in his hand.

But Curt wasn't quite done. "I thought we had something special. But you insist on keeping me at arm's length."

Dave had no explanation. "I'm sorry, but this is the best I can do."

"Well, it's not good enough," Curt said.

"It'll have to be," Dave responded, his face flushed. "I have no intention of leaving Charlie."

* * *

Anna loved Mexico. The weather, the sandy beaches, and the gorgeous sunsets conspired to create a romantic setting, making Anna ever more susceptible to Ernie's immense charms.

I must have been Mexican in another life, she thought as she awoke in the early morning hour nestled contentedly in Ernie's arms, at peace in a country other than the United States. *I've never felt so alive. So wanted.*

She remembered their night of lovemaking. Ernie's tender touch had offered a passion she'd only dreamt about. *It's all just too perfect*, she thought, listening to Ernie's gentle breathing as she too drifted back to sleep.

She next awoke when Ernie, showered and dressed, bent over to kiss her goodbye. Anna squinted her eyes. The scent of Lifebuoy lingered. *How gorgeous men smell in the morning.* Her eyes adjusted to the darkened room. If only she were able to spend the rest of the day tucked in his front shirt pocket. An adored possession. Near to the beating heart of the man she loved.

After Ernie left for work, Anna headed to the eat-in kitchen and poured herself a cup of coffee. She'd escaped the routine of her life in Phoenix, and much to her delight, had discovered Shangri-La, a world she'd only imagined, but never truly expected to find. And though thoughts of Henry periodically popped into her head—whether he was eating properly, getting enough rest—she quickly dismissed those concerns. *For goodness sake*, she reassured herself. *If Henry could survive on the streets of Phoenix, he can certainly manage in the comfort and security of my home. Besides*, she'd argue, *it's not like I've abandoned him. I'll be back in Phoenix soon enough.* She sighed. *Though I could earn a good living in Mexico if I worked with the resorts in town to schedule clients. That could be doable. Fifteen clients over the course of three days at $35 a pop. Great part-time money*, she fantasized. *That could be an option.*

By midmorning, Anna had readied herself to leave the apartment. Outside the front door of Ernie's building, and just across the road, was the beach. *So convenient*, Anna thought, trudging through the sand in her flip-flops. A dark-skinned, lanky man, in a tie-dyed tee shirt with shiny, shoulder-length, black hair, stood beside a tall stack of green loungers. Tied about his forehead was a brightly-colored bandana with the distinctive primary colors of red, orange, yellow, green, blue and purple. Anna opened her tote bag to search for her wallet. "I'd like a lounge chair, por favor. How much will that be?"

"Señora," the man said, a bony finger pointing in the distance, "this is not for you. You should go further down the beach. It is better over there."

Anna looked about. The sand was white and clean. The beach pristine. She'd no intention of walking further in search of a spot just as lovely.

"Absolutely not," she insisted. "I want to be here. Aquí!"

"No, no," the man said, shaking his head. "You are mistaken."

Anna withdrew ten dollars from her wallet and held it up. "Aquí," she repeated. "Aquí!"

The man at once relented, hoisting above his head a green lounger which he dutifully carried over to the exact spot Anna selected, under a large, rainbow-colored umbrella.

By eleven in the morning, the beach was filled with young men in skimpy bathing suits. These attractive men crowded together, boom boxes in tow, a cacophony of hip-hop, pop, and reggae filling the air. Anna averted her eyes, not wanting to stare, but no one paid her any mind. The beach had come alive. Dark-skinned natives worked the crowd selling cigarette lighters, suntan lotion, tee shirts, and native jewelry. Anna relaxed, enjoyed a cool drink, skimming through a magazine or two, and wondering what she'd done in her life to merit dying and going straight to heaven.

* * *

"Gosh, that really smells wonderful," Ernie said.

Anna wore a *Kiss the Cook* apron. With no make-up, and her hair pulled away from her face, she looked radiant. Ernie thought her the prettiest thing he'd ever seen.

He held a glass of Merlot as Anna stood at the stove and sautéed a mixture of mushrooms, snap peas, and corn, sliced fresh off the cob. The aroma of roasted chicken, rubbed with garlic, butter, and herbs, hung fragrantly in the air.

"So how was your day?" he asked, sneaking up and giving her a kiss on the back of the neck.

She squirmed as she transferred the contents of the hot pan into a red serving bowl decorated with green chili peppers. "Stop," she giggled, setting the pan down and then turning to face him.

He brought his wine to her lips.

She took a sip.

"So tell me," he implored her. "I want to know."

"My day was uneventful," she wistfully answered. "This is really the highlight."

"Cooking?" Ernie mindlessly asked as he reached for a snap pea and popped it into his mouth.

"No," Anna laughed. "Being here with you. Sharing a meal together. Now you're going to have to back up and give me some room," she said, taking his wine glass.

"What if I don't want to?" he playfully asked. "What if I just want to stand here and gaze into your eyes?"

She blushed. "Dinner will be ready soon. Just another ten minutes."

"Oh, another ten minutes," he said pulling her into an embrace. "Ten minutes, huh?"

"Ernie, you've got to give me some space. Really," she said invoking a serious tone.

"Okay," he relented, hands in the air. "It can't be helped if you're so enticing," he teased, as she handed the wine glass back to him.

Ernie took a seat at the counter, still watching Anna's every move.

She pulled a large glass bowl of mixed greens out of the refrigerator. With a dash of pepper, a sprinkle of salt, some olive oil and red vinegar, she dressed the salad, mixing it with a large wooden spoon and fork. Her expression changed suddenly as her coloring paled.

"Are you okay?" Ernie asked. Concerned, he insisted she immediately sit down on the sofa.

"Fine," she answered, despite the beads of sweat Ernie spotted breaking on her brow.

"No, there's no point in lying to me. I can tell something's definitely wrong."

Anna shook her head. "It's a little warm by the stove. That's all," she said, using the dish towel in her hand to dab at her forehead. "And I'm missing Henry."

"He's a good kid," Ernie acknowledged, surprised by his own admission. Anna broke into a big smile.

"I'm really glad you brought him," Ernie added.

"I'm so glad to hear you say that. He was scared to see you again," Anna admitted.

"And for good reason," Ernie agreed. "For months I blamed that kid for all my problems. Now, I look around, and with you here, I'm loving Mexico."

"But you know I can't stay," Anna clarified. "I need to get back to my life in Phoenix. I need to get back to Henry."

They hadn't talked about their relationship. Such a discussion seemed premature, and yet, the conversation had just taken a turn into that unchartered territory.

"I don't want you to go," Ernie blurted out, his appetite suddenly ruined. "I want you here with me. I know this seems all very fast, but I think we should be together. And if you're not quite certain, I say let's give it a bit more time."

Anna nodded. "Maybe we can do that."

Ernie honed in on the uncertainty of her response. "That doesn't sound much like a yes."

"Okay," she meekly replied.

"So it's settled." He pulled her into his arms. Her welcoming lips confirmed the answer.

* * *

Like many who fall in love, Anna assumed that everything in her life would be golden. And so it seemed. The days passed by gently. She awoke slowly, savoring the pleasure of a peaceful existence. In Phoenix, her life had been demanding, filled with people coming and going, requiring readings. Now, in the comfort and security of Ernie's affections, she let her guard down and relaxed. She experienced the day as it was meant to be lived. Calmly. Serenely. She lingered over a crossword puzzle. She read Dan Brown's *Angels & Demons*. On her iPod she listened to Beethoven, enraptured by the melodic beauty of his compositions. Her daily meditations were far less urgent, less necessary. Anna was hopelessly in love with Ernie and Puerto Vallarta, and a way of life she'd never known.

For Ernie, Puerto Vallarta too had been transformed. With Anna by his side, he began to appreciate the pace of the city. The tourists that crowded the streets and beaches no longer bothered him. He welcomed their presence, stopping to offer directions, recommending the best cafés for lunch and dinner. He adjusted to the humidity, enjoying the walks along the beach as Anna hunted for seashells, running in and out of the surf. Even the panhandlers no longer annoyed him. He came to recognize their faces and feel compassion for their plight.

His mood lightened considerably. He found great joy in returning home to find Anna lying on the sofa reading a Spanish-language magazine. Together, they spent the evenings sharing Spanish phrases, laughing, and making love. The rhythm of life pulsed with a vitality they both cherished.

But despite the calm Anna found with Ernie, her true nature could not be suppressed. At her core, she remained a gifted psychic, and whatever the spirits demanded, Anna was helpless but to obey.

* * *

Dave kept his thoughts to himself as he and Curt walked to the parking structure behind LA Fitness. Curt's nude stroll in the locker room after his shower had annoyed Dave. He'd spotted quite a few men admiring Curt and was certain Curt enjoyed the attention.

Curt double-clicked the car's key fob, unlocking the red Chevy Camaro.

Dave fumed as he settled into the passenger seat. "Do you really have to parade naked in the locker room? If you're interested in meeting someone new, just say so, and I'll be on my way."

"What are you talking about?" Curt said, seemingly surprised. "Parading? What does that even mean?" He inserted the key into the ignition. "I just happen to like my body. There's nothing wrong with that."

"Come on now," Dave countered, looking out the passenger window into the dimly lit structure where row after row of parked cars were sheltered from the scorching Phoenix afternoon sun. "You can do better than that."

Curt started the engine and stepped hard on the gas. Dave braced himself, one hand on the dash, the other flat on the ceiling. The car quickly reversed as Curt sharply cut the steering wheel before slamming on the brakes. Dave lurched backward and then forward. "Are you fucking crazy?" he yelled.

"Are you?" Curt shouted back. "Who the fuck do you think you're talking to?"

Dave ignored the question. "I remember what it was like to be in my thirties. You're attractive, but not really young anymore. You need to step it up to get noticed. I remember."

Curt pulled the car back into the parking space and turned off the engine. He pivoted about, leaning against the steering wheel, looking at Dave. "Wow, that's really mean. Poppa Bear giving you trouble at home? Is that why you're getting all pissy with me?"

Dave stared ahead. "Leave Charlie out of this. This is about you and me."

Curt squinted. A tiny vein popped in the middle of his forehead. "There is no you and me. There's just you and that lover of yours."

Dave was unsure what to say. His eyes focused on the metallic bumper of the Ford Super Duty parked ahead. A deep dent offered a funhouse distortion of the Camaro.

Curt spoke up. "Do you still want to come back to my place?"

Dave weighed his options.

"You don't have to come over, you know."

Dave didn't answer.

Curt slowly backed the car out of the spot.

They drove to Curt's apartment.

Once in Curt's bedroom, Curt kicked off his sneakers and slipped out of his gym shorts and tank top. Wearing only a black 2(X)IST jock, Curt sat on the edge of the bed. With a wave of his hand he beckoned Dave to come over, but Dave remained in place, standing by the dresser, watching Curt, trying to decide what to do next. Curt flashed a seductive smile, his white teeth signaling the time had come for Dave to submit. Curt leaned back slightly, palms down on the bed, seductively shifting his bulging crotch ever forward. Dave's eyes followed the movement. Dave came closer. Curt sat up. He reached out and gently massaged Dave's member to full mast.

"I bet you don't get this hard with Charlie," Curt said.

Dave stepped back. "You're really intent on ruining our time together, aren't you?"

"Okay, I won't say another word about your precious Charlie."

But it was too late. Dave had lost his erection. He was no longer in the mood. He pulled away, determined to leave.

"I just don't get it. When are you going to realize your relationship with Charlie is over?"

"Damn it, Curt. He's my partner. We've been together for over twenty years. I love him."

"If you love him, why are you here with me?"

"I'm not having this discussion again," Dave said angrily.

"I'm only speaking the truth," Curt taunted. "I'm all about the truth," his voice serene and innocent. "And by the way, if you don't like me walking around naked . . . you can go fuck yourself."

* * *

Anna sat on the beach amid the afternoon crowd. She imagined herself a beautiful butterfly in a garden of rare flowers. All around her were men of varying ages, shapes, sizes, and colors. Some lean, some muscular. Perfect tans. Handsome faces. All attractive in their own way. And though these men had no interest in her beyond a polite nod upon passing, Anna felt secure in their company. Safe, and protected; able to enjoy the scenery without any need to blend in.

Dark young men with trays of silver and jade eagerly circulated among the vacationers, working the beach, moving from customer to customer, selling their wares. Anna watched as they chatted up interest in their goods, flirting, laughing, attempting to extend interest and snag a buyer. And like honey bees, these vendors floated from flower to flower, exchanging goods for money, and sometimes, leaving the beach with a newfound friend.

One particular vendor caught Anna's interest. A mocha-skinned youth, tall and sinewy, black hair, shaved close at the sides, gelled high on top into a spiky Mohawk. He moved through the crowd with the grace and agility of an athlete, gently falling to his knees, offering a glimpse of his tray, and then with delicate balance, rising to full height. He wore an iridescent silver-green headband that matched his bathing trunks, catching and reflecting the sun's light, making his presence on the beach impossible to miss. The longer Anna eyed the young man, the more familiar he seemed. And since Puerto Vallarta was essentially a small town, she assumed she'd run into him before in any number of places. Shopping, walking the wharf, eating at a restaurant. He seemed irresistibly familiar. If only she could remember.

A soccer ball flew past her chair.

Anna watched as the owner ran by, kicking up sand and laughing. Distracted by the interruption, defenses down, Anna's brain retrieved an image. She at once remembered the hands that had gripped her legs so tightly. The man's quiet determination as she struggled to free herself.

The youthful vendor had been on that terrace with Maria.

He's Enrique.

She remembered it as clearly as if she'd been there. But then, she *had* been there. Maria had placed her there.

With a start, Anna realized she'd been directed to this particular spot on the beach to find Enrique. The moment had been orchestrated by spirit.

* * *

"I thought therapy was supposed to make me feel better," Charlie said as he wiggled about, his butt aching against the stiff base of the leather sofa. "Do you realize that the coils in this sofa are shot?"

Elston stared at Charlie from behind his smudged tortoise-shell frames. "You're working through important issues. Try not to give into minor distractions," Elston advised in his soft Midwestern accent. "Life takes time to understand."

"I don't have time," Charlie snapped, sliding a hand under his bottom to rub it. "And I don't want to rehash all this shit again."

"It's challenging work," Elston said, tilting his head downward to look at Charlie over the top of his eyeglasses.

"I suppose," Charlie agreed, "but for the sake of my sanity, I'm going to cut to the chase. Instead of dragging this out any longer, I'm going to talk with Dave."

With the push of an index finger, Elston repositioned his eyewear to the bridge of his nose. Though there was no outward expression in Elston's flat demeanor, Charlie thought he spotted a jubilant tapping of Elston's left foot. Charlie had reached a resolution; now he wondered if these were the moments Elston lived for.

There was a crease in Elston's brow. "Do you know what you'll say? Maybe we need an additional session to role-play."

"No, I can't wait," Charlie said. "It's got to be tonight. I was in the supermarket yesterday, and this woman was standing in line ahead of me. Well . . . she waited until the cashier rang up all her groceries before even searching for her checkbook. I went ballistic. *Are you kidding? I shouted. You couldn't have looked in that duffle bag of a purse when the cashier was scanning your crap? And a check? Who the hell writes a check?* It all just came flying right out."

"So you're feeling edgy."

"I'm frustrated. I screamed at Cox Cable. They placed me on hold three times when I called to ask about my bill. And when they emphasized the benefits of bundling, I lost control. *If it's such a great deal, why can't I read the goddamn bill?*"

"So you're speaking your truth."

"Oh yeah. I'm speaking my truth . . . to everyone but Dave. Someone's going to deck me if I don't get this under control."

* * *

Henry checked his phone. Paul had sent a text: Meet me at Starbucks. I have something for you.

Lately everything had become so confusing. Paul had been extremely attentive, texting Henry to check in on him, leaving messages on Henry's voice mail, stopping by to bring in dinner, watching television, caressing Henry, loving him.

He can't make me do anything I don't want. Henry thought, afraid of what Paul might ask and afraid he might do it. *I have free will.*

Really? Paul's voice in Henry's head answered. *I think I can.*

Henry waited at Starbucks. When he spotted Paul coming through the door, there was the old excitement. The thrill of being wanted.

"Here's the address of someone I'd like you to meet," Paul said as he dropped into the adjacent chair at the high-top.

Henry stared at the slip of paper.

"I don't know . . ."

Paul put his arm around Henry's shoulders and pulled him close. "What's there to know?" he whispered. "I'll be waiting for you outside. I wouldn't let anything happen to you. It'll be fun."

Henry froze.

"And when you're done, save a little something for me. We'll go back to my place. You can spend the night."

There was no point in resisting. If he wanted to be with Paul, he'd have to do it.

* * *

Charlie waited in the living room for Dave to come home. It was four in the afternoon. Dave had gone to the gym before lunch. "I'll just grab something to eat nearby," Dave had said. "Something fast."

Yeah, I bet, Charlie thought.

Charlie had dropped Daisy off for a late afternoon appointment at a Chez La Fab. She'd decided to go back to her perky blond color. "Grey is just too depressing," she'd said, running her fingers through her locks.

Timmy snuggled up to Charlie on the sofa. The comforting presence of the little poodle did little to ease the tension. Charlie's intent when Dave returned: quietly discuss their relationship; allow Dave the opportunity to explain. But the longer he waited for Dave's return, the angrier he got. By four-thirty, with still no sign of Dave, his frustration grew ever more intense. Unable to quiet his mind, Charlie was overtaken by an inner dialogue directed at Dave. *I don't think you're being fair. I'd never treat you this way. If there is something I've done to make you unhappy just tell me and I'll fix it. But don't lie and sneak around, because I can't ignore it any longer. I still love you, but I'm not putting up with this crap. I don't deserve it. It has to stop now. So you'd better figure out what you're going to do. You either want to be with me or not. But make up your mind. You can't have it both ways.*

Charlie bristled at the drama. He hated drama as much as he hated being the scorned lover.

This is about Dave, he reminded himself, unwilling to assume responsibility for the deterioration of their relationship.

And yet, Charlie still wondered if he was to blame. Dave had obviously needed something that Charlie had been unable or unwilling to give. That torturous thought weighed on Charlie's conscience . . . and made him madder than hell.

* * *

Charlie was in the kitchen preparing dinner when Dave's car pulled into the driveway.

White and red fingerling potatoes rested in a ceramic bowl. Charlie had planned to season them with a bit of olive oil, salt and pepper, and then roast them in the oven. Forgetting his plan, he reached for a potato masher. Nervous energy shot through him.

The potatoes didn't stand a chance.

"Hey," Dave said as he came in the door, a gallon of milk in his hand.

"Hey," Charlie replied without looking up, each rotation of the masher ever stronger.

"How was your day?" Dave asked, removing the milk from the plastic bag and placing it on the countertop.

"The same," Charlie said, adding butter and salt to the mix.

He was afraid to make eye contact with Dave. He was afraid he might cry.

"I dropped Daisy off at the salon and Bonnie will be picking her up. She's sleeping at Bonnie's tonight. Girls' night out or something."

"Good for them. I guess I'll get washed up," Dave said.

Timmy suddenly awakened from a nap in the living room, and came bounding into the kitchen. He jumped all over Dave.

"Hey, baby boy." Dave crouched to greet the poodle, stroking the animal's hind quarters as he excitedly leapt about. "And how was your day? That so! Wow. Isn't that terrific?"

"Can you take him for a walk?" Charlie asked. "I just fed him."

"I'll do it after dinner."

Charlie looked up. "Why not now?"

"I just got back from the gym. I'm kind of tired."

Then Charlie noticed the milk on the counter. "That's 2%."

"Damn," Dave said, checking the container. "I could have sworn I grabbed the fat-free."

"Well, I don't know what else you grabbed today but that's 2%."

Dave looked surprised. "Okay, no big deal. We can drink 2%. It won't kill us."

Charlie returned his attention to the potatoes. "Asshole," he whispered under his breath as the back door to the kitchen mysteriously popped open.

Dave walked over to examine the door. "We've got to get this door jamb fixed," he said, fingering the tab on the lock. "The tongue isn't quite catching."

"Great," Charlie answered sarcastically without missing a beat. "How about you take care of that. Call a handyman. I work all day. And then I cook dinner. And now I guess, I also walk Timmy."

Dave crossed his arms and leaned against the counter. "Bad day, huh?" His expression, pensive. "What's going on?"

Charlie had Dave's full attention. Metal masher held high, Charlie asked, his voice dripping with venom, "Why don't you tell me?"

Dave's face registered no reaction. "Tell you what?"

"Whatever you feel is important for me to know."

Dave shook his head, his face a frozen mask. "I don't know what you're talking about."

"Dave, I'm not stupid."

Dave's gaze fell to the floor. "How did you find out?" he quietly asked.

"What does that matter? I know. Isn't that enough?"

Dave nodded. "I'm not sure what to say," he admitted.

"Well, you can say . . . gee Charlie . . . I'm a fucking asshole."

Dave grimaced. "I know . . ."

"No. I'm not going to feel sorry for you. So you can take that sad sack look off your face."

"It was stupid," Dave admitted.

"Was stupid?" Charlie threw the masher into the sink with a hard crash. The clanking sound echoed through the kitchen. "You're still doing it. You've been doing it for weeks. This hasn't been a one-time indiscretion. Not like that would make it any better."

"This has been a really strange time for me. Not working . . ."

Charlie pointed his index finger in Dave's face. "Fuck you, Dave. Don't you dare blame it on that?" Charlie's voice escalated. "You don't get to complain because you're retired."

"How long have you known?"

"Awhile," Charlie admitted.

"What should we do?" Dave asked.

"Are you kidding me?" Charlie raged. "You're asking me *what we should do*. I'd say you better ask yourself that question."

Timmy nudged Dave's leg with his head. "Well, I better take Timmy for a walk."

But Charlie was too agitated. There was too much adrenaline coursing through his veins to allow Dave to walk away. He'd waited weeks, held his tongue, and now, he could no longer contain his fury.

"Over my dead body," Charlie shouted so loudly that Timmy took cover under the kitchen table, his tail between his legs. "You pack your things and get the hell out."

The color drained from Dave's face. "I won't leave. This is my home," he said calmly with just the slightest hint of a quiver in his voice.

"Oh you're leaving," Charlie screamed as his elbow accidently knocked over the 2% milk as he swung around. The container hit the floor and ruptured. Milk splashed everywhere. Timmy howled and scurried off. "Get the hell out of this house now," Charlie shouted, face red, tears rolling down his cheeks.

And without another word, Dave turned and headed out the back door.

17

....

What a prick, Charlie thought, slamming the kitchen door with a satisfying bang.

Tears in his eyes, he surveyed the mess.

The milk carton lay on its side, liquid spreading out across the floor. He grabbed a roll of paper towels and threw it at the milk, then knelt down to wipe it up. The floor was sticky. He wrapped up the chicken he'd planned to grill and placed it in the refrigerator alongside the bowl of pulverized potatoes. He pulled out the mop and bucket stored in the hall utility closet and poked at the hard, yellow-grey sponge, before heading back to the kitchen for the bottle of Mr. Clean stored under the sink.

He was surprised to find the kitchen door wide-open. He quickly closed it.

He filled the bucket with water and detergent and found himself grateful for the distraction. Though he hated housework of any kind, right then the act of cleaning seemed therapeutic and Charlie took pleasure in the shiny floor and a job well-done.

Hands on his hips, he stretched, turning side-to-side and then leaning backwards. *That takes care of that*, he thought.

He went into the family room, threw himself down on the sofa and stretched out. Within moments, he was asleep. When he awoke, he checked his watch and realized he'd slept for over two hours. He lumbered into the kitchen, not really hungry but wanting to soothe himself; sugar would do the trick.

Turning on the kitchen lights, he spotted the rear door. It was wide-open. *What the heck is wrong with this door?* He knew he had shut it.

He shut it again.

The door popped open.

He knelt and examined the doorjamb. The tongue of the lock was barely catching. He held the door in place and slipped on the deadbolt.

There we go, he thought. *Tomorrow . . . I'll call a handyman tomorrow.*

He searched the refrigerator. Nothing appealed to him. He rummaged through the pantry until he spotted a Keebler's Graham Cracker pie crust. *Hmmm . . . I bet that would do the trick.* He tore at the seal, pulling the inverted plastic cover away, and broke off a piece. He popped a small bite of sweet shell into his mouth.

Satisfied, he headed to the family room. Pie tin in one hand, remote control in the other, he turned on the television.

Turner Classic Movies.

Mildred Pierce.

Joan Crawford looked amazing. Charlie sat mesmerized, snapping off small pieces of pie shell, the black and white film throwing the only light in the room. And then, just as Mildred invites Wally to the beach house to frame him for Monty's murder, Charlie realized it was awfully quiet in the house.

He sat up and looked about.

"Timmy," he called out. "Timmy. Come here, boy. Come on."

Charlie waited for the familiar sound of padding paws.

"Timmy," he called again.

Concerned, Charlie got up. Timmy wasn't under the dining room table or sleeping in any of the overstuffed chairs. He wasn't in Charlie's office or under his desk. He wasn't in the three dog beds scattered throughout the house.

Charlie checked the bedroom. Timmy's crate was empty.

And then Charlie panicked. His heart raced, his stomach turned, he felt faint.

The kitchen door . . . the open kitchen door . . . holy shit!

* * *

In an apartment near 7th Street and Missouri, lying alone in Curt's bed, Dave was certain he'd made a terrible mistake. He felt uncomfortable. And though he was certainly familiar with the bed, he'd never actually spent the night. He'd always been too eager to get home, afraid Charlie might learn his secret. Now, Dave was unable to sleep.

Curt hadn't exactly made him feel welcome.

"What are you doing here?" Curt had asked, guarding the door.

"I've left Charlie. We had a big blow-out."

Curt looked to be weighing his options. After all the goading and nee-dling about Charlie, he looked as if he might not let Dave in? And then Curt smiled. It was a very *I told you so* kind of smile.

"Does that mean I can come in?" Dave asked.

Curt opened the door wide. It was then that Dave noticed Curt was dressed in a black Perry Ellis shirt, True Religion jeans, and black Kenneth Cole dress shoes.

"I have plans for tonight. I'm working the evening shift at Houston's."

"When did you start working at Houston's?" Dave asked, wondering how Curt could wear such tight-fitting clothing and still move around behind the bar.

"Is there a problem?" Curt asked, squinting his eyes.

"I just thought maybe we could talk."

Curt waved him inside, then grabbed his wallet and keys off the counter. "I've got to go. But you stay. I'll be back. Probably pretty late. Around three."

And then Curt left.

Dave was alone.

He didn't want to be alone.

The last thing he wanted was to be alone.

He wandered through the apartment, checking out the magazines and CDs scattered about. *Men's Fitness, GQ,* Lady Gaga, Rhianna, Adam Lambert and Jay Z. Dave glanced at the song titles on the backs of the jewel cases. He recognized none of them.

"You're really out of it," Curt had teased him the day Dave purchased a smart phone. "I can't believe it took you this long to get rid of that old clamshell. God, those things are antiques."

Dave had to admit they had very little in common.

Curt hadn't been alive when JFK, RFK, and Martin Luther King were assassinated. He didn't know about Stonewall, Judy Garland, or Elaine Stritch.

Dave hated Facebook and had no clue about Grindr.

And while Curt preferred Bravo, TLC, and *The Bachelorette*, Dave wanted to watch PBS and Turner Classic Movies.

Say Yes to the Dress and *Judge Judy* were the only things they could agree on.

"You need to stay current if you want to stay relevant," Curt had chided him.

Dave agreed he wasn't up on pop culture. But he did love politics and the *New York Times*.

Curt could never commit to reading anything longer than an email.

Dave opened Curt's refrigerator. Except for some condiments and a bottle of no-fat milk, it was empty. The freezer contained a bag of frozen Trader Joe's chicken breasts. Strictly microwave and serve.

Dave rummaged through the cabinets in the kitchen. Different sized glasses, odd dishes with various patterns from mixed sets. Propelled by curiosity, Dave searched through the drawers, reading scraps of paper that Curt could've pitched but had kept for some odd reason. Each had a name, phone number, and address scrawled on it. Curiosity piqued, he searched Curt's bedroom closet and drawers, unsure exactly what he was looking for. Perhaps some clue that he and Curt belonged together. A personal item that would make the connection a natural and wholesome union between two mature adults. He found no such clues. Only porn magazines stuffed in a box behind Curt's shoes.

By ten o'clock, Dave had crawled into bed. He tried not to stare at the Darth Vader clock on the bedside table. By ten-thirty, still unable to sleep, he sat straight up. Then Dave heard his phone, tucked inside the back pocket of his pants, hanging on the side of a chair.

* * *

"Hey, before you leave, I have a little something extra for you. Don't tell Paul."

Henry took the cash and slipped it into his back pocket. "Thanks."

"My pleasure," the man said. "You're really a sweetheart."

Henry blushed.

"Seriously. I wish all the guys I met were like you. You're special."

Henry smiled, somewhat flattered, as he slipped out the door of the Casita on the grounds of the Arizona Biltmore Hotel. It was a cool moonlit night as he walked along the dark pathway, back toward the main hotel. A young couple, who Henry imagined on their honeymoon, greeted him as he turned the corner. The two lovers held hands, giggling, sharing a sweet kiss. Henry envied them their spontaneous affection. How lucky they were to love and be loved without any concern for what others around them would think. *It must be a wonderful freedom*, Henry thought.

Then his cell vibrated.

"Where the hell are you?" Paul was in his car waiting for Henry outside of the hotel lobby.

"I'm almost there. Just passing by the spa."

Henry picked up his pace. And then he heard a whimper. Turning, he noticed a small dog crouched in the nearby bushes. Eyes bright, the little guy was panting and shaking.

"What are you doing out here all alone?" Henry said, leaning down.

The dog kept its distance, uncertain and shy.

Henry squatted. "Don't be scared, honey. Come to me." Henry extended a hand for the animal to smell.

The dog cautiously came forward. One step toward Henry, and then one step back.

"Oh you're a little skittish," Henry said, shifting from squatting to sitting flat on the ground.

The dog watched him intently.

Henry rolled over and lay flat on his back. He remained motionless as he offered sweet words of encouragement. The dog approached slowly, sniffing Henry's head, and then his eyes, and then his mouth. Then he licked Henry's cheek.

Henry petted the little guy's rump. There was a wag of a tale. Henry slowly sat up and the dog jumped into Henry's lap.

"You're so beautiful." he cooed, stroking the animal's head. "You like me. I can tell." The dog licked Henry's mouth. "You must be hungry. Where's your Mommy and Daddy? We better go to the hotel and find out. Someone must be worried about you."

Henry's phone vibrated.

"Where the hell are you?" Paul snapped.

"I'm heading to lost and found. I found a little dog." Henry stroked his new buddy's head. "I've got to make sure he gets back to his family."

"I don't have time for this," Paul said.

"Well," Henry boldly said, "I do."

* * *

"What is that?" Paul asked as Henry stepped into the car.

"What do you think," Henry answered. "It's a dog."

"Yes, but what's it doing in my car? He better not scratch the leather or I'll kill you."

"I've got him. Don't worry." Henry playfully lifted the dog's left front paw and swatted it in Paul's direction. Imitating Scooby Doo's voice, Henry said. "You're a real douche bag."

Paul scowled. "So what happened at lost and found?"

"No one had reported a missing dog. They were going to call Animal Control but I told them I'd take him home just in case someone calls later and notices their dog is missing."

"Does he have tags?"

"He does."

"Then what's the problem? Why didn't they just call the number on the tags?"

"Well, before I brought him in, I took his collar off and slipped it in my pocket."

"What? Why'd you do that?"

"Look at this face." Henry held the dog up. "Did you ever see anything so beautiful? I figured, if he belonged to someone at the hotel, okay, I'd turn him over. But if no one claimed him, then he's mine."

"Wow, you're a devious little shit. Talking about that, where's my money?"

Henry reached into his front pocket and pulled out $250. Paul took it and counted out $125. "Here's your split."

Henry slipped the money into his back pocket. "Now we can go buy dog treats," he said, snuggling the dog.

* * *

Frantic, Charlie had wandered the neighborhood calling Timmy's name. It was getting late, but he didn't care. He was nearly crazed with fear. Coyotes had been known to pass through the urban neighborhoods in Phoenix. He'd even seen one or two in the Biltmore. At the mere thought of Timmy cornered by a wild animal . . . Charlie threw up into a bush at Virginia and 25th Street. And then a stray thought crossed his mind. *What if Dave had taken Timmy?*

He texted Dave.

Within seconds, Charlie's phone rang.

"What's going on?" Dave asked. "Of course I didn't take Timmy."

Charlie explained about the open door.

"I'm coming over," Dave insisted.

"No," Charlie answered. "There's nothing more to do tonight. I've just combed the neighborhood. If he were here, he'd have come to me. I'm hoping a neighbor took him in. I don't think he's wandered far."

"But I should be there," Dave whispered.

"It's late," Charlie answered, keenly aware that Dave was *somewhere else* and *probably with someone else.* His anger spiked, he couldn't help himself. "Maybe you should've thought of that before you put us through all your shit," Charlie said, abruptly hanging up.

* * *

The next morning, Charlie posted a flyer around the Biltmore neighborhoods with a picture of Timmy. He called Phoenix Animal Control and contacted the shelters within a twenty-mile radius. He posted information on the web, including Facebook and Craig's List, and spoke to over ten different small dog rescue groups. Everywhere he called, he gave the same description. "Timmy has a puppy cut. He doesn't look like an apricot poodle. He almost looks like a cream-colored Bichon, so whoever picks him up may not even know he's a poodle. But he does have an embedded chip."

By noontime, Charlie was distraught. Daisy tried to soothe him. "I'm sure he'll show up soon. Someone will find him."

"If anything happens to him . . ." Charlie said.

"He'll turn up," she promised. "You have to have faith."

But Charlie didn't believe in faith. "I've got to get back out there. He must be frantic being out all night." Grabbing his car keys and a bag of treats, he rushed out the door.

* * *

When the young man selling jewelry approached Anna on the beach, she felt the hairs on the back of her neck stand up. There was no doubt about it. He was the young man in her vision.

She pulled her legs in tight to her chest and wrapped her arms about them.

"Good morning," he called, kneeling down next to her, offering a warm smile.

Anna only saw a sinister grin.

"We have many beautiful silver bracelets, all done by hand by local artisans. Perhaps this one would be nice." He lifted a bronze bracelet encrusted with jade. "Give me your wrist and let's see how it looks."

She shook her head no, but he ignored her. Instead, he reached for her arm, slipping the bracelet on her wrist. His touch was sheer electricity.

Images flashed quickly. Anna could feel the dizziness beginning. She had to get the bracelet off. She ripped at it as if she were wearing Lucifer's handcuff.

"Maybe that's not the right one for you," he responded. He pointed to another bracelet on his tray. "This one is fourteen-carat gold."

"No, I think not." Anna struggled to get to her feet.

"Are you all right, Señora?" he asked, genuine concern in his voice. "You seem unwell."

"It's the heat," she said, quickly gathering up her things. The beach was spinning. Her breakfast was in the back of her throat.

"Let me help you," he offered, holding her elbow, trying to steady her.

She jerked her arm away. "Don't touch me. Don't ever touch me."

"I was just trying . . ."

"I know all about you, Enrique," she foolishly blurted out. "I know what you did."

He paled. "Señora, how do you know my name? What are you talking about? I've done nothing." He was visibly shaken.

"I can see who you are." She grabbed her bag.

"Señora, you have mistaken me for someone else. I meant you no harm." He squinted in the bright sunlight. "Señora, I sell bracelets. That's all."

Anna glared at the young man.

He glared back. "You shouldn't be making scenes on the beach. You must be crazy. Are you another crazy American who comes to Mexico and thinks she owns our country?"

"Stay away from me," Anna warned, backing up.

"You're just an old lady on a beach, admiring all the pretty men, hoping someone porks you. But no one here is interested. You're old and ugly. You hear me, Señora? Old and ugly."

"At least I'm not a monster," she whispered, turning quickly to make her escape as the strap of her beach bag caught in the arm of the lounge chair. She lost her balance and fell onto the sand. The young Mexican came around from behind and placed his hands out to help her to her feet.

"Stay away," she screamed loud enough for everyone nearby to hear.

What had been a private interaction escalated to a very public display.

"I'm trying to help," he shouted back, matching her volume.

"I don't need any help," she insisted, rising to her feet. In seconds she was racing through the sand, up the beach, back to the high-rise.

"You disgust me," he shouted. "Go back to your husband. I won't have sex with you. You old sow, you make me sick."

The men who lined the beach laughed as she stomped away.

* * *

With Anna in Mexico, Paul had increased access to Henry. Henry no longer mixed with Paul's other friends. Paul made sure to keep the relationship separate and apart, stopping by at Anna's, bringing in dinner, keeping tabs on Henry and his new dog.

"I'm the only one who really cares about you, little bro," Paul said, biting into a Whopper as the dog circled the living room, sniffing about. "Look around. There's nobody else here but me. What would you do without me?"

Henry pulled the little dog up into his arms, holding him fast. "Buddy cares about me. Don't you boy?'"

"Buddy?" Paul's tone was mocking. "You know that isn't the dog's real name."

"He's mine," Henry protested. "I'll call him whatever I like. And he loves me." Henry offered the dog one of his French fries. It disappeared in a flash.

Paul wiped his mouth. "That dog only cares about eating." He took a long swig of his cola. "Now don't forget about tomorrow. I've got you set up for five o'clock. I'll drop you off at the hotel and wait."

Henry nodded. He'd been through the routine enough to know the drill. Paul arranged the "dates" and he collected the cash. He no longer felt guilty about the hook-ups. He rationalized his behavior as healthy sex-play. Paul made sure there were condoms and the guys were hot. For Henry, the lines between right and wrong blurred. The divisions between lust and love melted. In his loneliness, Henry was grateful for Paul's attention. There was an intimacy the two men shared, a shorthand that allowed Paul to cut through the polite boundaries that kept Henry from getting close to other people. The connection temporarily soothed Henry, even as he became increasingly isolated and forced to turn ever inward.

"Here's your cut from last night with that orthopedic surgeon." Paul handed over six twenties and a five. "Go buy yourself a Gameboy. You earned it."

* * *

Daisy thought it odd.

Charlie was inconsolable over Timmy but made no mention of Dave.

She wasn't sure what to make of his silence. Should she bring up Dave? In Charlie's current state, it seemed unnecessarily cruel. And so, Daisy took her cue from Charlie. She minded her business and said nothing.

She and Charlie lived together, side-by-side, talking about everything except Dave. She pretended all was as it had once been. Sitting together on the backyard patio, they lived a fantasy of denial; nothing between Charlie and Dave had changed. Never mind that Dave hadn't been seen or heard from. The two friends continued to have coffee overlooking the garden that Dave had planted.

The scent of basil drifted on the warm morning air. The birds gathered in the trees, their insistent cooing announcing the day was underway. The gardeners clipped the hedges, the trimmers creating a buzz throughout the complex. Golfers searched the greens for lost balls. Carpenter bees floated along the fences in search of the bougainvillea blossoms with the sweetest nectar. And all the while, Daisy waited patiently for Charlie to tell the truth.

* * *

The air conditioner shuddered to a halt. Charlie made a fast call for service and within two hours it was fixed.

Crisis averted.

After lunch, the hot-water tank sprang a leak and water flooded the garage.

"Why do these things always happen in clusters?" Charlie moaned.

The repair proved costly. The plumber barely looked at the tank before declaring it a total loss and going into his sales pitch. A new tank was installed, the old one hauled away. Charlie had the lingering feeling of being scammed. Later that afternoon, he checked Home Depot online, and confirmed he'd significantly overpaid.

And then, just after dinner, the garbage disposal jammed. It didn't require an expensive repair. It didn't need to be replaced. The red button at the bottom of the unit simply needed to be reset. No need to make a phone call. No need for service. No need to write a check. Charlie knew how to fix it. He'd done it before. Nevertheless, it was the last straw.

"Damn," Charlie howled at the indignity of life.

Daisy sat at the kitchen table, sipping a cup of chai tea.

"This goddam garbage disposal."

"Is there anything I can do?" Daisy asked, though she certainly knew less about mechanical repairs than nearly anyone.

"Oh, I've got it," Charlie said, cabinet door open, bending down searching the belly of the pump for the button. "Let me see. Oh yes, here it is."

The instruction booklet had warned that the InSinkErator should only be used with the sink stopper tightly in place. Charlie had removed it when the darn thing didn't work, using a flashlight to peer into its dark interior to see if there was a spoon lodged in its grip. That, of course, was before he remembered about the little red button.

With the push of an index finger, the InSinkErator jumped back to life. The sound of whirring metal blades accompanied a spray of flying debris. Carrot peels, bits of banana, old eggshells, and coffee grounds shot into the air. Instead of turning it off, Charlie instinctively covered his face. When he finally gathered his wits, his face, shirt, and hair resembled a Jackson Pollock painting.

"Oh my God," Charlie shouted, finally turning the disposal off at the switch. "Look at me."

Daisy could look at nothing else.

She grabbed a nearby dish towel. "Oh dear," she said, holding the towel out to Charlie.

Charlie didn't take the towel. He just stood there. "I deserve this," he said calmly. "I must have done something terribly wrong to someone somewhere. Now I'm getting it back in spades."

"Now, let's not be hasty. It's just an accident."

"No," Charlie insisted. "This is God's way of telling me I'm a terrible human being."

"Now, don't be ridiculous. God doesn't work that way." Daisy had never been a religious woman, but it bothered her when God's name was invoked to help explain something awful. "It's just a garbage disposal."

"No, it's more than that. Nothing in my life is working." Charlie slowly slid down to the floor, eventually leaning up against the dishwasher. "This InSinkErator is a symbol of my life. Dave's gone. Timmy's run away. My life is a freaking mess."

Daisy pulled a kitchen chair over to where Charlie sat. If she was going to give advice, she at least had to be sitting. Charlie looked up at her.

"So what are you going to do about it?" she asked.

"I've tried everything I know to do to find Timmy."

"That takes care of Timmy, but what about Dave?"

Charlie looked at her, blank-faced. "What's there to do?"

"Charlie. I'm ashamed of you. Surely you can think of something."

"I hoped Dave's fling would run its course."

"And what has Dave said?" She no longer worried whether or not it was her business.

"We haven't talked. We've screamed about it, but we haven't talked. I have no idea what's going on."

Daisy could hardly believe it. "You mean, you haven't discussed this with him?"

"I thought if I pretended it wasn't there, it would go away. And then the next thing I knew, I was telling him to get out."

"Oh my," Daisy answered.

"I know," Charlie agreed. "It probably wasn't the smartest move. But what can I do now?"

"You could tell him how you feel?"

"I can't," Charlie whined. "We're like strangers. It's just too humiliating. He's already tossed our love aside."

"Oh Charlie," Daisy scolded, "don't be so melodramatic. Tell him that twenty years is worth fighting for. Tell him how much you love him."

"But why should I?"

"Because he's probably missing you. I know men. They go through these phases."

"How can you be so sure?"

"Because . . ." Daisy swallowed hard. "I've been the other woman."

Charlie's eyes opened wide.

"And I know what you don't. What begins as a dalliance doesn't turn into love. At least it didn't for me. Oh, we had our good times, but in the end, he didn't love me. I was just someone he was passing time with. Someone he'd never marry. How could he? He'd never leave his wife. He just wanted someone to help him feel young again."

"Young again?"

"Yes, it happens to men and to women. There's that certain moment when you think you've grown old and you don't know what to do about it. You want to feel attractive. Young. Desirable. For men, it starts around forty, but can go well into their fifties and sixties. The angel of death is breathing down your neck and the only tonic seems to be someone new. Someone younger. It can work magic on an aging libido."

"Daisy!"

"Don't you think I know all about these things?" she asked in a tone that conveyed she was insulted. "I know as much as anyone about making love to a man. Lord knows I had my fair share of men. Too many to name. And far too many who were married."

"I can't believe what I'm hearing."

"Well, it's true. And it would be foolish to deny it at this point. Do you think I was born with this decrepit body? Wait till you're my age. Wait till you look in the mirror and see an old man, but still feel young. Life offers us these lessons. If you live long enough, you'll see."

"So, what should I do?"

"I've already told you," Daisy said. "Do what's in your heart. The rest doesn't matter much."

"I don't know," Charlie admitted. "It would be hard."

"The only things in life worth doing are the hard things," Daisy advised. "Now let's get you up off that floor. Whatever happens, at least you'll have spoken your mind. At least you'll have stood up for what you believe to be right and true."

"I suppose . . ."

"Come on now," she heckled him. "You've felt sorry for yourself long enough."

18

....

After her encounter with Enrique, Anna stayed away from the beach. His touch had unleashed flashes of gruesome death—men and women begging for mercy, severed limbs and heads. Unimaginable violence. Each soul, in its final struggle, had left a bloodied imprint of horror. The visuals were so graphic, that instead of sharing her fears with Ernie, she turned inward, struggling to understand what such depictions could possibly have to do with Ernie and Maria. And while Ernie's world expanded with the love he felt for Anna, Anna's shrank with the dread of discovering Enrique. She locked herself in the apartment, refusing to venture out to experience the beauty of Puerto Vallarta. Though she and Ernie shared a bed at night, each lived a different reality. Ernie drifted quickly off to sleep, content; Anna tossed endlessly.

* * *

"Have you heard from Henry lately?" Ernie asked after dinner as Anna wiped down the countertops and he rinsed off the dishes before loading them into the dishwasher. Anna had been unusually quiet during dinner. Now, she didn't seem to hear him over the running water. "Is it Henry that's been worrying you?" he asked louder, this time attracting her attention. "Or are you missing Phoenix and living in the United States?" He turned off the water and wiped his hands with a dish towel as he waited for her to answer. "Whatever it is, you might as well tell me. I'm bound to find out sooner or later."

Her face transformed. The light wistful look was gone. There was a darkness in her eyes. "It's about something that happened the other day."

Ernie crossed his arms. "What?"

Anna bit her lower lip. She took a breath and began. "Remember I told you that in my vision there were two men on the terrace with Maria?"

He nodded.

"I saw one of them on the beach."

"Are you sure?" Ernie asked excitedly. He could hardly believe it.

"Absolutely," she said, tightly twisting the paper towel that she used to wipe down the counters. "There can be no mistake about it."

"Then we have to go to the police," Ernie urged.

"Will they believe me?" Anna asked. "It isn't hard evidence."

"I believe you," he answered.

She smiled. He sensed that he'd said exactly what she'd hoped to hear. Believing her was tantamount to loving her.

"I'll talk to Sanchez," he went on. "See if we can get you in to meet the chief. Sanchez likes me. He'll help us."

"Whatever you think best," she said.

* * *

That night, Anna, unable to sleep, laid awake before eventually leaving the bed. She was ill at ease because she hadn't told Ernie the entire truth about her vision . . . about the other man . . . Juan . . . the man who had professed to be Ernie's father.

Why she hadn't told Ernie, she wasn't sure.

She stretched out on the sofa in the living room, lights off, the stillness of the blue-black night shrouding her in a sense of doom. Something wasn't quite right about Juan, something she didn't understand. An important detail that so far had eluded her.

* * *

Anna gasped. "What do you mean Sanchez is dead?"

"I stopped in at noon today," Ernie explained. "I thought perhaps we'd grab lunch together. But when I arrived at the police station, they told me the news."

Anna's face tightened. "How?"

"Hit and run. It was late at night, the desk clerk explained. Tourists drink and drive. Just a random accident." Ernie shook his head. "It's really hard to believe he's gone."

"Oh my God," Anna said, gripped by an intense fear. "How terrible."

* * *

Anna didn't leave the house.

She relied on Ernie to pick up groceries on his way home from work and made excuses about not feeling well enough to go out. She turned to Oreo cookies and Twinkies to anesthetize herself. Her self-imposed exile took its toll. Her shorts pinched around the middle as she struggled to get the zipper up. She switched to workout clothes. Lycra had more give.

She'd worked hard to get trim and she couldn't bear to have it slip away because of fear. Was she really prepared to let that happen?

Stepping out of the tub, she examined her body in the mirror.

She admired her calves; thank God there was one feature which remained immune to weight gain. Her eyes glided up her thighs to her hips, stomach, breasts, and face. Yes, it had started to happen. She could see the weight coming back on. And she was mad. Mad at herself for over-eating. Mad for allowing fear to rule her. Mad at taking the coward's way out by hiding. She had inflicted harm upon herself. It was an old pattern. But now, her life was different. She loved Ernie. She loved Puerto Vallarta. She loved life. She'd have to take fast action to reboot her courage.

She left the bathroom, crossed the living room, and opened the sliding door to the terrace. She was completely naked. It was ten in the morning. The sun was bright as she stepped barefoot onto the source of her original fear.

Her body was warmed by the ocean breezes. It was a gloriously clear day. She stepped forward and gripped the terrace railing. There was no electric shock. No overwhelming sensation. It was just a railing. She could feel the gritty texture of the metal on her palms. Her heart soared as she leaned forward. With the sun on her face there was no longer anything to fear. She'd taken back her power, her body, and her life. There would be no more spirit energy to interfere with her free will.

* * *

In the center of the bed, nestled in Ernie's arms, Anna broke down. She explained about the onset of agoraphobia that had trapped her in the condo. In the darkness, she opened up fully, sharing what she'd learned from touching Enrique.

Ernie listened, seemingly stunned that he'd been unaware of her plight. He released her from his hold and sat up in bed, sliding backward to lean against the headboard. "I had no idea you were so frightened."

She reached for his hand but he withdrew it.

"I wanted to tell you," she said. "I just didn't feel comfortable . . ." Her voice trailed off as she searched for the right words to explain her behavior. But none came. Instead, she blurted out her suspicion. "Is there any chance that your father is still alive?"

"I've told you all that I know about my father," he said defensively as he slipped his legs over the edge of the bed. His back was stiff, his feet on the floor. "Why would my mother lie about that? There'd be no reason to lie."

"Why does anyone lie?" Anna asked, afraid he was about to get up and leave the room. She could see the deep groove of his spine, dividing east and west. She loved his back. It offered strength and security. But now, it felt like a shield. He was blocking her out. Not letting her see him.

Ernie was off the bed, pacing. "My mother was a tough cookie. She always said what was on her mind. There'd be no reason for lies."

"Maybe she was trying to protect you." Anna patted his pillow. "Come back to bed."

"Protect me from what?" he said. "I don't believe that. No . . . that wasn't her way. Whatever shortcomings she may have had, she was an honest woman."

Anna pressed. "Does an honest woman illegally enter the United States?"

As soon as the words left her mouth, she regretted them.

Ernie reached for his robe. He was furious. "She did it for me. That has nothing to do with honesty. When a woman tries to find a better life for her child, that isn't a crime. She had the courage to take matters into her own hands. She wanted what America had to offer, for herself and for me. She didn't wait for someone to make it better for her. She was a brave woman and I was lucky."

Anna shook her head to the contrary.

Ernie was insistent on his vision of his mother.

"I'm just trying to understand all of this. I don't want to fight with you." She extended her hand in a plea of reconciliation.

Ernie's posture softened. He removed his robe and dropped it on a nearby chair. He came back to bed.

She slid over, closer to him. He put his hand in hers.

"I'm sorry," he said, "but I can't guess what's going on with you. You need to tell me the truth."

Her head rested on his shoulder.

"You shouldn't be afraid to share anything with me. You should have told me about all this sooner."

Anna pulled away and took a breath. She bit her lower lip as she weighed her options. And then, she decided to just let go of it. To tell Ernie the entire truth. "Well then, you should know that the other man in my vision *was your father.*"

She waited as Ernie absorbed this new information.

He was irritated again with her. "Now why didn't you tell me that right off?"

"I'm sorry," she said, knowing that she'd have to let go of her secrecy, allowing Ernie to see her, flaws and all. "I was scared and I didn't want to upset you."

"We're in this together," he whispered. "And let's not forget, Maria was my mother. If you learned something about her death, I have a right to know."

Anna nodded.

"Don't you trust me?" Ernie asked.

"This has nothing to do with trust," Anna replied.

"Yes, it does," Ernie said. "When you trust someone, you confide in them. You tell them your fears and your worries. We can never really be together if we aren't telling each other the truth. I love you. And there's no point in my loving you if you're going to keep things from me."

It was the first time Ernie had mentioned love. The word shot between them with a force that amazed her.

"Do you?" she asked, partially proud, partially needing to hear it affirmed once more.

"Yes, I do," he said, using the gentle touch of his thumb and index finger to lift her face up, so that he might look into her eyes. "I love you. I should've told you sooner. Don't look so surprised."

"It's just so unexpected," she answered, thrilled beyond measure. "I hadn't thought any man would ever love me. I'd almost given up."

"You're a warm and loving woman. How can you think you aren't worthy of love?"

Anna clasped a hand to her mouth. She didn't want to ruin his *I love you* with talk of her insecurities. It was the wrong time and place for that conversation. At this moment, she wanted to linger in the discovery that he loved her.

Ernie smiled. "You should know by now that I love you and I can't be without you. And if we continue as we are, I'm going to ask you to marry me."

Anna yelped with joy. "Is that a proposal?" she asked, excitedly jumping out of the bed.

"In time, yes," Ernie said with a broad smile as she danced about the room.

"You know you shouldn't tease a girl. It's not nice," she said, leaping back into bed with a hard bounce.

"I'll remember that," he laughed.

* * *

The instant Charlie caught sight of Dave, he brightened.

They'd agreed to meet at The Vig, an outdoor café, for Sunday brunch. Positioned under an orange tree, Charlie sipped a dry martini straight up. It was only noon, but he needed the fortification. As soon as he'd handed his car over to the valet, his nerves had begun to fray. He remembered Daisy's words of encouragement. "If you're true to your feelings, Dave will respond." Charlie hoped Daisy was right.

As Dave approached, Charlie reached out for a hug. "I've missed you," Charlie said. "How are you doing?"

"I'm okay," Dave answered. His energy low. "Any word about Timmy?"

Charlie regrettably shook his head. It was bad enough Dave had gone. The thought that he'd also lost Timmy only further compounded the hurt. He quickly changed the subject. "Thanks for meeting me," he said as a waitress made a beeline for the table.

"What are you drinking?" Dave asked Charlie, and without waiting for the answer, told the waitress, "I'll have the same."

The outdoor patio filled with young fashionable adults in designer lululemon gym outfits, Nike tee shirts and shorts, giving off the impression that they'd just come from working out at the nearby 24 Hour Fitness or any number of private pilates studios in Arcadia. There were few children, except for the occasional newborn strapped to his mother's chest like a papoose. Waitresses weaved in and out among the closely packed tables, handing out menus, serving drinks, taking orders.

Charlie tried to relax. He'd practiced what he wanted to say and hoped he didn't appear too eager or rehearsed. He wanted Dave to come home. He wanted to tell him that no matter what had transpired, he still loved him. He wanted to leave The Vig that very afternoon with Dave by his side. He was prepared to ask. He was even prepared to beg.

What's he thinking? Charlie wondered as Dave scanned the menu. He'd seen many couples at restaurants sitting across from each other, not talking, and always assumed they'd probably said everything there was to say to each other. But now, with Dave, the silence signaled a greater problem.

Charlie took a sip of his martini and braced himself. "Dave, I want you to come home," he admitted, his heart racing. He leaned forward and clarified in a low voice, "I don't care what's happened. I just want you to come home."

Dave's gaze wandered.

The waitress brought Dave's martini and took their order as Charlie pretended everything was just fine. In reality, he didn't have much of an appetite. He was too upset to bother with eating.

"I don't know where we went wrong," Charlie continued. "I'm prepared to hear you out and own my share of it. But I want us to be together."

Dave looked into Charlie's eyes and sighed. It was a gentle breath.

Charlie couldn't decide if Dave was agreeing or merely signaling he understood what Charlie was saying. They had only just started to talk and already Charlie was feeling frustrated. He rested his face on one palm and stared at Dave for clues. "Is there anything you'd like to say to me?" Charlie asked.

"I'm sorry," Dave offered. "About this whole situation."

"That's a start," Charlie replied.

Dave stared hard at Charlie; he appeared to be at a loss for words. Then he looked away, saying nothing more.

"Okay, you're scaring me," Charlie said. "I'm not hearing you say you're ready to come home. This silent act . . . aren't you going to talk to me? Do I have to do all the work?"

Charlie's sadness turned to anger. The buzz from the cocktail wasn't helping matters.

"I don't know what to say," Dave answered, his mouth twisted.

"You don't?" Charlie said, growing annoyed. "You could start by telling me why, after all our years together, you suddenly prefer someone else's bed." He nervously looked around to make certain his voice hadn't carried. "And why haven't you called? Why do I have to make all the overtures?"

He wanted to reach across the table and shake Dave senseless.

"I'm just surprised," Dave said. "I didn't think you were going to ask me to come home. I thought we were meeting to work out the details of the separation. I need time to figure this all out."

Charlie lurched back in the chair. He felt as if he'd just taken a sucker punch to the gut.

Dave now leaned forward, voice barely audible, pace quick. "I know this is all my fault. But I don't seem to be able to help myself. I don't know how you can even look at me. I've made a mess of things."

"Yes, you have," Charlie agreed, relieved by Dave's admission. "But it isn't something that can't be fixed. Come home," Charlie implored, deciding to give it one more shot. "Just come home. We'll work it out."

Dave locked eyes with Charlie, and then glanced away, as if he were considering Charlie's suggestion. In silence, the two finished their martinis.

"I hate myself," Dave finally said. "I hate my life, I hate what I've become, and I hate what I've done to you . . ."

It wasn't easy for Charlie to sit at The Vig surrounded by happy people, voices raised in shared laughter, enjoying brunch. Dave had caused Charlie a lot of pain, but to Charlie, it now seemed that Dave was presenting himself as the injured party, and that he was helpless, the apparent victim of his own bad behavior.

". . . But I'm not ready to come home yet."

Charlie stiffened. "Why?"

"I just can't right now. I'm not even sure I can explain it."

"Try," Charlie said.

Dave rubbed his eyes. He looked as if he was struggling to wake up.

Charlie waited as Dave seemed to gather his thoughts. His patience running thin, he said nothing. He was too eager to hear Dave's explanation.

Dave took a deep breath. "When I walked away from that job, my life seemed to implode. I said I'd retire . . . but to do what? I had no purpose. Nowhere to go in the morning. No one to talk to. I was totally lost. I had no idea how to spend the day. Time practically stood still. It was a devastating experience. I was drowning and I needed something to anchor me."

"Something or someone?" Charlie asked.

"*Something . . .*" Dave said, a bit exasperated. "But then *someone* showed up who made me feel better. Better than I'd expected to feel about being this age. And I felt powerless to stop myself. I know it sounds ridiculous. My career may be over but . . . *I am still alive. I'm still the same man. My sexual appetite is still strong.*"

"Oh Dave," Charlie responded, shaking his head. "That's so adolescent. What can that really mean in the long run?"

"Right now, *it means a lot,*" Dave emphasized, eyes pleading for Charlie to understand.

Charlie turned away, as if by doing so he could erase Dave's words. "No. I will not accept this," he said. "There must be some way for us to patch this up. After all, I've been pretty good about this whole thing. I haven't asked too many questions. I've given you your space. I don't know many guys who would have been half as understanding."

And then Charlie spotted *the tell.* The tic that signaled Dave was done talking. Over the years Charlie had seen it many times. It showed up when the conversation got too heated. Dave pursed his lips in such a way that his mouth stretched from side to side. If you didn't know Dave, you might think he was struggling to smile. Charlie wasn't prepared for *the tell.* There was still so much he wanted to say; kind things to persuade Dave; loving things to reassure Dave. But now all that went out of his mind. Instead, he fought to contain his rage.

I could kill him. I could break off a branch of this tree and beat him to death, Charlie thought. If his eyes had the power to incinerate, Dave would have been a smoking pile of ash.

"I'm going to go," Dave said, standing up.

"No . . . no . . . don't go," Charlie said, an order more than a request.

"I've got to . . ." Dave said.

Charlie's voice grew loud and hostile. "Don't you dare walk away when I'm talking to you," he threatened, having learned those words from his mother. Wasn't that her line? Inwardly, he cringed, while outwardly, he'd drawn the attention of those sitting nearby.

"No scenes, please," Dave said, wincing. "Let's just go our separate ways for now. We both need time."

"I don't need any time," Charlie announced to everyone on The Vig's outdoor patio.

Dave threw a twenty-dollar bill on the table. "Later," he said, heading for the exit.

* * *

"I'm not sure what's wrong with him," Henry explained to the veterinary technician as he placed the little dog on the metal examining table. The animal whimpered and shoved its head into Henry's underarm, seeking to escape. Henry stroked the little guys back. "He's been throwing up and has a nasty case of the runs."

"How long has this been going on?" the young woman asked as she lifted the dog up by its hindquarters and inserted a thermometer.

"Since last night."

"Has he gotten into anything in your backyard, or maybe on a walk?

"No," Henry answered. "Not that I've seen."

"Have you suddenly changed his diet?"

Henry blushed. He was overwhelmed with guilt. "I found him wandering in the Biltmore," Henry admitted, "so, I don't know what he typically eats."

The tech checked the thermometer. "He's normal," she said, reaching for the forlorn animal's head and scratching under his chin. "There you are. You like that, don't you? What a handsome boy you are," she cooed.

Henry winced as her voice got higher and higher in pitch.

He sat and waited for the doctor to come in. The little guy wandered the room, alternatively sniffing the floor and growling at any sound emanating from the hallway. As footsteps drew closer, the dog hid under Henry's chair. Henry bent over to make eye contact with the poodle. "Hey bud, what are you doing under there? Come on out. You'll be fine."

When the door finally opened, the dog went off like the fourth of July. Henry was so startled by the intensity of the barking that he pulled a muscle in his neck reaching down to grab the poodle out from under his chair.

"Whoa, another happy customer," the vet said, amused by his new client's howl. He offered his hand to Henry. "I'm Dr. Davis."

"Hey," was all that Henry could manage over the fierce barking. "He's really a sweet little guy."

"He's protecting you," Dr. Davis said, as Henry struggled to get the poodle to sit on the examining table. "That's always a good sign your dog is healthy. So is he a rescue?"

"I found him," Henry admitted.

"No idea who the owners are?" he asked, examining the poodle's ears.

"No. No idea." Henry thought about the tags and collar he'd thrown away.

Dr. Davis felt the belly. "Ah, he's tender. What have you been feeding him?"

"He had some leftover hamburger and a few French fries. He ate some melon too. I guess I should have been more careful."

"No wonder his tummy's upset."

Dr. Davis felt around the dog's neck.

"This dog has a chip."

He pulled the skin taut just over the right shoulder. "Barely noticeable, but there it is."

* * *

Dr. Davis's staff scanned the chip and located Timmy's name and phone number in the database.

"Wouldn't you like to stay and meet the owner?" the vet asked. "I'm sure he'd like to personally thank you."

Henry declined. "I don't think so," he said, scratching Timmy behind the ears. "No. I better say goodbye now, while I still can." Henry lifted Timmy off the exam table and hugged him. "I'm going to miss you, fella. Now you be a good boy."

As he left the clinic, Henry was overwhelmed with sadness. He thought of the dog he'd left behind with his parents. Tears rolled down his cheeks. *Gosh, how I hate my life.*

* * *

Daisy sat at the small kitchen table as Charlie rehashed, for the third time, his encounter with Dave. She winced each time he repeated the story. Not so much about the actual details—those were bad enough—but at the energy Charlie put into the retelling. He seemed emotionally devastated, and yet manically animated. Each revision hiked the energy ever higher.

After thirty minutes of sitting quietly and listening, she took her best shot at jumping in, just as he was about to start again from the beginning. "Charlie, it sounds awful," she said in a soothing tone. "I'm so sorry."

I'm sorry seemed to be the wisest response. Daisy didn't want to take sides. She had no idea if and when her two friends might get back together, so she had to remain neutral. She hoped some active sympathy might stop Charlie from going on and on.

For the moment, it seemed to work. Charlie stopped talking. He looked at her, eyes glassy and distant. She was relieved. He was beginning to drain her energy. She had no doubt after their talk she'd need a long nap.

And then he started the story again.

He was still at The Vig, looking into Dave's eyes, humiliated. Trying to understand why he'd tolerated Dave's transgression. Why he'd been so forgiving. And why Dave had been so willing to give up what they had together.

Daisy tried again.

"Maybe he's confused . . . gotten himself into more than he bargained for. Maybe you need to give him time to find his way back."

Charlie appeared to absorb Daisy's suggestion. "We've been together so long," Charlie said mournfully. "I can't imagine life without Dave."

Daisy's patience had run out. "You listen to me, Charlie. You're more than your relationship with Dave. Yes, that's all good and wonderful, but you're more. Every day relationships end. Some because of death, some because of divorce, some due to neglect. No one knows why these things happen. Look at me. I've managed to survive Lyle and he isn't the only man I've lost. We human beings have a natural resiliency. Where there's life, there's hope."

"But how do you go on?" Charlie asked, his eyes searching Daisy's face for the answer.

"Well, you just make up your mind," she said, adjusting her posture, sitting taller. "You wake up one morning and make a decision. Are you going to lie down and die? If not, then you choose life. You dig down deep and you refocus. You work to improve the lot for your fellow man. Nothing is more healing than giving to others."

"I don't know," Charlie muttered. "That seems like a tall order at the moment."

Daisy sipped her tea. Charlie looked absolutely miserable. Her heart ached for him and she wondered if perhaps she should reach out and talk with Dave, but then, she thought better of interfering. If Dave wanted to come back, that would strictly be up to Dave to figure out.

And then the phone rang.

It was a veterinary technician from Adobe Animal Hospital on the line.

* * *

"We can save money if we double-up," Jack said, seated on the edge of Bonnie's white sofa. He wore a pair of khakis and a red Tommy Bahama shirt covered in blue and grey palm trees with silver cockatoos. With his golden tan, he looked like an escapee from a far-off Hawaiian island as he examined the appetizer tray Bonnie had placed before him on the glass coffee table. Using a toothpick, he speared a green olive stuffed with blue cheese and popped it in his mouth.

Bonnie handed him a glass of merlot. "This isn't about money, Jack. I want you to really *want to be with me*. I just don't want to be your transition honey."

"What the hell does that mean?" Jack asked, his face twisted into a mask of disbelief. "I just can't understand the separate quarters. I'm practically here all the time. How long is this going to go on before you commit?"

Bonnie sighed as she tucked a strand of hair behind her ear. "Jack, as I've said before, I *am* committed. But I don't want you to be with me just because I'm available. I want you to make the choice to be with *me*." She took a seat at the far end of the sofa, slightly shifting about so that she faced Jack, her white skirt hiked up a bit displaying her shapely legs.

"That makes no sense," Jack pushed back, slicing a small piece of Brie and placing it on a cracker. He offered it to her. "If I didn't want to be with you, I wouldn't be here. Of course I want to be with you. For Christ's sake, I want to marry you."

Bonnie declined the cracker, crossed her arms, and gave Jack a dismissive look. "Of course you do," she said somewhat sarcastically. "That's what men say when they jump in and out of relationships. That's how people ruin their lives. They marry too quickly. They live together too fast. They don't give life a chance to confirm that they belong together. I've been down that road Jack. I don't want to wake up one day and find that we've both made a terrible mistake. And neither should you."

Jack wondered if she felt trapped. Perhaps it was a longstanding pattern in her love life that once a man got too close, wanted more, instead of welcoming him, she'd put up roadblocks. Worried about her freedom. Equivocated on the relationship.

Maybe that was why she was still single.

But instead of sharing his suspicions, Jack listened as she expounded on her belief that after a longstanding marriage, a man should be independent to avoid defaulting to the next available female.

Jack scratched his head. "For the life of me, I have no clue why you're making this so complicated."

"When was the last time you were alone?" she quizzed him.

"This morning. I was in the bathroom, shaving, looking at myself and thinking, shmuck, what are you doing in this rat-trap? Why aren't you living with Bonnie?"

"Is that how you talk to yourself?" She giggled.

"Only when I'm annoyed," he answered.

"You poor thing," she said, sliding up close to him. She gave him a kiss on the lips. "You really are struggling, aren't you?"

"I am," he admitted. "I never liked being alone. I don't like it now."

"It will give you a chance to find out what you really want. To know who you really are."

"I know who I am. I'm the guy who wants to be with you."

"You are with me," she stated the obvious. "You're just not living with me."

Jack was getting nowhere. It was a circular argument without a resolution. He dropped the subject. The conversation turned to dinner, where to eat, whether to make a reservation, and if he wanted another glass of wine.

While Bonnie put the snacks away in the kitchen, Jack waited. Seated in her living room, he looked about.

How does a man get into a woman's apartment and stay?

Jack wished he knew the answer.

He wished he was younger. He wished he had more money. He wished Bonnie loved him more.

And then, he wondered whether she loved him at all. Maybe it was all a ruse. She needed someone to pay for dinner, take her to the theater, and bed her whenever she wanted. He was at her beck and call, always available, always attentive, while she kept him at a distance. Maybe Bonnie was *stringing him along.* Maybe she was taking advantage of his situation. Maybe she didn't truly love him.

It hurt to think he was being played.

"Almost ready," Bonnie called out.

He finished his wine and kept his suspicions to himself.

* * *

Enrique was startled to see the crazy American lady back on the beach, lounging in her usual spot, head buried in a book. He'd nervously looked for her every day, and after a week, assumed she returned to the States.

He'd been relieved.

The thought of seeing her again had worried him, kept him up at night. He was afraid she might go to the police. *But how*, he wondered, *could she possibly know*? None of it made any sense. And still, he felt threatened by her presence.

Americans are so childlike, he thought, derisively. *They believe the world is either good or evil. That's a luxury for those with a full stomach and a warm place to sleep. I live in the real world. You take what's offered. You do what you must.*

He'd been orphaned at eight and raised by his grandmother. She'd warned him not to follow in his parents' footsteps. They'd died violently, victims of the Mexican drug wars. She'd scared him with her talk of demons lurking about to seize the unclean . . . those who sinned against God . . . the mumbo jumbo of superstitious old ladies. And yet, at night, unable to sleep, he'd lie in bed, fearing the shadows, afraid the demons his grandmother so vividly described, with their batlike wings and sharp claws, were gathering to drag him off to hell.

He tried to concentrate on selling his goods but his eye kept wandering to the sole female form on the beach.

Strutting through the crowd shirtless, chest pressed forward, he carried a four-by-three wooden display case. The interior was lined in black felt. A leather strap rested on his sturdy neck, assuming the primary weight of the display, freeing his slender fingers to hold up selected pieces. "Bracelets, rings, jewelry. The work of native artists. Beautiful Mexican craftsmanship," he called out, searching for anyone who made eye contact. It was so much easier to approach if someone seemed interested.

And yet, try as he might, he couldn't ignore the crazy lady. She wasn't looking his way, but she dominated his attention.

A pasty-faced Canadian caught his eye and smiled. Enrique's jet-black hair glistened in the sun. His over-developed pecs bounced as he knelt before the middle-aged tourist on the bright red towel to offer his display of jewelry. "Señor, would you like to buy a bracelet?" he asked politely, flashing a brilliant smile.

Once again, he looked over at Anna. But this time, she was looking back.

His heart raced as his inner voice raged. *She has no right to try and expose me. How dare she? Perhaps she knows too much for her own good. Perhaps she's already gone to the authorities. Maybe I'm being watched.*

He ignored the Canadian and suddenly rose to his feet.

He quickly looked up and down the beach. There were no police in sight. It was just another beautiful morning.

Enrique glared at Anna. She didn't scare him. Nothing scared him. This was his country. If she didn't like it, she should get the hell out.

* * *

Charlie rushed into the veterinary office. A German shepherd growled. Its owner pulled tightly on the leash and apologized. Charlie barely heard the dog as he leaned against the reception desk. "You have my Timmy," he said with a mix of relief and exuberance.

"The little poodle?" the receptionist answered. "He's in the back. Why don't you take a seat and we'll bring him right out."

* * *

Dave sat on the edge of the tub and watched Curt who stood naked at the sink. Shaving cream, hair gel, eye cream, moisturizer, and bronzer lined the counter. A Norelco electric razor rested nearby for a fast touch-up on stray body hair. It was hard work to look perfect, but Curt seemed to have it well in hand.

"I'm tied up tonight, so you're on your own for dinner," Curt reminded Dave as he ran a brush through his hair. "If you want, we have Trader Joe's enchiladas in the freezer."

"Thanks, I'll manage," Dave replied, mesmerized by Curt's routine.

Curt was out of the house three or four evenings a week. At first it had been to meet up with friends whom Dave didn't know. Dave accepted Curt had friends. He didn't expect to be Curt's entire life, and yet he couldn't help but wonder about those friends. Who were they? Curt had no pictures in the apartment, and as far as Dave could tell, he never seemed to be on his cell phone having a personal conversation.

Dave assumed Curt's friends were young, attractive men who drank, danced, laughed, and probably did drugs. Dave had been there, done that, and he reasoned that Curt deserved his time to play, especially since it would soon be coming to an end. A man in his thirties, no matter how youthful in appearance, eventually tires of partying. Late hours and wild evenings start to show on your face and physique. So far, Curt had been extraordinarily lucky. He could pass for years younger than his real age. In ten years, he would no longer be able to pull that trick off. Dave knew that time had a way of teaching gay men the joy of spending their evenings at home.

It's a short walk from a twink to a daddy, Dave thought, watching Curt step through a spray of cologne. *When it's all gone, and one day it surely will be, what's left? Would Curt spend his remaining years showing photos of his younger self, attempting to parlay the value of his lost youth? Could he hold his own if his pecs sagged, hair fell out, and those chiseled abs swelled to the size of a basketball? What then?*

Dave squinted and tried to imagine Curt older. He'd played the game before, but mostly in reverse with older men, wondering what they must have looked like in their youth. Only a few, the Chad Everett types, retained their good looks. It was disheartening to think about what time and bad genetics could do to the best looking people.

"You're awfully quiet tonight," Curt said, preening before the mirror. "What's going on in that head of yours?"

"Nothing. Just sitting here, watching you get ready," Dave said.

"Yeah, but I can hear those wheels turning. What's wrong?" Curt asked, taking a step back. "What? Do I have something hanging out of my butt?"

Dave mused, cocking his head. "Is that a tail? Is there something you haven't told me?"

"A tail? What are you talking about?" Curt asked, turning his back to the mirror in an effort to see what Dave was looking at.

"I'm joking," Dave answered, "just joking. Calm down. You look fabulous."

"I don't like those kinds of jokes," Curt said indignantly. "I don't think they're funny. I don't even get why you'd say something like that."

Dave nodded. He'd heard it before. Curt had no sense of humor. Not about his looks, his life, or their age difference.

"Stop looking at me," Curt ordered, clearly irritated with Dave's teasing. "You're like a hungry dog waiting for a treat. You used to be so much fun before you moved in here. Now you spend all your time hanging around watching me. You need to get a life. Get out of here for a while. You must have some friends, somewhere."

"I have friends," Dave said, crossing his legs and arms as he swayed from side to side on the tub's edge.

"Careful," Curt warned, noticing Dave's imbalance. "I don't want it said that an old guy fell in my bathroom and died."

"Now don't be mean," Dave answered, uncrossing his arms and placing each hand on the white porcelain to steady himself.

"So why haven't I met your friends?" Curt asked, as he slipped into a pair of black Calvin Klein briefs. "If they're anything like you, they must be a hoot."

"Hey," Dave said, taking offense. "What's that supposed to mean?"

"Oh, nothing." Curt's attention was redirected to the mirror. He examined his reflection as he buttoned a white dress shirt and tucked it into his jeans. "Not bad," he said, shifting his head from side to side as if there were dance music playing. He turned to Dave and beckoned. "Now come here and give me a hug."

Dave obeyed.

Curt smelled wonderful as Dave pulled him close. The mix of pine and musk thrilled his senses. The tautness of the younger man's body instantly signaled Dave's sexual desire.

Curt pulled back and gave Dave an impish grin. "Do you have any cash? I'm running short."

Dave opened his wallet. "I can spare forty."

"How about sixty?"

"I've only got seventy."

"So." Curt reached into Dave's open wallet and took sixty dollars. "That leaves you with ten. And you're not going anywhere."

"When am I going to see the fifty you borrowed the other night?"

"I'm good for it."

"And the rent money. You were good for that, too, when I covered you last week."

Curt's tone turned serious. "It's like I always say, *you play . . . you pay*," and Curt's right hand went down to his crotch. "You want some of *this*, then you pay the rent every now and then."

Every now and then, Dave thought. *Is this what I signed up for? Is that all I am to you? A meal ticket?*

"How did you manage before I got here?" Dave wanted to know.

"Very well, thank you." Curt smiled giving Dave a peck on the lips. "Okay, I'm out of here."

"When will you be back?" Dave asked, following Curt.

"What, am I on a schedule?" Curt answered, hands high in the air. "We talked about this. I will be here when I get back. You're not my mother."

"No, I'm not," Dave agreed. And then it slipped out. "At the moment, I'm not really sure what I am to you."

Curt walked directly up to Dave. They stood toe to toe. "Are you trying to tell me something? Like, you're unhappy?" His tone, dead serious.

Dave shut down. He hated confrontations. Charlie knew that. Curt, had no clue.

"Do you plan on saying anything?" Curt asked. "Anyone home?"

Dave stared into Curt's cocky eyes. He was speechless.

"Okay, I'll take that as *I'm sorry*," Curt said as he headed out the door.

After Curt left, Dave drove over to the Arizona Biltmore Hotel. He missed the old neighborhood. He missed Charlie. He walked the winding paths of the hotel, passing the swimming pool and the lush gardens. Guests and staff nodded hello. He felt welcomed and comfortable. It was a relief to be among friendly people. To be anonymous and yet pretend he still lived in the Biltmore. Here, he could reclaim his former life. Sit at the hotel bar, Dewar's in hand, and imagine nothing had changed.

* * *

Henry stood in front of the double oak doors of the Southwestern adobe mansion, one of the many that dotted the suburbs of Paradise Valley, with its high twelve-foot ceilings, carved wooden beams, and cacti lining the entryway. A small sign along the pathway warned intruders of the security system.

He rang the doorbell. It'd been so long since he'd last been inside the house. He wondered if anything had changed.

Jello, the sixty-pound Yellow Lab, was first to reach the door.

Henry remembered how Jello's loud bark had echoed through the house. His jubilant announcement of visitors made the doorbell redundant.

Henry knelt down and placed his palm on the sidelights that ran alongside the heavy oak door. "Jello," he called to the excited animal. "Look at you. You're so beautiful."

Jello leapt wildly in the air, spinning counter-clockwise and then reversing.

"It's me, Jello. It's me," Henry enthused as the animal whimpered with excitement. "Oh, I missed you too." Henry laughed. "I did, honest."

The Lab jumped up and placed two paws on the glass, tail wagging wildly.

Footsteps followed.

A woman's voice rang out. "Be quiet . . . okay . . . we know . . . yes . . . someone's at the door."

Jello let out a whine of sheer delight as Henry's mother opened the door. She gripped the animal's collar tightly as she locked eyes with Henry.

"It's me," Henry said, as if the woman who stood before him might have failed to recognize him. "It's me, Mom," he repeated, excitement in his tone. "It's so good to see you."

There was a quiet moment as Henry's mother seemed to drink in the image of the young man before her. Henry almost thought she might step forward and hug him, pulling him across the threshold, telling him that all was forgiven and she was sorry for having made such a mess of their lives.

But then, that moment passed.

She raised her chin, jaw turned slightly to the right, as a fierce expression settled on her face. Henry had seen that look before. An expression of profound disapproval—one brow raised sharply, eyes dark, unwelcoming, lips tightly drawn. Henry's heart seemed to stop as he realized nothing had changed, and that probably, nothing ever would.

"Why are you here?" she asked, her face screwed up so tightly it was a wonder she was able to speak at all.

"I wanted to see you," Henry explained, his voice barely audible. "I missed you."

"You can't come in," she said, yanking tightly on Jello's collar, firmly in control of the animal by her side.

"I'm back in school," he offered, eager to appease. "I'm getting good grades."

But his education was no longer of interest to her. "I'm not letting you into the house. Not as long as you choose to be a homosexual."

"Mom," Henry pleaded, "I've told you. It's not a choice."

She took a deep breath. "It most certainly is. You can pretend this horrible thing is born in you, but I know the truth. I know that as a baby you were perfect. You chose this because you're a coward. You're afraid to live your life as the man God meant you to be."

Frustration crept into Henry's voice. "But that's what I'm doing. I'm gay. That's who God meant me to be."

"You should be ashamed of yourself," she hissed. "You've thrown your life away and you have only yourself to blame."

Jello whined. Despite the tension about his neck, the dog tried to come closer to Henry. Henry thought the Lab would have gladly licked everyone's face to mend the rift and make it all better. But his mother pulled hard on the collar, yanking Jello into a sit.

"You're not going to break my heart," Henry said in a quiet, deliberate effort to try and control his emotions. "You've done a terrible thing by throwing me out. You're the one who should be begging me for forgiveness. God will want to know where you came off judging me. You shirked your responsibility as a parent. You abandoned me. You're the one who's done wrong."

The woman's eyes flashed. "How dare you speak to me like that?"

Barely able to control himself, he started to yell. "You're not going to win. I'm going to rise above this. I'm going to prove you've done a terrible injustice. And when I do, there'll be no forgiving you."

The woman slammed the door with such force it sent Henry back on his heels.

He pounded on the door, indignant at being treated so harshly, his tirade fueled by months of suppressed anger and frustration. "Let me in. Let me in," he cried, tears cascading down his cheeks. He continued to bang on the door with all his might as if by sheer will he could destroy the barrier that divided them.

"Get away from the door before I call the police," his mother shrieked as Jello barked furiously. "And don't you come back. We don't want your kind here."

Henry had never spoken back to his mother before. Never raised his voice to her. But he'd also never felt such rage toward another human being. And though he'd been tossed out, he had hoped that one day, his parents would welcome him back. They'd come to understand. Realize the error of their ways. But now, he understood a line had been crossed and his family was gone. He was alone in the world. All alone. No one cared about him. And it suddenly seemed that no one had ever really cared about him. Not his mother, not his father, not Anna, not Paul. They had all gone through the motions but the truth was undeniable. He was unlovable. Simply unlovable.

* * *

Jack stewed over Bonnie's refusal to allow him to move in. And though they spent much of the weekend together, Bonnie strictly adhered to her privacy during the week, insisting Jack sleep at his own place.

"I don't get it," he pressed after dinner at The Capital Grille. Jack had hoped that an expensive meal might set the right tone for another try with Bonnie.

"We've been all through this Jack," Bonnie said, taking a forkful of key lime pie.

"Is it something Daisy said?" he pressed, blindly guessing at any other reason than the one Bonnie had already given.

"Don't be silly Jack," Bonnie answered, rolling her eyes.

"Oh . . ." Jack nodded as if he were onto her now. "That's it. *It is my aunt.* She told you something. Something awful that's given you pause."

Bonnie laughed. "Honey, trust me, if I'd been concerned about how you treated Daisy, I wouldn't be sitting here."

Jack paled. "Hey, I was the one who interceded and got her that settlement check. And I promised to repay whatever was missing from that account."

Bonnie licked her lips, snatching a bit of whip cream that had edged in the corner of her mouth. "You say it like you're the big hero in all of this.

Jack, you need to face the facts. Whatever happened to Daisy, you share the responsibility."

"Okay," Jack agreed, one hand in the air, conceding the point. "Okay. I'm not going to defend myself. What happened was wrong. Fine. But just remember, Daisy walked away from our family, and for whatever reason, my mother really disliked her. So you can't believe anything Daisy says about me because she doesn't know me. She was the black sheep of our family."

Bonnie held a fork in the air. "Oh Jack. She only speaks well of you."

"Really? Why do I find that hard to believe?"

Bonnie gave Jack a sheepish grin. "Because you're not a trusting person."

Jack burst forth with new energy. "Now I know she's the reason you won't live with me," Jack pressed. "Admit it."

"Jack, you're being ridiculous."

"No," Jack said pointing a finger, his temper flaring, "That old bitch has it in for me. I knew settling that lawsuit wouldn't be the end of it. She's holding a grudge – isn't she?"

"Your birth mother?" Bonnie announced, her glare fierce and uncompromising. "That dear woman who you've been maligning gave birth to you. She loves you Jack. She may not have raised you, but that sweet woman would never do anything to ruin her chances of being close to you. Never."

* * *

Henry skipped school. He was too upset to leave the house.

He thought of calling Anna, begging her to come back to Phoenix, but then he didn't think anything he might say would do any good. Besides, he reasoned, if she truly cared about him, she'd never have stayed in Mexico so long, leaving him to fend for himself. He couldn't remember the last time they'd spoken by phone, and though she did text often, it was mostly to convey instructions and reminders of what he needed to do to take care of the house.

No, he thought angrily, *there's no point in calling Anna. As long as I water the plants, make sure the roof doesn't leak, I've served my purpose. She doesn't care about me.*

And then his cell phone rang . . . a sharp, high-pitched ringtone that jolted him.

He was suddenly excited. *Could it be Anna? Maybe she'd sensed he was upset . . . picked up on his vibrations . . . and decided to call. Maybe she was coming home after all.* Instantly his mood lightened. *Thank God*, he thought as he reached for his cell, only to see the name displayed on the screen. Crestfallen, he accepted the call anyway.

"I'm coming over," Paul announced, his voice determined, unyielding.

"No," Henry objected, "I'm tired. I won't open the door."

"Well you better, or I'll break in a window."

Thirty minutes later Paul pushed his way into the darkened house. "Go get dressed," he ordered. "We're going out tonight."

Henry knew that Paul meant he'd set up another "date."

"I can't," Henry said, "not tonight."

Paul glanced about the house. "What are you doing anyway? Feeling sorry for yourself? Have you even eaten today?"

Henry could only stare back.

"This is ridiculous," Paul said, taking Henry into his arms. Henry melted into the warm embrace. "Your being all alone here when there's money to be made. I've set up an appointment. Now go wash your face."

Henry pulled away. He wasn't going anywhere. "I'm not in the mood," he said, the high-pitched voice betraying his emotions as he held his ground.

"Not in the mood?" Paul repeated, his face contorted into an expression of disbelief. "Who do you think you are?" He stared into Henry's eyes. His look, threatening.

"I'm me," Henry shouted. "I'm someone who's tired of being bossed around. Go find someone else to make money off of. I'm done."

Paul grabbed Henry by the arm and gave him a shake. "You think you're the only one I have to deal with, don't you? You think I have all the time in the world to play games with you, begging and pleading, and letting you put your hands all over me? You think you're so important that I can't manage without you?"

Henry took a breath, but said nothing.

"Well, you're not the only lost boy," Paul bragged, still holding tightly onto Henry's arm. "There are others. And I could let any one of those other kids do your job tonight. Some of them are younger and better-looking than you."

"Then send someone else," Henry said, pulling his arm away. "Call someone else," he shouted, rubbing his arm where Paul had gripped it, proud to have found the courage to stand up for himself. "And while you're at, lose my number."

"Oh, you're going," Paul said, as he slipped an arm about Henry's neck and pulled him into a headlock. "I've had just about enough of you. You're coming with me before I get real nasty."

Bent over, looking at the floor, Henry struggled to maintain his balance as Paul tightened his grip about Henry's neck.

"I'll beat the shit out of you if you give me a hard time," Paul said, pulling Henry roughly down the hallway,

Henry stumbled along, leaning heavily on Paul, his face pressed against Paul's waist. "Why are you doing this?" he cried out in pain, desperate to keep pace, afraid he'd fall.

"We got places to go," Paul said, as he released Henry and shoved him into the hall bath. "And I'm not putting up with anymore of your bullshit."

Before Henry could answer, Paul had a grip on Henry's shoulder. A tight squeeze into the muscle brought Henry immediately down to his knees. Paul grabbed the top of Henry's hair, and with a knee planted firmly in Henry's back, yanked his head back. Henry's eyes came to rest on Paul's inverted sneer.

"If you don't pull yourself together and stop all this nonsense, I'm going to shove your head in that filthy bowl. Now, have I made myself perfectly clear?"

19

....

"I've made a terrible mistake," Bonnie managed to say before she burst into tears in the doorway. Daisy quickly ushered her into the kitchen, away from Charlie's prying eyes and ears. Some conversations were best left to the women.

"Okay, take a breath," she softly said, as Bonnie took a seat at the table. Her mascara ran dark below her bottom lids as she searched, and then retrieved from her bag, a small packet of tissues. Daisy gently rubbed her back, heartsick that the relationship with Jack had probably run its course. She had so wanted the two to be together. Now she couldn't help but feel sad. Sad for Bonnie, sad for Jack, but mostly, sad for herself.

She placed a glass of water in front of Bonnie. "Alright now. Take a sip and gather yourself."

Bonnie did as she was told, in between sips, dabbing at her eyes.

Charlie appeared in the doorway. "What's going on?" he asked spotting the two women huddled together. "I wondered where you went," he said to Daisy. "Answering the door doesn't take that long."

"Oh Charlie," was all that Daisy could manage as she wondered how to tactfully ask him to leave his own kitchen.

Charlie instantly zeroed in on Bonnie. "Are you okay?" he asked. "What's going on?"

Bonnie inhaled, covered her mouth with a damp tissue and gurgled a bit of something that neither Daisy nor Charlie could make out.

"I think she and Jack had a fight," Daisy offered.

Bonnie vigorously shook her head to the contrary.

"Oh," Daisy looked over at Charlie, eyes wide, now uncertain what all the fuss was about.

"Jack knows," Bonnie managed to eke out as she looked at Daisy. "I told him. He was pressing me, and one thing led to another, and before I knew it, the cat was out of the bag."

Daisy gasped, a hand resting on her heart.

Bonnie continued. "He just got up and walked out. I assumed he was coming over here. Is he here?"

Daisy shook her head.

"Told him what?" Charlie asked just as the doorbell rang.

* * *

Jack appeared at Charlie's front door looking haggard. The color gone from his face, his eyes, dull and dead. "Is she here?" he asked in a flat monotone.

"Bonnie?" Charlie asked, smelling alcohol on Jack's breath.

"No. My Aunt Daisy."

Charlie pointed his chin toward the kitchen. "She's talking with Bonnie now. She's pretty upset."

"I want to talk with my aunt."

"Well you can't right now," Charlie said, stepping in front of the door. "How about if we wait until everyone cools down a bit."

Jack eyed Charlie's stance, seemingly deciding whether or not to push past, before relenting. "How about if I wait out here?"

"Sure," Charlie agreed, pulling the door shut as he stepped out onto the front walkway. "Why don't you tell me what's going on. Maybe I can help."

Jack offered a sardonic smile. "Nobody can help."

"Well, you may not know this, but Dave and I split up, so I just might have some insight to share."

Jack cocked his head. "What are you talking about?"

"Me. My relationship. I understand about these things. Shit happens."

Jack squinted at Charlie. "Daisy's my mother," he announced with irritation. "Bonnie knew all along and kept it from me. And my own parents . . . never let on."

Charlie froze. He had no clue what to say next.

"So don't tell me about your troubled relationship and expect me to take your advice."

"Crap," Charlie said. "I had no idea."

* * *

"Oh dear, this is a mess," Daisy said as she pulled up a chair next to Bonnie.

Bonnie reached over and squeezed Daisy's hand. "You never did intend to tell him, did you?"

"No, I didn't. I couldn't see much benefit in it."

"But it is the truth?" Bonnie eyes focused on Daisy for confirmation.

She shook her head. "Oh yes."

"And they say the truth will set you free."

Daisy exhaled. She thought such platitudes provided a poor excuse for hurting others. "Personally, I think everyone prefers a little white lie. What I don't understand, is why you felt compelled to tell him?"

Bonnie looked down, her face coloring. "I seem to have a unique way of blowing up all my relationships. I really shouldn't be trusted with men."

* * *

"I'm glad you finally know," Daisy told Jack. "But I should have had the courage to tell you myself."

At Daisy's request they had all gathered in the living room. Jack and Bonnie on the sofa, Daisy and Charlie in the matching club chairs facing them. Timmy curled up at Daisy's feet.

"I shouldn't have said anything," Bonnie sheepishly admitted, speaking to Daisy. "I betrayed your trust."

Jack looked askance at Bonnie. "I'm the one who should have your allegiance. You should be asking my forgiveness"

"Well," Daisy said, "The best kept secret *is the one never told*. Now it's all out in the open. And I suppose I'm glad. You actually did me a favor." Daisy nodded to Bonnie. "No harm done."

"Not much," Jack said, a scowl on his face. "I don't understand how this could be true."

Daisy leaned forward, elbows resting on her knees. She hadn't thought it would be easy to tell Jack. Now she realized why she hadn't. He looked absolutely miserable.

"Well it is true," she began. "I was young, scared, and I let them run me off. I didn't think I could manage a baby. But I do remember holding you and never wanting to let go." Her arms interlocked as she once again held her baby. "You haven't had children. But if you had, you'd know exactly what I mean. There hasn't been a day that I haven't thought of you. Not a day."

Jack looked nonplussed. "Then why didn't you ever reach out to me?"

"Oh I tried in the beginning. But my letters were returned. And then I just thought you were better off without me. The longer I kept the secret, the more it seemed as if I'd imagined it all. That it was never real. Like it had happened to someone else."

"You should have kept trying." Jack insisted, anger in his eyes. "I always felt like I didn't belong. Like there was something wrong with me."

Daisy clasped a hand to her mouth. She struggled to regain her composure. "Oh Jack. Forgive me. I had no idea you were so unhappy."

Charlie intervened, directing his comments to Jack. "But look how lucky you are now. You've found each other again. We don't all get a second chance to be loved. And to have Daisy as your mother, for me that would be a dream come true."

Jack stared at Charlie. "I had a mother," he answered with disdain.

Daisy agreed. "Yes, that's very true. I may have given birth to Jack but being a mother implies much more. Jack, if you don't want to use the word mother, I completely understand if you'd prefer to call me Aunt Daisy."

Jack nodded. "This whole thing will take time to get used to."

"Of course, dear," Daisy said, her smile filled with warmth.

"But I can't see any reason for me to call you anything other than mother," Jack quickly added as he glanced over at Daisy. There was a glimmer of fondness in his eyes. "I don't think I'll ever be able to look upon you as my aunt again."

* * *

Anna marveled at her courage. Earlier, she'd been afraid to leave Ernie's apartment. Now she was at Police Headquarters with an appointment to see Ricardo Esteban, the chief of police.

Puerto Vallarta was in the midst of a heat wave. A warm, damp breeze swept the waiting room, coming from a buzzing rotating floor fan in the corner. Anna hoped the visit would be over before she melted into the cheap plastic yellow chair that seemed permanently affixed to her rear end.

"Anna Garrett," a male voice called out. "This way."

She followed the policeman through a doorway that ushered her into a large room of uniformed men seated amid a maze of gunmetal desks, and then through a long dark hallway, to a private office at the rear of the building. After a gentle rap on the door, he nodded his head for Anna to enter. Then left.

She opened the door.

"Ms. Garrett," said Chief Esteban as he came around his mahogany desk. "How nice it is to meet you." He took her hand in his. "Please forgive me for keeping you waiting."

Anna felt a growing sense of claustrophobia as the door closed behind her. The air held a sour scent—a mix of hair tonic, body odor, and cheese enchiladas. The only light, coming from the ceiling, was fluorescent. Its gentle flickering hurt her eyes as she struggled to adjust to her new surroundings.

"And to what do I owe the pleasure of this visit?" The chief smiled, offering Anna a seat.

"I have important information about the death of Maria Gonzalez."

"Yes . . ." said the chief, now seated behind his desk and leaning eagerly forward, seemingly interested in whatever had enticed her to visit on such a hot day.

"I want to report a murder," Anna blurted out.

"A murder," the chief repeated in a grave tone as if such things rarely occurred under his jurisdiction. The faintest belch escaped his lips. "Forgive me," he apologized, scrounging through his top desk drawer before pulling out a roll of Tums.

"Yes, a murder," Anna said. "It happened a few weeks ago at my home." She blushed as soon as the words escaped. She hurried to correct herself. "Well, it isn't exactly my home. It's the home of the man I live with."

Esteban removed two Tums from the tiny packet and popped them in his mouth. "And whom may I ask is that?" he said chewing on the tablets, a gentle look of amusement crossing his lips.

"Mr. Ernie Gonzalez," Anna answered in a voice which sounded excessively girlish to her.

"Ah . . . the son of the woman who jumped from the high-rise?"

Anna wrung her hands. Esteban was eyeing her suspiciously. She sensed he was playing with her. "But that's it," she said, this time with conviction. "She didn't jump. She was thrown."

Esteban blinked twice. He retrieved from his pants pocket an old gold pocket watch. He placed it on the desk. Anna assumed he was about to check the time, but instead of opening the watch, he just left it there in full view.

Esteban cleared his throat. "We've investigated that case and found it to be suicide."

"But I know it wasn't." Anna took a breath. "I *know*," she said again with fierce determination.

Esteban leaned forward in his chair and gave her a sidelong glance. "Now how could you possibly know that?"

Anna hesitated but a moment. "The victim told me so."

Esteban shot backward in his chair and let out an explosive laugh. "Seriously?" he asked, his brown eyes wide in condescension. "So you have spoken to the deceased?" The tone of his voice was playful and amused.

"Yes, I have," Anna said, lifting her chin, unafraid of his scorn. "I have the gift. I can speak with the dead."

"Very interesting work I'm sure," the chief replied, standing to indicate the meeting was over. "Well, I do so appreciate your bringing forward this valuable information. We will make certain to add that to the files," he said.

"But you haven't heard me out," Anna protested.

"Oh, I think I've heard all that will be useful."

"You think I am making this up?" she stammered, as Esteban came around from behind his desk.

"No, not at all," he said, placing a hand on the back of her chair. "I'm certain you believe this to your very core."

She knew he wanted her to leave. But she wasn't about to move. Instead, she looked up as he hovered nearby. "You're saying I'm a charlatan."

Esteban extended his arms wide. "Ms. Garrett, I wish I could believe you. It would be wonderful if every crime victim could simply step forward and give me the name and address of the perpetrator. It could save me hours, not to mention"—and again he gently burped—"forgive me." He swallowed hard. "It would make my job so much easier."

"But I do know," Anna insisted. "I've already identified one of the men. His name is Enrique. He works as a vendor on the beach in front of my building. He was on the terrace that night. He held my legs." Anna quickly corrected herself. "I mean . . . Maria's legs."

Esteban took a seat on the edge of his desk. "That sounds very dangerous," he calmly said. "Confronting someone who you suspect is a murderer is not the wisest thing to do."

"Oh," Anna assured him, "I'm not afraid." She held her head high. "He thought I was deranged."

At once she realized the absurdity of her statement.

The chief flashed a broad smile. "Perhaps it would be wiser not to talk about such things," he said.

Anna was not about to back off. "I'm not afraid," she said, indignantly. "Fear not . . . want not."

Esteban glared at her. "What did you say?"

"I'm not afraid," Anna repeated.

"After that . . ." the chief wanted to know.

Anna had no clue. She shook her head slightly and shrugged her shoulders.

Esteban lifted the pocket watch from his desk and popped open the cover. He showed Anna the engraved inscription inside.

Fear not . . . want not.

* * *

The sweet scent of barbequed chicken hung in the air as Dave prepared a green salad with a simple oil and vinegar dressing. On the kitchen counter, a glass of merlot awaited. He opened the oven door and admired his handiwork. Everything was perfect. The glass table in the small kitchenette was laid out with the new white Crate & Barrel china that he'd recently purchased for the apartment. Water glasses, silverware, and two votive candles completed the presentation.

He sat on a bar stool and watched as the light slowly faded from the room. Shadows danced on the walls as the edges of the apartment slipped away. It seemed as if time stood still as he waited for Curt to arrive home.

At 8:00 p.m. he poured himself another glass of wine before finally getting up and turning on the lights.

He was no longer hungry.

He packed up the food and placed it in the refrigerator before retreating to the sofa, where he settled in, leaving the kitchen table untouched. He turned on the television. HGTV was running back-to-back episodes of *Flipping Out*. He stared into space, not thinking of anything in particular . . . happy not to think at all. By 9:30, shoes off, stretched across the length of the sofa, he drifted off to sleep as Jeff Lewis complained about something or other.

He awoke at 11:30 to *Property Brothers*.

Curt was still not home.

Curt had had a habit of mysteriously disappearing but he'd yet to stay out all night.

Dave checked his phone. No messages, no texts.

Where can he be?

He called Curt's cell which went directly to voice mail. "Where the hell are you?" he demanded to know, instantly regretting his tone.

Dave had tried to ignore Curt's many late nights, but he'd be damned if he'd overlook his disappearing completely without a word. Mostly, Curt tended to blame his lateness on last minute requests to fill in as either a waiter or bartender around the Valley. "They have my number on speed dial," he'd grumble. "If I say no, they don't call again." But when Dave asked which restaurant or bar he'd been working at, Curt quickly changed the subject. "Don't tell me you're actually jealous of my job?" he'd taunt Dave. "You know I can't afford to hang around all day like you. I need to earn a living. Unless you have some other suggestions . . . I have to work."

Dave didn't like Curt's tone. He especially didn't like Curt painting him as the bad guy.

"That's not what I'm saying," Dave defended himself. "If you're going to be late, just let me know so I don't worry. Call if you're late. It's just a matter of courtesy."

But by this point Dave had given up. There was no point in ramping up the tension between them. It was clear Curt was either too absent-minded or inconsiderate to call. Dave reconciled to the reality. But he didn't like it. He didn't like it one bit.

When Curt finally came in, Dave was in bed, tossing and turning. He checked the clock. It was 2:00 a.m.

"Where have you been?" Dave asked, rubbing his eyes.

"Who are you . . . my mother?" Curt said, by now a familiar refrain. He made his way to the bathroom, dropping clothes along the way. "I'm taking a shower," he called out.

Dave got out of bed and picked up after Curt, putting the shoes, shirt, pants, and socks where they belonged. Curt flung his briefs at Dave before stepping into the shower.

Sitting on the edge of the bed, Dave waited. When Curt emerged, towel wrapped about his waist, Dave tried again. "So, how was your evening?"

"You don't trust me," Curt said in the tone of an indictment.

If you want someone to trust you, Dave thought to say, *be trustworthy*, but he couldn't get the words out. "No, I trust you," he said in contrast to his true feelings.

Curt just shook his head.

"It's late," Dave said. "Time for sleep."

He thought perhaps Curt was right. Maybe he was too possessive. Maybe he'd feel differently if he was closer to Curt's age, distracted by a job, earning a living. He understood Curt had built up a following as a freelance bartender/waiter, but couldn't exactly figure out why he didn't have a full-time job.

"I'm sorry," Curt said, dropping the towel and slipping under the covers. He nestled up to Dave, burying his head in the crook of Dave's neck.

The tension faded. Dave no longer cared that Curt had been late or why. He only wanted to touch and be touched. To feel the warmth of Curt's body against his. Whatever problems they might have were best left to the daylight.

* * *

"What do you mean, he laughed at you?" Ernie asked after hearing about Anna's visit to the police station.

"At first he laughed," she clarified. "He thought I was crazy."

They had agreed to meet for dinner at the resort. Slowly the dining room filled with vacationers. Men wearing pastel-colored shirts and khakis; women in light summer floral dresses. The more they talked about Maria, the more anxious she felt. She glanced at the specials as the waitress delivered Ernie's margarita. He took a sip and announced it delicious. But the arrival of the drink didn't derail the conversation. Ernie continued to push.

"Maybe I better stop over there myself and have a talk with him," Ernie said.

"No, please don't," Anna pleaded, fear building inside her. "I've told them what I know and I think we need to leave it at that. The next step is up to them."

"We have to do something," Ernie insisted. "My mother didn't kill herself. We know that."

Anna lowered her voice to a whisper. "But this is dangerous. We're not the police, and we have no idea what's going on in this town."

Ernie ran a finger around the salted edge of his glass. "Anna, let's not forget who we're talking about. I'm responsible. Had I been there, it would never have happened."

A chill ran up Anna's spine. "Or you would have been tossed off the terrace too," she said, her eyes welling up. "God forbid anything happens to you. I couldn't bear it." She reached across the table to grab his hand.

He smiled tenderly. "If that was going to happen, it already would have. You'd have never known about it. You'd still be in Phoenix, living your life, not mixed up in all this nonsense."

Anna shuddered. "You are my life," she said. "There was no life before you. There'll be none without you."

"I love you," he whispered, sliding his chair closer to her. "You mean the world to me."

She strengthened her resolve. "I'll try again tomorrow," she vowed. "I'll make him listen."

"But how?"

"I'll find a way. Once he's heard me out, he'll re-open the investigation. I know he will. I can feel it in my bones."

20

....

Two nights a week, Charlie volunteered to answer phones for a suicide prevention hotline and true to Daisy's words, his focus shifted from thinking about Dave to helping others.

There was a renewed lightness in the house.

In the evenings after dinner, he and Daisy retired to the living room where Charlie was engrossed in Daniel Goleman's *Emotional Intelligence* while Daisy browsed her favorite magazines—*Newsweek, The Smithsonian, AARP,* and *Vanity Fair*.

Timmy once again dropped his pink ball, which Daisy had nicknamed *baby*, by Charlie's feet, tail wagging, whimpering to get Charlie's attention.

Charlie immediately reached over and tossed the ball.

"You're spoiling that animal," Daisy said, shaking her head in mock disapproval.

"I know," Charlie answered, sliding off the sofa onto the carpet into a seated, cross-legged position, to better play with the dog. Timmy nudged the ball with his snout and yelped, demanding Charlie throw *baby* again. "At least he sleeps during the day and doesn't bug me when I'm talking to clients. Isn't it amazing how he's learned to speak? He's so smart."

"Yes," Daisy laughed. "A real genius. So tell me dear, are you enjoying that volunteer position?"

It was an odd question Charlie thought. Who could rightly enjoy hearing the trouble of others?

"Enjoy is the wrong word," he gently explained. "Let's just say it has given me another perspective. Everyone has their challenges."

"Amen," Daisy opined, barely looking up from her magazine. "Life is that way. Some of us hurdle from one crisis to another. Others take life as it comes and manage to persevere."

Charlie thought about the gay kid who he'd spoken with the night before. "There's a lot of loneliness out there. People struggling on their own. You have to be very brave to manage by yourself. It scares me to think that one day I might be alone."

Daisy stopped reading. "You know, I never thought about it until I broke my hip."

"Really?"

"Absolutely. If you're engaged in life and healthy, those kind of thoughts don't cross your mind."

"Unless you're a worrier."

"I suppose," Daisy said with a broad smile on her face. "But look at me. Even with all the things that I've gone through, life is still wonderful. Always remember that. You don't need to be alone. No one does. It's a choice Charlie. Just another choice."

"Yes," he answered, uncertain if he agreed with Daisy, but in awe of her persistent optimism.

* * *

Charlie wasn't supposed to give out his personal information to any-one calling the hotline, but after talking with the kid again, he broke the rule. His heart went out to the boy who desperately needed an adult to confide in, and Charlie felt eminently qualified to assume that role. So when he picked up his cell phone on the third ring and heard the kid's voice, he wasn't at all surprised.

"I know it's late . . . but I need to talk."

The boy sounded tense. Charlie had a bad feeling. He wondered what he'd gotten himself into. "It's not too late," Charlie said, checking his watch. "It's only nine o'clock. I'm just sitting here reading the paper. Where are you?"

"I'm at Biltmore Fashion."

"Oh," Charlie said, relieved. Biltmore Fashion Mall was hardly the setting for a desperate kid determined to do away with himself. With its upscale boutiques, anchored by Saks Fifth Avenue and Macy's, and its central court, which hosted late night movies and yoga classes, Biltmore Fashion was the height of luxurious shopping in metropolitan Phoenix. The mall was an open-air extravaganza with misters that ran continuously through the summer, creating a cool haze that enveloped shoppers.

"Are you outside the Apple Store?" Charlie guessed.

"Yes, on the bench right outside," the kid said in an astonished tone. "How'd you know?"

"What self-respecting teen could pass up the Apple Store?" Charlie reasoned.

Friday nights came alive at Biltmore Fashion as Phoenicians eager to escape the confines of air-conditioned homes crowded together to enjoy the evening. Shoppers mingled with young families and tourists; flip flops, shorts, and expensive tee shirts were the attire of choice for those either out to dinner or just taking a walk to enjoy a frozen yogurt on a hot night. Dogs of all sizes gathered around the perimeter of the central fountain, some playing, others sleeping, as the warmth of the night depleted the energy they'd stored up during the day.

Charlie parked his car and hurried along the pathway to the central court. There he stood, taking in the buzz of activity. A movie was being shown on a large screen; young people on blankets covered the grass; older folks sat about on portable lawn chairs. It took Charlie but a moment to recognize George Peppard and Audrey Hepburn in *Breakfast at Tiffany's*. He stopped and stared. Beautiful people deserved to be admired.

Charlie strolled over to the Apple Store. Children of various ages stood about, some even on tiptoes, to touch the display stations anchored to the white laminate tables. Young adults packed the aisles. *It's like they're giving something away*, Charlie thought as a young man approached.

"Are you Charlie?"

Charlie nodded, somewhat surprised. He'd expected an awkward looking teenager with bad skin and greasy hair. But the young man before him was his height. He had shoulder-length black hair, strikingly handsome chiseled features, and deep-set green eyes. His build suggested someone with a college sports scholarship. He looked to be twenty or twenty-one.

Charlie instantly thought he was being played. Was this some kind of twisted game? A bait and switch?

"I wondered if you were really coming," the young man said, extending his hand in a greeting. "I was worried you might not show."

Charlie squinted as he furrowed his brow. "You called. Why wouldn't I be here?" he asked disingenuously, unsure if this was the kid to whom he'd been talking with earlier.

He had no intention of being played for a fool.

The young man's eyes glistened with a sincerity that Charlie was unaccustomed to with strangers. "It's just that most people are unreliable," he said, so matter-of-fact that Charlie let the comment pass as a truth.

The voice seemed to be the same. Charlie recognized the timbre.

"People?" Charlie asked, directing the young man over to a bench just a quick few steps away. "Like who?"

The young man sat down and rubbed his hands on his shorts. "You know. Parents, social workers, friends." He looked down, deflecting Charlie's critical gaze.

"So why did you need to see me tonight?" Charlie asked, taking in the young man's every move.

"I'm scared," he said rubbing his hands together. "Maybe this wasn't such a good idea. I probably should have stayed home."

Charlie pressed, his tone defiant. "A big guy like you? It's hard to imagine you'd be scared of anything."

They locked eyes. To Charlie, it seemed to be some kind of weird test. Who would look away first? Charlie held the gaze, all the while thinking that maybe the rules they set up for volunteers were in place for a good reason. Maybe he should never have given the kid his cell number or agreed to meet him. Maybe he was going to be robbed.

"I know I don't look like the type to be scared," the young man admitted, "but I am." His eyes welled up to reveal a genuine pain. "I've always looked older than my age. More mature. I'm not sure it's done me any good. People tend to expect an awful lot of you based on what you look like. If I was small and spindly, maybe I'd have been able to pass. Just get by. Maybe I'd have been too weak to speak up for myself and stayed home with my folks. Maybe then I'd have felt more comfortable in my own skin. I'm not sure," he said, looking to Charlie as if he might have the answer. "I guess it doesn't matter. I'm who I am. I'm just me." The young man shifted a shoulder and took a deep breath. "Nighttime is the worst. I worry that it will always be like this. This intense loneliness. I'll never get past it."

Charlie had to test the kid. Make sure he was who he said he was. The voice matched, but the physical looks were so off-putting. Young men who looked like jocks didn't have life and death problems. "So where are your folks?" Charlie asked.

"You're not a very good listener. I told you last night."

"Sorry," Charlie apologized. There was now no doubt in his mind the kid was telling the truth. At once, he felt foolish for his subterfuge. "I remember. Your folks tossed you out when you told them you were gay."

"Right," the kid answered.

"So, who do you live with now? You didn't tell me that last night."

"I live alone. I used to live with this woman, but she's in Mexico. I go to school and she sends money."

"Sounds kind of lonely."

"It's very lonely." The kid looked down. The pain was evident.

"Why don't you move in with some friends?" Charlie asked.

"I can't," the kid answered. "I have to take care of the property."

"Then get a roommate."

"Again, that's a no. The owner doesn't trust strangers in her house."

"Hmmm . . . okay," Charlie said, finally acquiescing. "You're coming home with me. At least for tonight. No monkey business. I'm not kidding." Charlie squinted and pointed an index finger in the air. "If I discover you're one of those mass murderers, drug dealers, or psychopaths, and if you dare to steal anything from my house, I swear I'll kick your ass."

The young man made a horrified face. "That's quite an invitation."

* * *

"You're awfully quiet tonight," Ernie said, putting his fork down. Typically Anna was all conversation, all the time.

"Am I?" Anna had been lost in thought throughout much of dinner. "I've been thinking about Phoenix."

"About Henry?" Ernie wondered.

"Mostly. And about going home. I've been gone too long."

Ernie leaned an elbow on the table. His chin rested in his palm. "Can't you imagine this as your home?"

She glanced about the apartment. "It's lovely. But it's not home."

"Don't you want to be with me?" he asked, hurt by Anna's sudden desire to leave.

"Oh Ernie, I do," she answered excitedly. "If we married, you could come back to the States with me. It would be so wonderful."

Ernie shook his head. "But I don't want to go back to the United States," he said. It was a fact that he'd grappled with ever since he and Anna had gotten together. He didn't want to go back.

"You don't?" Anna said. "But why? We can have a wonderful life in America. And Phoenix is your home."

Ernie's expression hardened. "Not anymore," he said firmly. "I'll never go back to Phoenix. And I'll never return to the United States."

Anna suddenly became panicky. "But why? I don't understand. I thought after all we've been to each other, you'd be eager to get back to America."

"I don't expect you to understand, Anna. I'm not even sure I can explain. But Anna, they don't want me in America. I'd feel unwelcome."

"Who are they?" she implored.

"The people of the United States. And I can't go somewhere that I'm not wanted."

"But this time it'll be different. We'd be married."

Ernie just shook his head. "It wouldn't be different for me. I'd never feel safe there. I'd always be *the undocumented immigrant*. Someone to be looked down upon. I have a wonderful job here. I'm respected. I won't go back to an America that doesn't want me. I won't," he said in an explosion of emotion.

"But Ernie, I can't stay in Puerto Vallarta forever. I have a life, a business. I have to go back."

"I know," he said, desperately trying to figure out a way to bridge their two worlds. "I don't want you to go. But I understand that you need to do what you must. But I will be waiting here in Mexico. Here, where I belong."

* * *

Side-by-side, Charlie and Henry crossed the parking lot to Charlie's car.

"By the way, I don't live alone. I live with this older woman, Daisy. She's a senior but has a mind as sharp as a tack. Don't bullshit her. She has a built-in bullshit meter."

"Is she your mother?" The kid grinned from ear to ear.

"She's not my mother," Charlie said sharply. "My mother's dead and buried. Daisy's just a friend."

"So you live with an old lady? Wow. You really must have mommy issues."

Charlie rolled his eyes. "Hey, think whatever you want. Just don't call her *an old lady*."

"How did you wind up living with her?" the young man wanted to know.

"It's a long story. She can tell you over pancakes tomorrow," Charlie said. "Here we go. Here's my car." Charlie double-clicked his key fob. The lights of a white Ford Explorer flashed.

"Pancakes?" the kid called out as he opened the passenger door and climbed in.

"Yes, it's Saturday, and on Saturday we eat pancakes." Charlie gestured to the kid to put on his seat belt.

"Where do I sleep?" Henry asked as he buckled up.

"The sofa in my office pulls out to a sleeper. And one more thing," Charlie warned, as he backed out of the spot. "No slipping into my bed during the night. My door will be locked, so don't even try."

The kid laughed. "No offense, but you're a bit old for me."

"Good. That's how I like it," Charlie emphasized. "It's bad enough that I broke the rules giving you my cell number. I certainly don't need you thinking I'm sexually attracted to you."

"But aren't you?" the kid teased, seemingly amused that someone of Charlie's advanced age might be hot for him.

"Not in the slightest," Charlie admitted. "I don't do anyone under fifty. So, if you're under fifty you're safe."

"Fifty? Do people still have sex at fifty?" the kid asked, as they approached 24th Street and Missouri.

"Barely," Charlie joked, though he suspected the boy believed him. "By the way, what the heck is your name? We've been talking all this time and I don't even know your name."

"Henry."

"Henry," Charlie repeated. "Is there a last name?"

"If the pancakes are good, I'll tell you."

"Great," Charlie said. "Just what I needed . . . another food critic."

* * *

Dave didn't bother to leave a note. The empty closet and drawers would provide explanation enough. He'd finally come to his senses. Too many nights spent waiting for Curt, wondering if he was coming home at all. Whatever sexual chemistry they shared couldn't make up for Curt's lack of loyalty. And then there were the text messages. Dave hadn't wanted to spy on Curt, but he had to know. Out until all hours, saying he was bartending. Seeing friends. Eventually the entire story came out.

"I thought you cared about me," Dave said, holding Curt's phone up. He'd scrolled through the nude selfies Curt had sent. "Explain these pictures on your phone. Who sends these kinds of photos to friends?"

"I do," Curt insisted. He grabbed his phone back. "Now why should I change my life for you? You're still emotionally hung up on that ex-lover of yours. Well, I'm not him and I'm not taking care of you. If anything, you should be taking care of me, and I haven't heard you making any such promises."

Dave struggled to understand. "Promises? What are you talking about?"

Curt's eyes flashed with anger. "You expect me to spell this whole thing out for you. Why do you think I'm with an *older man*?" The words burned in Dave's ears. "In case you haven't noticed, there's a bit of an age gap here." Curt snapped his fingers. "If you want one hundred percent of my attention, then you need to take care of me one hundred percent."

"What?" was all Dave could manage to get out as a numbness settled in.

"You're too thick for words." Curt pointed a dagger-like finger. "If I have to spell it out, you're too dumb to understand."

Dave was bewildered. He doubted he'd ever known Curt at all.

"And besides," Curt angrily continued, "you have no right looking through my phone."

Dave winced at the very memory of the exchange. He was certain Curt had been the biggest mistake of his life.

How could I have been such a fool?

As Dave closed the front door of the apartment, there was a genuine sense of relief. This awful chapter was finally over. He'd arrived with nothing and was leaving with just enough to fill one suitcase. Most of his things remained at Charlie's. He'd lacked the courage to collect them. Now he was glad he hadn't. How does a couple divide up all the things shared over twenty years together? It was easier to leave everything exactly where it was.

Dave sat in his car and stared at the building where Curt now lived alone.

What had this experience really been about? It wasn't about love. He doubted he'd ever loved Curt. So what had he been doing? Why did he allow what should have been a one-night stand to turn into something which destroyed his relationship with Charlie?

Dave backed the car out of the driveway and headed toward the top of the street. He wondered what he should do with the rest of his life. For years he'd relied on Charlie for his well-being. It was Charlie who anchored him. Charlie who knew what to do, what to say, and how to manage through difficult situations. Those were Charlie's gifts. Charlie could go with the flow, take a bad situation, and make the best of it. Dave hadn't needed to worry about the future. He only had to rely on Charlie who supplied the forward momentum. Now he needed to rely on himself.

He checked into the Courtyard by Marriott on Camelback, grateful for the peace and quiet and absence of Curt.

* * *

Henry shifted positions. The sofabed in Charlie's office released a high-pitched squeak. The long metal rods that supported the thin folding mattress cut sharply into his back. He twisted and turned, dislodging the sheet, in a hopeless attempt to find a comfortable spot. With a kick, he freed his right leg from the light blanket and rolled onto his left side. It was no use. He couldn't sleep. He sat up and surrendered to the mess that was now his bedding.

I should have never come here.

He rubbed his eyes, more uncomfortable in these new surroundings than he had been at Anna's. His anxiety was palpable. He could feel the energy shooting through his limbs, his fingers and toes practically vibrating. He contemplated finding Charlie, but remembered Charlie's words, and decided against it. He was sure that no matter what he did, or how he might reach out, in the long run it wouldn't help. He remembered the night in the church tower. Anna calling to him as he searched the sky, afraid to jump. *I wish I'd done it then*, he thought bitterly. *If I had, it would all be over now.*

He bit his lower lip and prayed to die.

* * *

Jack awoke with a start. Bonnie was lying next to him, gently snoring. He glanced over her shoulder to check the clock. It was 3:00 a.m. Ever since leaving Enid, he'd been unable to sleep through the night. Even here with Bonnie, sleep eluded him. He yawned, adjusting his head in the soft pillow, trying to find the sweet spot. There was a slight twinge in his lower back which required him to shift positions. A full bladder now informed his next decision.

Out of bed, he made the short walk to the bathroom. In the dark, he backed up to the toilet and with a plunk, sat down. Bonnie had asked that he sit since his aim had been somewhat shoddy. He'd been willing to concede the point, but now, it seemed as if every request was just another hurdle to overcome in her many objections about their living together.

Back in bed, he was unable to fall asleep. Lying in the dark, he agonized over their relationship. Had she been disloyal, keeping Daisy's secret? Worse, had she finally told him the truth to hurt him? The context, now seemed critically important.

Bonnie shifted, pulling the blanket right off of him.

Uncovered, he doubted she'd ever really loved him; that she'd ever truly loved any man.

* * *

Dave tossed and turned in his hotel room, unable to find peace from a busy mind. At 6:00 a.m., he rose, showered and dressed, and hopped into his car, heading to Frank & Albert's at the Arizona Biltmore Hotel to grab an early breakfast. It was time to treat himself with a little kindness. He hadn't yet figured out the next step beyond the delicious cornflake-crusted French toast with warm maple syrup. What he would do with the rest of the day was anyone's guess.

The waitress refilled his coffee cup as he dug into his food. He tried to put aside his thoughts as he savored the warm goodness. But he couldn't. Accusations played in his head, the voices loud and unrelenting. *You're such a fool. Ruining your life . . . and for what? To feel wanted? A final fling? Meaningless sex with someone who didn't even want you?*

Dave pushed the plate away. He'd lost his appetite.

Dave had always believed that no mistake was so terrible, it couldn't be fixed. No error so permanent, it couldn't be corrected. If he threw money at a problem and solved it, it wasn't really a problem. But now he understood that there were different kinds of problems in life. Some, couldn't be fixed with money. Some, just maybe, couldn't be fixed at all.

"Can I get you anything else?" the waitress asked.

Dave stared straight ahead. He shook his head. It was such a simple question, and yet, the answer was too overwhelming to contemplate. He needed his life back. He needed Charlie. He needed to go home. That was it. All the rest, well, who cared? He needed his family. And Charlie was his family.

Dave paid the check and walked through the art deco lobby and on through to the hotel's beautiful lush grounds. Convention goers were beginning to throng about, enjoying the facilities and the promise of another beautiful day in paradise. Room service zipped by on their bicycles, delivering meals throughout the vast complex of the hotel property.

Dave took a moment to drink in the early morning beauty of the Biltmore. He'd figured out what he wanted to do. Now he needed to do it. For the moment, his mind could rest before he contemplated his next step.

* * *

When Anna awoke, Ernie was gone. A note on the counter explained he had early meetings and hadn't wanted to wake her. A fresh pot of coffee greeted her. Ernie had set the brewing time, anticipating she'd wake at sunrise. She sat at the counter, drinking her coffee, looking out on the new day, enjoying the view of another spectacular morning in Puerto Vallarta.

She'd waited a long time to meet a man she could truly love and who would love her. A man who'd be able to express his adoration with such tenderness. She thought of how they had met in Phoenix, and how they might never had reconnected if Ernie's mother hadn't died so tragically. It was odd how something good could come from something so bad. And how people can meet at different points in their lives, not recognize one another as important, and then later on, mean the world to each other.

And now she needed to face the facts.

Though she loved Puerto Vallarta—the people, the beaches, Ernie— she missed Phoenix. It had been weeks since she'd last been home. Being with Ernie had opened her eyes to a whole new life, but she still owned a home and had a business. And she wasn't prepared to give it all up.

And then there was Henry.

She had an uneasy feeling. She'd left messages at the house but Henry hadn't returned her calls. She wondered what he was up to and when he might call back.

She stepped out onto the terrace. The ocean air caressed her face. She believed life had a way of presenting itself; if one was alert to the possibilities, the road appeared to the weary traveler. But the challenge in finding love had confirmed her belief that even she, who understood the flow of universal energies, was destined to live the same struggles as everyone else. There was no pass for the psychically gifted. She might be able to read the signs for others, but for herself, she had been effectively blindfolded, stumbling about, still unsure of her place on life's path.

* * *

"Well, good morning," Charlie said, spooning wet pancake batter into a hot Presto griddle as Daisy entered the kitchen. "Sleep well?"

"Why yes," Daisy answered. She spotted Charlie's efforts in the breakfast nook. "Oh, how lovely."

The small glass table was covered by a crisp white tablecloth and matching linen napkins, rolled into the shape of a swan, and placed atop Charlie's best china, used strictly for holiday celebrations. A cactus with three delicate orange blooms occupied the center of the table. There were three place settings.

"We have a guest," Charlie said, pouring orange juice into three tall cocktail glasses as the bacon sizzled on the stove. "He should be up anytime now."

Charlie transferred the first set of pancakes to a plate and then popped them into the oven. Even the maple syrup had been gently microwaved so that it would be nice and warm.

Daisy sat on a bar stool at the kitchen counter while Charlie poured her first cup of coffee into a large mug. "I knew you two would get back together," she said breaking into a bright smile. "I'm so happy. This is wonderful news."

As Daisy sipped her coffee, Charlie tried to underplay her mistake. "It isn't Dave," he said in his most casual tone, as he placed the juice next to each setting. For a moment, he couldn't help but wish otherwise.

Daisy's face registered immediate remorse. "Oh, Charlie, forgive me. I wasn't thinking. How awkward. I'm such a fool."

Charlie smiled, trying to make light of it. "No harm done. Our guest is a teenager named Henry who needed a place to stay last night. I received a last minute call from a Teen Center," he said, concocting a story, "and his guardian is out of town. So I volunteered to take the young man in."

Daisy smiled warmly. "Charlie, you're a wonderful human being."

Charlie shrugged. He hated lying to Daisy, but felt it was important to protect Henry's privacy.

"Well that's odd," she said, as Charlie refilled her cup. "I didn't hear you come in last night. Timmy must have barked. How did I manage to sleep through all that racket?"

"Funny you should mention that," Charlie said, as he transferred the cooked bacon from a skillet to a plate lined with a paper towel. "We both know how high-strung Timmy can be. Well, he didn't bark once," Charlie said. "Not once. Instead, he let out a low cry and then jumped into Henry's arms and started to lick his face. I've never seen anything like it. Timmy acted as if they were long lost pals."

Daisy appeared shocked. "Our shy Timmy?"

* * *

Anna stepped out of the lobby into the bright morning sunshine. Her plan, to do a little marketing. There, parked in front of the building, was a black sedan.

Puerto Vallarta was crowded with little, ugly, utilitarian cars. Few people drove anything that equaled the luxury models of the United States. And though the black sedan was out of place, Anna paid little attention to the automobile until the doors suddenly opened and she was surrounded by two men. One, a tall, older man, in his seventies. The other, Enrique.

"We've been waiting for you," the older man said, grabbing her by the arm. "Get in the car."

Anna winced as she was pushed toward the rear door. "Let go of me," she ordered.

"Do as I say," the man said, twisting her arm tightly behind her back, "or I'll break your arm off right here in the street."

Anna could do no more than cry out in pain before she was shoved into the back seat. The older man hopped in beside her and closed the door. Enrique got in the driver's seat and started the engine. In no time the car was making its way through the busy streets of Puerto Vallarta.

* * *

"Well this must be an unusual young man if Timmy didn't bark," Daisy whispered as if speaking of a potential suitor. "How old is he?"

"He's not quite seventeen."

"So young," Daisy said solemnly.

"Yes," Charlie confirmed, "but he has a surprising maturity. You'll see when you meet him."

"Oh, I can't wait," she said.

"Well, that should be any time now." Charlie looked at the wall clock. "We came in last night about eleven. Now it's nine. That's a lot of sleep for anyone."

"The smell of breakfast will wake him up," Daisy assured Charlie. "Young people love to eat almost as much as folks my age."

"I guess." Charlie smiled.

"So he must be in high school."

"That's right."

"Oh, how nice," Daisy answered. "I wonder what they're reading these days. Chaucer. Hemingway. Steinbeck."

"Now promise me you won't pepper him with questions. I want him to feel welcome. Promise me."

"Yes," Daisy conceded. "You're right. That would be rude."

Charlie's pancakes came out picture perfect. He placed bacon along the edges of the platter before sprinkling a dusting of powdered sugar on top. A fruit bowl, filled with cantaloupe, watermelon, and red grapes finished off the table. It was a lovely offering. The smell of fresh Starbucks coffee filled the room.

"Okay, it looks like we're ready," Charlie said, admiring the table and his renewed culinary creations. "Pretty good, even if I say so myself."

"Oh, Charlie, you've outdone yourself," Daisy said.

"I hope so," Charlie replied. "I want him to understand that we're a family."

"That's sweet," Daisy answered. "Now sit down next to me," she said, patting the bar stool on her side of the island. "I want to talk with you."

* * *

"What's going on?" Anna pleaded. "Where are you taking me?"

"You have a big mouth," the older man said, his gray hair greased back, a deep scar running down his cheek. "You make lots of threats."

"Let me go," she insisted.

"You're not going anywhere," he said, grabbing her by the wrist and sharply twisting it. "Not until you tell me how you found out about Maria."

"I can't talk while you're hurting me," she cried in agony.

The man pulled on Anna's arm even tighter. "Then you better learn how. And fast."

The pain was so intense Anna was afraid she might pass out.

"Now quickly. How did you find out?" he growled.

"I'm a psychic," she wailed, eager for him to ease up on his grip.

"A what?" the older man asked.

"A psychic. I pick up on people's energy."

"So what does that have to do with Maria?"

"She came to me. I could sense her energy, her final exit. I could see it all."

The older man burst into uproarious laughter. "That's your proof?" he croaked as he rocked back and forth in peals of laughter. "Enrique, what's wrong with you? I thought you said she had proof."

"But Juan, she does," Enrique insisted.

"Ridiculous," Juan replied. "I'm letting her out at the next corner."

"But she can identify us."

"Who cares? She's crazy. No one will believe her."

* * *

Charlie took a seat at the counter next to Daisy.

She glanced down at her coffee cup as she struggled to find the right words. "Charlie, you know I would do anything for you. And we *are family.*"

He nodded, a concerned expression on his face.

She cleared her throat. "And because we're family, we want what is best for each other."

"Of course," Charlie quickly answered.

"And that's why, my darling, I'm going to move out."

Charlie was stunned. "What are you talking about?"

"If Dave is ever to come home, it's got to be just the two of you. I love you, you know that, but you have to allow Dave space to come back. And you, my darling, need to stop collecting people."

"Collecting people?"

"Me, this young man. We're getting in the way of your finding your way back to Dave."

"But you were the one who suggested I get on with my life."

"Yes," Daisy said. "Guilty as charged. But if you and Dave get back together, you can't have all these people about your neck, draining your attention."

"I didn't know I was doing that," Charlie said rather indignantly. "I don't suppose there's any way I can talk you out of it."

"I'm sorry, no. I've been thinking about one of those lovely retirement villas in Scottsdale and with Lyle being so generous, leaving me financially secure, plus the settlement from Jack, I can manage nicely."

"I'll hate to see you go," Charlie said, already somewhat resigned to Daisy's plan.

"It's for the best. It's time for me to move on. And I'll only be in Scottsdale. It's not the other side of the world."

* * *

Anna eyed the old man's knobby fingers. "My God. You're the other man," she suddenly realized.

"You have an overactive imagination," Juan replied.

"No, *it was you.*" Anna closed her eyes. "Your hands were on my waist. I looked down and I could see them. You were standing right behind me."

"You?" Juan mocked her. "You don't look dead to me."

All the pieces were now falling into place. "No, but you killed Maria. She was an innocent woman and you murdered her."

"Innocent," the old man snarled, the tone of his voice changing instantly to indignation. "Was she innocent when she stole my only son and fled to America? She was lucky to die the way she did. I wanted to cut her head off and feed it to the pigs."

Anna was confused. "But Ernie's here in Mexico. He's alive."

"Ernie?" the old man spat. "Who the hell is Ernie?"

* * *

Charlie smiled weakly, a mild depression coming over him at the mere thought of living alone. "Well, I better slip this platter into the oven to keep it warm," he said, changing the subject. "When do you think that kid's going to get up?" He checked his watch. "It's already ten. I should wake him."

"Oh no," Daisy pleaded. "Let him sleep."

He rolled his eyes in disapproval, then headed down the hall to his office. He knocked gently on the door. "Henry, time to get up. Breakfast is ready. Pancakes. Come and get them while they're hot."

"Oh, it's a shame to wake him up," Daisy said aloud, mostly for her own benefit.

"Come on, Henry," Charlie knocked again. "I know you're in there. Time to get up."

"When I was that age," Daisy called to Charlie, "I used to sleep and sleep. Oh what I wouldn't do for one of those nights again."

Charlie banged louder. "Henry, it's me, Charlie. Time to get up. Let's go."

Charlie returned to the kitchen with a worried look.

"I wonder if we lose our ability to sleep as our internal clocks wind down," Daisy mumbled, taking another sip of her coffee.

Charlie's face flashed sudden concern. He darted back down the hall and tried turning the knob. The door was locked from the inside. He raced past Daisy, through the rear kitchen door to the back of the house, just outside his office window. He couldn't look in. The curtains were drawn.

Daisy continued to talk, oblivious to Charlie's altered demeanor. "Oh to sleep. How I miss it," she called out. "Those wonderful mornings when you'd wake up so refreshed and grateful to be alive."

In a blind panic, Charlie ran back into the house, past Daisy, and down the short hallway. He charged the door with the full force of his weight. The door didn't budge. He stepped back and wildly started to kick the door in.

* * *

The old man glared at her. "What are you babbling about?"

"Your son," Anna answered, certain that he must know the truth. "The man I live with. Ernie. Ernie *is your son*."

"Not my son," the man answered in clear denial. "My son was Juan Pedro Gonzales."

"She must have changed his name," Anna said, struggling to understand how there could be any confusion.

"My son," the old man snapped, "never made it across the Arizona desert. He died in the back of a truck in that sweltering heat. His mother survived because she squeezed herself upfront where the truck was cooler. She knew how to survive using her God-given talents."

From the front of the car, Enrique pleaded with the older man. "Please, Tío. We have to do something with her. She knows too much."

The older man scoffed at the suggestion. "No . . . she's a fool. No one will believe her. Drop her at the next corner," he demanded, as Enrique slowed the car.

"Get out," the old man ordered once the car came to a stop.

As Anna stepped out of the vehicle, police sirens blared from all directions. Flashing lights encircled her. The police seemed to be everywhere, guns pointing at the vehicle. Anna screamed and fell to the ground. Within moments, Juan and Enrique were on their knees, hands in the air. Anna could see the Chief of Police walking through the intersection.

* * *

Daisy rushed to join Charlie in the hallway. Timmy was at their heels excitedly leaping and barking in unison with every one of Charlie's fierce kicks.

Daisy grabbed at Charlie's arm. "Charlie, have you gone crazy? What's wrong? What's going on?"

He ignored her pleas, as he continued, ash-faced and breathing heavily, focusing all his might on the door. "Stand back," he shouted as he thrust forward one last time, his foot landing squarely on the doorjamb.

* * *

"Are you okay?" Esteban asked Anna, helping her up.

"Barely," she said, straightening her blouse and rubbing her sore arm. "How did you know?"

"We've been watching you."

"But I thought you didn't believe me."

"At first I didn't. But then I gave it some more thought. You knew the inscription inside my pocket watch. How could you know that? Was it a coincidence? My mother gave me that watch when I graduated from the police academy. And she always had an uncanny sixth sense about life. So I had two of our men watch you. I thought, if something was going to happen, it would happen soon."

Ernie broke his way through the crowd that had gathered. "Are you okay?"

Anna practically fell into his arms. "They were going to let me go," she assured him. "They were just scaring me to keep me quiet."

"You're lucky," Esteban informed her. "These two are suspected of a slew of murders in Puerto Vallarta. We've never had evidence on them. You were the first witness to live to tell the story." The chief opened the trunk of the car. "They had plans for you. See that electric saw and the plastic bags? You could have wound up in a garbage dump or floating in the ocean, a meal for our hungry sharks. We've found quite a few of these black bags torn to shreds after the sharks catch the scent of blood. These guys are butchers."

Anna shuddered at the sight of the rusty saw, its teeth covered in dried blood.

"Not to worry now. We have them," Esteban assured her. "This car should produce enough evidence to solve the disappearance of the others who weren't quite as lucky as you."

"And what about Sanchez?" Ernie wondered.

Esteban rubbed the bridge of his nose. "I'm afraid Sanchez was a victim of his own dirty doings. He'd been destroying evidence, helping these guys cover their tracks. And then he got greedy. They just got to him before we did."

* * *

After one last kick, and the sound of cracking wood, the door burst open.

On the floor by the sofabed, Henry laid in a pool of blood. Nearby, broken glass from one of the paperweights on Charlie's desk.

"Oh Lord," Daisy cried as she peered past Charlie, a hand on Timmy's collar to keep him back.

"Dear God," Charlie shouted, as he fell to one knee by the body. "Call 911. We need an ambulance."

* * *

Charlie paced nervously as he awaited word from the doctors. He'd followed the ambulance to Phoenix Children's Hospital, and hadn't thought to change his blood-stained shirt. After finding Henry, he'd rushed to the kitchen to retrieve two dish towels which he'd used to wrap each wrist. Now hardened, caked-on blood was everywhere. On his knees, elbows, and even on his cheek and forehead.

"Charlie, you have to clean yourself up," Daisy said, when he finally sat down next to her in the private family waiting room. Henry's cell phone was in his hand. Digging into her purse, she pulled out a packet of Kleenex. Offering the packet to him, she said, "At least wipe your face. There's a mirror over there." She pointed toward the other side of the room.

Charlie took the packet from her but didn't move.

"This is just about the worst thing that's ever happened," he said. "That kid needed professional help, not a place to stay for the night. I should never have given him my cell number. What was I thinking? This is all my fault."

Daisy was not about to agree. "Thank goodness he was in our house. It gave you a chance to save his life."

"But why did he do it?" Charlie said, leaning over, his faced buried in his hands. "It doesn't make any sense. He was talkative and then when Timmy greeted him, he seemed so happy. It just doesn't make any sense. None of it."

"Well, I don't rightly know," she said, "why someone so young is willing to give up on life. There must have been some powerful reasons. Whoever can ever really know what's in someone else's head? He's the only one who can answer that question."

"I just wish I understood," Charlie said, removing a tissue from the packet. "We spoke, and I listened, but I don't think I truly understood . . . not the depth of what he was saying. No matter what issues I had with my parents, I was already an adult when I came out. How do you deal with that kind of rejection as a teenager? Young people should feel cherished and protected."

"Should," Daisy repeated in agreement.

The conversation ended with a knock on the door. Bonnie peeked around the corner. She had Jack in tow. "Are you two okay?"

Charlie looked at Daisy. Daisy immediately spoke up. "I called Bonnie when you were talking with the clerk in the emergency room. I thought with Bonnie's healthcare background it might be good to have her here."

Charlie nodded.

"And I brought Jack," Bonnie said. Jack held a palm up in the air as a quiet hello. "If you want, he can run and grab something to eat. And Jack . . ." She turned to him and nodded.

Jack held up a paper bag which he passed to Charlie.

"Daisy thought this might come in handy," she explained. "It's a clean shirt. You might want to put it on so that you don't scare the little children."

"Thanks," Charlie said, as he removed his shirt and tossed it on the coffee table. "That's very nice of you," he said slipping on Jack's shirt.

Bonnie smiled. "Ah, that's better," she said, giving Charlie a hug. "So how are you two holding up? Any news yet?" She looked from Charlie to Daisy.

"Nothing," Daisy answered.

"I'm sure they're doing everything they can," Bonnie said. "We might as well sit down and relax. It could be quite a wait."

As they settled in, there was another knock at the door. All conversation stopped.

Charlie called out. "Yes . . . come on in."

* * *

Anna had left Puerto Vallarta as soon as she had received Charlie's call. Rattled beyond words, she'd gone from the police station, where she'd just given a statement as a material witness, directly to the airport, and without any luggage, caught the two-hour flight to Phoenix.

"Hello, my name is Charlie Huff."

She'd expected to hear Henry's voice based on the caller ID.

"You don't know me, but I'm afraid I have some bad news."

Charlie had searched Henry's phone, upon the advice of the hospital staff, hoping to locate Henry's legal guardian.

As she boarded the plane she reflected on her behavior. *I should have never left Henry alone. How could I have been so selfish?* Taking her seat, she was wracked with guilt. *Please God. Please. Let him be okay.*

It had been a fast goodbye with Ernie. Barely enough time to discuss when they'd next see each other. Everything was so up in the air. But first, she had to take care of Henry. He'd quickly become her number one priority. *Oh Henry, I'm so sorry,* she thought as she drifted off to sleep, gently rocked by the vibration of the jet as it lifted off.

Within moments, she was startled awake by the voice of the older man.

"My son is dead . . . he never made it out alive from the Arizona desert. He died in the back of a truck . . ."

The words had been stored in the deepest recesses of her mind, just waiting to be retrieved. Words spat out with such fury, Anna couldn't help but record them, although at the time, she was certain he was mistaken.

"My son is dead. My son is dead. My son is dead . . ."

Anna struggled to make sense of it. Enrique must have known of Ernie. Everyone from the doorman in the building to the leasing manager knew about Ernie. It stood to reason that Juan should have known Ernie was alive. And yet, the old man's pain was so genuine; those four simple words embedded in her brain.

My son is dead . . .

What would make him think his child had died crossing the desert? She was now certain Juan knew something she didn't know. That Maria had lied. That the little boy had, in fact, died.

Anna struggled to put two and two together.

If it's true that Juan's little boy had died when Maria tried to smuggle him out of the country, who then was Ernie?

* * *

When Anna walked into the family waiting area, she was greeted by four strangers. Each held an expression of anticipation, seemingly wondering who she was and waiting to be introduced. "Hello," she said, breaking the tension. "I'm Anna Garrett. I'm Henry's legal guardian."

"I know you," Jack said, pointing at her. "You're that psychic on 19th Avenue. Oh my God."

Charlie leapt to his feet and introduced the others. He explained, "I had Henry's cell phone. I didn't even know his last name. Luckily, I was able to find Ms. Garrett among his texts."

"Please call me Anna," she insisted.

Jack gloated. "I had a reading awhile back with Ms. Garrett. Couldn't make heads or tails out of it at the time. I doubt you remember," he said, looking at her with a new respect. "That was one expensive proposition. But . . . it all proved to be true. Odd. How did you do that?"

Anna shrugged, deflecting his question. "What have the doctors said?" she asked Charlie.

"We're still waiting," he answered.

"Why don't you come and sit over here next to me, Anna," Daisy offered, scooching closer to Bonnie who occupied the other end of the sofa. "How terrible this must be for you. Please know we're all here to help."

* * *

Daisy took Anna's hand and held it in her lap. A doctor had at last arrived, and though he asked to speak to Anna alone, she requested the group remain. "After all," she said as she looked about, "you've all spent a good deal of time worrying about Henry."

Charlie fidgeted in his seat as Dr. Parsons, the emergency room psychiatrist, a dark-skinned Hispanic man with a shaved head and multiple tattoos on his neck and arms, explained the intake process required by the state for those under eighteen who attempt suicide. "So there's no need for you all to stay," Dr. Parsons wrapped up.

"But will he be alright?" Charlie wanted to know.

Parsons shifted his gaze from Anna to Charlie. "Henry's fortunate. He really only sliced one wrist; the other was more of a surface wound," Parson's explained. "Slitting your wrists is very painful. Most patients don't go deep enough to actually sever the vein. Henry made the mistake of cutting across, leaving a messy and bloody wound. Had he sliced deep and down the vein, well, it might have been a different outcome. And being right-handed . . . he is a righty?" Anna nodded to the affirmative. "Well then, he used his dominant hand to make the first slice into his left wrist, making it nearly impossible that the weaker, now damaged left hand, could do the same to the dominant hand. Anyway, he won't be seeing any visitors today. You might as well all go home."

"But there was so much blood," Charlie felt compelled to point out.

"Yes," Parsons said standing, ready to take his leave. "He's lost quite a bit of blood. But he's a strong, young man. And with the transfusion, he should be fine."

Charlie blinked twice, shaking his head. "I'll never get that image out of my head," he muttered, mostly to himself.

"I guess there's nothing more to say," Daisy remarked once the doctor left, as the five adults remained.

"I bear the blame for leaving him alone," Anna finally said, breaking down and bursting into tears.

Bonnie gently placed a hand on Anna's back. "You can't blame yourself. It's not your fault any more than it's Charlie's fault."

Upon hearing his name, Charlie snapped out of his fog. "I thought we were all past this. When I was growing up, if you were gay, you were isolated. That's just how it was. But today . . . with the Internet . . . everyone's so out and proud . . . this isn't how it should be. Gay kids shouldn't be killing themselves."

"The gays have come a long way," Jack remarked. He'd been standing apart from where the group was sitting, leaning against the windowsill.

Bonnie glared in his direction. "Oh Jack," she sternly snapped. "*The gays*. What a thing to say. Like we are not all *just people*."

Jack's hands were in the air. "I didn't mean anything by it."

Charlie ignored their exchange. "God this makes me mad. I didn't live through AIDS to see our young people kill themselves before they even live."

"We really should do something about this," Daisy affirmed. "It's horrible that we are allowing these kids to die."

The five adults looked at each other.

"We absolutely have to do something," Jack said in a determined voice, so loud that Anna, Charlie, and Bonnie all looked at him with a surprised reaction.

"Jack used to be a teacher," Daisy reminded everyone. "His heart's in the right place."

* * *

Anna prepared a hot bath. Exhausted from the day, she climbed in, closed her eyes, and slipped backward, allowing the tub pillow to support the full weight of her head. Her muscles relaxed as the warm water did its magic.

One deep breath and the vision of another place and time began.

She was peering through living room curtains and watching a little boy ride his tricycle up and down the sidewalk. He was a beautiful child with thick black hair and immense brown eyes. She sensed that she'd seen him many times before from that very window; dreamt about him; wondered what it might be to hold him in her arms.

"Maria, where are you?" an old woman's voice called out. "I'd like to go for a walk around the block."

The window was located on Palmcroft Drive, a quiet, circular street, lined with palm trees and wrapped about 9th Avenue, a main north/south thoroughfare through the elegant Encanto neighborhood of Phoenix.

"I'm coming," she called out, dressed in her white uniform as she headed up the stairs to the second floor bedroom. *If only, she* sadly thought, still longing for her child; his image firmly fixed in her mind's eye.

Without references, she'd been lucky to find a live-in job. Mrs. Johnson, the woman who had hired her, was an elderly widow who needed help with daily activities such as bathing, dressing, and going to and from doctor's appointments. For a short time, she became Mrs. Johnson's treasured companion, and in turn, her conversational English skills improved.

She was eager to work and grateful to have found the Johnson household, and yet, even that small blessing couldn't make up for all that she'd lost. She doubted anything could fill the void in her heart. A deep gloom dominated her spirit from the moment she opened her eyes in the morning and remembered. Had it not been for Mrs. Johnson and her immense kindness, she wondered how she'd have managed to get through the day.

And still she watched the little boy as he played with the neighborhood children on the lawn of the house across the street. No adults in view. Smaller than the other children, his skin tone decidedly darker. *How old must he be? Three? Four? Certainly no older than that.* When a black woman in a white uniform appeared at the screen door and called his name, how brightly he smiled, abandoning his playmates as he scrambled into the house. A cherubic face atop a chubby little body, hands waving, voice in high-pitched laughter.

The morning that Mrs. Johnson died, she was bereft. Mrs. Johnson's attorney showed up midday, provided her with an envelope containing two hundred dollars in cash, and a reference letter. He requested she vacate the premises, allowing her just enough time to pack her things, before he returned to lock up the house.

The little boy was outside, holding a water gun and racing about wildly, shooting at make-believe playmates. As she walked past, he called to her. She thought she heard, "Stop. Take me with you." She grabbed him by the hand and lifted him up into her arms. At once, she felt an intense calm as she held the child in a tight embrace and rushed down the street. Moments later they were riding on the 9th Avenue bus heading toward their new life together.

* * *

Charlie waited for Dave at Pane Bianco on Central. He arrived early, sitting patiently at a rear table, more excited than he cared to admit. When Dave walked in, Charlie waved him over.

"Hey," Dave said, pulling up a seat. "It's good to see you. How have you been?"

Charlie thought about telling Dave all about Henry. But seeing Dave made Charlie so happy, he didn't want go there. Instead, he merely smiled and basked in the presence of Dave. "Fine," he dutifully answered. "I've been fine."

Over the phone, Dave had explained to Charlie that he'd ended the relationship with Curt. But Charlie didn't know any of the details.

So how are you holding up?" Charlie asked with genuine interest.

"I've been better," Dave answered, checking out the menu, avoiding Charlie's gaze. "I've been quite the fool."

"Oh," was all Charlie could manage in mocked surprise.

Dave broke into a wide grin. "Okay, I deserve whatever's coming. Fire away."

Charlie nodded. He wondered what Dave actually did deserve. Would it be too soon to take Dave back? After all, he'd been deeply hurt. He wasn't quite sure.

The waiter took their order.

Dave sipped his water. Charlie thought he spotted a bead of sweat gathering at Dave's brow. He knew this lunch was important. He'd have to watch his tone. He didn't want to drive Dave away. Dave had made the overture and Charlie knew it'd been difficult. He didn't want Dave to decide the effort wasn't worth it. Charlie bit his lower lip, unsure what to say next.

"I want to apologize," Dave started, eyes fixed on Charlie.

"You broke our trust," Charlie instinctively answered, immediately wishing he'd said nothing until he heard Dave out.

Dave blinked twice and took ahold of the water glass. "That's right," he said, "I did."

Charlie stretched his neck. He had to ask the next question. "How do I know you won't do that again? What's changed?"

Dave looked startled. "I thought you wanted me to come back?"

"It's not about what I want Dave," Charlie said, suddenly irritated. "It's about how you plan to behave in the future."

The waiter brought their order. An arugula salad with goat cheese and candied pecans for Charlie. A panini with speck, tomatoes, and mozzarella was placed before Dave.

Charlie exhaled. Suddenly it all seemed so clear. "You know Dave, I'm not really sure I can do this today."

Dave's eyes popped. "What are you talking about?"

"There's a kid over in Phoenix Children's Hospital who has had a rough time. He's made me think twice about what's real and what's not," Charlie said, much to his own surprise. "I thought, us being together would be enough. But life is too short. If you're coming back because it's easy, hey, don't do me any favors." Charlie's voice began to rise. "I love you Dave. I probably always will." Charlie stood up, ready to walk out. "But I'll be damned if I'm going to live the rest of my life with a man who refuses to grow up. We're mature men, Dave. It's time to learn that love is not something you toss aside on a whim. The person you hurt, won't always take you back."

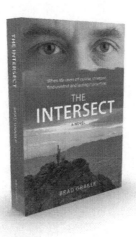

Thank you for reading *The Intersect*.

If you enjoyed the novel, please join my network of friends by going to my website at bradgraber.com and signing up for sneak previews of future works as well as a "deleted scene" from *The Intersect*, sure to prove entertaining. The website also provides a reader's guide, character review, information on upcoming book tours, and how to contact me to be a speaker at your next organizational event or book club. You can also follow me on twitter at @jefbra1 or send me an email at brad@bradgraber.com

Happy reading!

Brad